The Crucible

Part Six of

Changels Genesis

by Peter King

Peter King Publishing
Wellington, New Zealand

SPECIAL NOTE TO READERS

The Crucible is the final part of Changels Genesis

Dialogue that originates telepathically is rendered in *italics*.

The transition between the narrator's present (in the present tense) and past (in the past or perfect tense) is marked by an elipsis ... centered on an empty line

When the location changes through teleportation ("bending") there is a new line and a '[+]' symbol.

Non-English words have been hyphenated on their first use to expose the syllabic structure and ease pronunciation. The exception is Karearea (falcon) which is always hyphentaed e.g.Ka-rea-rea. Maori words ending in the 'e' have been given a non-standard accent acute (e.g. Tané) for the same reason.

Translations Sam (the narrator) understands are parenthesised e.g kara-kia (prayer). Non-English words are hyphenated to aid pronuncuation.

Changels Genesis is fact based fiction. Facts have been indicated with a superscripted dagger symbol[†] There is a three page fact and fiction section at the end of this part of the story.

THANKS AND ACKNOWLEDGEMENTS

I would like to acknowledge the advice and support of the Wellington chapter of the Romance Writers of New Zealand, in particular Kris Pearson.

Finally I must acknowledge my father, John, who assisted with some early proofing; my mother, Dell, for teaching me long ago the art of dispassionate editing; my sons (Lars, Torsten, Joshua and Oliver) who inspired me to write; and finally, my wife, Jenny, for her patience and support.

Hell is empty And all the devils are here.
— **The Tempest, Act 1, scene 2**

CHAPTER SEVENTY FOUR: DISCOVERED

So Sam, you were right. That stuff with Khadiyeh it's ... it's ... Are you saying *God's* on your side," Sue blurts out, disbelievingly.

We are still in her kitchen. Sue's been listening intently throughout. I think now that she had finally met Dr P and decided to join, she just wants to get to the bottom of all the possible weirdness that might come her way with us.

"Noooo way," I laugh.

She visibly relaxes with that. I can tell she finds it all a bit spooky. Not that we didn't, but it makes her think we're some kind of cult and that makes her nervous. She smiles because I laugh. I go on.

"I mean, I don't know what we ... saw or whatever it was," I shake my head.

"Hekator said the smaller your idea of the Universe, the quicker you are to call everything bigger than you're used to 'God'. I mean our galaxy has hundreds of billions of planets and it's one of hundreds of billions of galaxies so the Universe is bigger than big. Whatever Khadiyeh's friends are ... they're millions of years old and their command of nature is way beyond anything we can even imagine. They really are just beyond our understanding. We call them Ophanim because that is the old Hebrew word for

1

the most powerful angels like Ezekiel saw. We prefer that word because 'archangel' just sounds too weird, even to us, because we have no idea what they are really."

Sue nods, so I went on.

"But, you know ... Khadiyeh ... she's ... Well, I mean strange stuff happens around her. And sometimes she helps us and sometimes we help her. And sometimes we don't agree. Why her? I have no idea and it's not worth us worrying about. Tarik got really into it but in the end he couldn't make sense of it either."

"But what you thought you saw wasn't God?"

"No. That was Jibreel, or Gabriel in English, or his spaceship or whatever the hell it was."

Sue thinks for a moment, "So ... Nah ... You're right. It's too ..." she shakes her head.

"Exactly. Even for us it's too... We just park it and deal with whatever Khadiyeh does when we have to."

"OK, but who were the other guys? The ones from Tarim who could read you?"

"Yeah, they were a bit more interesting. Shall I go on?" I ask.

"Yeah, do."

•••

The shock of surviving the cosmic weirdness of Jibreel only to find ourselves caught by the mysterious psychic Yemenis we had first met in Tarim was too much for me. I was ready to jump out of the truck back into the desert storm.

"It's those guys from Tarim!" I called to Tahira who was in another truck. Scott, next to me, was looking from me to the man's head not sure whether we should bale.

2

"*Relax Sam! Calm Tahira!*" Khadiyeh said in our minds. She was in the same truck as Tahira. "*Jibreel has summoned them. They will do as he asked.*"

As if that meant something to me.

"Why don't you uncover your faces. You look like bandits," the mysterious young man in the mirror said to us in Arabic. His words were echoed by his powerful thoughts.

"Too small for bandits Abu Qassim," the driver replied smiling, looking at me in the mirror for a second.

I wondered how he could drive at all in these conditions. All you could see was the red tail lights of the Land Cruiser a few meters in front as we wound among the dunes. It was the blind leading the blind.

"*So do we lower our facescreens or not?*" I asked wondering if it would be a security breach.

"*Lower them,*" said Khadiyeh and the guy with the dark eyes and trimmed beard in front at exactly the same time.

"Only a thief needs hide his face," the young man said. He really did have some kind of eye makeup on.

I thought "your women hide their faces all the time," but we lowered our face screens anyway.

"An American!" the old bearded driver exclaimed looking around over his shoulder at Scott. I wished he would look where he was going.

"He's not an American, Abu Wahid, he's British. They look different," the bored younger man said without even glancing at us.

"How can you find your way in this storm?" I asked via the suit in Arabic, astonished.

"Ha ha. Old Bedu magic," said the driver laughing at my

3

astonishment.

"The lead truck has a GPS. It's American magic," the younger man sniffed.

"Now you spoil my story Abu Qassim," the driver said laughing and putting on a show of being disappointed.

"I have heard *all* your stories Abu Wahid. All the way from Dubai. What I would like to hear is these boys' stories. Why are they on top of a dune in the Rub al Khali in the middle of a storm?"

The madeup eyes were back in the mirror. The intensity made me nervous.

Scott and I looked at each other. What could we say.

"We came to protect Khadiyeh," I said.

"Ah yes, the girl. But you are not of her tribe. Where did you come from?" he asked.

"Far away," Scott said quickly.

"Yes ... far ... far away ... but to the east, I think, not the west," he was reading us.

"From Oman?" the driver asked. "Are you from Oman?"

He had been to Oman many times. He was the kind of man who liked to talk and needed to bring the conversation back to himself. The younger man just stared again in the mirror.

"Australia," said Scotty suddenly. "Perth."

The older man had nothing to say to that. The younger man glanced up into the mirror again looking like he didn't believe him.

"You are very young to be in the desert," the old man reasoned. He seemed to be very slow or something. We were wildly out of place but he didn't seem to get it at all "Where is your family here? You should go to them," he told us seriously.

4

"We stay with Khadiyeh," I said.

"Where does she live?" asked the young man.

"Uh ..." I was not sure.

"*I must return to my parents house in Thaubah,*" Khadiyeh told us happily.

"She lives in..."

"Thaubah. Yes. It is on our way," the young man told the driver.

"Where are you going?" I asked.

"Tarim," said the driver.

I said nothing. Then because the driver hated silence he said with practised bluster. "We drive to Tarim. We bring machinery parts. For motorcycles and pumps. They throw away old ones in the Emirates and we take them to sell."

It was a lie. He was practicing it on us because he wasn't used to telling it yet.

Actually they smuggled Qat, the favourite drug of Yemenis working in the north. And they smuggled back guns and ammunition.

"Our business is our business," said the young man, grimly looking at us in the mirror. I wondered if they were El Qaeda.

The young man's eyes were in the mirror again.

"Our problem is Saleh, not Americans," he said.

"Saleh!" spat the old driver angrily.

The Yemeni president was obviously not their favourite person.

"But that is not a business for children," he added.

"Our guests only look like children Abu Wahid," said the young man. "There is much more to them than they let on."

The driver laughed.

"Spykids three," he said looking back at us and laughing. He obviously found this very funny. "You seen that? I got it for my

5

niece in Oman."

This driver was bothering me more than the serious dude sitting next to him. He seemed crazy and loose. He wasn't dangerous but I just wondered how he could drive.

"Guys I don't know exactly what you are doing there and how you found the Yemeni girl. But we need to wrap this up and you need to come home. You've got school," Grandpop interrupted. There was a brief pause.

"*I am safe now. Thank you all my friends. Go to your school. These friends will see me home safely for they know Jibreel watches over me tonight,*" Khadiyeh said.

I looked at Scott. He looked at me and shrugged. We started to seal our facescreens. The eyes in the mirror looked away.

"So tell me Abu Wahid where does your son work again in Dubai?" the younger man said to the driver, "I think I was asleep with my eyes open."

He was clearly distracting the old, loose dude.

"Ah Abu Qassim it happens. The desert drives you crazy. He is working on the Burj Khalifa. It will be the tallest building in the world."

"No! How could he be so fortunate as to get such a job?" said Abu Qassim with just the smallest hint he was winding the older man up again.

I caught a glance from him. He nodded and then looked back at Abu Wahid who was explaining at length his great cunning in getting his son a job.

"*Let's go,*" I said to Scotty, and we folded away to nothing.

The jumpstation tank flared a couple of times as I made my way out.

"De-brief guys … de-brief," Grandpop was calling.

We noticed that Dr Prosperov, Dr Gursoy and Mrs Jones had come down to the briefing room too. I found myself a seat. I was just starting to realise I was starving. The others came in and sat down.

"Please to explain process of finding Khadiyeh bint Sulimen al-Hadrânî ?" Dr P began impatiently, still sitting in a chair. He seemed to be annoyed we'd beaten him to it.

Hekator and Hekati appeared in hologram form. They were curled up in what looked like a huge squishy ball of tiny green leaves and pink flowers. I got the impression they were in bed but it was hard to know with them.

Slowly we explained what had happened. It was Ashley who interrupted to say we were very hungry. It wasn't long after that Mr Trân came down with Aunty Liz, Mitra and Zoe with a whole heap of food. It slowed things down while we ate but it felt sooo good.

When it came to the bit with Jibreel we discovered something strange. For a start our Control had recorded nothing. We couldn't believe it. We could all describe what happened and all our descriptions matched but the suits and Control just recorded us sitting on a dune getting frightened and excited.

"There is an explanation," Hekator said when we'd finished. We all looked at him.

"Khadiyeh has her own friends and they are more powerful than any of us," he shrugged.

"It is something we have seen on your planet before. It is also one of the reasons for the treaty against intervention. Humans have, for some reason from time-to-time, attracted the interest of the Ophanim."

"We don't know very much about them. They are even more

developed than us, as we are than you. All we know about them
is they span the galaxies. This is something well beyond us.
Dealing with one galaxy with 325 billion star systems, 120,000
light years across is big enough. How they cross the universe is
something we are only beginning to understand.

"Do they not visit you?" Tahira asked Hekator.

"Not for thousands of years. But there is one of us, you know
who has met them. Raman met them when he was your age.
He's asleep at the moment but I will tell him of your experience
when he wakes up."

"But what about the guys who picked us up afterwards. Who are
they?" I asked.

Hekator looked confused.

"They seemed like you from the recording," Hekator said.

"Khadiyeh said Jibreel had called them," I added.

Hekator looked at Hekati who shrugged.

Tahira had a theory.

"We saw zees people in Tarim. I zink I know what zhey are," She
said looking a bit nervous. "I zink zhey are Al Djinn."

Hekator glanced at Hekati. They didn't look surprised.

"Who's Al Gin?" Ashley asked like it was some bartender's name.

Dr Gursoy started to laugh. Tarik grinned too.

"The Djinn … genies you call them," he said.

"Genies?" I asked " you mean like the guys in the magic lamps
who give wishes."

It sounded ridiculous.

"No … Al Djinn, people of smokeless fire," Tahira said seriously.
"Zhey are real. Zhey are even in the Koran."

"Djinn *are* real," Mrs Jones said. "I have met one or two before
in London. They don't like the cold though. They have many

powers similar to the Fae."

"Aren't they Fae?" I asked, looking at Hekator.

"No ... the Djinn are not one of the races of Fae," he said. "Nor are they allied with the Aesir. They are refugees of a destroyed world. They are the last survivors of a world the Aesir called Jotaheim and we called Genaheim. They were as advanced as we are but were dispersed by war. Their home world is wrecked now. Some came to your world and settled among you after Fae or Aesir withdrew. They have never considered themselves parties to the non-intervention treaty but they have largely lived by it anyway. They are a very proud race who keep apart from Fae, Aesir and humans."

"We know they have small settlements on other worlds as well. They travel as we do among them. Unlike us they are immune to strong radiation and prefer hot climates to draw energy directly from the sun. But we do not really know much about them except that they are drawn to the Ophanim. They are fascinated by them but, of course, have no power over them."

"Should we regard them as hostile?" Grandpop asked, getting down to business.

"No. They are not hostile, but they aren't helpful either. They are neutral. They are very proud and disdain us all – Fae, human and Aesir. They live among the poorest humans. But they want to be left alone and as they are dangerous enemies and live in places full of solar radiation where we cannot go, we do leave them alone. I believe the Aesir and their synthetic descendants generally do the same."

"Are we going to tag Khadiyeh?" Ashley asked.

"*Can* we tag Khadiyeh?" I asked.

"Is prudent to try," Dr Prosperov said.

"I zink we should ask *'er*." Tahira replied.

I liked that idea.

"It's not like we could hide it from her anyway," Tarik agreed.

"Is most unusual case," Dr Prosperov mused. "Is obvious is woman in foresight but ... I have nothing to link her," he shrugged.

"I think Gennady we should take heart from the fact that she approached us," said Dr Gursoy said quietly. "After all she was not without alternatives. Several alternatives in fact. In some ways I think you could take this as a rather significant endorsement of your entire programme."

"Is good thought Ali," Dr P smiled. Then he looked thoughtful again.

"Yet, as you know, I am always seeing alternatives," he said quietly to himself.

The meeting broke up and we got changed to go to school. But because of us being tired and stuffing around it was morning break when we finally got there. Grandpop went in to talk to the teachers. He said he would tell them a story about the bus breaking down on the drive. It can't have gone down so well because we saw him leave looking a bit chewed out by Mrs MacLean. But luckily we didn't get in trouble for that.

What we did get in trouble for was daydreaming. None of us could concentrate on *anything* Mr Wakefield said. And whenever we closed our eyes we'd get a flashback to Jibreel. I noticed we were all doodling wheels with eyes. Mr Wakefield even threatened to call our parents and demand we got enough sleep in front of the whole class. It was another ugly us-and-them moment.

And it was true. We did need sleep. By the end of the day we were wrecks. In the bus Asal and Rewa were playing some clapping game but the rest of us were dozing. Homework and chores disappeared in a blur. I was too stuffed to even notice some ghost flicking the switch on my vacuum cleaner all the time. At dinner Grandpop decided we should forget missions and go to bed. So we did. I climbed into bed and had the most amazing sleep I ever had.

I woke in the morning feeling totally righteous. It was a strange feeling. Like everything had fallen into place and I knew who I was, what I was doing and what had to happen next. And strangely enough one thing I knew had to happen was I had to help Emma find those dak plantations.

It was a sunny day but with a cool wind. Summer was starting to slowly give way to autumn and the storms would start soon. School was school. Our daily routine was pretty much normal. We had dinner and then it was into our suits and down to the briefing theatre.

We agreed that Tahira and me should visit Khadiyeh to see if she would agree to being tagged. We would take Shaheen to provide an eye over the area. Tahira thought he'd like a morning flight in Yemen. Control had tracked the convoy we had been picked up by and seen Khadiyeh dropped at her parent's house at two in the morning. The reunion had started badly until Khadiyeh's mother saw the burn on her hand. I couldn't believe she had been able to cope with the pain but maybe she could somehow stop it, or something, because she hadn't complained once during that strange and alarming night.

While me and Tahira talked to Khadiyeh, Ashley and Cam would take Hooty, and Scott and Tarik would take Buffy, into the park on Aotea to look for Ax's weed plantations. They would mark them for Emma with sea shells on the path so she could find them, and report them to the cops. We were also considering tagging Emma herself so we could find her quicker in the park. We were still a bit uncertain about that because it was a bit close to home. For tonight's tasks we didn't see any particular problems when Grandpop asked, so we trooped off to the jumpstation and bent space.

[+]

Me and Tahira arrived on the top of the big red canyon above Khadiyeh's parents' house which was below in the valley. It was a big place, and the morning sun was still casting long shadows. Even so there were plenty of vehicles on the road and, of course, dawn prayers had been an hour ago.

Tahira released Shaheen who was a bit impatient and keen to fly. He'd been fed before we left, but he took one look at the place from Tahira's pouch and just wanted to get into that huge blue sky.

From where we stood the drop to the valley floor was quite a way. We were on the edge of a cliff about thirty or so meters high, but below that was a steep bank covered in loose rock that was about another hundred meters. That sloped down to a few houses, the one on the right being Khadiyeh's parents' home.

The easy way down was to fly. But on a bright morning that would attract attention. There were certainly a number of people around, including a couple of boys from next door playing in the wide dry river bed.

We talked about it and finally agreed the easiest way was to bend into the house. That meant getting Shaheen to stop riding his thermals and check in the windows. At first he wasn't so keen. Then, after Tahira had scolded him once or twice, he flew over and dropped like a brick, pulling up just at the last minute. The boys looked up and noticed as the falcon flew to the top window of the house.

Tahira told me that Khadiyeh was inside and had looked over at the falcon as it landed on the window ledge. She had been folding clothes.

"She's talking to Shaheen," Tahira said.

We were standing, looking down at the house. I saw the bird suddenly rising, flapping for height.

"C'mon, she's inviting us down," Tahira said, passing me the LZ. We flashed into a small clean room. It was about five meters by four. There were four divans on the floor and some curtains, now open. Around, and under beds, stuff was stored. The room had two windows and stairs down to the next level.

Khadiyeh surprised me because she was wearing trousers and a knee-length long sleeve top. She wore her brown hair up with ringlets hanging past her ears. She was pretty but not stunning and looked almost like any other kid our age, although she was still very small. I noticed she had a new dressing on her burn.

"Sam! Tahira! Uncover your faces," she said in Arabic, smiling. We did, and she came up to us to look more closely. I realised then her eyesight was not that great.

"You are prettier that I expected," she said to Tahira

"And Sam is very handsome," she smiled turning away. She went and sat down on one of the divans.

"Why have you come to see me?" she asked.

It was funny talking to her because her powerful mind echoed her thoughts.

"*To see how you are, of course,*" Tahira smiled coming closer and kneeling down in front of her.

"I am getting better. My hand is very burned but Jibreel, praise God, has reduced my pain. My mother has put honey on it to repair the skin."

"Were there any problems when you came back?"

"My mother was a bit scared of visitors at first because my father is away, but when she saw that I was hurt, and they were keen to leave me, she was relieved. She was angry when she saw what my husband, Ali, had done to me. But she is fearful of what my father will say when he comes back from his trip. He was paid a bride price, and he can't pay it back."

"Has Ali tried to come and take you back?"

"No, I don't even know if *he* knows I am gone yet."

A young face appeared on the stairs. It was a girl with bright brown eyes.

"Mummy … mummy there are people talking to Khadiyeh in the bedroom," she shouted running out again.

Khadiyeh smiled.

"That's Alia, my sister. She's four."

There were voices below. Alia's excited high-pitched little voice and other kids voices followed by a mother's voice telling them to quieten down. A lot of clomping feet on the stairs and three faces looked at us. Khadiyeh laughed.

"Alia, Fatima, Nasreen. These are my friends Tahira and Samuel."

The kids goggled at us. It was quite cute really. Their mother called up to them and they confirmed that Alia had spoken the truth. We heard their mother climbing the stairs.

"You may have to look special for my mother," Khadiyeh thought in our heads.

A woman's brown face appeared. She looked old. Her black hair had touches of gray in it. Her face was lined and thin but her brown dark eyes, though tired, were warm.

"Khadiyeh? Who are these people?"

"Mother, these are angel children. They have come to see how I am. They helped me escape from Ali."

The woman's smile froze on her face. She looked at us. I don't think she thought we were angels.

"I am 'Pure'. This is God-has-heard," Tahira told the woman gently in Arabic. The original meanings of our names suddenly seemed perfect. "Your daughter is very special in the eyes of God," she added.

The woman stood still, looking at Tahira. She wasn't sure whether she was being tricked or not.

"Can you *really* fly?" blurted out Nasreen, who was about nine.

"Yes," Tahira smiled.

She looked at me. It was no use saying. They had to see. We cranked down the gravity to ten percent and glowed brightly as we let out our wings. The family's eyes were popping out and their mouths fell open. Tahira changed her suit to rippling gold, I changed mine to silver. Then with a few strong strokes of our wings we lifted up into the air and hovered in their bedroom about half a meter off the ground.

The mother sank to her knees with a small moan, mostly of fear. The kids' faces told a different story. They were overjoyed.

"Mum! Mum! It's true! Khadiyeh wasn't making it up!" Nasreen was yelling excitedly.

But the older woman had started crying. She seemed to be very frightened. She was whimpering and begging for mercy. I looked at Tahira and we stopped. The glow died and we switched back to hoodies and jeans as we dropped to the floor letting our wings fold away behind us.

"Mother don't be frightened," Khadiyeh said, going over to her. She was still trembling and shaking, not daring to look at us. We backed out of the way as she led her mother to her bed.

"They are children. They are children and our friends. They aren't here to punish anyone," she said.

"No … certainly not," Tahira agreed warmly also coming closer and approaching Khadiyeh's mother, gently stroking her. Slowly she stopped shaking and crying and started wiping her eyes and laughing a little. It was strange looking at the two girls. While Kadiyeh's mother was looking in awe at Tahira, I couldn't help noticing how … well the only word I could think of was "serene" … Khadiyeh looked. Tahira might be a fake angel, but Khadiyeh looked like an honest to God saint.

The kids were a lot less frightened by us than their mother, although little Alia had run to Khadiyeh when her mum had suddenly become frightened. Fatimah and Nasreen were more curious than afraid. I think it was because they could see we weren't adults so no matter what we did they thought they understood us.

Nasreen came up to me and asked if he could touch my clothes. I didn't mind. He ran his hand over the soft carbon fibre surface. Fatimah did the same thing to Tahira.

"Why have you come?" Khadiyeh asked us.

"Um …" Tahira had forgotten.

"We want to give you some medicine," I told her.

"Medicine?" she asked.

"Yes for your burn and to help you … help you … call us when you need help," I said feeling like an egg.

Khadiyeh smiled. She saw straight through me.

"I don't need 'medicine', Samuel. I have all I need," she said.

"Uh ... um ... OK," I found myself saying.

Khadiyeh's mother was looking at us in confusion. You could tell we weren't being angelic enough. But ... well ... it wasn't us who claimed we *were* angels.

"But thank you for coming," she said.

And she meant "thank you for coming to show my mother you exist".

I looked at Tahira. She looked at the window.

"*Back to the hilltop*?" I asked her silently.

She nodded. We got up and backed away.

"It's good that you are well. Call us again if you need help. We will always try to come," Tahira said.

"Thank you Tahira. Thank you Sam. And please thank the others for their kind thoughts. God willing I will not need rescuing again."

"God willing," Tahira agreed.

We sealed our facescreens and bent back to the hill above the house. Shaheen was miles away and didn't really want to come down.

"Well, that didn't go too well," I said.

"She got what she wanted," Tahira disagreed. "She could show her mother she hadn't been lying."

"But what about her father and this creep Ali, her so-called husband."

"She knows how to call us. She's been doing it for a month," Tahira shrugged.

As we waited for Shaheen we watched the day heating up. You could see the haze forming. I don't know if it was me after that

17

sleep, or if Jibreel had changed something, but there seemed to be something wonderful about Yemen. Something powerfully alive. It almost seemed to breathe.

Shaheen was a pest to get back into his pouch but finally we got him in. Then we went home.

[+]

The others had been more successful. They had competed to find marijuana plots and had both found four. They were well hidden off the main track which was incredibly dark at night because of the over-hanging bush. Without a good torch, or night vision like we had, you could get seriously lost. And if that wasn't bad enough there were cliffs and holes off the main tracks. Emma would have to be very careful.

Dr P was disappointed that Khadiyeh had not wanted to be tagged but accepted Tahira's argument that unlike all the others Khadiyeh knew we existed and also could call us, so there was less need to tag her anyway. I think he just wanted some control but Khadiyeh didn't want to give us any.

We felt pretty good that night but the next day we were in for a shock. School that morning was the same as ever. It was a slightly windy day but otherwise sunny, We were outside at lunchtime when a car pulled up at the beach opposite. My father's henchmen Ray and John got out first followed by two skinny, mean-looking, brown dudes covered in evil-looking tats. Ashley took one look and freaked.

"Holy f___! It's them! They've found us! Hide me! Jesus H f___ Christ! What do I do? Oh shit! oh shit! oh shit!"

It was MS13.

18

"They won't come in here," I said as we went around back into the library.

"Don't you bet on it," she said. "Back home dey come into schools and shoot people."

She was really scared.

"We need to call Renwick," Tarik said. "But Mrs Thomas won't let us."

"It's easier than that," Scott said taking charge in that calm way he had. "Ash, stick your finger down your throat and spew. Report sick and they'll call your mum anyway."

"Good one Scott!" agreed Tarik.

"Not with us *all* here. Boys go," Cam said.

She was right. It looked too sus if we were all crowded around.

"We'll distract them," Tarik said.

We trooped out and went back outside.

"Split up," Tarik said.

So we split up. We were in a line of Tarik, Scott and me. The men had crossed the road to the fence. John was pointing out Tarik and me to the skinny dudes. They smiled in a way I didn't like. They were going to use us to get Ash. Unfortunately for them they missed Scott who just blended in with all the other white kids.

But these dudes worried me. For a start they were seriously mean-looking. Drug addict thin, and hard, like some fighting dogs I'd seen gang guys with. Their tats over their faces showed they didn't care about anything but their gang, and they weren't scared of anything. Certainly not Sergeant Smith and a bunch of soft white teachers.

The two tat-faces swung easily over the low fence, and started across the field like dogs hunting. We went to intercept them.

They were halfway across the field as Tarik and me circled around to them on opposite sides. But Scott walked into the soccer game in the middle of the field.

"Visitors have to report to the office," Tarik yelled out at the men.

"Huh?" the man nearest replied, putting his hand to his ear pretending he couldn't hear to get Tarik to come closer.

Suddenly Scotty intercepted the soccer ball, flicked it up into has hands and ran toward the men. Marshall and his friends had been ignoring us and the men but now an excuse to chase and beat up Scott started yelling "Givusitback!".

Both of them were distracted by about twelve kids suddenly rushing towards them led by this blond kid.

"Now," yelled Tarik and rushed at the guy nearest him. I rushed my guy. Scott drop kicked the ball in his groin from about two meters. While he was distracted to his front Tarik ran forward from the side and rugby tackled this guys knees bringing him down. Distracted by his mate going down I tackled my guy's legs and brought him down from behind too.

All the kids were confused. Me and Tarik were rolling out and jumping away from the gang guys we'd floored. Scott had already started running back through Marshall's mob who stood unsure what to make of the men on the ground. They, of course, were furious and as they got up pulled out their long knives. Marshall and his mates took one look at these and ran. We led the way.

"He's got a knife," someone yelled.

Mr Wakefield was on duty and came around the corner of the building to see two men in the field and all the kids running away and yelling about a knife. It was kind of funny. His eyes went wide and he ran, actually turned and ran. Tarik, me and Scott regrouped by the corner Mr Wakefield had fled around. The gangsters hesitated. This was not going to plan at all. They weren't meant to have the whole school in uproar until *after* they had grabbed Ashley. Now everyone was hiding from them, the authorities were alerted, and they still hadn't got Ash. Mrs Maclean and Miss Green came up behind us.

"What's going on? Mr Wakefield's calling the police. Who are those men?" Mrs Maclean asked.

The arrival of teachers had sealed it for the gangsters. They wouldn't think twice about killing Mrs Maclean in a second if she was between them and Ashley. But she was between them and *finding* Ashley, and that was going to be hard with the whole school in an uproar. They knew they were better to cut their losses and pretend it was all a big misunderstanding. The knives vanished back into their pants. They started to retreat. But Mrs Maclean was not giving up. She walked out across the field all by herself giving slow motion chase and demanding the men stop and explain themselves like a stupid aggro goose demanding to know why the farmer was carrying an ax.

We watched anxiously, worried we would see them stop and stab her. The gangsters didn't exactly run away but just walked back to the fence and joined the others on the other side while Mrs Maclean hissed after them. She went all the way to the fence demanding answers. The men got into their car and drove away. When Mrs Mac came back across the field looking grumpy we cheered her quietly.

It wasn't much later that a whole bunch of cars showed up. One was Sergeant Smith and the others were from Renwick. Patricia and Zoe were in the Range Rover, Grandpop and Ken were in

Ken's Pinzgauer. Patricia went into the office while Zoe parked the Range Rover. We wanted to go over to them but the bell rang early so we had to go to class. We saw the Range Rover leave but Grandpop and Ken were parked up outside the school.

In class I noticed Emma was looking over at us a lot as we sat down. Everyone was chattering about what had happened. There was a lot of play acting and laughing. Mr Wakefield looked angry and demanded silence. He said he wanted to understand what had happened just now.

I thought "Tarik and Scott just took on two killers from MS13 while completely unarmed and you ran away, you big turkey," but I said nothing. Of course Marshall had to tell it differently. The way he told it we'd attacked two adults as they came into the school then made out the men had knives and started a panic.

All eyes were on us. Marshall was grinning, evilly.

"They did have knives. I saw them," Emma called out. A few others agreed. Mr Wakefield yelled for silence. Then he addressed us.

"Did you tackle those men?" he asked Tarik.

"Yes."

"Sam?"

"Yes."

"And Scott you kicked the ball at them."

"Yeah that was me," he grinned.

There were a few appreciative chuckles around the room. But Mr Wakefield was looking very serious.

"I think you had better go to the Mrs Maclean's office and explain yourselves to her and Sergeant Smith."

"Expel 'em," Marshall muttered.

"Off you go," he said.

I felt cold and hot the same time. Cold because we were in trouble in a way I'd never been in trouble before, and hot because I was pissed off that Mr Wakefield was punishing us for being brave enough to confront gangsters he ran away from! We walked out while Mr Wakefield was telling everyone to be quiet. I caught Emma's eye. She knew the truth too.

We walked over to the office. We half felt like taking off but we decided to go in and face the music. Mrs Maclean was talking to Sergeant Smith. She looked over at us.

"What do you boys want?" she asked.

We explained what Mr Wakefield had said. When we came to the core of it Mrs Maclean was puzzled.

"So you tackled them before they showed their knives."

We looked at each other. Well, there was no point denying it.

"Yes," we agreed.

Sergeant Smith looked at us carefully.

"Why?"

We looked at each other again. But I had the best answer.

"I recognised them as being in Ax Stephen's gang," I told them. "They weren't allowed in the school that way. We knew they were up to no good."

Sergeant Smith and Mrs Maclean looked at each other.

"You don't just tackle adults that come into the school," she said forcefully. "You direct them to the office."

"I did," Tarik said evenly. "They pretended not to understand,"

Sergeant Smith bent down to us. He is quite tall.

"Look guys. I can't decide whether what you did was very brave or very rude but don't do it again. You were really lucky you weren't stabbed. If you see something bad happening, tell an adult. Don't try and stop it. You can get yourselves in trouble and no-one wants to see you get hurt," Sergeant Smith said.

"Yes sir," Scotty said.

We all copied Scott and acted meek. Mrs Maclean took her cue from the police.

"All right you can go back to class now. But like Sergeant Smith says I don't want you to do this again. We do not attack people in this school. Not even trespassers. Especially not trespassers. Do you understand?"

"Yes ma'am," said Scotty and we echoed again.

As we went out of the office we heard Mrs Maclean telling Sergeant Smith she was unhappy that thugs were traipsing into her school. He replied he'd asked Auckland for reinforcements but so far there was nothing but paperwork. We walked back to class. Mr Wakefield had given everyone a silent reading task so we couldn't talk until after school. But when it was time to pack up Emma came over quickly.

"What's going on?" she asked me quietly.

"Outside," said Cam who sat next to me. She looked at me. I nodded.

We walked out and drew over to the empty field. Emma came too.

"Why did you tackle those men?" she asked.

"They were after Ashley," Scott replied.

"Where is she?"

"Home. Safe," Scotty answered.

"Look what is happening? Maybe I can help or something," Emma appealed.

We looked at each other. She was a useful ally.

"OK, what's happening is two of the world's most dangerous drug gangs is 'ere on Aotea," Tarik began.

"And they're after Tarik and Ashley," Cam added.

"And they've teamed up with my dad's gang who knows every trick in the law book," I finished.

"Why are they after you?" Emma asked seriously.

"Politics. Things is very serious back in Turkey at the moment," Tarik told her.

"With Ashley it's big money and the honour of a Mexican drug syndicate," Scott said.

"And the police can't do anything because they haven't broken the law yet," I pointed out.

"Hmmm maybe," Emma added. She was thinking of the plots in the bush. She was weighing up telling us what she was up to.

"So what are you going to do about it?" she asked.

"Try and get them arrested," I said.

"Sergeant Smith can't arrest all of them by himself. They'll kill him," Emma said. She looked around. "He's really worried. He told my dad."

She decided to show her cards.

"Look, the only way he can get more cops is if he can show there's a big drug operation here. But he can't spend time looking for their plots himself so I've been sneaking out at night looking for them. If you guys help we can find them. Then we tell Sergeant Smith and he can get a big drugs bust organised."

"Sounds like a plan," Tarik agreed.

"So do you want to help me?" she asked.

"Uh ... yeeah," I agreed a bit doubtfully.

"It's just it's a long way uphill to the park from our place," Scott said scratching his neck. "Take about an hour to get there and an hour back. If we started at nine when we've finished our chores we wouldn't be back before twelve. That's assuming our parents didn't stop us."

"We could use our bikes," I pointed out.

"So you might save half an hour back," Scott allowed.

"And zen zere is looking in ze dark," Tahira said wrinkling her face as if she was worried this might lead to a chipped fingernail. I almost laughed. Tahira the amazon playing the princess. But she was doing it to distance herself from me and Emma.

"Look, it's a good idea and we can try but we can't promise much," I said.

Emma was confused. She knew we were tougher than we were making out but she couldn't understand our being so cautious.

"Well, if you want to team up, call me," she said, a little sourly. She turned to go. Tahira caught my eye and gave me a "get on with it then," look. I chased after Emma.

"Emma ... um ... look ... something you should know.."

She turned to look at me.

"From my father ... I learned this ... they sometimes mark plots with sea shells on the path."

She eyed me for a second.

"Why?"

"So they can find them in the dark."

"Really?" she asked, doubting it.

"Yeah," I said.

"Will you be able to come out?"

"Uh ... well, I'll try. Aunty Liz is a bit nervous about us at the moment. She thinks Ax will try and grab us."

That seemed to make more sense to Emma that anything Scott had said.

"Yeah, OK."

"Look, see ya."

"Yeah ... seeya Sam," she replied, and we parted.

I joined the others. We walked on for a bit, then they burst out laughing.

"*What*?" I asked, embarrassed, as we met up with Rewa and Asal who were talking to Ken and Grandpop at the gate.

"Nothing mate," said Scott.

"You are *so* cute Sam," said Cam.

"I thought *I* was," said Tarik.

"Zhou are many theengs Tarik but 'cute' ees not one of zhem," Tahira said.

"What *am* I then?" Tarik added as we got on Betty the bus.

Grandpop was driving today. Bernard and Ken were guarding in the Pinzgauer.

"You're brave, smart and sexy," Cam reeled off as she pushed Tarik up the aisle towards the back seat.

"Hey, I can live with that," Tarik grinned.

"And also..."

Cam turned in the aisle and pushed Tarik hard into a seat.

"You're mine!" she said and jumped on him.

We all went "wooooahhhhh" as she kissed him.

The rest of us found seats.

"You boys were really brave taking on those men," Cam told us, after she stopped kissing Tarik.

"So do we all get some of what Tarik's getting?" Scott grinned.

"Find your own," Tarik said from beneath Cam.

"Forget it!" Tahira said as all eyes fell on her.

"I'll kiss you Scotty." said Rewa.

"What!" I exploded, outraged. "You're too young."

"So are you!" she replied.

"She's not much younger than you, Sam," Tahira said.

"But she's my younger sister," I argued.

"Zat doesn't mean you own her."

"No but..."

"Oo do you zink you are telling er oo she can kiss or not?"

"But it's..."

"Rewa can kiss Scott if she likes," Tahira laid down the law.

"I don't want to now," Rewa put in.

"That's OK Rewa," Scotty smiled.

"I will!" said Asal getting up.

"Sit down! No you won't!" exploded Tahira.

Everyone jeered at Tahira who had a hard time justifying herself the rest of the way home.

When we got home we found there was a bit of tension in the house. Patricia wanted to take Ashley away because officially they weren't here anyway. Dr P thought this was probably wise, but Ashley didn't want to go. She felt that if we could deal to gunmen and gangsters the world over why should she run from these ones? Everyone was arguing about it as we did our chores and got ready for dinner. It was clear we kids were less afraid of these guys than the grown-ups. Dr Gursoy was also surprisingly staunch.

"We were chased halfway around the world. There is no point running back around the other half," he said.

A compromise was reached where we agreed that all of us would get sick during the week. That would give us scope to find some more of Ax's plantations and deal with the foreigners.

"OK people," Grandpop began when we were gathered in the briefing theatre after dinner.

"A good defence is pretty much the same as a good offence and the main thing you need is intell. So tonight we will need Buffy and Hooty, as well as Cam and Tarik's bugs and we'll need them all over Ax and all his merry men."

"For back-up Tahira I want you to fly overhead. Sam you're the mobile reserve but I want you to keep an eye on Emma in case she gets into trouble."

"Ooooooo," Tarik and Scott murmured. Ashley and Cam hit them.

"Yeah, I know it's 'oooo' guys, but she *is* helping us and what she's doing is seriously dangerous," Grandpop said.

"Still, Sam make sure you can bend out pronto if we need you."

"OK," I said, trying hard not to go red.

"Yeah no ..." Tarik began.

"Shuddup Tarik," Grandpop growled.

"Yeah, you can't talk," Scott added.

"Anyway, Sam you may as well go find Emma as she'll be heading out soon. The others have to go over their plan."

I had a funny suspicion Grandpop had made things work out this way so I didn't end up near Ax again, but I went off to the jumpstation as asked.

"Where would you like to go Sam?" Control asked.

"Ah...what's the time?"

"Eight twenty four."

Can we check out the entrance to the park by Emma's place?"

The walls of the jumpstation suddenly looked like the path. It was dusk and getting darker by the minute.

"Bit further up the path?"

The scene shifted. There was no-one around.

"Here's good," I said.

"Bending in three, two, one."

And I was out of there.

[+]

I arrived in the gloom of the bush.

It was a bit lonely really. The moon was rising full in the east. It looked quite lovely. I thought about bend-diving to check out the area but it was a waste of time really. Then I thought about sneaking down to Emma's place. That had more appeal. I thought about the pros and cons and couldn't see a downside so I set off.

It was only about five minutes down the road. I noticed that I picked up some dust from the gravel road on the way which was a bonus because it would have looked sus to arrive outside her window all clean. I didn't bother getting camouflaged until I got close to the house. It was getting pretty dark now so I didn't need adaptive blend camouflage. A good dark green was enough. I fluffed up my feet and nipped down the path to the back and hid in the hedge. There was no-one to see me.

Then Emma came into her room, turning on the light and drawing the curtains. I watched Emma's silhouette come and go through her bedtime routine and eventually her mother said goodnight and switched off the light at nine. She gave it quarter of an hour and opened the window.

By now I was onto thermal imaging. The moon was up but with no streetlights or other buildings around it was still pretty dark. The drop out her window was about as far as she could reach. She emerged like a long black shadow.

I suddenly realised I didn't have a torch. If I'd had one I could have signalled her silently by putting a spot of light on the wall. I didn't need one of course, but that would look pretty sus to Emma. I wondered if I dared do that with my beam, and decided against it.

PART SIX: THE CRUCIBLE

"Grandpop any chance of a torch? I forgot one," I asked.

"I'll see what I can rustle up. But I'll only be able to send it ahead or Emma'll see it arrive," he said.

"Uh yeah ... OK ... thanks Grandpop."

Emma had slipped out of her room and was now sneaking up the path past her parents' room and then past the living room which glowed orange behind the curtains. I let her go ahead out of sight and then padded silently after her.

Yet, even with fluffy feet, it was impossible not to make a noise on the gravel road that shone white in the moonlight. I had the advantage though, that I could hear when she was moving, so I moved at the same time. She moved in short spurts of about fifteen to thirty meters darting quickly in the warm summer night. I was taken a bit by surprise by how quickly she moved and had to run faster to keep contact.

She looked back behind her searching the fourth time she stopped. She was at the foot of the drive up to the carpark and she must have heard me. That turned out to be lucky because she missed the bright flash of light on the path.

"Put your torch by the gate," Scott said and vanished again. Emma turned back, aware of something out of the corner of her eye. She looked back and then moved again. I followed. I reached the bottom of the drive as she reached the top.

"Emma!" I whispered loudly.

"Oh!" she cried and froze.

"It's me, Sam," I said coming out into the middle of the gravel drive.

"Don't *do* that to me!" she whispered angrily.

"I came down to meet up with you, but we must have passed each other."

31

"Why didn't you call?" she complained hoarsely.

"And talk to your dad?" I asked in my natural voice as I crunched up the hill toward her. My voice sounded loud out here, but then we were far enough away from her house not to be heard. All you could hear were cicadas and the odd owl in the distance.

"I didn't expect you to come," she said honestly as I reached her. I shrugged.

"Why are you wearing that bag?" she asked critically.

"Just brought a few things to avoid getting lost or something."

"Well, we have to move fast so it better not be too heavy."

"Nah, it's light."

We walked together up to the start of the track. It was still like we were meters apart even though we were really so close we could have touched one another.

"I left my torch up here," I said as we came to the gate.

I passed off not finding it for a moment pretending it had fallen. Finally I found it. It was pretty small compared to the big lantern Emma had brought but it was an excuse rather than a tool. I let her go first and she lit up the dark under the trees and among the bushes as we walked up the hill.

"We'll have to go quite a long way in," I warned as I put the way-points Control fed me into the suit's navigation system. "About an hour I'd say."

"How do *you* know?" she asked.

"Nobody plants anything close to an entrance. To easy for someone looking for a place to pee to find."

"Well, keep your eyes open on the way anyway," she said.

We walked up the hill steadily. It was strange walking along in the dark like that. Everything looked weird with bright highlights and dark, dark shadows. It was lucky we both knew the track well because it could have been a bit freaky otherwise. At first we just walked and looked. It was like we were checking each other out, really. Both a bit shy of letting our guards down. But then Emma started to ask me questions about Ax and about Renwick. Finally she got down to her basic suspicions.

"So, do they smoke it there?"

"They?"

"That Japanese woman and the others?"

"No … I don't think so."

She stopped and looked at me seriously.

"*Really*, Sam?" she asked voice full of doubt.

"Straight up, Emma. They don't."

"What about you … and the others?"

I smiled.

"Of course not," I said looking her in the eye.

"Yeah, OK," she said looking around. She thought I was lying.

"Hey," I put my hand on her shoulder, just gently to stop her looking away. She looked at it and at me. I looked her in the eye and dropped my arm.

"We don't do drugs, Emma," I said.

She looked at me uncertainly.

"What about when Charli and I found you up by the old forts throwing sheep shit at each other. You were all off your faces."

I smiled.

"We were totally exhausted. Exhausted and relieved. We'd been working non-stop for months. We'd finally stopped."

She set off again.

"All summer."

"Yeah."

"So what were you so busy doing?"

"A bunch of stuff. Some of it a bit like this to be honest."

"Looking for dak plots?"

"And other stuff."

"Like what?"

"Like ways out of being chased by gangs if you must know."

"Did you find any?"

"Yeah ... a few. We found some of the plots you're looking for too."

She spun on me turning the brilliant light in my face. I winced.

"Why didn't you report them."

"Because it wasn't harvest time then. There was just a bunch of little plants in a clearing. Who could the cops arrest? It's almost harvest time now, so now's the time to get them."

"And you really know where they are?" Emma asked. She was getting excited in spite of herself.

"Some of them. Not all."

"OK, well let's see 'em then."

"OK, but it's still a while in."

We walked on. We crossed a bridge, then kept going. It was a good walk in daylight. It would have been good by moonlight too, if Emma could see anything. We passed 'the cliffs' and went inland.

'The cliffs' were a short part of the path where it ran along the edge of a cliff with a steep bank on the other side. We had a fantastic view to the horizon in the east and all along the island. Somewhere down below was the road back to Renwick. The cliffs had had a fence once, but it had been broken ages ago and nobody ever fixed it. After 'the cliffs' the path went inland into the hills and gullies. Emma stopped to take in the view. We were about ten minutes from the first plot.

"Sam?"

"Yeah, what?"

"Did you snog Tahira?" she asked looking out to sea.

I looked at her for a moment. Then dropped my gaze. I was wilting.

"Yeah," I admitted to my shoes.

"Thought so," she went back to walking faster than she had been.

"But you snogged David," I said following after her.

"I know ... I liked it too," she added.

I felt awful trailing after her.

"So what's the problem?" I asked.

"Problem? Who says there's a problem," she said snarkily to the bush as we left the cliffs behind.

"You ... judging by the way you walking fast enough to win the hundred meters."

She spun on her heel.

"Just because my boyfriend is six hundred kilometers away and your girlfriend is six meters down the hall doesn't mean there's a problem," she shouted.

It was very quiet in the bush in the dark after that. It seemed all the creatures in their branches, nests and burrows were thinking about what she'd just said.

"Tahira doesn't want to be my girlfriend," I admitted.

"What? Why not?"

"She likes me but she's...she has someone else. Like you. Someone...who's far away...far, far away."

"Oh," Emma said, thinking about it.

She walked on.

"Really?"

"Ask her. She won't mind."

"Why should I? *I've* got a boyfriend."

"Six hundred kay away."

"At least he cares."

It was crunch time.

"I care. I wouldn't be here if I didn't care."

"Hmmm where are these plots then?"

"The first is just around this bend."

I nearly missed it myself. It was that well hidden. I pushed through, checking for wire, but they had relied on hiding this patch. Emma pushed behind me. After ten meters we came on a plot of plants taller than we were, about twelve meters square. It was spooky in the torchlight. The smell of the heads was unmistakable. These were very, very ripe. Maybe too ripe.

"What do we do?" I asked.

"Mark it and tell Sergeant Smith," she said, hair swishing.

We backed out.

Emma had brought a hunting knife. She went to carve an x.

"Don't do an X," I warned. "Do a heart. Less sus."

She nodded and carved a heart with TR and DJ on it, just to tweak my nose.

We moved on to the next plots and marked those too. The moon was getting steadily higher. I couldn't help thinking it was over a month since we had been ambushed in Armageddon.

"Let's look for more," Emma said.

I rather doubted there were any. If Scotty and Ashley couldn't find them I doubted we would. But to humour her I agreed, and we set off moving higher up the track. We were starting to get seriously into the bush now. The trees were high and the ground

– despite what Emma's dad and his department had done to smooth it out – was rough.

To my surprise we did find another set of plots. There were three altogether which we marked. Emma was quite excited now.

"Sam, it's midnight. The others have finished. Ax's gang's been in bed for two hours now. Are you OK to bring Emma down by yourself," Grandpop yawned.

"*Yeah, no problem,*" I replied silently. Then I added "*How come they went to bed so early?*"

"I dunno. Maybe they're getting up early."

"*Why?*"

"I dunno."

"*Maybe they want to harvest this lot. It's ripe enough.*"

"Could be. Well then don't keep her up all night. She's meant to have school tomorrow. Even if you don't."

"*Yeah, OK.*"

I turned to Emma.

"Hey Emma, what's the time?"

"I dunno, why?" she asked pressing on, torch out.

"Well, the moon came up about half eight and it's up there now. So I reckon it's after midnight."

"Really?"

"Yeah, I reckon. And we've got school tomorrow."

"You can cope with being tired at school. You were last year. Anyhow this is fun."

I said nothing. I followed her as she kept searching. I spotted another mark by Scotty and Ashley and we found another plot. Emma carved another heart.

"Why were you so tired then, anyway?"

"Tahira's friend was here. We did a lot of this sort of stuff."

"You met him!"

I decided not to correct her. Tahira didn't need *that*.

"Yeah."

"What's he like?"

I had to think about this.

"Nice. Really good looking too. Taught us a lot. Very unusual though. Liked to go out at night a lot."

"Was he older?"

"Yeah. Quite a lot older."

"Oh, OK," she thought about it.

"So why did she snog you?"

"Well, I didn't want to at first."

"*Yeah right!*"

"No, I didn't. I knew she was using me as a substitute."

Emma looked at me. She seemed a bit guilty.

"Really," she asked evenly.

"True," I said.

"So why did you give in?"

"Oh, it wasn't like that. We just both needed substitutes at the same time. It just sorta happened."

Emma was searching the same place over again. She moved on trying to be above it all. Then it came.

"So who was she your substitute for?" she asked almost in a murmur, trying to act like she didn't care, looking into the dark. I felt a bit bad about this because she was almost walking into it by herself.

"Can't you guess?" I said looking at her.

She was hotter than she had been all night, both to my eyes and to my thermal vision. She looked at me, and then away, shyly.

"No," she murmured.

"You, of course," I told her quietly.

I don't know why I even said it, to be honest. It wasn't true. I'd snogged Tahira because I needed to feel love after the bus ambush. But talking like this was turning Emma on and it was turning me on too. She didn't look at me. There was a long silence.

"We should go home," I said, looking at the moon.

Suddenly the torch went out. The moon was looking kind of raggy in a sky with some clouds. Right now it was out of them and bright.

Emma sighed.

"It's nicer without the torch," she said.

"Yeah," I agreed. "But darker."

She snorted. Then she was laughing her head off.

I couldn't help joining in.

"but darker," she repeated laughing again.

"God, you're an idiot sometimes, Sam," she said wiping her eyes. I smiled at her. I liked to see her laugh. It had been a long time since she had been so relaxed around me. Her eyes danced around me. You didn't have to read minds to know what this was about.

What amazed me later was how confident I was. I don't know where it came from. Maybe it was being shot at. Maybe it was Tahira. Whatever it was, I found it so amazingly easy. I walked up to her looking her in the eye. Her breathing was quick and shallow. Her chest rose and fell in a nice way.

"What?" she asked.

"Come and dance. Dance, by the light of the moon."

I put my arms out. She was uncertain, so I put my arms around her and gently pulled her close, then hugged her. Her arms closed tight around me. She let out a long sigh.

I kissed her neck. She murmured but didn't let me go. Her eyes were closed. I pressed my forehead to hers. It was her lips that sought mine. We kissed, softly at first and then hotly and more passionately.

She tried to pull my hood off, but, of course, it didn't come. Finally she broke away.

"What is the matter with this thing?" she laughed nervously.

"It doesn't come off."

"What? Why not?"

I shrugged and pulled her close again, but she pulled away.

"Why doesn't it come off?"

"It's all one outfit. The bag doesn't come off either."

I thought I may as well tell her now rather than let her find out later.

"It's all one?" she asked curiously.

"Yeah...one big romper suit."

"What do you wear *that* for?"

"It's really comfortable."

"It's weird. Where did you get it?"

"Tahira's friend's family makes them."

She looked at me nervously.

"Maybe we should be getting home," she said.

I thought, just like Tahira, get me all turned on and then get cold feet. But I shrugged and smiled.

"That's what I said an hour or so ago," I reminded her.

Actually it was two hours ago. It was two in the morning. The night felt dark and old.

Emma switched the torch on again and I let her lead the way back down the hill. I was feeling strangely lightheaded. I knew

I was tired but I had this weird sense of hope that I should have worried about.

It took quite a while to find our way down the hill. The torch was getting weaker now and the beam was turning yellow. For a while I held Emma's hand but after a time she let go to speed up. It wasn't that she didn't like me but she did want to get home. As we got further along the path we sped up – Emma leading the way – so that over the last two hundred meters or so we were running down the slope.

Then a hundred meters from the exit I realised something was wrong. Putting on extra power I caught up with Emma and put my arm out to grab her.

"Emma! Stop! Stop!" I whispered as she ran ahead.

"Lemme go!" she said, not loudly but louder than the quiet bush around us. She wriggled free and continued running down the path, her trainers pounding loudly on the dry clay. I stopped and ducked quickly off the track.

I heard her feet, then a brief shriek, quickly muffled. There was a struggle.

"Let me..." Emma started.

Then a struggle which ended quickly.

I could just hear, muttered in a low growl through the undergrowth, "That's a big knife for a little girl! Now you be good Emma or I'll throw you down a hole so deep even daddy won't find you again. Got it?"

There was a pause.

"Right, get up, but not a squeak. Understand?" he snarled quietly.

They seemed to get up.

"Boss? Boss up here! We gotta small problem," the man called out in a hoarse whisper. The voice was familiar.

I had already heard the grind of wheels on gravel, the crunch of boots, the tell-tale clinks and muttering sounds of a large group of men gathered below. Now I heard the crunch of a pair of boots up the path.

"What's the problem, Ray?" said a voice I knew too well.

"This."

"Emma! Hmm, what say you tell Uncle Ax what you were doing up in the park at three in the morning?"

We'd got it wrong. Tonight *was* harvest time.

I couldn't sleep so I went for a walk," Emma lied.

"She was telling someone else to let her go before she ran into me. There are two pairs of footprints," Ray disagreed.

I switched to adaptive blend camo and started sneaking closer through the bush.

"*Grandpop?*" I called silently.

"Control here Sam."

"*I've got a problem. The gang have got Emma.*"

"Sam you must not reveal any secrets. You have been identified. You must not use adaptive camouflage."

"*Whaaaat?*" I asked unbelieving.

The very time I needed it Control was telling me to switch it off.

"Switch it off Sam, I am rousing Mike."

I switched it off and went back to dark green before he started switching things off I might really need.

I couldn't see through the brush but I could hear Ax was sniffing Emma's hands. All I could smell was dirt and bush.

"What's that in your pocket?" he asked.

The rest of the gang were joining him on the path. There was a pause as I moved closer and they did something.

"You just bought yourself a shitload of trouble missy," Ax told her sharply.

I couldn't see what it was but I guessed she'd taken a seed head as evidence.

"Anyone got something to tie her?" he asked the others.

"Here boss," said someone

He grabbed her and was quiet for a moment as he must have tied her hands.

"Take her up the path. If she struggles or screams, do her," he said to Ray.

"Right. C'mon you," he said.

"OK boys there's at least one kid in the bush hiding. Spread out nice and wide and move forward so we can net him. Don't let him get away. These kids have found our gear."

While Ax was organising his men Ray was pushing Emma up the path towards me. It was a trap. If I jumped Ray the others would be able to trap us both. On the other hand the men were distracted with forming their line. Ax had turned to climb the path. It was now or never as Ray came level with where I was. When he was five meters away I decided to go for it. I charged out behind him, leaped, grabbed his head from behind, and pulled it hard after me into the bush on the other side. Ray was twisted off his feet and let go of Emma to defend himself. He landed heavily on his back. I was still on my feet and ran off into the bush. Emma was jerked back but remained on her feet and started running.

"GETTEM," roared Ax and started off after us with the rest behind him.

Emma was never going to get away with her hands behind her back. I needed a weapon. There wasn't a single rock in sight so I broke a small tree off and turned back to the path. Ax was running up the hill after Emma. I chased after him with my bushy spear. Behind me, the others were coming up fast.

I caught up with Ax and shoved my tree into his legs. His thighs were three times thicker than the slim trunk but it was dark and he didn't see it coming. He tripped and fell and I let the tree drop with him.

"Run Emma," I yelled after her as she ran into the dark.

Ax had turned to look at me. The others, including Ray who had jumped up, could see me too, and were closing fast. There were about twenty altogether but none of them had Kalashnikovs. The bad news was:

"Sam?" said Ax from the ground.

"Sorry dad," I said and ran off the path into the bush.

I was hoping to draw them after me where I had the advantage. I could see reasonably well when the moon was out, better than they could anyway. I was faster, stronger and being small didn't hurt either. But the others were right behind me and I had to run.

I drew them up into the bush for five, maybe ten minutes. It seemed like forever. Then there was a shrill scream. They had Emma!

"*Control?*"

"They're coming down Sam."

The others weren't even changed. I'd be on my own for a while yet. I changed direction and started heading towards where I'd heard the scream. The guys behind me were falling further back, mostly because it was dark but also because I was simply faster. There was another scream followed by Emma yelling and swearing. I raced on towards where they were. I was leaving the guys behind me for dead. Then, very close by, another scream followed by Emma screaming threats and insults in a voice strained by fear and hatred. I could also hear laughter. I burst into a clearing.

Emma still had her wrists tied but she had managed to get them in front of her. That would have been great if they hadn't caught her. Now she was hung up from a branch kicking hopelessly while Ray whipped her with a rope. I was furious. I rushed forward when I was suddenly tripped and fell, just before Ray. I spun over in time to see a big shape loom out of the darkness.

"Sorry son," said a voice.

And then something hit me in the face and I ... well I don't know what happened.

I woke up to find myself over someone's shoulder. Someone big. I couldn't tell if it was Ax or not. We were walking back into the park. I felt dizzy. One of my eyes wouldn't open. I was trying to remember why I was there.

"Sam, lie still, " said Grandpop. "Cam and Tarik are overhead. The others are in the bush. Just relax and get your head together."

That was proving rather easier to say than do. I didn't feel so well. Suddenly I vomited in spite of myself all down this guy's back.

"Aw yuck," he said and threw me on the ground.

"He puked on me," he said while the others jeered and laughed at him.

I just lay there disorientated and groaning. The guy went to kick me. I couldn't do anything.

"Pick him up or I'll more than puke on you," Ax's voice said somewhere.

Grumbling the man picked me up again. We walked on. But slowly I started to feel a bit better. The dizziness was still there and my eye was closed but my head was clearing.

"*Sam? Are you OK?*" Scott asked.

"*Not the best, to be honest, Scott.*"

"*You're coming up on the cliffs. We'll have to bend ahead.*"

"*Sure.*"

"*Are you still in the air guys*?" I asked Cam and Tarik.

"*Closer than you think,*" Tarik said.

"*What's happening with Emma.*"

"*She's up front ... wait, they're stopping,*" said Cam.

"Untie her. Bring that boy of mine up here," Ax called.

I was carried past a bunch of others.

"Put him there," Ax ordered.

I was lowered to my feet. I found myself standing next to Emma. I staggered and she stepped towards me and held me up. I looked behind me and realised we were right on the edge of the cliff where the fence was broken. Just centimeters behind us was a ten meter drop to trees that fell rapidly away down a steep, steep slope for hundreds of meters. It made me sway.

"Right you two. This is your last warning. We're busy and we don't have time to f____ around. Any more interference from you and that's it. Son or no son, you're f_____ dead!" he snarled.

Then, suddenly, he shoved us off the cliff. Everything seemed to happen in slow motion.

Emma flailed and screamed. I grabbed her as I fell backwards. I was underneath. I realised as Ax disappeared out of sight of my one good eye that there was a danger I could break my neck if I fell head first. Immediately I began to engage gravity neutralisation holding Emma in front of me to cover the glow but there was no way to avoid it. We had to somersault.

"*Distract them!*" was my only thought to the others.

47

The first half-second passed. I vaguely heard a loud noise in the distance. I twisted Emma under me. We kept falling. The gravity neutralisation increased. Emma was still screaming and clutching me. We were still accelerating downward but only quarter as fast as normal. Emma came up again in my arms. She'd stopped screaming and was rigid. She knew something weird was happening. Then the treetops sailed past far too fast. I began to curl my legs underneath us.

The tree next to us was thickening out. The top of the steep slope was coming into view. I had to extend my legs down. I was running out of time. My legs were half down when suddenly time sped up again.

I hit as I held Emma in my arms, my legs absorbed the impact. We skidded down the bank as I continued holding her on the edge of losing my balance. I slid briefly under the cover of the trees and then slowly straightened up still holding Emma like a baby, as I glowed a deep blue.

"*Woooaah Sam! Incredible!*" yelled Tarik.

In my arms Emma's eyes were wide. She stared at me for a second and then gasped because she had stopped breathing.

"Shhh," I said to her, and stopped glowing.

She nodded. Her body was stiff as wood.

"*What's happening,*" I asked the others.

"*Scott, Tahira and Ashley are drawing them. They're trying to catch them. They haven't a hope in hell,*" Tarik told me.

"*Emma's going to have questions,*" I said looking at her. She still hadn't moved.

"*I bet,*" Tarik replied.

I gently put Emma down. She just sat at once. I backed off but because of the slope our eyes were level. I felt weird squinting at her out of my puffy eye. She looked at me for a while and then craned her neck at the cliff behind us. I had been hoping it would look smaller, but ten meters of cliff plus another ten of steep bank is a long way to fall. She looked at me again.

"Sam?" she asked in a small voice.

"Yeah?" I asked a bit defensively.

"What's going on?" she asked, almost frightened of the answer.

"Um ... well ... I'm sorta looking after you."

"Sam ... we just went over a cliff and ... and you caught me."

"Yeah ... pretty cool eh?" I smiled as if I'd been amazingly lucky. She half-smiled, "Sam, it's impossible. We should be down here with broken bones but there's not a scratch on us."

I blew out stale air I'd been holding in.

"Yeah ... amazing eh?"

"You were glowing Sam. You were glowing and ... and we took way longer to fall that far than normal."

I should have zapped her with the amnesia ray. I had time and I knew I was meant to. But I couldn't do it. I wanted her to find out why I'd been so distant.

"Emma you have a choice. Either you trust me and keep the biggest secret in your life or ... or..."

"Or what?"

"You forget about this."

"How can I *forget* about it?" she asked angrily.

"I can *make* you forget it. I'm *meant* to make you forget it," I told her.

She got the threat. Her eyes flickered for a moment.

"Sam you probably just saved my life. Of course I trust you."

"Then you'll have to be patient. I can tell you a little but I can't tell you everything now. You have to trust me and be patient."

"OK."

"It's not kids stuff anymore Emma and its way bigger than a small time dope dealer like my dad. He's just a pain in the arse. This is totally f_____ serious."

"OK, I get it."

I sighed. Control was not going to be happy.

"Grandpop am I right to trust her?"

"It's OK so far Sam. We'll see how she goes. We can fix her later if we have to. But we will have to tag her."

"OK."

Emma was looking at me.

"Are you listening to someone?"

I nodded.

"Who?"

I thought about different ways to answer that. "Grandpop" sounded lame, like I was playing.

"We call it 'Control'"

"It?"

"Yeah, Control's a system."

"You mean like a computer or something?"

I found myself doing a so-so head shake the way Dr P often does.

"or something," I replied.

"How can we get out of here?" I asked Grandpop.

"It's four in the morning. You guys must be buggered. I reckon the best way is for Tarik and Cam to give you a lift," Grandpop said.

"Give us something to do," Tarik agreed.

"What are they saying?" Emma asked.

"We're sorting out a lift home," I told her.

"Really?" she asked brightening up.

"By helicopter?" she suggested.

I smiled.

"Way too loud."

The two speeders were black. They curved over out of the stars and came up behind me straight and level, silently. They looked dark, powerful and spooky as they sat there in mid-air.

"*Taxi*," Cam laughed.

I smiled. Emma's face was slack with shock.

"*What* are those?" she asked fearfully.

"Our rides."

"You mean we get on top of them?"

"Yeah."

I went over and sat on Tarik's speeder. It wasn't comfortable but it would do.

Emma came forward looking very cautious.

"This is way weird."

"It's OK, just hop on."

She straddled Cam's speeder the same as I had.

"How do you make them go?" she asked.

"*You* don't," I grinned. "Tarik and Cam are inside them. We're just carrying you this way because it's the easiest for such a short distance."

"They're *in* them!?" she asked, amazed.

"*Tell her I'm her horsey*," said Cam.

"Cam says she's your horsey," I repeated.

"Really? Cam's in there?" Emma smiled.

Cam flashed a smiley on her top.

Emma laughed nervously.

"So hang on," I told her.

"What to?" she asked panicking slightly.

"Whatever you can," I replied.

Tarik and Cam turned and slowly went off level toward the sea for a short distance before turning left to run up towards her place. The east was starting to lighten. We had to be quick.

Cam and Tarik kept the speed down to about forty kilometers an hour and the height to only about ten meters. It was fast enough for Emma to start out worried, but slowly get more confident. Although it had taken half an hour on foot the trip out only took five minutes. They circled the speeders around and let us off on the road outside Emma's house.

Emma got off and I led her back.

We stood back from the black boxes. They looked so cool.

"They've got to go now. It's getting light," I explained.

"*Going up,*" warned Tarik.

The two shot up into the sky inertialess and vanished among the stars.

"Shiiit!" Emma exclaimed loudly at the speed in spite of herself.

We were alone on the road as the sky began to brighten out to sea and the darkness changed to gray.

"What do we do now?" Emma asked.

"*How are you guys going?*" I asked Scott, Ashley and Tahira.

"*We've had enough. We're back home. They're probably giving up by now,*" Tahira warned.

"*They're scattered all over the place,*" Ashley yawned.

"*They didn't harvest anything much, that is for sure,*" Scott agreed.

"*Did they see you?*" I asked.

"*Of course not. They heard us but they couldn't see us. They just thought there were more kids in the bush,*" Scott said.

"*Scary kids,*" Ashley said sleepily.

"*Or ghosts,*" Tahira added.

"*So the only live kids they saw was me and Emma?*"

"*Yep,*" agreed Scott.

"*And they think we're at the bottom of the cliff,*" I summarised.

"What does it say?" Emma yawned.

"Oh, I was talking to the others. They led the gang on a goose chase all around the park. Of course Ax and the others still think *we're* at the bottom of the cliff."

"So what do we do?"

"Tell your dad. He'll want to know what happened to you. Just say we got you away after Ray whipped you and we hid and then got lost in the bush."

"Do I tell him about the plots?"

" 'Course. Tell him everything except about falling off the cliff. He won't believe it anyway and that will sound like a lie. If you ever get pressed say you just remember waking up on a bush."

"What about you?"

"Me?"

"Should I tell him about you?"

"Sure. Closer to the truth the better."

She smiled and shook her head.

"It was a helluva night Sam."

I shrugged. My eye made my face feel lopsided.

"Do you want a leg up to get back in your window?"

"Yeah. That'd be great."

We turned for her house and crunched down the road, slipped past the sleeping house to the back. The curtains were still drawn.

I braced and cupped my hands for her foot. She put it in, drew close to me and said.

"Thanks for looking after me, Sam."

Then she kissed me gently, released and stood up. She grabbed the window ledge and swung herself in. The curtains were in her face as she pushed through and vanished.

Then her dad said, "Well, *you* sure have a lot of explaining to do young lady."

I wasn't sure whether to beat it or not. But I decided I'd stood by Emma this far. I'd better stand by her now. Tama pulled open the curtains and glared at me. I was a bit embarrassed.

"Hi Mr Reeves."

"What the hell have you two been up to?" he demanded suspiciously looking at my eye.

The explanations took an hour and a half. At first Tama didn't believe us but when he saw the marks on his daughter his suspicion we were sneaking out to have sex turned to anger. He was angry with us for getting into something over our heads but he was also angry with Ax. He was angry with Sergant Smith and the cops too. He raged, and grumped, and went on, but finally by five thirty he was exhausted. We were falling asleep on our chairs too. Finally he decided we needed to sleep. He'd talk to Sergeant Smith later.

He sent Emma to bed and drove me back home to Renwick. Most of the way back he said nothing but as we got close to Renwick he started up.

"Sam I have to thank you for helping Emma to get away from those bastards."

"I couldn't leave her Mr Reeves."

"Not every boy would do that And I appreciate it took a lot of guts to stand up to your old man like that."

I shrugged.

"Do you like Emma, Sam?"

"Yeah, sure," I answered automatically without thinking. The sun was rising gold and pink. It looked fantastic.

He glanced away from the road at me.

"I mean do you *like* her, Sam?"

"Oh … well, yeah. Sure, we like each other."

"Did you kiss her?"

I said nothing and looked a bit embarrassed.

"Thought so," he said grimly as we drove down the hill.

"OK, so listen up Sam. I don't mind you seeing Emma at school, at home, or anywhere else where adults are around. But so help me if there's another stunt where you sneak off at night with her I will ask your Aunt to come down hard on you and if she doesn't I'll have the lot of you out of that house quicker than you can say it's name."

We drew up at the front steps.

"Have I made myself clear to you young man?"

"Yessir, Mr Reeves."

"Good. Now get some rest. Sergeant Smith will probably come and talk to you later."

I got out and he drove back up the hill. I stood there looking at the dust from his wheels settle. The air was cool and fresh. The birds in the bush were singing their hearts out. The sea was roaring too as it bashed into the beach. I'd been up for twenty three hours and I was totally whacked.

I fell asleep in the changer apparently. All I remember is waking up in my room at two in the afternoon feeling like a tractor had driven over me a few times. I lay in bed for a while thinking about stuff. Then I checked out my face. My eye was this huge

55

purple thing. It looked awful. I went back to bed.

Emma had definitely kissed me. That was good. But she'd pulled away. I didn't know about that. Why? Was she not sure? Did she still like David?

Then there was Ax. He'd pushed us off a cliff. But then when they'd heard other kids and tried to catch them they got nowhere. He had wanted to harvest the plots but it had been ruined. That meant he thought we were out there suffering and he was running out of time. He was going to be majorly pissed off.

So was Emma's dad. Why was it that adults always imagined kids were out to have sex all the time. Was that what they did? I had to admit I really liked it when Tabika or Tahira or Emma wanted me close. I loved being turned on too. But I just couldn't square being naked and doing it with those girls. What would you say? It just seemed really embarrassing and gross. Plus when I was honest with myself, I wasn't sure I was ready. Still, that didn't seem to stop Emma's dad having weird ideas about us.

Mum smiled at me. She seemed to think I'd work it out in time.

I was dreaming away when Aunty Liz came to my door.

"Hi sleepyhead," she smiled.

I looked over at her.

"Hi Aunty Liz."

She came in and sat by my bed.

"That was quite a night you had."

"Yeah," I agreed.

"Tama Reeves rang."

"Oh yeah?"

"He was very uptight. I had to calm him down."

"OK."

"Of course he imagines a whole heap of stuff that didn't happen, while I can see exactly what did."

"Oh," I wondered if that was good.

She smiled.

"You made me proud Sam. You stopped Ax, and you saved Emma. Your Grandfather's stoked."

"Oh good."

"Sergeant Seay's coming pretty soon so you'd better get up."

"Oh ... OK."

She got up and went to the door. Stopped, smiled and turned.

"You look like you're a pretty mean kisser too. No wonder the girls like you."

I felt myself going red.

She smiled and left. I admit I was smiling to myself all afternoon after that.

Sergeant Smith knew he had a problem. He was a bit nervous when he met me. Aunty Liz and Grandpop were in the front lounge as well. He listened hard and tried a few questions that were meant to catch me out. Finally after he'd written it all down he stood up.

"Tama went up the track about ten and found all Emma's marks and the cannabis. The drug squad are due pretty soon and the helicopter will be taking out the plants."

"I can't say I think you kids were all that wise doing what you did. These guys are not to be messed with. They could easily have killed you, or injured you and left you in the bush and nobody would have known where you were. So although we owe you for being lucky, don't do it again. They won't give you

57

another chance."

"Have you arrested the gang?" I asked.

"They'll be taken in for questioning. One of them may rat on the others. The problem is only your evidence links them with the cannabis and even then not very well. A good defence lawyer could make it hard for us to get a prosecution."

This was not so good. Later on we heard the helicopter and the police launch was out to sea for a while too. But as Grandpop said, all we had done was get Ax mad. The danger would come when he tried to get even.

When Rewa and Asal came home they told us that the cops had taken away the whole gang. Everyone seemed to be pleased about that. But they added that the Americans and the Turks were now waiting together by their cars on the beach. They had followed Ken and Grandpop's Pinzgauer all the way to the top of the turnoff down to Renwick. There was no doubt they planning something.

None of us had gone to school. In theory we all had the spewing virus Ashley had faked to escape MS13. I called Emma to see how she was.

"I've got a helluva headache but apart from that I'm fine," she said.

"You know your dad doesn't want us to go out together at night," I told her.

"Yeah, but he doesn't mind if there are adults around," she hinted.

"What do you mean?" I asked.

"Well, you must have some spare rooms over there," she said.

"Yeah, sure." I agreed.

"So maybe I could come over and stay the night some time?"

"Ah yeah ... OK, I'll ask," I said.

"Yeah, but not right now. Dad's still jumpy. He's really worried the gang's going to be coming back to get us."

"Well, you're safer from them here, than there," I pointed out.

"Yeah, but he thinks we ... well, you know."

"No, I don't."

"He thinks we're going out to ... you know."

"Oh."

There was a pause. We both listened to the other trying to get up the courage to say something and then we both spoke at once.

"I really like ..." she began.

"I really missed ..." I started.

We stopped.

"You go," I said.

"No you," she answered.

I thought for a moment.

"I really missed our times together after last summer. It was a lot of fun."

"Me too Sam. I didn't know what ... well you ..."

"I know ... But you're right. If you had a sleepover you'd ... well you'd learn a lot about us here. It'd be pretty educational."

"That's what I thought," she said.

"So let's work toward it when you're dad's a bit more relaxed," I suggested.

"OK ... Can't wait," she said.

"Me too."

"OK, well ... see you at school I guess," she finished.

"Yeah ... See you."

I came off the phone feeling better than I had in weeks. There was a knock at the door of the apartment. It was Tahira wearing her hair in a scarf.

"Missers Jones says we 'av to do our cleaning," she told me.

"Oh, OK."

I followed her down to the cleaning cupboards. We got our vacuum cleaners and dragged them to the top floor.

"Djhou are very 'appy wit yourzelf," she noticed.

"Yeah," I admitted.

"You kessed Emma," she said. It was not a question.

"Hmm," I smiled.

"But she was distant, yes?"

I thought for a second she was reading me. But she was smiling to herself at my expression.

"How did you...?"

"Because eet eez obvious."

"Why?"

"A girl does not change at once. She ees not a big lightswitch to be turned on or off. She likes you, yes, but she does not know of your commitment. You av to give something. At ze moment she 'as not given you first place in er 'eart. Zat you 'av to win."

And smiling at her own genius at romance she turned on the vacuum cleaner making a reply impossible.

I thought about that while we worked. I wondered what I had to give. I realised I had no idea, but I wasn't going to ask Tahira this time. I wanted to work it out with Emma.

After chores and dinner we had a general meeting down in the briefing theatre. Rewa and Asal came too because it was about keeping safe at school. Grandpop started off.

"After the way the two foreign teams joined forces today to watch you we suspect they may act independently of Ax's gang," he let that sink in.

"OK, so as every soldier knows, it's better to attack than defend. Sitting around waiting to get hammered is bad tactics and bad for morale. No base is invulnerable, not even this one. You have to harass the attacker and rob him of his surprise and coordination. It all comes down to get him before he gets you."

"Now unfortunately from what Ali and Patricia tell us these guys are not very easily intimidated. They expect a level of violence which ... well ... it wasn't good for me, and I'm not going to let you guys go there. So we can't do anything which will horrify them because that's what they're used to."

"We could zap them and put them somewhere else but that would make them send more to kill everyone. Secrecy is their friend not ours. What we want is for the cops to catch these guys and expose them for what they are. So the first thing we need to do is introduce our friends to Sergeant Smith. Not for anything huge, but for enough that they get uncomfortable."

"So the plan is to break into the place they are staying, and steal stuff from their rooms. Passports, credit cards, cash, phones. Not cameras or computers. Stuff they can mostly replace but which involves lots of form filling and shagging around. The break ins have to involve damage so the owner has to make insurance claims and repairs. Then we plant the stuff on Ax's guys."

"That will start some fireworks and get Sergeant Smith involved again. So the plan is to do that tonight about two in the morning so you guys can sleep in your suits. Now meanwhile Bernard has been amusing himself setting traps along all the bush paths from the Chapel to the House."

Bernard grinned as he stood to speak.

"It is nothing lethal but the sort of things poachers use to take

61

large animals. We don't think they will drive down because it's too obvious. Even so Ken's put his barbed wire net back out on the road so if they do try it, they won't get far. But hopefully anyone trying to sneak down the paths tonight will spend quite a lot of time trying to get untangled."

We smiled as Grandpop took over again.

"Our hope is that while our visitors are doing this, you'll be robbing their units."

We all laughed a bit about that.

"However ... if ... and we have to plan for this ... if they get past the traps we need to be ready in case they try and break in here."

"We've given Control access to the window washing system that keeps the salt off, and to the sprinkler system. He can turn it on to give any visitors a thorough soaking if they get close enough."

We were enjoying this.

"So if they get inside ... no ... listen.."

Tarik was acting out how we would get them.

"If they do ... get inside we do have a problem," he said seriously. "We can use the amnesia rays but they need a good size bruise on the head to go with them. So if they get inside we need a good story which doesn't involve you guys but involves me, Bernard and Ken."

"Because we can't be sure they won't be armed the plan is to let them come up to levels two and three and ambush them in the corridors with the umbrellas. Then we'll thump them. If they do anything anti-social like try and light fires downstairs we'll send you guys in to zap them first."

"So who wants to do the burglaries?"

"Ash and I have Hooty and Buffy for support. We make sense," said Scott

"Cool. You're the burglars. Sam and Tahira you'll be called up if they come before three. Cam and Tarik if they come after that. I'll get up with Nguyen to keep him company in the morning."

"OK, so for tomorrow everyone takes their ground kit to school. Don't all wear the sunnies at the same time or you'll look sus. Just keep everything in your bag and keep it close. Tarik and Ashley keep a low profile. Cam and Scott watch your buddies. The rest of you keep your eyes open and keep in contact."

"Right Scott and Ashley you stay behind to look at the burglary mission. The rest of you teeth, toilet, suits and bed."

And that was it. I went to bed and woke up at seven the next day feeling really great even though my eye was still puffy. But it turned out that this time it had been my turn to miss out on all the fun.

What happened was most of Ax's crew missed the ferry back after being released by the cops because there was no evidence they had done anything. Ax and Ray were still being questioned but a few of the gang came back on the last ferry drunk and in a grumpy mood because they had lost a lot of money because of the raids. Two of Ax's gang agreed to help the foreigners get us, probably hoping to cash in a bit with them. The other three were too drunk to be any use to anyone and were left behind.

The two MS13 and the two Ergenekon spies set off with their shotguns and their two local guides at one in the morning. They arrived at the Chapel about fifteen minutes later and cut the phone lines to Renwick. Then they started through the bush. About five minutes later the first of Ax's gang guys was hoisted ten meters off the ground in a net. Apparently he yelled enough to wake the dead. His mate stayed to help him down.

Now alert to traps, the MS13 and Ergenekon spies, kept going.

Scotty said you could tell the Turks were way more used to being soldiers in forests than the Americans. So the next victim of Bernard's traps was an MS13 gangster who tripped a wire and got a stinging nettle flicked up into his face. He wasn't too quiet either as he blundered around unable to see out of his swollen face. The same guy then tripped all by himself and gashed himself on an old branch which could have happened to anyone but convinced him he was in a minefield of improvised weapons. That impression would have been reinforced the next minute by one of the Turks getting caught by a cunningly placed neck snare which brought a large log down on his head, stunning him. The stunned guy and the blinded guy were left to look after each other.

The remaining Turk and American decided the road had to be safer then going through the woods so they cut across to the gravel and started cautiously down the road. They were trying to get the vicious barbs of Ken's razor wire car trap off their shoes when Ashley and Scott bent into their unit at the motel.

Ash and Scott smashed through the cases and searched through all their baggage, tossing it around. They found the passports and a large wad of American money. There were no phones or wallets around so they assumed they had taken them with them. The Turks' had hidden their stuff and Ash and Scotty had to turn the whole place over. But they came away with wallets, passports and money.

The next trick was to plant the money on the other gang members. Scott bent into the toilet and hid the money under the mattress of some large hairy man snoring his head off in bed. Then they smashed windows into a whole bunch of motel units using their claws and vanished up to the Chapel above Renwick.

By this time Ax's guy in the bush had managed to injure himself badly getting out of the net, one of the Turks was concussed and one of the MS13 was hobbling badly. They were heading back to the cars so Ash and Scott split up and let the air out of *all* their cars' tyres and bent home.

Meanwhile the remaining Turk and MS13 gangster were trying to find a way into the house. When they got close enough Control made sure they were drenched by the sprinklers.

Still, these guys were tough. A little water was not doing to stop them. They had shotguns and they were getting pissed off. After walking around the sleeping house a few times they found a ladder in Gunter's workshop put it up to the front windows and decided they'd smash their way in. Unfortunately the windows were a sandwich of thick plastic and glass so they couldn't do a thing to them with the shotgun butts. They even nearly brained themselves when they tried to use a sledgehammer which bounced off the window. Luckily they realised firing the shotguns would wake everyone so they didn't try them.

They circled again and realised the windows of the front gallery about eight meters above the front entrance was just in range of the ladder and *those* windows were ordinary glass. The skinny MS13 gangster was the lightest and quickest, so he went up while the big Turk held the ladder.

For some reason we'd forgotten about the ghosts. To us they were an unpleasant nuisance like rats or ants. You coped with them even though they were depressing and annoying. The American – well he was Spanish American, they both were, obviously got a helluva shock when hideous Private Archibald Brown suddenly appeared, because he bellowed with fear and fell off the ladder eight meters to the concrete steps where he lay

65

with badly broken ribs and a broken arm.

The remaining Turk decided that the fun was over and carried the badly injured American back up the road, forgetting about the lower razor wire net Ken had set and stepping on it heavily dropping the already injured American in his surprise. There was a lot of screaming.

At this point Grandpop woke up and turned on the gallery lights. He tried the phone and found it cut. The badly hurt attackers got away to their rental cars and drove all the way back to their units on flat tyres. When Grandpop got down to the control desk he found Scotty and Ashley laughing with tears pouring down their faces, and sent them to bed.

So by the time we got to the bus in the morning we were feeling pretty good. We convinced Grandpop to let us play gangsta style music and all put our sunnies on and danced about to that. Control had no idea why we wanted to do that.

When we got to school Emma noticed we were all excited and sidled over. Scott and Ashley retold what had happened while we made sure nobody else listened in. She high-fived Scott and Ashley. And it was from then on that I think we accepted Emma into our group.

CHAPTER SEVENTY SIX: A SURPRISING PRISONER

Lunchtime!" Sue says decisively, getting up from the couch, where she's been lying.

"And then I'm going out. I need some space," she says muffled from the passageway.

I sit for a moment in the living room, but then feeling stupid I get up and follow her.

She's opening the cupboards.

"Looks like it's beans on toast," she says. "There isn't much else left."

She puts the kettle on and offers me some tea.

"Yes please. So whaddya think?" I ask, feeling unsure of myself.

"I think ... it's not getting us much closer to solving the case," she says inspecting a near empty cupboard.

"Well no ..." I admit.

She opens a can of beans, tips them into a pot and sticks it on the stove.

"I mean Sam where is all this going?" she asks a little grumpily.

"I dunno. I'm just telling it how I saw it."

"Hmmm," she says stirring the beans, thinking.

"And Ax was never charged over mistreating you and Emma?"

"No."

"Why not?"

"There was a whole bunch of lawyer stuff I didn't understand. Something to do with me and Emma being unreliable, whatever that means. It pissed us off."

"And the cannabis?"

"The police took it."

"Yes of course, but did they charge Ax with growing it?"

"No. They couldn't. Nothing except us linked him to it."

"Hmmm."

"Gavin Smith got two new cops to help him for a while though. Their first job was investigating the break in at the motel. They never did find the American's money we planted though. The hairy guy must have kept it well hidden. The MS13 who was hurt – his name was Reno something – went to hospital in Auckland and then went home. The other guy – Hernandez – he stayed with Ax."

"What were the Turkish guys' names?"

"No idea, I never saw the passports."

"So did Ax come back at you guys?"

"No, he vanished with Hernandez."

"Vanished? " She asks, surprised.

"Yeah. We didn't see him for a whole month."

"Where did he go?"

"It turned out he went visiting in Menazanilla, Mexico."

She looks at me frowning at such a strange twist. Then she gets it.

"Oh shit!" Sue breathes. "I assume he wasn't there on holiday."

"No, you got it. He went to meet up with the Sinaloa drug cartel."

"So he was trying to get into the big time?" she asks.

"Yeah. He had a plan. It was pretty simple really. Aotea is over an hour out of Auckland harbour for ships from Menazanilla, Mexico. Menazanilla is a Sinaloa smuggling port handling Cocaine and Meth ingredients from China and quite a few ships call into Auckland from there. Up the road from Renwick is Port Hobson where yachts, some of the bigger fishing trawlers and game fish launches moor. Of course the Hauraki Gulf is full of small craft day and night. As Ax saw it where better to intercept ships from China before they reach customs and take delivery of stuff dropped over the side. He was going to offer a customs bypass service because those ships get searched pretty heavily and the Mexicans were used to milk powder from New Zealand coming through."

"Hmmm could work," Sue admits.

Sue takes some bread and stuffs it into the toaster and goes back to the beans.

"I should've fried some onions with it," she comments to herself. She looks at me like I'm a new idea.

"Do you like onions?"

"Yeah," I shrug, "I like onions."

"Oh well, too late."

The toaster pops. She grabs some plates, pokes her nose into the fridge and pulls out a tub of margarine. There's barely any left but she scrapes it onto the bread. Then spoons beans onto it. She gives me the plates and I take them to the table while she puts on the jug. She joins me at the table with knives and forks.

I hadn't realised how hungry I'd been getting and we scoff the lot in a minute.

"I think ... I need to check some stuff out," she announces.

"At work?"

"Yeah."

"Won't they … you know … be angry because you didn't tell them where you were?" I ask.

She picks up the plates and takes them to the bench. I get up and Sue starts to do the dishes. I grab a tea towel.

"Probably. But I'll have some good progress to report."

"Like what?"

"That I met with Dr Prosperov and everyone else, and they aren't dead and very much alive, at a secret location. That should shut them up."

She finishes the dishes and pulls the plug. I finish drying. She's smiling but it's more a getting-ready-for a scrap smile than anything else. She's going to shock the cops but she had a head full of ideas.

She suddenly looks at me as I look at her.

"I keep forgetting you can do that," she says directly, warning me off.

"Do what?" I ask, innocently.

"Read my mind."

"I wasn't," I say defensively. She keeps looking at me.

"Well, OK I can, but only vaguely. If I want a particular bit of information I can get it and if I want a sense of where you're at I can get that, but minds leap all over the place. Dr P's was always on the go so we could never read his."

"Hmm. Yes. I suspect from the games he had you play that he knew how to do that already, and he does it on purpose too."

"Why?"

"It's just a hunch. I can't be sure yet. Don't try and read me. It might be wrong and for the moment I'd rather I kept it to myself."

"It's hard *not* to think of something." I point out.

She grins at me.

"When did you first meet that French Interpol Inspector. The one you saw again the day before yesterday. The one on the moon?"

"Du Croix? In Belem, Brazil, there's a kid in the jungle there somewhere, we still haven't found yet."

"How far are we away from that?"

"Oh that wasn't until July 2008. But then we didn't have much to do with Du Croix until we needed his help with Diana."

"I thought she went back to Moldova."

"They did, but it's a shithole, so they decided to have another try at escaping."

"When?"

"They waited for winter to pass. They decided their biggest mistake had been not to wait for good weather. They wanted to be able to sleep outside if they had to so they didn't go 'til the beginning of April."

"And we're up to what? March?"

"Yeah, nearly. The Khadem's hadn't started fasting yet."

"But when did you meet Inspector Du Croix again?"

"Not til September."

Sue's calculating.

"And that was the last of MS13 and Ergenekon?"

"Of Ergenekon, yes. It was too late for them. When Tarik planted the archive back in Turkey so it could be discovered by the right people it made such a stink Ergenekon were seriously being laid-into back home. They couldn't be bothered about New Zealand and the Gursoys anymore. But it was different with the Robinsons."

"How?"

"Well, they took the job off MS13."

"Who did? I thought that it was MS13 that Patricia's brother had stolen from."

"Well, that's what the Robinsons thought too, but that guy Heysoos was in with the old Mexican Gulf cartel. When that split with Los Zetas he ended up with Sinaloa in Menazilla. So when Ax shows up they make the connection so Ax offered to take over from MS13 and build a link across the Pacific."

"And how do you know this?"

"He told Rewa."

"Rewa! I thought he was under a court order not to approach her?"

"Yeeaahh, well ... they spent some time."

"When?"

"Before he died."

Sue's looking at me strangely.

"When did *that* happen again?"

"Umm not til December, last year."

"Hmmm," Sue muses. Then she snaps out of it.

"OK," she says and grabs her phone from the bench, dials and orders a cab. Then she goes into the bathroom where I find her putting on makeup.

"What will you tell the cops about me?" I ask a bit nervously. She glances at me briefly.

"That you're back with your Aunt."

She puts on some lippy, looking at herself in the mirror.

"Won't they want to talk to Dr P?"

"Of course."

"What will you tell them?"

She checks herself again in the mirror.

"That I don't know where they are because I was blindfolded. All I know is that it was by the sea, somewhere within an hour of Whangarei."

She starts with mascara.

"How's your head?"

"Pretty good actually," she says.

I watch her as she lines her eyes.

"Well not *good*," she admits to the mirror. "But a whole lot better than you'd expect after someone performed brain surgery on you. How's your hand?"

"Yeah, it's sore but the suit is very good for healing skin."

"What will you do while I'm gone?" Sue asks putting her eyeliner away.

"Dunno. Might see what's happening with Nathan."

"That would help. I'd love to know what he remembers."

"I'll see what I can find out."

"OK," she pauses for a moment." Look Sam ..."

"Yeah?"

"Umm ... just watch your back eh?"

"What do you mean?"

"Look ... I'm not sure exactly what's happening here, but there's a bunch of stuff that doesn't add up. I don't think you know everything you should. I don't want to say more now."

There's a worried look on her face. I'm suddenly struck by how much she cares for me.

"Thanks Sue," I say, and mean it.

"I'll be back around six," she adds.

I pull up my hood, close the facescreen and bend back to Hastings.

[+]

The lightning crackles, then the water sluices and the air blows.
I come out to find Hekator, Grandpop and Dr P sitting in the
control lounge. They are still talking when I walk over.

"So there's nothing for it, we just have to be fast," Hekator's
saying.

"Hi Sam," he nods.

"Hi, what's happening?"

"Things are bad for Nathan," Grandpop tells me.

"The growth in Sue's head was going to completely take over her
brain," Hekator explains. "Nathan's is much more advanced. We
can't just kill it as I had first hoped. We will need to bring him
aboard the Vimana Ashanti for immediate medical attention,"
Hekator nods at me.

I was supposed to get something from this. I didn't.

"Oh," I shrug.

"Problem is Nathan is compromised. Information immediately
returned to Administration," Dr P starts to explain.

"Yeah," I nod, not making the connection they seem to expect.

"So we need you to zap him, bag him and send him to Ashanti,"
Hekator says. "We have to take him by surprise. Anything he
sees may well be linked back to the Administration."

"Oh, OK."

"What about his grandmother?" Grandpop checks. "They may
well try to get to her if they guess that Nathan is being treated."

"Perhaps is best to evacuate both," Dr P suggests to Hekator.

"Then you will need an alpha crystal," Hekator says to me.

"Will I?" I shrug, having no idea what that is.

"It's a small red crystal. You press it on their foreheads for
a moment for it to stick on, then it puts them in an alpha
suggestive state. I'll get the doctor on Ashanti to send you some."

"Sure," I nod.

"Other than that, its up to you to work out how you lift him from where he is now and put him back ... wherever you want to put him."

"Can we plant memories?" Dr P asks.

"Yes. But simple ones are best," Hekator says. "But the first priority is to remove that growth."

"Do you think you'll ever be able to get it out of Sir Michael?" I ask.

"If it's fully developed it would kill him."

That was depressing. But Hekator looked upbeat.

"But actually Sam that is a good suggestion because he would be an excellent candidate for an experimental procedure I've been thinking about."

"What's that?"

"Well, I can't remove the whole brain tap, it's too invasive and connected to be killed or removed, but I can change the communications interface that it connects to so that it doesn't talk to the Administration anymore. It's a weakness with their design. You see they've focused on growing links into human brains so they can monitor and control. But they haven't needed to secure the whole system because they hide the communications interface deep in the lobe by the amygdala where it's inoperable with your technology. But using our technology I can cut off and even replace the communications interface. I can't do it without them knowing but I can do it while the patient's asleep so they won't be able to retaliate by killing him or making him attack."

"So you're cutting it off at the roots?" I ask.

"Yes, that's a good analogy."

It amazes me how clever Hekator is at getting around problems that look impossible to solve.

"That's great Hekator," I tell him.

"If, of course, the ethics court agree, and they haven't become bitter after they were overridden over Sue," Hekator grins grimly. "I won't be able go back to the Council again. Anyway we'll worry about that when we get to it. I'd better go back to Ashanti. Good luck Sam."

He folds to nothing and vanishes.

"How is new recruit Sam?" Dr P wants to know.

"Umm ... she's going back to work. She's going to pretend we're hiding up North."

"Good. Is plan," Dr P nods.

"Will talk with her tonight. Will leave you to organise retrieval of Nathan," Dr P says to Grandpop, and with that he turns and takes a disc up.

Grandpop waits til he's out of earshot and says quietly, "The others are really jealous Sam. They'd rather not be at school."

"Who wouldn't?" I shrug.

"Well, enjoy it while it lasts. OK, let's take a look at Nathan."

It was half past eight at night in Florida and raining hard. The palm trees were shaking in the driving rain and cars were swishing through the streets outside the motorlodge, which stood in an empty looking car park. Nathan and his Grandmother had eaten pizzas and were watching TV in their second storey room.

"What's it like outside?" I ask.

We change our view to the car park outside. The wind and the rain make all the cars shiny, reflecting the orange sodium lights, and the shadows of the trees dances on them. We look around.

There's a black Ford Transit van with tinted windows. It looks very sus'.

Grandpop circles it but he can't get closer. Control's appears. "Mike, I think that one could be dangerous. I won't put the dimensional probe inside it. I'll x-ray it from here instead," he says.

On Grandpop's big wrap-around screen, projected on nothing, the van appears to glow, then the shapes of three men, sitting inside appears.

"Hmm, I wonder what *they're* doing?" Grandpop asks.

One of them appears to make a call on his cell.

"That's interesting," Control comments. "That phone is connected to the local cellular service but it hasn't initiated a call. That suggests that phone is similar to the ones we have and has a quantum modem as well."

"You mean he's not human."

"He may be human but his phone wasn't made on *this* planet. It also suggests they detected my x-rays."

"Can we search around Nathan's neighbours?" I ask.

"Given the Administration appears to be waiting for us I don't think that is a good idea. The dimensional probe can be seized. That may be what they are hoping for," Control says.

Grandpop sighs.

"It's like fishing ... We really need Hooty and Buffy on this."

"Yes I would agree. Their links can't be grabbed," Control agrees.

"But Scott and Ashley aren't back until four which is ..."

"Midnight in Florida," Control agrees.

"Well Sam, looks like you're off the hook. You can't do this by yourself after all. We'll need the whole team. What would you like to do?"

I remember what Sue asked about Nathan's medical records. "I'm wondering about those medical records of Nathan's. I'd like to visit the Mediscan lab and see what they have."

"Sure. Let's have a look," says Grandpop.

Control brings up the Mediscan building. He ran a few checks then the viewpoint moved inside. It's after business hours so there's a small crew still at work in the lab but the administration area is dark because everyone's gone home. There's no security cameras or anything inside.

"Looks OK," Grandpop says. "Take a key."

He pulls open a drawer of Control's USB keys. I take one, roll over to the cabinet and bend space-time.

[+]

The office is completely dark. Immediately I feel alert because you never know what can happen. It's a two storey industrial area in Virginia outside town. Through the windows I can see other buildings, some with their lights on. I feel the busy spirit of the place. This is an office where they moved things through fast. I try to relax and take things carefully.

I look around the desks. There's a lot of PCs but Control wants the server. After exploring a bit I eventually find a small server rack and plug in Control's USB key. Control does his thing while I check the place out.

The corner offices are locked but they are easily opened with my pinky key. I go through them all checking drawers and cupboards. There's a lot of papers, books and boring personal stuff. But after half an hour I find something interesting: a small fridge in someone's cupboard. It seems odd so I look inside. I find beer in front but at the back a box of blood samples. I pull them out and check them over.

There's nothing written on them, though each sample has ID numbers and dates. They're obviously out of place. There's a big, busy lab for this sort of thing downstairs. This was the admin area. Why should any samples be stored up here? Especially samples without proper labels. Grandpop's interested too. "Good work Sam. I reckon we tag that and see where it goes," he says.

I squirt tracking fluid onto the bottom of the box from my forefinger, and wait for it to dry into an invisible tag. Then I put it back where it was.

I check the office for the name of its owner and find a box of cards with Dr Daniel J Johnson on them. I think it's his office. Then I put everything back the way it was when I came in, lock up, pick up the USB key and fold back to the decontamination booth.

[+]

I go over to Grandpop.

"That looked pretty useful Sam."

I agree and sit down. After a short while Control appears.

"Dr Johnson has an interesting email correspondence with the school nurse, Mrs Sanchez. He asks for double samples for certain students but she doesn't ask why and he doesn't explain. Nor does he have any emails with anyone else about them."

"I think we need ..."

"A fly, yeah OK," I say, getting up.

Grandpop reaches into another drawer and looks through rows of small clear containers

"A little one, I think," he says to himself.

He picks one but instead of giving it to me, takes it to the cabinet.

"It's a new trick of Hekator's," he explains, "the case defines the payload and shields the fly for the transfer but is destroyed on entry. That way we can inject a fly with a much smaller field density," he says coming back to the desk.

"OK, Control off you go."

There's a tiny flash in the office I've just visited and a small flycam window appears in space in front of the office scene. Control flies the flycam to a bookshelf and parks it there.

"Why don't we do that for Nathan?" I ask.

"We will but not for a while yet. After lunch. Hopefully it will have stopped raining."

I forget that it's only eleven thirty here in Tasmania.

"How's Sue?"

"She's a bit cranky today ... she finds listening to me annoying now."

"You must be getting a bit sick of her too by now too."

"Well, it's not so much her, as all this waiting around."

Grandpop laughs briefly.

"I remember the young ones in Vietnam said the same thing," he sighs and ruffles my hair.

"You always get waiting around, Sam. Get used to it. Take advantage of it. Why don't you get that suit off and just chill. You've been on edge for two weeks you need to take some time out. Sue's probably the same."

"What can I wear?" I ask.

"Wear your ground kit." he suggests.

I didn't really want to, but he had nothing else for me to do so I go up and get changed. He's waiting for me outside the changer. We go up into the greenhouse and then over the lawn to Hastings Hall.

I get a second lunch of Tom Yum soup with all the adults and the little kids. Then Mrs Jones suggests I make up for my absence by doing the others cleaning. It isn't exactly exciting but I did owe them – especially Tahira – so I set to work.

I have tons of time and it's kind of nice to get to know this place. You notice things when you clean. Scuff marks here, patterns in the carpet there. The adults come by and tease me or stop to chat. They're mostly in the library working on what they call our 'reintegration strategy' which means our plans for being seen alive in New Zealand and then escaping again so *they* lose track of us somewhere in the world. They're talking pretty hard-out about all this adult stuff to do with immigration law and account transfers.

It makes me realise there's a lot more to escaping the Administration than just jumping in a tube and disappearing. They're old, so officials in other countries want to know their history. Making one up isn't easy.

After three hours cleaning I'd pretty much done everything. I go downstairs and Ken suggests I have a spa.

"I've hardly got any clothes." I point out.

Aunty Liz agrees we need to do something about that but there isn't time yet. Ken says the ground kit dries quickly enough, so I stripped down to the underwear and get in. After all the stress of the last few weeks it was definitely worth it.

I was just getting out when Ken tells me he's off to pick the others up from school and asks if I want to come along. I want to see where I'll end up so I go with him.

We drive down the long drive. Automatic gates slide open and we head out onto the road. The road's gravel, just like at

Renwick, and runs downhill until it meets the seal. From there it runs along the coast and through forests. The trees are tall and light. The bush is messier and not as heavy as the bush back home and it seems way more cheerful and less scary. We go over a hill and come into a bay where a pier juts out.

"Your grandfather's boat is the one at the end," Ken points out. It's an aluminium workboat, not unlike the two others moored there. It's just the sort of thing I knew he loved. Not fancy, but practical.

The road turns inland and the country opens up into farmland. It's so like home I have to pinch myself: the crappy little houses; the cute churches; the rugged pubs and shops. It all seems so familiar and I wonder if this was how Scott or maybe Ashley had felt when they'd settled into Aotea; knowing you came from a poor, unimportant place and arriving in another just like it. The drive to the school takes half an hour, which is longer than I expected. Plymouth District High is a small set of run down brick buildings off the main road. There's a bus and a bunch of cars full of mothers, and some fathers, in the carpark. The surprising thing is how many of them are Aboriginal. It seems every third face has the darker skin tones and shape of the original people of the land – the "tang-ata when-u-a" we call it in Maori. It's a shock to realise I'm no longer one. But they aren't really any different to anyone else. They have strong Australian accents and just gossip and laugh with the people they knew. We're hard to miss: a Mongol and a Maori kind of stand out here. An aboriginal woman comes over to talk to Ken. She says her name is Moira and she's on the school parents association. She asks about us and where we come from. I tell her it's very like Hokianga, and she's interested in the fact that I'm Maori.

She reads to me as a friendly, gossipy type who just likes people to get along so I like her straight away.

She's a bit unusual though. Most of the others – black and white – are stand-offish. They're wiry, hard looking people with hard eyes. They shake Ken's hand and call him "mate" but don't smile. Moira takes us into the school. I turn back and catch one of the men pulling his eyelids in imitation of Ken's while the other's silently laugh. That isn't so different to Aotea either.

The school building is just plain tired. Nobody's spent any money on it. It didn't seem surprising there's talk of closing it. The white woman in the office seems to know Moira quite well and she gets some forms for me to fill in. Ken asks, but the woman says the principal, Dave Hamlin, is teaching. Then the tinny bell rings starting the rumble of classrooms packing up. We go to room eight where the others are. They're surprised to see me, but pleased as well. Apart from the whites I notice there are five aboriginal kids in the class, plus us lot. The teacher, Mrs Driver, is a fat, white woman wearing pink, pearls and way too much makeup. Ken introduces me using my new name: Stan Hawke. She seems friendly enough but she wonders what problems I'm hiding.

We leave the classroom and gather up Asal and Rewa before heading back to the Transit. The others are giving me heaps about missing out on school but Ken points out I'd done all their cleaning, so they ease up after that.

In the carpark I notice Moira has collected her son. He's tall, about fifteen, in a white shirt, and good looking. I notice Tahira notice him too, but I'm distracted by Rewa who asks me when I'm moving in. I tell her I think it's this weekend.

The Transit's a lot more cramped than Betty. We have to stay in our seats and wear the seatbelts. I sit with Rewa and we talk about her day at school. She says it isn't much bigger than Aotea but teaches from kindergarten level all the way to final secondary. She and Asal have made friends with two white girls: Kate and Fiona. She says they have a mixed age class of twenty two kids. There are only six teachers for one hundred and forty two kids. Her teacher's name is Mrs Houghton who's a bit strict, especially with kids who aren't white.

I ask the others about Mrs Driver.

"She is very crude," Tahira says disapprovingly.

But Tarik thinks she's funny, as does Scott. Ashley and Cam think she's trying too hard to act like a man. I ask about the other kids.

"They think of us as the rich newcomers," Scott says.

"The black kids don't like us, and da white kids dey don't like us either. Dey're all embarrassed? Dey tink we rich," Ashley explains.

"No, not so much rich or poor," disagrees Cam. "Their world is small and comfortable. We make them think bigger. That makes them feel small. So they don't like us making them feel small."

It was logical and sensitive as Cam always is.

"Yah, it was the same on Aotea," Tarik agrees.

"Except Kevin," Tahira puts in. "He already thinks bigger."

"That's true," Ashley agrees.

"Who's Kevin?" I ask.

"He's the Aborigine guy in Grade ten. He's very popular," Scott says, raising his eyebrows, thinking of Tahira and a few other girls.

"Ee's cool," Tahira says. "He doesn't take shit."

"He gets shit from those O'Grady brothers," Tarik disagrees.

"And his cousins William and Fred like to try and bring him down too," Scott agrees.

It sounds just like back home again to me. Scott and Ashley relate to it too.

When we get in it's four in the afternoon. Grandpop's waiting and tells Ashley and Scott to go get Hooty and Buffy and meet the rest of us over at the base. It's nice to be working with the others again. I don't feel so lonely any more. Ken follows us too. When Ashley and Scott join us in the briefing room Grandpop gets Control to put up the hologram. Ken stays at the back to watch.

It's still dark and raining in Florida. We're watching over a whole bunch of two storey holiday apartments surrounded by parking lots. A connecting road leads back to a main road that goes through a shopping area. The whole place is a patchwork of built-up areas, empty lots, and bushy bits which are often swamps.

We're about a kilometer away from the second storey motorlodge room Nathan and Ashley's grandmother are staying in. It's late so they're probably asleep. Outside, the big black van we x-rayed before is still sitting there, the Administration agents inside probably watching for any sign of us. Grandpop sums up the situation.

"So this is where Nathan and Margaret are staying. They're both asleep. This van is a suspected Administration observation point. From the flies we think the ground floor apartment below them is in Administration hands too. Our job is to get Nathan and Margaret to the Vimana Ashanti without losing them or any of us."

"The obvious problem is that the Administration is expecting us. Control suspects the Administration are using Nathan and Margaret as bait and have field detectors and possibly wormhole stabilisers ready to grab us when we pounce."

"Mike?" Control interrupts.

"Yeap?" he replies.

"There's an Administration fighter overhead now, as well."

Our view pulls back and we begin to realise Control has zoomed in from a long, long way away. The view tilts and barely three kilometers above are the unmistakable three blue lights of the gravity deflectors of a triangular UFO fighter just below the clouds.

"They don't seem too bothered about being seen, tonight do they?" Grandpop comments to us.

"Means we can't bend dive in, too," Scott points out.

"And they have an aerial view over the approaches," Grandpop grumbles. He sits back, rubbing his chin.

"Well this is getting pretty hard isn't it. Let's see, what can we do?"

"Distraction?" suggests Tarik.

"I can't risk anyone being caught, Tarik," Grandpop warns.

"No, look at it this way. They are expecting us to bend in. What if we drive in?" Tarik grins.

"In what?" Grandpop asks, thinking speeders.

"In a car."

That's a surprise.

"But you can't drive," Grandpop objects.

"Sure I can. An automatic anyway. What if we're a bunch of street racers. We drive in and ram the van. It's the last thing they'll be expecting."

Grandpop's thinking about it.

"Hmm, certainly has a few good points to it. Control if the kids ram the van could they bend out?"

"They may not be able to if the fighter responds quickly enough," he warns.

"If we look like we're just ordinary racers they won't realise anything's up. We could even get the police to chase us," Tarik suggests.

"They might well stop you too," Grandpop warns. "Those guys are professionals. You're a fourteen-year-old kid who's just seen too many movies."

"But it would explain why we were driving fast to the fighter."

"Only one car would hit the van," Grandpop says, thinking aloud.

"I could drive ze uzzer car," Tahira volunteers.

That meant I got to ride with her. I wondered whether I liked this idea.

"I dunno," says Grandpop." It's dangerous – and I don't mean for you. There are people on the road over there who would be at risk."

"There hasn't been a lot of traffic on that main road behind you Mike. In fact I haven't seen any." Ken points out.

"Do you like the idea?" Grandpop asks, doubtfully.

"Well, it's a good distraction but to be honest I think I could drive the racer car more effectively. Normally I'd suggest Mariko for the other one but it's not something you do when pregnant. But the real problem is it doesn't solve the main problem.

How do we get to Nathan and Margaret if the fighter closes in, distraction or no distraction. If they decide their ground based grab team are knocked out they'll just move the flying one lower.

They obviously don't care about being seen."

"Yeah, it's a good distraction," Grandpop agrees, "but if there's any driving to be done I'd rather have an experienced driver do it. Sorry guys but it is actually a skill, cars aren't speeders, they don't drive themselves. OK, so let's just say we can take out the van. But the next question is what do we do about the fighter."

I think about giving it something to chase like one of us in a speeder. Then I remember Ka-rea-rea.

"Grandpop! Ka-rea-rea! Have they taken him yet?" I call out. Grandpop looks around over his glasses. Control appears.

"At present Ka-rea-rea remains in the parking building."

Grandpop thinks for a minute then asks Control, "Hmm that could certainly distract the fighter. But I'm confused. Do we need to pretend Sam hasn't rejoined us?"

I speak before Control can.

"Nah, that trick's busted. They know I was with Sue when I was meant to be in Ka-rea-rea. But they still have the feed from Sue's fake brain. They still hope to get us by getting Sue into Hastings." I say.

"Hekator is filtering Sue's experience but he is still transmitting most of it to the enemy," Control says.

"How detailed is that?"

"It includes awareness of her surroundings, her emotions and her physical wellbeing, but nothing from her higher consciousness. That hasn't developed yet."

"What does that mean in practice?"

"They know what she sees, feels and hears but not what she thinks."

"Hmm, so Sue's a potential source of distraction as well?" Grandpop checked.

"If they are confident that her transmissions haven't been tampered with."

"Is there any reason why they should?"

"None we know of."

"So to make them hope she's working for them we should make her part of the mission. Maybe *Sue* could race Ken?" Grandpop suggests.

"She'd be perfect," Ken agrees.

"Grandpop, if we're going to use Ka-rea-rea to distract the fighter it will take two hours to get him to Florida," I warn.

"Good point. But, he isn't doing anything useful in a parking lot."

"Uh Mike, its only five in the evening in New Zealand. Ka-rea-rea can't fly out of that parking building in the middle of rush hour," Ken points out.

"It will be obvious to the Administration where Ka-rea-rea is headed and when he will arrive. The probability of interception over that time frame is very high," Control says.

That's true. Compared to a Fighter Ka-rea-rea is a hummingbird against a falcon. But at four thousand knots he'd be a very slow hummingbird as well. Then I realise something.

"Hang on," I shout excitedly, "how fast can Ka-rea-rea *really* go if we don't worry about field intensity. I mean he's *already* tagged so there's no point hiding him now."

Everyone gets the idea but only Control knows the answer.

"At maximum inertialess field intensity the design can reach 240,000 knots but only in a straight line. Angling around a large gravitational mass like the Earth cuts that speed to only 48,000," Control says.

"So he could be there in … ?" Grandpop asks.

"Ten minutes," Control calculates.

"Hmmm, well that's a lot more useful. Ten minutes is enough time to react but not so much that they can intercept." Grandpop pauses for a moment thinking, then turns to me and growls over his glasses.

"Sam, we need to get Sue to that parking building and pick Ka-rea-rea up pronto. We can't hang around waiting for Auckland to shut down on a Friday night. We need to move him somewhere quiet."

"Where is she?" I ask.

"Not sure, ask Control. OK, your job is find Sue, get Ka-rea-rea. Get him somewhere you can launch him. Somewhere out of Auckland. Stay posted there will be more. Off you go."

"OK."

I run off to a pole and slide down to the cabinets.

The display by the jumpstations is empty. Another Control appears.

"Where's Sue?" I ask.

"She's in a meeting at Auckland Central police station.

"Is her car in their garage?" I ask, remembering it from when Kevin drove me from there.

"I don't know. Which vehicle is hers?" Control asks calmly.

"White Nissan Pulsar. Numberplate is uh ... PNR163Q."

"Ummm ... yes."

"Can you put me in it?"

"If you crouch."

"OK."

[+]

I dash over to the cabinet, get in and crouch down. The world folds away, spins through the realm of presences, and returns me in a flash of light to the back seat of Sue's old car. I lie down on the back seat and switch on my blend camouflage. From the outside I'm practically invisible.

"Would you like to rejoin the meeting Sam?" Control asks me.

"What? Oh! Yeah, OK."

Suddenly I appear in the briefing room as a hologram like Control. The others see me looking at myself because its weird to be a ghost. They smile and point at me. Grandpop looks over his shoulder at me but keeps talking.

"So Tarik and Cam are with Ken in the car. Your job is to make sure Ken's OK and help him escape. If we get Sue, Tahira and Sam will do the same thing with her. Ashley and Scott you are the stakeout team with Hooty and Buffy. You'll have to find a spot a few kilometers from the target or else they'll see you arrive. The whole operation relies on good timing so I'll monitor and coordinate. Sam, you launch Ka-rea-rea when we're twenty minutes out.

"OK."

"Once we've taken out the fighter and the van, Tarik and Cam will bend in and zap Nathan and Margaret. We don't have time to mess around explaining. Hekator doesn't want Nathan conscious on the Vimana anyway. Ashley and Scott you will watch their backs for new arrivals who might interfere. Tahira and Sam you are the guard and will counter-attack any interference."

We nod.

"OK, so we're waiting on Sue. Sam do you want to give her a call and hurry her up?"

"Uh ... OK...Control?"

"We don't have a node in New Zealand, Mike. I will have to link in from California. Standby."

I wait for about ten seconds, then I hear various clicks followed by the sound of Sue's phone ringing. Actually come to think of it I can also hear her ringtone too.

"*She's coming! Kill it!*" I tell Control. The connection to Hastings vanishes as well.

"Sue Williams," I can hear Sue say as her footsteps get closer.

"Hmm funny," she says.

A car drives past and toots.

She comes up to her car, fiddles with her bag, gets out her keys and gets in.

"I wonder where the little bugger is now," she mutters to herself. It makes me smile. She throws her bag onto the seat next to her.

"Behind you," I whisper.

She jumps. I can't help sniggering.

"Shit Sam! don't do that!" she says angrily, her blue eyes in the mirror. She can't see me because I'm too well blended in. She looks around for me. It takes her a moment to work out where my head is.

"Why are *you* here?" she asks finally.

"We have a mission in Florida and need you to help."

"*Florida?*"

"Yeah, but first we need to go to the parking building and pick up Ka-rea-rea."

"What? Now?"

"Yeah."

"What's all this about?"

"Nathan."

That changes her mind a bit.

"Oh! What about him?"

"It might be better if you act like you aren't talking to a missing kid wearing camouflage in the back of your car," I suggest.

"Yeah," she says pulling back. She put her keys in the ignition and checks the rear vision mirror.

She starts the engine and starts to pull out.

"Took a bit of a caning over being absent without leave," she comments over her shoulder.

She wants some concern shown.

"You OK?" I ask briefly.

She waves someone else on with her fake smile.

"Well, let's say I wrecked a five year career and if I thought I was staying I'd be gutted," she says out of the corner of her mouth as she manoeuvres out of the park and into a short queue of cars.

"But as I'm about to resign, I guess I can cope with the crap."

"Haven't you resigned?"

"No, not yet. I think it would be too sus."

We move forward to the exit slightly.

"So what's this about Nathan and Florida then?" she asks.

"He's bait. He's in the holiday place we put him but there's a men-in-black van outside and a Service fighter overhead."

"A fighter?"

"It's a Service UFO. Triangular. Very dangerous."

"And why do you want to walk into the trap?"

"To get Nathan out of *their* control, of course."

"Is he worth the risk?"

"It looks like everyone thinks he is."

"So what do I have to do?"

There's a sudden tap on her window. I freeze. The window comes down.

"Talking away to yourself?" laughs a man's voice.

"Yeah," Sue agrees nervously.

"Look Sue, about today, I know its upsetting to get a reprimand but don't let it get to you. We've all had them. Sometimes you have to take a chance on things. I think you did the right thing. Don't let it stop you taking risks otherwise you'll end up in a dead end like Kevin. You're one of our best young detectives. Don't give up just because the department can be a bit anal sometimes."

"Thank you Sir."

"OK, I just wanted to let you know we are looking out for you."

"Thanks Sir."

"Goodnight Sue."

"Goodnight Sir."

She winds back the window. A shadow passed away. Sue exhales slowly. I could breathe again too.

"Who was that?"

"Detective Chief Inspector Peter Thompson. Kevin's boss's boss."

"He likes you."

"Yeah. I didn't even think he knew who I was."

We lurch out of the garage into the gray overcast day but stop again, waiting for the car in front to join the jam.

"So what's the plan?" Sue asks.

"You and Ken are stealing cars, racing them and then Ken is ramming the men-in-black stakeout van. At the same time I try to distract the fighter with Ka-rea-rea."

"You want me to *steal* cars and *race* them?"

"Yeah – as safely as possible."

"Whose cars?"

"I dunno. Some street racer's I spose. They'll have to look the part."

"How do you rob a street racer?" she asks turning into the jam.

"Find one who's stopped at a light or to chat with his mates. Zap everyone. Throw them out and drive off. Pretty easy really."

"Hmmm," she says, thinking. "Have you any idea how many laws that would be breaking?"

"No, but at least we get two racers off the street."

"Yeah, I know but it's just not a way of thinking I'm used to yet."

"I mean if you don't want to do it, Ken can do it himself, it just won't look as natural. If there's two cars it'll look more like a couple of racers."

"And all the time Ka-rea-rea is headed for Florida? Won't that look sus?"

"No, he arrives first."

"Oh, OK."

"So what do you think? I ask."

"I think ... I'm hungry and need a shower."

"Yeah, I'm starving too. Can I sit up now?"

"No, stay down, Sophie from accounts is behind us."

"OK."

There's a silence as we drive through Auckland's busy streets.

"Sam, Mr Trân wants to know what you guys want to eat," Grandpop asks.

I passed the message on. Sue asks for something she can eat while driving.

"Mr Trân says you're getting sushi," Grandpop tells me.

"He's sending sushi," I relay.

"This has to be the best takeout service in the world," Sue smiles.

I'm glad she sounds like she's starting to relax.

"Can I sit up now?"

"Yeah, she's gone."

I change to street clothes and sit up, putting on my safety belt.

"How far away are we now?"

"About seven minutes in this traffic. What floor are we going to?"

I had to ask Control. As he's telling me it's level seven a travel box flashes onto the seat next to me. Sue swears in surprise. It's like an enormous photo flash going off. On the street a number of people glance in our direction but see nothing.

I open the box. Inside are two pretty bento boxes tied with ribbon, and miso in sealed cups.

"Food's here," I tell her happily.

At the next lights I pass Sue an opened box. She puts it on the seat next to her.

"Ohhh this is fantastic," she says, sipping the miso.

It *is* good. We munch sushi as we edge along in the queued traffic. Then, finally, Sue gets a break, roars along the straight, gets a green and then swings into the dark of the parking building. We stop to take a ticket and start zooming up the ramps while the other cars are heading down.

It's now almost half-past six and the building is dark and pretty empty. I direct Sue to the right level and over to the fenced off electrical thing Ka-rea-rea is sitting on. We pull up next to it. Sue sighs and turns to pick up her food again. I tuck into my sushi too.

A car park does not exactly provide a great view. There's a few other cars on the level. Not too far away a man is sitting in a silver car talking on his phone. He looks very relaxed, like a businessman talking to his wife at the end of the day.

"So what do we have to do?" Sue asks.

"Just move Ka-rea-rea onto your roof."

"How?" she asks, eyeing the fence with barbed wire on top.

"Easy! I just ask him to fly here," I tell her.

"Oh, of course," she says sipping her miso.

We eat the rest of our sushi.

"That guy keeps peeking at us," Sue says quietly. I try to read him. I get nothing. Damn. He's a biobot.

"That's because he works for *them*," I tell her in a low voice, looking away so as to stop him realising we've spotted him.

"Grandpop we need a sleeping bag for Sue, just in case," I ask.

"On it."

The travel box folded into nothing.

"At least these sushis are good," Sue said eating her second to last.

A big black Ford Explorer with tinted windows comes up the ramp onto the level. It makes me nervous.

"Don't look. We have company. They'll be armed."

Now I knew who this guy in the silver car had been talking to. The Explorer rolls forward cautiously. The tinted windows hide those inside. They know we're there. They're hoping to take us by surprise.

"What do we do?" Sue asks.

"We have to distract them from Ka-rea-rea. On 'go' dash for the staircase just behind us and head *up*."

Sue's looking back at me but she stretches out ready to kick open the car door.

"Why up?" she asks casually as her hand drifts to the door handle.

"They will assume we want to go down and escape."

"OK."

"Three, two, one, go!"

She's way quicker than I expect. She's out of the car and sprinting across the driveway in front of the Explorer before the guy in the silver car or I were even out the doors. His mistake is watching her. I zap him and he goes down. The guys in the Explorer start piling out, their cellphone shaped weapons at the ready. I dash after Sue who's already disappeared through the bashed looking white door. Laser targeting dots from the cellphones are everywhere as I sprint after her. The buzz of invisible lightning hits the door as I push it open. Another hits the wall just over my head in a puff of concrete dust. I dash through the door. It's heavy with a safety glass window. I leap *down* the whole flight of stairs drawing them away from Sue. I hit the far wall on the landing with my shoulder and leap the second set of stairs as the first agent opens the upper door and another buzz puffs dust off the wall above my head. I leap the next flight of stairs under the shooter as he starts after me.

"I need an LZ *in* the Explorer," I call as I land and wrench the next level door open. Another buzz hits the door I'm holding as I run through and slam it behind me, coming out onto the next level.

"No good. He's speeding for the down ramp to intercept you," Grandpop warns. It's true, I can hear the screech of the Explorer's tyres above.

"Cancel that. Make it with Sue."

[+]

The LZ information hits me and I fold to nothing an instant before the man following me reaches the door and the Explorer turns onto the deck. I leave the realm of presences and flash next to Sue who's waiting on the floor above Ka-rea-rea by the lift. An old lady is waiting with her and her mouth falls open, looking at me.

"Sorry ma'am," I tell her and zap her in the eye with the amnesia beam. She stands there, mouth open, eyes glazed.

"What's happening?" Sue asks.

"I led them down," I gasp.

"What do we do now?"

The scratched blue lift door opens.

"We get in," I say bundling her inside. I hit the 'close door' button. The lift smells of piss and one of the neon lights flickers. The old lady wakes just in time to see the door close in her face. I extend my pinky key and lock off the lift with the key.

"Now we can get them," I smile at Sue.

"How? We're locked in a lift," Sue asks confused.

"We have Ka-rea-rea, remember?"

I close my eyes and activate the small craft. He takes a little while to come up and unpack himself.

"Sam?" he asks.

I have him adopt a camo pattern so that he looks like he hasn't extended himself. Then I call Grandpop.

"*Where are they?*" I ask him.

"They've been searching under the cars. Now they've decided you took the lift. Two are headed down. The Explorer with it's driver, and two on the side are coming back for Ka-rea-rea."

"*Could someone else pick up the two who went downstairs?*"

"*Sure,*" Tahira replies.

"*Thanks Tahira.*"

Through Ka-rea-rea's sensors I see the Explorer roll up the ramp slowly. Even with Ka-rea-rea's sensors I can't see the driver through the tinting. There are two 'men' on either side walking along and looking around under the few remaining cars. The driver pulls the Explorer in beside the silver car and their fallen comrade.

"*How are you doing Tahira?*" I ask.

"*I just arrived in the women's toilets and they smell,*" she says.

"*Hang on. I'm checking the exit.*"

Ka-rea-rea's has the two guys outside the Explorer sighted.

"What's happening?" Sue asks impatiently. All she can see is a grubby lift.

"Shhh just aiming here," I tell her, with my eyes closed.

The driver of the Explorer gets out and comes behind the back of the vehicle into my line of sight. Now I have all three. He turns and looks at Ka-rea-rea. I can't believe it! It's Father Rocelli! The other two join up with him. He opens the back as the other two pick up the fallen agent from the silver car. As the other two men bring their friend to the back Rocelli stands clear and again glances at Ka-rea-rea.

I realise he's noticed Ka-rea-rea looks different, just as *he* realises I have them in my sights. I fire at once. Microsecond laser pulses hit three heads, ionise the air and send brief electric charges that knock all three down with puffs of steam.

"*Father Rocelli and two others down,*" I tell Grandpop.

"*What's he doing there?*" Tarik says.

"*I know. He was in Lichtenstein just three nights ago,*" I reply.

"*That helps. The other two are coming back off the street, inside ...*" Tahira reports.

I open my eyes. Sue's looking at me.

"What?" she asks.

"Remember Father Rocelli?"

"Yeah," she says uncomfortably.

"He's unconscious by your car."

"Huh?"

I put the key in the lock and turn. The door opens. The old lady looks at us and then wrinkles her nose in disgust as we get out. "Should be ashamed of yourselves," she mutters as she passes us, thinking we had locked her out to be alone. We dash to the stairs and head down to Ka-rea-rea's victims.

Meanwhile downstairs...

"*One ... two down*," Tahira says.

"*Now I have to drag them into the* mens'!" Tahira complains.

"*I'll do it*," Tarik tells her.

"*Thanks*," she replies.

"*Watch out for the old bag in the lift*," I warn.

We come out of the stairs and go over to the cars around Sue's to find four men lying on top of each other behind the Explorer, still with its rear door up.

"Well, that looks pretty bad," Sue says.

"Let's stuff them into their cars," I suggest.

So we pick them up and drag them back to their doors and shove their heavy drooping bodies into their seats.

"I hope no-one sees this," Sue mutters.

It's harder on her because they're bigger than she is and my suit gives me extra strength. I get two in and Sue was just going back to drag Rocelli when Grandpop calls in.

"Sam, he's a keeper."

"Hang on Sue," I tell her.

"What?" Sue asks.

"Mike's got instructions," I tell her.

"OK, but I have to move this tank of his out of the way. Grab him will you?" Sue says dropping Rocelli.

I drag him away from the back of the Explorer and lie him on her car's trunk while Sue gets into the Explorer and Grandpop fills me in.

"Hekator wants us to take him for interrogation. But we can't bend him until we have Nathan. So you guys will have to keep him," he says.

"*OK. Look, I have to talk to Sue, she may find that a bit illegal given she's still a police officer,*" I warn him.

Sue parks the Explorer next to her car, hops out and then goes to her car. She seems a bit grumpy again.

"*Can you talk to her about it? It'll sound better from you,*" I suggest.

"Put me on so I can," Grandpop tells me.

"*Ohh kay ...uh ... how?*" I wonder.

"On your suit skin."

"*Oh, right.*"

I go around to Sue who's eating the last of her sushi. She looks out the window at me. I put the video link from Grandpop on my chest like a TV. Sue lowers the window laughing up at me.

"Oh my God, you're La-la!" she laughs at me.

"Tell me about it," I mutter.

Grandpop repeats to her what he'd told me while I close my eyes and fly Ka-rea-rea to the top of Sue's car and extend his legs and grabbers so he looks like an ordinary roof rack capsule. Sue asks Grandpop a few questions. She's a bit bothered but finally agrees and Grandpop signs off.

"Shall we put him in the boot?" I ask Sue.

"Nah, he might suffocate. Put him in the back seat."

I drag Rocelli into the back seat and belt him in. He slumps so I have to rearrange him. Then I get into the front seat and we'r off.

"Where are we going?" I ask, mouth full of my last sushi.

"If we're lucky we'll catch the last ferry to Aotea."

"Why there?" I ask, surprised.

"Quiet place to launch that box of yours, and I have a few things I want to check."

"You'll have to be quick, the last ferry leaves at seven."

"Oh, I will be."

She reverses out and takes off down the ramps. It's 6:35 p.m when we leave. Sue drives with determination and cunning. I just shut up and watch. She doesn't need me yapping. We just seem to zip through traffic and get through lights without breaking any laws. We arrive with minutes to spare, buy a ticket to board the 7 p.m. ferry – the last car on the last ferry of the day.

"That was some driving," I tell her, letting my breath out at last. Sue smiles as she packs up.

"Do you think Mr Trân made any dessert?" she asks. I ask. Five minutes later there's a flash in the car and not long afterwards we're enjoying a chocolate cream pie with a latté for Sue and a mocha for me. I place the red alpha crystal they've sent on Rocelli's forehead. It sticks fast and glows dully red, looking like a Hindu bindi. I hope it works. Rocelli awake is seriously dangerous.

"So how was your day?" she asks to pass the time.

"Good," I reply and tell her about it.

"How about you?"

"Well, apart from the fact I have to show up in uniform on Monday for an official reprimand and the case has been turned over to organised crime so that I can go back to my actual job everything's hunky dory."

"Organised crime?"

"Yeah ... well, that's the story isn't it. You're all hiding from international criminals. I'm youth aid not international criminals so I have to write them a report and turn it over to them. I'm off your case."

"Well, that sucks," I say.

"It's what happens. In the real world you get moved off interesting cases all the time. They knew I was angry. I mean I do everything a detective should, then, having busted the case open, they reassign it because I'm 'out of my depth'. They have no fricken idea how out of my depth I've had to go. I've been to whole other planets to solve this! So they pat me on the head and want to put me back in the kiddies play pen again."

She exhales heavily. Then she goes on.

"Back with Rachel it was another thing I would have sucked up, and drunk too much, but, you know, now I have options I can't see why anyone should! So I'm resigning. They can pretend I haven't got what it takes if they like, or even investigate me for corruption, but they won't find a thing. So I guess I'm in now, boots and all."

"And kidnapping priests," I add.

"Yeah and kidnapping alien priests with crystal pacifiers and stun rays. What the hell! That's sounds more like me anyway! By the way when do I get one?"

"I dunno, probably when we go to Florida."

"Good!"

There's a pause. Sue settles back in her chair and closes her eyes.

"That was a yummy pie," she sighs.

"The food Mr Trân makes is just so much better than at the police canteen," she adds.

She looks very cute with a smile under her nose and crumbs on her face.

"So tell me more while we're waiting," she says.

•••

March was pretty quiet. The Khadem's had nineteen days of fasting. Ax had gone and the gang hadn't come back. Jeanne was staying at the clinic in Goma and learning about babies; Diana and Elena were still shivering over their stove in their little flat; Nathan was putting up with his drunk mother in Washington and calling his grandmother in Capitol Heights when he could; and in Umm al Fahm Sarah was keeping her head down and trying to blend in because the war in the Gaza strip was getting meaner.

Khadiyeh had convinced her father, Rashid, not to send her back to her husband, Ali. Her father was still trying to work out what had happened that night and constantly asked his neighbours if they too had seen two figures appear in a flash of light and vanish again. Meanwhile Ali had tried to stir up tribal anger against Khadiyeh's family, but his family and neighbours were telling him to drop it. As far as they were concerned Khadiyeh was involved with powers they didn't want to cross, and it was easiest to leave her alone.

Ali could divorce Khadiyeh anytime, as any Muslim guy can, by simply telling her he divorced her three times, but he preferred to keep what he saw as an insult against his honour as a debt to use against Khadiyeh's family and tribe for later.

So we spent a lot of our spare time staking out Uri's planes as they flew aid into Africa trying to work out what they were up to. When they arrived at night we could bend dive into the airstrips before they landed, and try and blend into the crowd that seemed to appear out of the ground, as soon the planes were heard.

The night dives were easy. What was hard was the bony people with angry, desperate eyes when we reached the ground. They literally had to fight for everything. There were dead bodies too. Thin, thin people who had nothing left to fight with, who had given up. The small kids were the hardest. They tore at your eyes and stayed with you long after you went to bed.

The refugee camps stank in the most awful way and the spirits were angry and bitter. Quite often we were driven off, not by the smell, or the desperate beggars who thought we might have something for them, but by angry ghosts who resented our being there at all. Gradually we realised that even among these desperate starving people, there was politics. The men and boys with the guns, and the drugs that kept them awake and kept the pain of hunger down, were still fighting. The women and old people despaired of ever seeing their land again, or any place where they could plant crops or raise their goats in peace.

All over the world people were rioting about food prices. Every day the news had reports of some new place where riots had started. The problem seemed to be the high price of oil and some countries replacing food crops with energy crops for biofuels. For people in richer countries like New Zealand it made people grumble, but in Burkina Faso and the Sudan where we were going, it made food too expensive. People were basically being told they were too poor to eat, and that made everyone angry.

For us kids it was an experience which changed us all. Ashley tried to bring them things but it was hopeless. We couldn't feed them *all* and we couldn't choose between one hungry kid or another. We started to appreciate even the smallest things which we had and they didn't. Things like clean water, safe food, warmth and most of all not having to hide whenever some guys with an AK-47 drove into the camp recruiting boys for their army. We all knew how much these kids dreamt of going to school and learning so they could leave their awful lives behind them. It even made us almost appreciate Mr Wakefield. Almost.

As summer slowly turned cooler and yellower heading into autumn 2008, Mr Wakefield had stopped letting us run around and made us concentrate on our projects more. We started searching the web for more information about old Olympics. It was then that we first came across old videos of the Nazi Olympics in 1936 on Youtube.

Perhaps it was because we were trying to understand what Hathaway and Rocelli were doing that we found them so interesting. The films were about an idea of human perfection as they lingered on the bodies of white athletes. The anger of Hitler when the black American sprinter, Jesse Owens, won the one hundred meters was amazing. It made no sense to us – but then, I guess given the only white among us thought like an African, it wouldn't.

We kept clear of Hathaway. We were frightened of him and weren't bothered about admitting it. But we kept a closer eye on Father Rocelli. He seemed to be doing some very strange things. His main job was travelling around the various missions, orphanages and churches having meetings and bringing things.

He seemed to be well liked by everyone and he always had a smile on his thin lips. But we soon discovered he also did other things. Things that weren't quite so obvious.

Our job was to release flies, put down bugs and tag things. We never hung around long enough where Rocelli was concerned to watch him. Watching him was what the parents did while we were at school. It was Bernard and Zoe who focused on Rocelli – Bernard especially because he was raised in a church orphanage and he was particularly interested in the man he called "the serpent in the garden".

Bernard discovered Rocelli's secret jobs. The first one was simple. When a priest was accused of child abuse he would organise for him to be moved to another country. That way by the time national authorities were ready to arrest the priest he was gone. Bernard had known of unsafe "fathers" in his own orphanage but he'd kept away from them. He'd wondered how they'd never been caught. When he found this out he was angry and started watching Rocelli even more closely. He, Patricia, Scott and Ashley worked on this, I was more involved with Hathaway.

Anyway, they found that another of Rocelli's jobs was taking children into orphanages. Not all of them were orphans either. Some had young mothers, others only had fathers. Rocelli organised for them to be taken away from their parents; often at birth, by telling the mother who had just given birth that the baby had died.

But his really dark secret was not all the children went to orphanages either. Some went to clinics where Hathaway's people worked. Others were given to women who acted as couriers and took them to Europe. There they were looked after in other orphanages. It was very strange.

At that time we didn't know what this was all about. We had a bad feeling about it but we didn't know exactly. It wasn't until Frau Muller explained about the Bruderschaft that we finally began to understand what was happening.

I spent more time on the planes. Hathaway was busy. He was working with Virion and the Huuygens and a number of other groups to get stuff onto the planes. Most of it was legit aid. As I said we tested loads of it and it always came back clear but we simply couldn't believe a guy like Hathaway would do anything to help the people he had almost managed to wipe out.

Hathaway was very hard to track. He noticed the tiny lights which accompanied Control's spy wormholes and after Tel Meggido we daren't try and read him. He was always armed. Somehow nobody noticed the FN five seven pistol in his carry-on luggage when he flew. He seemed to have similar powers to read people as we did and he was much more ruthless, even though he smiled a lot.

At this stage we hadn't had any contact with the Administration apart from laying the moonbase sensors and a couple of UFO scares including the encounter on Pica da Neblina. But we were becoming aware that both Hathaway and Rocelli were both working with, and hiding things from, the Administration.

The first Administration agent we encountered was in one of the planes Hathaway was flying over Sudan. The planes were pretty well packed with pallets which were loaded along the eight meter length of the fuselage. There was a passenger area behind the cockpit which was sort of walled off from the pallets but which had a door on it. If we bent onto a plane in our afternoon, it was early in the morning local time so the passengers were generally asleep, so we could take samples from the pallets without being interrupted.

Tahira was quietly breaking into a pallet while I was standing guard, squashed between the side of the aircraft and the pallets, when suddenly the door into the passenger compartment opened. We both froze and as it was really dark in there, and we were using blend camouflage, we were pretty sure we wouldn't be spotted.

I was about halfway along on the right side of the plane with Tahira behind me when this guy peers around the load holding his cellphone out in front of him, glowing with the light from its screen facing away from me. I thought it was pretty weird to come into a darkened cargo plane to take a picture of the cargo when he hit me with a stun beam. Not only could he see me, he was also using the same technology as we were!

The beam wasn't strong enough to stun me through the suit's insulating carbon armour. I could take a charge way bigger than that! So I zapped his phone with my beam. The shock made him drop it where it clattered to the floor, its light gone. But I knew that a pistol would be next even if it wouldn't do an old aircraft any good to fire bullets around inside. I also knew it wouldn't do me any good to be hit by them either.

At the same moment, Tahira, who was now by one of the bubble windows in the side of the plane called out a warning.

"*Light closing very fast,*" she said.

"*Let's go,*" I agreed.

A muzzle with a laser below it had appeared around the side of the pallet. If I hung around a bullet would surely follow. In a second we had gone.

[+]

A bit later we watched Control's remote recording.

A lumbering old AN-32 plane was flying through the starlit sky. From miles away we saw a bright light zoom up on the plane as if it was standing still. The UFO was about a third the size of the plane. A pink light appeared from the bright UFO light and lit up the aircraft. Then the UFO quickly orbited the old aircraft's fuselage shining the pink light on it, searching for us. Then the pink light went out and the UFO light quickly elevated up into the stars again.

Unfortunately Control would not risk trying to watch the person who had tried to zap me, but we did realise that, whoever they were, they worked for the Administration and could sense our arrival.

•••

I stop.

"I think I should tell you the rest of this on the top deck," I tell Sue. She opens her eyes, her head on the headrest of her reclining seat.

"Why?" she frowns.

"It's better for seasickness and I can't be sure this guy's ears aren't still working."

Sue looks behind us. Father Rocelli is slumped over in his seatbelt. She turns around and grabs an awful woollen blanket she kept there and pulls him down like he's sleeping. Then we get out of the car and lock up.

The sea's a bit rough and the ferry is riding the chop as she leaves the shelter of the harbour. Spray's flying over the few cars on the open deck. The sun's setting, which is good because it means we can start the main mission to rescue Nathan when we arrive at Renwick in three quarters of an hour's time.

We climb up the ladders and internal gangways to the upper deck. It's chilly for Sue but she doesn't seem to mind. We watch the view of Auckland, its lights coming on as dusk sets in, slipping behind us. Sue goes downstairs and buys herself a packet of fags and a beer, with a ginger beer for me. Then we settle down in a sheltered corner.

"You're my windbreak," she informs me.

I shrug. Doesn't bother me.

"Anyway this was more to the point than usual. So Rocelli's been shuffling children around?"

"Yeah."

"I have a bad feeling about where this is going," Sue says.

"Well, you're right. But we may get more out of Rocelli directly."

"How?"

"I've no idea, Hekator's sure to have had some idea how to get him to talk."

"I can't get over the fact that I've just finished a shift on the job as a police officer and now I'm kidnapping someone. An indictable crime punishable by about fifteen years."

"You were also involved in a shootout. It just didn't make any noise," I point out.

"And it didn't kill anyone, I hope," she asks.

"No, of course not. We can't kill. Not on purpose, anyway. Grandpop's killed lot's of people and he won't bend. He's not even psychic but he gets the nightmares. I hate to think what it would be like if *we* killed anyone."

Sue studies me for a moment.

"Is that why the Fae only give you the suits?"

"I dunno. Could be, eh? Even Tahira – and she's way meaner than me, or Scott who's killed animals – even they can't actually *kill* anyone. It's a bit of the disadvantage because no-one else we deal with has any problem with it."

"I see it as a strength, myself," Sue says.

I shrug.

"Anyway, on with the story. You have..." she looks at her watch. "Half an hour.".

"OK, so I was just coming up to Easter which was toward the end of March 2008."

"Sure, what happened in Easter?"

•••

Easter 2008 the transit bases in Sizwe, Khakoborazi and La Roundel finally came online. It meant we could bend speeders and change in or out of suits there. That meant our speeders could now reach most of the planet within an hour.

All the bases are pretty small. There was room for about two speeders and two changers, one briefing holodeck and a jumpstation with a small oil bath. The difference was the oil bath was charged so any tags that could be hurt by electromagnetic energy would be fried instantly on arrival. There's a micro sun and a small ecosystem of plant furniture there so that the temperature, air pressure and oxygen levels are comfy even though the bases are up serious mountains or in desert caves. Hekati travelled to all of them over the Easter break and got them running. They are interconnected and they were connected to Control. We tested them with all with the speeders and they worked fine. We also tested the changers while Hekati looked on. She wanted to be sure they worked properly before we used them operationally. Each site took a few hours to get going before Hekati was happy. Then she just smiled at us, told us to "have fun." and vanished.

We did. Me and Scott tested Sizwe in Egypt by flying Ka-rea-rea and Inkwazi down to Goma and back. We flew low over Libya and didn't bother with warp invisibility. We were doing about three thousand knots at about one kilometer altitude. The sonic booms would have been wicked but it was way cool.

Tarik and Cam went to Khakoborazi and had a good time flying through the Himalayas. They followed some amazing geese through the high passes and flew all the way to Afghanistan where they decided to avoid the American airforce and came back again.

But it was Tahira and Ashley who flew and dived in the Caribbean from La Roundel who had the best time. I think Dr P had given them a hint because they flew to the Azores on the other side of the Atlantic and dived. They were gone the longest but when they came back they had a couple of cut diamonds the size of peas with them.

Dr P was waiting for them with a big smile. It turned out he had sent them after a Portuguese Carrack or merchantman called Nau Chagas which had been sunk by the British in June, 1594[†]. She was a treasure ship full of jewels and precious metal plundered in South America. He and Control had found her using x-ray sweeps and sent the girls to check what they had found.

The ship was very deep down. Almost two kilometers so it was dark and cold. She had a huge hole in her side and her cargo was scattered. There was a lot of mud but it was light and silty and our sensors saw straight through it easily. So we spent a fun Easter playing Easter egg hunts for sunken treasure, and man! There was a lot of it!

We got to the point where we couldn't be bothered picking up anything spilt. We just packed caskets and boxes into big travel boxes and sent them home. Then after four hours in the dark we flew back to Roundel above the Atlantic night and using the minibase jumpstation bent ourselves and the speeders home.

In that weekend we gathered up about twenty million in gems, and twenty in gold and silver each, while Dr P made another hundred and twenty as well, and there was still plenty more down there. So everyone was pretty cheerful by the time we had to go back to school.

I gave Emma a diamond and ruby ring and pearl and sapphire necklace I'd found in a casket with a stone big enough to get her on the cover of a women's magazine. Zoe said it was worth about three million. She squealed so loud everyone on the playground looked at us. Then she kissed me full on the mouth. She hid it, as I told her, but she was grinning her head off all afternoon.

I was a bit shocked how happy it made her. Strangely that made *me* feel less sure of *her*. I talked to Tahira about it while we were cleaning that evening.

"But what turns her on isn't the thought, its the amount of *money*!" I complained.

"So you buy er 'eart," Tahira shrugged.

"Yeah, but *anyone* can do that. All you need is a big pile of expensive stones."

"But not *anyone* gives 'er expensive stones."

"But they don't have to care about her to give her expensive stones."

"Why not?"

"Well ..." I was a bit confused. Obviously they had to care to give expensive stones. "I um ... But all it depends on is how many stones you have. If you have heaps you could buy dozens of girls hearts."

Tahira wasn't so sure.

"You could buy zhere *attention*. But we are not *stupid*. Our 'earts we keep for ze one we love."

"So you think Emma loves me?"

"I zink if you keep treating her like zat she will."

"So I just give her more and bigger pretty stones?"

"No, no, no! You show er, she iz special! A big pile of stones iz just a big pile of stones. Surprise. Thoughtfulness. Zat is what matters."

I felt a bit reassured by that. It actually turned me on that she was so happy with me. I thought it wasn't so hard to make her feel special.

But that was the easy side of finding more treasure.

When we went back to the airstrip in Dafur having all that money only made us feel worse. Here we were, scooping up a fortune in stolen treasure from the seafloor, while these people were starving for want of food that cost a tiny fraction of the fortune we had just made. Of course we could see the real problem wasn't a lack of money but too much fighting. Nobody could grow food in these conditions, but we still felt we should do more. Ashley was especially fired up and said something to Dr P. Dr P was, as usual, coldly rational when she argued the injustice of the situation.

"Suggest you give to relief agency. Sell gems and donate to charity. Suggest UNICEF."

Well, that made us feel stink. We wanted *him* to give up some treasure but he was pointing out *we* had the ability to do something ourselves. We felt stink because we felt a bit selfish about our gems. We had collected them down in the dark muddy bottom of the sea. It had been work not fun. Still Ashley shamed us, and she was right, it was impossible to step over kids bodies and do nothing.

We collected together a pile of gems we didn't want and took them to Dr P. He waved us away to Zoe saying he took his advice from her himself. She said the next trick was to get Kimberley process certificates.

Kimberley certificates were needed to prove diamonds aren't being mined to fund wars in Africa. Zoe took over the whole operation because she knew all the right people in Zimbabwe to get certificates. Zimbabwe has a whole industry in changing war or blood diamonds for its own supposedly clean diamonds and then selling them to De Beers the giant South African diamond company. She had to make a bunch of calls and organise it.

Some of her contacts still wanted to know where she had gone and where her diamonds had come from. We had to do a bunch of drops and thefts so they realised they were being watched and could end up in huge trouble if they robbed us. Anyway by May she had managed to organise the whole thing so that twenty million American dollars worth went to UNICEF and four million went to her friends, who were pretty stoked about it and immediately left Zimbabwe while they could. But by that time, of course, Ax was back and we had bigger problems closer to home.

•••

CHAP+ER SEVEN+Y EIGH+: EX+RAC+ING NA+HAN

We're starting to approach Port Carlyle and Sue's getting edgy again. She goes to the loo and leaves me on the deck to watch my old home get closer and closer. I have mixed feelings about the place now.

Now that everyone has moved to Hastings it's no longer home. It's just a place where I lived for two years so I feel no great loyalty to it or most of the people on it.

On the other hand Emma still lives there and I had – well, there was no other way of describing it – I had grown up there. I had arrived a kid running from my father and left, well – if not yet a man, at least a pretty experienced teenager – and perhaps that gave me a feeling of respect.

Sue's obviously bringing me here for a reason. There's plenty of other places around Auckland we could launch Ka-rea-rea. I'm not sure quite what she has in mind yet. The presence of Father Rocelli also makes things tricky. I don't trust anything about him. He could so easily be a walking bomb or have a beacon inside him, or both.

I'm certain he's not in New Zealand by choice. Somewhere Inspector Du Croix is behind this. He'll be sure we're after Nathan and he'd be very happy to find either our new base or the Vimana Ashanti.

All these thoughts remind me how tricky our enemy is. Maybe the defences they've surrounded Nathan with are just to make us work harder to get him and they had already put tags in him, just as they had allowed us to think we had tricked them, when all the time Sue's brain had been set up to infiltrate us. I call in to Grandpop.

"Grandpop, do we know Nathan isn't carrying a beacon now?"

"No, but don't worry Sam, Hekator's already thought of that."

"It's just I'm pretty sure Rocelli isn't here by choice. I think Inspector Du Croix sent him as bait. He's using the Bruderschaft to get us. He was happy to tell me that when he dropped Ka-rea-rea off."

"Which is why you, Ka-rea-rea, Sue and Rocelli are all together Sam. At the moment every source of information *they* have reinforces every other source. Sue's impression stream, Ka-rea-rea's location tag, and whatever they have in Rocelli are all focused on you, giving the others freedom to operate undetected. Don't worry we aren't underestimating Du Croix. And we haven't forgotten you either."

"Where should I put Rocelli while we deal with Nathan?"

"Renwick's vault. They'd have a hard time getting in there if they've got a UFO waiting to ambush."

That's true.

"Is someone coming to get Sue with a bag?"

"Actually we've got something special for her to wear."

"What's that?"

"Well, it's a special outfit for adults Lana designed. It's not as complete as the Lana you guys have, but it's better than a sleeping bag. Sue can wear Zoe's one until we can get one for her."

"*Have you all got them?*"

"No, just me, Ken, Zoe, Bernard and Patricia. They're the only ones I wanted able to operate in the field. They can look after themselves."

"*Cool. Well, we're almost there so we should be at Renwick in half an hour.*"

"Sam, we're going to send you a scanner to check Rocelli over with so could you go to the toilets now?"

"*OK.*"

I bump into Sue as she's coming back to get me. We agree to meet back at the car. I go into the battered ship's loo and close myself in a cubical. A moment later a small travel box flashes into existence right in front of me. I open it and take out a blue crystal, set in a silver handle. I shrug, because it makes no sense to me, pocket it, and leave the travel box to vanish by itself. I get to the car just as the ferry's about to land.

"You took your time," Sue complains.

"Just got something from Grandpop for 'Big Ears' in the back". Being the last on makes us the first off, so pretty soon we're driving out of the car park and up the hill into the orange lights of Port Carlyle. As we pass through the village Sue remembers something she's forgotten to pass on.

"Based on what I told them Kevin's putting out a media release tonight asking for anyone who has seen the Renwick families to dob them in. They want to talk to Dr P about the fire. There's some evidence of accelerants. They think you were left as a decoy. He's pretty pissed off."

"Why would we burn down Renwick?" I ask.

"Apparently it was going to be part of a Waitangi treaty settlement for the tribe. Tui O'Reagan Tukarere is really angry about it and calling for changes to the deal because of the loss. They were going to get the Department of Conservation farm and the Renwick as part of the settlement. Renwick was officially insured for only half a million before it was renovated but was estimated to be worth five, probably because of all Gunter's work. The deal was all set to go when the fire happened."

"Really?" I ask. This is all news to me.

"Uh huh," Sue says.

She's letting me make the connections. It's very convenient that Renwick had to be abandoned just as we were about to lose it anyway. Almost convenient enough to look like it had been planned that way.

But if that was so the Administration would have to have been part of it. Because Ashley *had* been tagged and an attack carrier *had* been launched. I'd seen the things. And the Service wouldn't launch an attack carrier to help Dr P with shady property deals. And if the evacuation *had* been staged it meant Dr P was working with the Administration which made no sense at all.

Almost as if she'd read my mind Sue interrupts my thoughts.

"So what do you know about Inspector Du Croix. And does Dr Prosperov ever talk to him?"

"Um ... I don't *think* they know each other. But... well after Easter 2008 Dr P and Dr Morozov started doing all these trips. He said he needed to move to get a better feel for the other kids we were looking for and he did come back with better information which meant we found another two. But to be honest, exactly what he was doing, I don't really know. And I don't like to talk about it with Big Ears here in the back."

Sue glanced back. "He looks asleep to me."

"Yeah he is, but he may not be the only one connected to his ears. I could feel it when I was talking to Sir Michael although I'm not so sure about this one so better to be safe than sorry."

We're coming up to the school. Pretty soon the tar seal and the street lights would be left behind. That could make us vulnerable. It would not be hard for them to jump us on a deserted country road on an island like Aotea. As the beach side car park comes into view I speak up.

"Sue, could you pull over here please?" I ask.

"Why?"

"I'm not sure about the road ahead. Another saucer could be waiting for us. And I need to use this thing." I say, pulling out the scanner.

She glances at it.

"What does it do?"

"Scans Big Ears for things. What? I dunno."

Sue checks me, then the road. She slows down and pulls over into an angle park facing the sea, opposite the school.

"*Grandpop? Is the sky clear? It would be dead easy to jump us.*"

"I know Sam. We're already checking."

"*Don't forget the sea too,*" I add.

"What's the story?" asks Sue.

"Just making sure Rocelli's mates aren't waiting for us."

"Oh, OK."

I turn around and point the blue jewel thing at Rocelli and vaguely thought "OK, so do it."

The blue jewel pulses with light, then stops. It takes so little time I wonder if it's worked. I'm about to do it again when Hekator comes on my channel.

"*Thanks Sam,*" he says. "*He's got no communication inside him.*"

"*None?*"

"*No the device detects tiny field disturbances. He's completely clean.*"

That's good news. A bit surprising too. A moment later Grandpop's back.

"Looks OK for the moment Sam. But tell Sue to step on it."

"Grandpop says the road to Renwick is clear now but we should make it quick."

Sue raised her eyebrows. She reverses out.

"Does that cop Smith patrol at night?" she checks.

"Yeah, but it's too early now."

"And the road is..."

"Clear," says Grandpop.

"Clear," I repeat.

"Good," Sue says and puts her foot down.

I'm glad I trust Sue. I didn't know anyone could drive a gravel road like that, and I've lived on them most of my life. Technically she never breaks the hundred kilometer a hour speed limit but she gets pretty close. She's sliding her car sideways around the corners like a rally driver, laughing and having fun. I don't mind admitting I'm shitting myself, and I'm really glad I can bend out because if she gets this wrong we will be off the road and over the cliff like Ax was when he died.

Normally in Betty with Mariko driving it's a twenty minute trip. Sue does it in five. We slide to a stop outside the dark smudge of Renwick's ruin in a cloud of stone dust.

"Now what?" Sue asks, smiling.

"That was *mean!* Where did you learn to drive like *that*?" I gasp, breathing at last.

"Police college. And I used to do rally sprints as a teenager."

"You are so much cooler than I thought,"

"I'm not a bad shot too," she adds, "but what do we do now?" she asks getting out. I get out too.

"Ah, well the plan is to get 'Big Ears' here into Renwick's vault."

"How?"

"Don't worry, I'll do it. Just keep an eye on the sky. If you see any weird moving lights anywhere, follow me down real quick."

"Will do."

I open the rear door and lift Rocelli out of the car. I carry him over Renwick's wreckage and pick my way through to the hole. The hole looks dark and deep. I can't help remembering the last time I'd entered it in Ka-rea-rea when I'd been surprised by the others. I really don't want any surprises this time. It makes me hesitate a moment but I don't have time to worry about it. I jump, carrying Rocelli like an oversized baby, and float down under antigravity.

There's no light down there so I light up my suit a little more. Then I realise I can't open the vault because my suit covers my hand and the vault needs my print. So I stow Rocelli on the cellar floor where the little red dot on his forehead blinks in the dark. It's a long way to the hole and the debris's unstable. He won't be getting out of there by himself in a hurry. Then I jump back out of the hole, and walk back through the wreckage. Sue's just waiting, sitting on her car.

There's a sudden flash and Tahira appears carrying a travel box. I come over as she opens the box for Sue.

"Your suit eez like a sleeping bag because eet protects you when you bend, though eet is slower than our suits because eet 'as leetle power and is passive," she explains.

Inside there's what looks like a soft gray leather motorcycle suit and a completely gray motorcycle helmet. Tahira takes out the clothes and puts them on the front of the car next to Sue.

"Where it eez a bit like our suits eez it 'as adaptive camouflage, impact resistance and built-in tools in zer gloves and boots. Ze 'elmet 'as an old 'ead-up display and communication system. Zere is also a dazzle beam weapon in ze 'elmet en case zhou 'av to escape. Zhou aim by looking. Eez better zhan ordinary clothes ..." Tahira shrugs.

"OK, so is there a changer or something?" Sue asks uncertainly.

"No eet eez just three pieces. Zhou wear like normal clothes."

"So I have to get undressed," Sue checks.

Tahira shrugs.

"Zhou can change in zhe car. I need to talk to Sam anyway."

Sue takes a deep breath then jumps off the car and grabs the clothes as the travel box silently folds away to nothing. Tahira leads me away as Sue gets into the back of the car.

"Sam, zere is a slight change of plan. Control tracked Nathan's blood sample you found in za fridge to anuzzer lab. Is unnamed place also in Virginia. Zat is your new destination for Ka-rea-rea."

"Huh? But when do we get Nathan?"

"When Administration ez distracted."

"I don't get it."

Tahira rolled her eyes and started again.

"Ze plan is for you to fly Ka-rea-rea to zere secret lab in Virginia. When we have drawn attention to protecting lab we rescue Nathan. Got it?"

"Ummm yeah ... but won't they wonder why we are using our only tagged speeder?"

"Of course, but zhou will be going very fast to place zey are sensitive about, and zen zhou will vanish."

"Vanish? How?"

"Dr P 'as a plan to remove ze tag."

"Really?" I'm surprised.

"Yes. Zen per'aps we can keep im," she smiles.

"And what about you and Sue?"

"We bend to Florida but what 'ekator will pass on will make it seem like Virginia. It will confuse zem."

"But ... will I be able to bend out of Ka-rea-rea?"

"Yes ... but you must be quick. Zhen you can fly 'im via Control. Zer big ball connector Hekator gave you before Control was back online is no longer necessary."

"Oh, OK. But ... I still don't get this. Why use Ka-rea-rea at all?"

"Because ee attracts zem. Zhou are big, fat, juicy target going to sensitive place. Is like impressions from Sue zat Hekator is passing on. We give some informations zat are wrong and some zat are right, to confuse zem. So not to tell Sue about change."

"It's confusing me." I complain.

"*Situation normal*," laughs Scott in my ear.

"What's confusing you," Sue asks coming over.

She's wearing the leather motorcycle gear and her helmet. She looks pretty hot.

"The plan. Apparently I have to fly Ka-rea-rea. We meet there."

"Hey, we've got a car for Sue and Tahira," Cam calls. "We're just getting the driver and her friend comfy."

"Sam, we need you there in ten minutes." Grandpop calls.

I look at Sue. It's funny to be getting ready for a new mission next to the wreckage of Renwick. The smell and sound of the sea and all the stars seem so familiar. I still wondered about what Sue had said about Renwick being taken off us.

"OK, well good luck you guys," I tell the other two.

They wish me luck too. It feels strange. I look around, then call Ka-rea-rea off Sue's car. He floats over and settles in front of me. I open up Ka-rea-rea. I get in and close Ka-rea-rea and realise my hood has to be down to fly him. I lower it, lift off and hover about ten feet in the air tilting the nose up so I'm ready to go. I'm still bothered about my hood. It means I can't bend immediately. If I have to bend I have to get my hood up fast. This was going to be a problem.

"Sue and Tahira, get over to Cam and Tarik and drive your car to meet up with Ken," Grandpop tells them.

They look at each other. Tahira takes Sue's arm and they fold to nothing. I'm like a rocket ready to launch but my snag is serious.

"*Grandpop to bend I have to twist my head off Ka-rea-rea's control interface. That means I'm blind while my hood comes up.*"

"Yeah, you'll have to time it right," he agrees.

"*Do I have to fly this Grandpop?*" I ask him privately.

"No, you could do it remotely if you want," Grandpop says.

That would mean me hiding on a beach while everyone else put their lives on the line. Plus, *they* might come rescue Rocelli while I was focused on Ka-rea-rea and catch me too.

"*Nah, just give me a minute to get my bail technique sorted.*"

"*Hey, Sam!*" Sue calls on an open channel, "*This is so cool! We really do have a little red corvette!*"

Sue sounds like she's starting to enjoy herself.

"*Though I'm not used to driving on the right. It feels weird,*" she adds.

"*Just remember, driver is always in the middle of the road. You get used to it,*" Ken tells her.

I practice twisting my head and telling my suit to close up. It's annoyingly slower than putting my hood up with my hands. But its too cramped to do that. From head off to hood up and sealed takes five seconds. That's five seconds a Service fighter could use to lock on to me using the trace Du Croix attached, use that pink light to stop me bending, and catch me for real. Then I'd be looking at suicide options on the moon, but for real. That knowledge makes me gulp. And given that in five seconds a fighter could move fifty kilometers, easy, I had better keep my eyes wide open.

"*This is harder than I thought.*" I tell Grandpop.

"Yeah, look Tarik and Cam are inside that lab now. It's pretty creepy. Could you get going." he asks. There's a note of worry in his voice and it isn't for me.

"Gee thanks a bunch," I think.

I reconnect with Ka-rea-rea. The beach and the night return to me. The moon is three quarters full and now quite high. The sky is clear. This was going to be the fastest I'd ever gone. Control was feeding Ka-rea-rea a flight plan and letting me in on the details.

I start climbing slowly. I make Ka-rea-rea check he is completely fine. I don't want any problems taking me by surprise. Then as I get to about four kilometers over Aotea, with Auckland twinkling behind me in the background, the checks are finished and everything's good, so I punch it.

I thought I'd been fast before, but no, *this* is fast! Before I've even blinked the clouds are way below and the blue haze of atmosphere is gone. I'm between the pale blue of the atmosphere and the endless liquid black of space above. It's scary. Almost like the first time I skydived.

The Pacific below makes Earth look like this huge blue marble with white cloud patterns over it. It's so big, and even at this speed just goes on and on. In less than sixty seconds I'm a thousand kilometers from Renwick at an altitude of four hundred kilometers where low earth orbit satellites fly and I'm still climbing. Somewhere below is Raoul Island but its too small too see and I'm going too fast to look for it. Normally speed feels righteous but this is just scary. I'm leaving Earth and it's drifting away below me, getting further and further away.

After five minutes I'm over the specks of Kiribati's islands 5,000 kilometers from Renwick, 1,200 kilometers above the big dark ball of the Earth below me. Three minutes later I'm at my highest point: 2,000 kilometers up over the little islands of Hawaii.

Suddenly Ka-rea-rea spots a craft far below me.

It's big and moving pretty fast, though not as fast as me. I feel sick. Fast, I might be, but any Administration craft could have me in seconds. I feel horribly pinned inside Ka-rea-rea and I start to think about bending out. Then to my huge relief, I realise it isn't an Administration craft at all. It's ours! It's the international space-station with one of NASA's shuttles docked to it.

It makes me feel a little bit proud that old and clunky as it is, we can make spacecraft. I soar over it, tiny and invisible, and it falls behind as I begin to descend again towards California, which is covered in dense gray cloud in the darkness of night.

I realise I've been so tied up in my own experience I'd forgotten to listen in to what's going on.

"What's happening?" I call.

"This lab is spooky," Cam says from Virginia.

"Why?"

"It's full of cameras and locks. We've got flies out, but even they have a hard time getting through. In some places there are patients. Well, I sure hope they're patients, because they're locked in. And you wouldn't think hospital orderlies need to carry Tasers would you? Hang on, we've found a new LZ."

I cross the shore of the continental United States, somewhere in the cloud below. I'm invisible to all the US Air Force radars even though I'm the same shape and size as a missile warhead.

"Tarik's found a computer to tap into," Cam reports.

I'm descending gradually. It's 2 a.m where I'm going and the lights of California below are under dense cloud. Beyond that, it's mostly dark deserts and mountains.

"The fighter's moving," Scotty warns.

"Gone!" Ashley echoes.

That's scary. It reminds me with a jolt that while the US Airforce can't see me, the Service knows exactly where I am. I feel my breath become fast and shallow and try to stop it.

"Where'd it go? Sue and Ken are you guys ready. Let's go!" Grandpop orders.

"It went north, not west," Ashley answers.

"Sam? Are you listening?"

"Sure am."

"Tarik, Cam! Get ready to bend. He's headed for Virginia."

I suddenly feel very nervous as I rip through the sky, now back down to 400 kilometers over the frosty state of Oklahoma. Before, I had felt happy heading towards my friends, now I feel nervous I'm getting into trouble faster than I can get out of it.

"Cam and Tarik! That fighter is overhead! Get out now,"

Control said.

"*Where?*" Tarik hesitates.

"*You're joining Ken,*" Control tells them.

"Ken? Sue? You have five minutes. Tahira stick with Sue," Grandpop relays.

"*Hi guys,*" says Ken. Tarik and Cam must have arrived in his car.

"*Sam, stick the course,*" tells me.

I'm 250 kilometers over Nashville and feeling very nervous. All I can think of is a fighter and pink light enveloping me, which is not a good thought at all.

"OK Sam, this is the tricky part. We want you to do a conventional re-entry, but upside down."

"*What? Why?*"

"Because the re-entry heat will destroy Du Croix's tag."

"*Oh! Of course!*" I realise. This makes me feel much better. At the right angle Du Croix's little bandaid is going to be crispier than burnt toast.

"Stand-by. Control has re-entry parameters for you. You'll slow quite a bit. We're aiming for four kilometers a second which will yield 4,000 degrees Kelvin. That should do it. Oh, Hekator says it will get quite hot and bumpy."

"*Roger that.*"

I roll Ka-rea-rea over and start pulling up towards the dark ball of cloud covered Earth that fills my view. Camouflage is no use any more. I would be radiating so much heat and light it would be pointless for the tiny diamonds that lit the adaptive camouflage to try and look like their surroundings. They'll probably get covered in soot anyway. Control feeds in the flight path. I don't really have anything to do because Ka-rea-rea is flying to Control's direction.

"*We've got company,*" Sue warns.

"*There's a police car chasing us,*" Tahira explains.

"*Can we run this red?*" Ken asks.

"Yep. Nothing coming either way," Grandpop tells him.

"*Good.*"

"*Ken, speed up will ya, this guy is going to try and get around me,*" Sue calls.

"*How far out are we?*" Ken asks.

"Two minutes."

My view was starting to go bright red. Then Ka-rea-rea retracted his sensors and I couldn't see anything. I could only feel us being buffeted around the sky as we came in like a meteor, but I could hear everything that was happening in Florida.

"*Woah! He took a swipe at me,*" Sue complains about the cop car.

"*That's not safe!*" she adds with professional annoyance.

"*He hasn't started shooting at you yet,*" Grandpop warns.

"*What! There's a child in this car!*" squawks Sue.

"*Stop panicking,*" Tahira replies, obviously grumpy at being called 'a child'. "*I'll take him out.*"

"No Tahira," Grandpop tells her. "We want the cops along for the ride too. This is perfect. Two street racers and a cop. They won't expect Ken at all! You're one minute thirty out."

Ka-rea-rea is now up to 4,012 degrees Kelvin outside. Inside it was over forty and my head was getting pretty hot too. We were bumping and slipping all over the sky. At this temperature even Ka-rea-rea's diamond armour will start burning so I'm pretty sure the tag was frizzling up.

"Scott and Ashley, how are we doing?" Grandpop asks them about what's happening at the target.

"All good. Hooty's in a tree nearby. The van's still sitting there, fat dumb and happy. Buffy's been flying around the flats. The downstairs flat seems to be clear. There's just some boxes in it," Scott said.

"Check them out guys. How about Margaret and Nathan?"

"They're asleep."

"Cool. I want to know what's in those boxes." Grandpop says.

"Sam, are you down yet?"

"Nearly."

"OK Sam. The fighter's moved to intercept over Virginia. Distract them. Play hide and seek. Bend out whenever you need to. Ken! It's the next hard, hard left. You'll be there in ten seconds. Slow for it!"

I was now down to 40 kilometers altitude and three kilometers per second, about three times higher and faster than a normal fighter jet. My sensors were back up, but there was a lot of cloud so there wasn't much to see. Below they were having a snow storm. However I was too far north. If I kept on my current route I'd be over Washington D.C in three minutes. It was time to make a turn. With inertialess engaged for a moment that was easy.

"Brace!" Ken shouts suddenly.

There's a pause.

"Holy shit! Are you guys OK?" Ashley calls.

"Hate to be in that van," Scott comments.

"Bending out with Ken," grunts Tarik.

"Sue don't hang around, step on it, let the cops deal with the van guys," Grandpop tells her.

"Is Ken OK?" Sue asks, clearly worried.

"He's had better days," Ken replies through clenched teeth.

"*Broken leg by the look,*" Cam fills us all in.

"*How are you Cam?*" Tahira calls.

"*OK. Tarik got it harder than me.*"

"*You OK mate?*" Scott asks him.

"*Just bit my tongue,*" grunts Tarik

"*Ow,*" Scott sympathises.

"Guys, gotta get into Nathan's apartment." Grandpop says. "Cam and Tarik, in you go. Sue and Tahira lose that car and the cops and come home."

"Sam, what's happening?" Grandpop calls.

"*I'm six minutes from Florida.*"

"Cool. Keep an eye out. The fighter can't be far away. Get ready to bend."

"*What's that Mike?*" grunts Ken about something.

"A little surprise from Hekator."

"*Mike, help*!!" Cam yells.

"Shit!" Grandpop swore. "Tarik and Cam zap Nathan and Margaret as planned. Scott and Ashley keep that watch up. Tahira take this black marble to the downstairs flat. Throw it through the window."

There's a pause.

"*What's happening?*" I ask.

"Pink light from the downstairs flat. They'd set a field disrupter like the one that nearly got you in Greenland to go off if anyone bent in. and Tarik and Cam are in it. The fighter will be headed this way, for sure," Grandpop tells me.

"*What's Tahira doing?*" I asked.

"Killing the field disruptor," he tells me.

"*Hooty sees cops, fire and paramedics coming,*" Ashley reported.

There's another pause.

I feel a twinge behind me. It's weak but getting stronger. Ka-rea-rea's telling me there's a gravitational field being warped by a UFO.

"*I've got a fighter at five o'clock,*" I warn.

"Is he closing?"

"*Uh?*" the twinge got stronger, "*yes!*"

"Draw him Sam, but don't make it easy."

"OK guys. We're going to implode the bottom flat with a very small black hole ... Cam and Tarik, watch out, the floor will sag or collapse. Tahira, ready? ... Excellent ... Toss it in and clear out! Run, run away from there!"

Another pause.

"WOAH!" yell Tarik and Cam

"*The whole bottom flat's collapsed. The building's just pancaked. Paramedics arriving,*" adds Scott.

"Wow. That was more powerful than I thought. Tarik and Cam zap Nathan and Margaret. Tahira, you and Sue are bringing in the sleeping bags. Get them to the Western end of the apartment."

But I'm too busy to listen now. The fighter's gaining fast. He's a hundred kilometers away and closing. It's time to act. I go inertialless, zig east, drop to two kilometers per second at five kilometers altitude. I let him see it. Then I drop inertialess and switch on warp invisibility. That will make things tricky for him. Just to be annoying I veer south.

"*Tahira, Sue! Go!*" Grandpop orders.

"*Two black vans on the way,*" warns Ashley.

"Pack up Buffy and Hooty you two. You're nearly done. Move to target two," Grandpop tells them.

"*Christ! What a mess!*" says Sue.

"Just bag them and go," Grandpop calls.

"Sam, how are you doing?" he adds.

"*He's closing,*" I tell them.

I've nearly reached the coast when I feel another twinge in my left shoulder.

"*Another fighter!*"

I zig west.

"I think you've found our other friend. It's too hot! Time to go, Sam! Tell Ka-rea-rea to stay warp invisible and outrun them. Get back to four kilometers per second. Keep him heading south."

I pass on the instruction, then pull my head off the interface.

In the time the suit took to close I'd gone thirty kilometers and both the fighters were angling toward me. Cramped in the dark box I couldn't help wanting to know what was happening outside but finding out could be fatal. There could be no antimatter explosion to negotiate with on Earth. I knew this was, finally, the end of my beloved Ka-rea-rea. In the darkness for just a half second I said goodbye, and then folded into nothing.

[+]

Lightning, rain, wind. It seemed to take ages.

"*Why isn't the sleeping bag working?*" Tahira asks from the wreckage of the motor lodge in Florida.

"*It's the scanner, it won't bend if it thinks he's bugged. It's found something inside Nathan,*" Hekator says. "*Hang on I'm coming.*"

Then the cabinet door swings open and I'm out. Cam and Tarik are gathered around Ken, who has his leg up on a squab with Patricia tending to him. Grandpop is still staring at the screen.

"Sam, they're nearly on Ka-rea-rea. Get over here!" he yells.

137

I dash over.

"Sit down, Control can link you in for instructions."

I find a spot behind Grandpop while the others are talking about getting Ken to hospital.

"Hang on mate," Grandpop says over his shoulder. "Just need to sort the others. Ashley and Scott? Have you got him?"

"*Yeah, he was a bit surprised,*" Ashley says.

"Not as much as *they* will be."

"*OK, Hekator he's bagged,*" Scott reports.

"*Wait Mike, Nathan is serious.*" Hekator warns.

All this was going on as the link to Ka-rea-rea came up. The link via Control was never as good as Hekator's bowling ball thing for being there. The others are really distracting too.

Luckily I already know my next move. I make Ka-rea-rea dive down from five kilometers to five hundred meters up and slow way, way down. Now Ka-rea-rea's field is tiny, and my warp invisibility is still impossible to see over two hundred meters away.

I have him start following a suburban street. There's traffic on it. That might put them off. But it doesn't. Showing typical Service disregard for being seen, the triangular UFOs come down low too, and start scanning hard for Ka-rea-rea. The intensity of their powerful but short pulses would halo the warp invisibility field as surely as if they were within two hundred meters. Ka-rea-rea would be lit up like a Christmas tree every five seconds. I switch warp invisibility off. Adaptive camouflage won't work because Ka-rea-rea's covered in black soot. So I drop Ka-rea-rea right down to five meters to hide in amongst the houses.

But the UFOs come down too, floating eerily over early morning Florida. I start a shell game as I slip around houses, trees, sheds and even cars. I'm really looking for another vehicle with a roof-mounted pod which looks like Ka-rea-rea. If I can do that they'll have a very hard time spotting him.

The fighters are just above the rooftops. Even though it's early I'm sure they're attracting attention. Perhaps that's distracting them because they're having a hard time finding Ka-rea-rea.

"*Sam?*"

It's Hekator.

"*Yeah,*" I say, still concentrating.

"*I'm inside the wreckage of the apartments with a lot of your kind outside. I've evacuated Nathan's grandmother but they've put a beacon bomb inside Nathan's stomach. If he bends they'll blow up him and Ashanti.*"

"*OK,*" I say. The fighters are really close.

"*I'm going to bend Nathan's bomb out of him and inside Ka-rea-rea. But you need to get him away from the surface. If they don't detonate the beacon, we'll set Ka-rea-rea to invert the antimatter vortex in two minutes. Instead of an explosion it'll be an implosion like the device you used on the building.*"

"*They're almost on me Hekator,*" I warn.

"*OK, So on my 'go', break at maximum field for the sky.*"

"*Make it quick,*" I tell him.

"*Three, two, one, go!*"

Ka-rea-rea bursts out from under a verandah and narrowly misses a fighter as he blurs into the stars.

"*Bomb bent,*" Hekator said.

There's a pause.

"*Has it detonated?*" Hekator asks.

"*No, they're almost on him,*" I report as the fighters gain behind him.

"Right, Sam, set the vortex to maximum power growth, inverse polarity in two minutes."

"There's a warning."

"Ignore it."

"Done."

"I'm taking our patient now, Good work, Sam."

Suddenly I lost contact with Ka-rea-rea. One second I'm receiving and the next, he's gone. I shake my head and stand up. Then I look around.

On Grandpop's big screen, from a distance of ten kilometers Control has picked up the pink light from the fighter flashing above the clouds. A commercial jet is about fifty kilometers to the east. The image is a long, long way away and Control struggles to keep it as the two sets of triangular lights rise at unnatural speed out of the atmosphere. Then one set of lights vanishes. The other falters, then rises again.

There's a flash of light. Hekator appears on the floor among the cabinets as two, then a third begin, flashing with lightning. He has a big grin on his face.

"That went very well indeed," he says coming over.

Scott and Ashley step out of a cabinet each.

"Woah, Ken! Are you OK?" Ashley calls out.

"Hi Hekator," she adds as she runs up to Ken.

Scott follows, nodding at Hekator on the way.

The other cabinet opens and Tahira and Sue pile out. Sue's looking a bit frazzled. Tahira too runs to Ken.

"Man! That was one mother of a crash!" Ashley tells him.

Sue comes up by Hekator.

"Alright Sue? How's the brain?" he asks.

"Ummm ... spinning a bit actually."

I'm catching up with what Ken had done.

"You gotta see it Sam. It was awesome," Scott tells me.

"Control, show Sam!" Ash says.

The big, wrap around screen shows Hooty's view from about fifty meters away in a tree. There are a bunch of cars parked about and a driveway that twists around among a lot of two storey accommodation blocks. The large black Ford Transit is sitting there by itself. Inside *their* surveillance team. There's a roar of engines, a lot of sirens and flashing lights reflected on glass.

Then, from the main road that feeds into the twisting driveway, a flashy looking black SUV appears suddenly. There's just time to realise there's a red sports car and a police cruiser with lights flaring chasing the SUV, when the SUV swerves suddenly and smashes straight into the back of the big black Transit van at high speed. The impact shunts the van forward about fifty meters, while the SUV loses half the driver's side under the hood, loses speed and drifts after it, the windshield covered by airbag.

Both the red car and the police cruiser slow right down. Then the red car speeds away, while the cruiser stops, lights flashing. The video stops. The total time is five seconds.

"Is your leg injured?" Hekator asks, making the connection.

"Broken," Ken grunts.

"Well, I'm not surprised. That wheel recess needs rethinking," he pauses for a moment. Ken pulls a face of disbelief.

"Can you fix his leg, Hekator?" Ashley asks.

"Yes, but I wouldn't do anything your doctors wouldn't. Mechanical breaks are something your body can heal well if helped appropriately," he glances at Patricia and adds. "Your

141

mother knows more about treating Ken than I do. Though you should ask Control to do a scan because he easily can," he adds.

"But doncha have like some kind of potion or somethin?" Ashley persists.

"A potion? I'm not a magician Ashley, I'm an engineer! Broken bones are best cured by splinting and rest," he glances at Ken, whose face is twisted with pain. Then he realises.

"Oh, sorry," he says and takes Ken's hand and presses his thumbs onto it three times in different places. Ken sighs as the pain subsides.

"I forget you don't know basic acupressure," Hekator mumbles.

"So Hekator, how are Margaret and Nathan?" Grandpop asks.

"Fine, thanks to you all. I had to remove the bomb from Nathan but they're both on the Ashanti. They're working on the growth now. The first stage plan was to use a 5D beam to cauterise the transceiver. That'll be done by now. Then we'll send in the phages to recycle the growth before it necrotises. Simple. Exactly like a basic brain tumour really."

"And Michael?" Grandpop asks.

"Same, except we only disconnect the transceiver, and he didn't have a bomb."

"Michael?" I asked.

"Scott and Ashley picked up Sir Michael for the same treatment." Grandpop tells me.

"Can we trust him?"

"He won't be conscious Sam," Hekator explains.

"Might put him in the same hospital as Sian," Grandpop smiles.

While this is going on I check Sue. She looks like she's struggling. I raise my eyebrows at her. She gives me a small smile. That's no good, so I speak up.

"Hey everyone, that was Sue's first mission with us. No training! Straight in the deep end eh?"

"That's true," Grandpop agrees, turning to her.

"You did bloody well," he adds to her, "really good driving."

"I'm just glad you didn't let this idiot try it," Cam says of Tarik, her arms around him.

Everyone laughs. Tarik pretends to look offended.

"Actually Sue, would you mind helping me take Ken to hospital?" Patricia asks. "I just need someone to drive the van."

"Sure," said Sue.

"Gunter will do it Pat. Sue has to get back to Renwick. It's not over yet," Grandpop interrupts.

Sue looks surprised.

"We have to find a place to interrogate Rocelli," Grandpop reminds her.

"Hekator are you interested?" he adds.

"Yes, very much. But Mike, I suggest I see to him now, and return him safely to you in the morning. He may be somewhat dangerous at the moment."

"I'd like to come," Sue says quickly.

Hekator turns to Sue smiling a patient smile. She goes pale as he 'says' something to her. I wonder if he's following up his own investigation again. The one Queen Morganne doesn't like.

"Oh ... OK," she admits, " It's not that important. It can wait for morning."

"You two deserve to rest and get used to your new home," says Hekator, "and don't worry Sue, I will be recording the primary evidence, not tampering with it."

Sue's a tad embarrassed. There's a silence.

"So Sue *can* drive Ken?" Patricia asks, uncertainly.

Sue shrugs "Looks like it," she says.

I join the others getting onto discs and going back to the changers. It feels so good to be back with them again.

"You seriously need some new clothes," Scott tells me as I get back into my ground kit. It's all I have left.

"I had some. But they all got lost," I tell them.

I wonder what Leonora did with them in the changer.

We go back to Hastings and I find Rewa's still up, watching TV and having a hot chocolate before bed. I get one too and slouch down next to her. The others are either watching TV or watching Cam take out Tarik at pool.

"Are you staying tonight?" Rewa asks, still staring at the TV.

"Yep. I think I finally am," I sigh.

"Yay," she says softly.

I edge along the couch and squeeze her. She snuggles against me. We don't say anything. We don't need to.

Half an hour later Rewa's almost asleep. Aunty Liz comes in and tells us to go to bed. My room has no view at all, which is a bit of a loss after Renwick. Still, it's warm and comfortable, and it could have been anywhere, just sensing the familiar minds of my family and friends around me is just so comfortable I'm asleep within minutes of my head touching the pillow.

CHAPTER SEVENTY NINE: INTERROGATION

For a moment after I wake up I can't remember where I am. The light and sky seem different. The room, just so unlived in. But I hear someone moving about outside my door and I get up to find Aunty Liz drinking a cup of tea and reading a magazine.

I come out feeling a bit dazed.

"Hello Sam," Aunty Liz smiles.

I feel so fuzzy I just amble over to her. She gives me a hug, which feels nice.

"Sleep well?" she asks.

"Yeah, great thanks. Is there any tea?"

"In the pot."

It's Nana's old pot.

"Did you take this with you?"

"Yeah, it was about the only thing I *could* grab."

"You must have looked pretty funny clutching a teapot."

"Probably did. But everyone had something. You only realise what's really important when you absolutely have to leave nearly everything behind."

I sit down next to her with my tea.

"I wish I'd been there."

"So do I, it would saved us a lot of worry about you."

She takes a sip.

"On the other hand Sam you've done amazingly well. Dad's very impressed, and so are the others."

I shrug.

"I didn't have much choice really."

"No, none of us have."

There's a silence as we reflect on that.

"I'm very grateful to Sue for looking after you."

That's not right!

"I looked after *her* half the time," I point out.

"Yes, you did. You're growing up Sam."

I feel sort of good, and sort of dumb about that.

"I wonder if they cleaned Nana's house?" I say, thinking about the gang.

Aunty Liz looks sad.

"It can't be cleaned Sam. It's contaminated now. It'd be better if they'd burned it down too."

I feel sad about that.

"Seems like all our past is being rubbed out, bit by bit," I say.

Aunty Liz smiles, "Ay ... but a new net goes fishing, eh boy?"

It's an old Maori saying. She meant a new generation makes a new future.

"I need to learn more about that stuff," I say, half to myself.

"What stuff?"

"Our Maori stuff?"

"The old people always wanted to teach you. It was dad who was against it. But he's changed. This place has changed him heaps. He really likes it with everyone here. He says he feels reborn."

"Yeah, he seems much less grumpy than I remember him."

"It's the war."

That confuses me.

"What about the war?"

"He hated himself because of the war. He never talked much about it but I know he did things he … well … things he wasn't proud of. Working here … with you kids … to make the world a better place … he feels like he can finally do something good with that experience. It's changed his world. He's happy in a way he's never been happy before."

It's true. That *was* what's different. But it raises a big question for me.

"What about you Aunty Liz? Are you happy?"

"Aw you know … I'm always happy to see my whanau growing up and happy."

I look at her. She's being shy.

"When I was alone in that police station I read Sue's mind," I tell her.

She starts to go a bit red. She won't look at me.

"Sue thought she *had* to put up with her girlfriend being a bitch because that was the best she could get. I knew she could do better," I tell her, getting up.

Aunty Liz is really embarrassed now. She's never really talked about her own love life to us, ever. She's always hidden it from Grandpop and away from us. Always taken second place. Always sacrificed.

"She's totally straight-up Aunty Liz. That's what she wants too. Some-one to be straight-up. It's all she ever wanted."

I leave her to go get dressed. When I come back out she's in her room. I go down to breakfast where I find Rewa, Grandpop and the others tucking into scrambled eggs, sausages, hash browns, onions, and stuff. Being Saturday everyone's in a good mood.

147

Even Ken who's stumping around on a crutch with a cast on his leg and a toy parrot on his shoulder which Ashley had put there. I notice Sue isn't there, but it feels so nice laughing and joking with the others it doesn't bother me.

After a while Dr P appears. He's wearing jeans and looks relaxed. He claps Ken on the shoulder and then pretends to be surprised by the parrot. He tells us Nathan and Sir Michael have been successfully disconnected from the Administration network but it will be another day before it's clear whether the bacteria which dissolved the mindtap material are working without side effects. However, he says Sir Michael and Sian will soon be reunited, the only problem will be whether they can return to their old lives or not.

Ashley's cousin, Nathan and grandmother, Margaret, are in the same boat, although being younger and practically unknown the problem for Nathan is reduced. There's all sorts of discussion about where Nathan and his grandmother should be returned to, with options ranging from Hawaii to Louisiana and perhaps even Canada. One thing that is for sure, Washington DC is out. Dr P sidles over to me when Ken's talking.

"Please to come to my office in five minutes," he says quietly, just to me. Then he joins in the discussion again.

Not too long afterwards he leaves. I have a strong idea that he wants to talk about Sue. I wonder if he's having second thoughts about her. Anyway, a bit later I leave the café and head through the library to the front building to find Dr P.

Dr P's new office is a bit different to his old one. It's on the ground floor and the only view is of the carpark. There's another larger room behind his office which he's using as a lab. Dr Gursoy is in there. But Dr P's office still looks like it had just been dumped there.

The desk and chairs are new. The screens are new. There's no Samovars or telescopes. The walls are just white and boring. I knock at the open door.

"Sam, please to come in, and be comfortable," he says in a carefree way.

I come in and take a chair, but notice he closes the door behind us. He doesn't wait to get back to his chair before speaking.

"Sam … you slept good?" he interrupts himself.

I shrug, "Yeah … fine."

Dr P puts his fingertips together and to his mouth like someone praying. He's thinking about what he wants to say to me as he sits.

"Good … good. Sam, there are things I need to tell you," he says. He looks at me for a moment, like a chess opponent.

"Is about return plan."

Now he has my attention.

"Objective is to complete mission you started by closing story of Renwick in New Zealand. To that end all staff must depart New Zealand using own passports under surveillance of Customs and Immigration and arrive in other nations under similar surveillance. In this way is no question of mystery or disappearance. However is best if Police not aware of departures recorded by other departments until too late."

"Now, appears New Zealand Police wish to interview me regarding fire at Renwick House. Is possible am to be arrested again in New Zealand. However is useful opportunity to distract Police today while others make get away."

"So all staff on flights out of New Zealand today and tomorrow. Mariko, Gunter and Mrs Jones fly to Tokyo; Khumalos fly to Singapore; Khadems and Gursoy's to Dubai; Ken and Robinson's to Buenos Aires. Your family, mine and Tran's fly to Sydney tomorrow possibly when I am arrested. Reason is so that is clear evidence everyone alive and everyone has left New Zealand. In this way, is no more mystery."

"But my distraction not enough. Is needed for rearguard to make as appear everybody remaining in hiding today and perhaps tomorrow also. Therefore am asking for you to volunteer to assist. As soon as staff completed flights you return here."

"What about Sue?"

"She has notice period, so to come much later."

"OK."

He looks at me for a moment.

"So, is yes?"

"Yeah, sure," I shrug.

"Thank you."

He has something else to say but seems to be trying to think how to say it.

"Detective Williams is excellent operative. Very thorough detective."

"Yeah, she's got an amazing memory for details ..." I enthuse.

He smiles thinly.

"Yes. Is very good. She is to interview Enrico Rocelli. She wants you to help."

"Oh! OK," I agree happily.

He seems to be thinking something, I start to probe. His eyes flash as he notices. Then he grins that wolfish grin.

"Let me admit now," he begins uncomfortably, "you and she will discover ... inconsistencies."

I didn't quite understand. He sits back, although he's trying to relax, and relax me, there's a tension in the room.

"Your friend, Mr Ceder, is correct. Whole situation is multi-dimensional. Like chess in three dimensions. To win chess means gambit, means sacrifice. Not all friends always friendly. Is many secrets within secrets. Is embarrassment and shame on all sides."

He pauses, and sighs.

"Is not always possible to do right thing, in right way. Sometimes we must take course of expedience to avoid greater evil."

I wasn't sure if he's talking about Queen Morganne, or Rocelli or what. He checks my face again.

"Please to keep in mind wider conflict," he ends, pulling a thoughtful face.

I'm confused.

"So … do I go somewhere?" I ask, interrupting his cloudy thoughts.

"Yes. Miss Williams is at rental house in Port Carlyle on Aotea island with Rocelli. Hekator has finished with him."

"Is he safe?"

Dr Prosperov looks at me, thinking again. Then he shakes his head.

"No. He is never safe. Is sent for reason. Reason is opposed to us. Hekator says he has no tag or bug or bomb but does not make him safe. Our opponents are clever and subtle. Truth is matter of emphasis and perspective. His purpose is to cause damage to us perhaps as you cause damage in moon. Always to remember."

He seems a bit mean about this. Meaner than he has to be. I'm a bit surprised. He seems a bit surprised at himself as well. And

151

strangely uncertain.

"So ... should I get changed?"

He nods. I get up and turn to go, and then I remember something and turn back to face him.

"Thank you for coming for me in Liechtenstein."

He looks at me, surprised. His face softens a little.

"Is rare occasion when self and symbiant in absolute agreement," he tells me.

I'm gobsmacked. It never occurred to me before that Dr P and Lucky disagree on anything, and now he's saying it's rare that they agree. I wonder how he can do it at all. I stare for a moment and then realising it looks weird say, "thank you," again and leave his office.

I meet Rewa and the others coming into the library. They're planning their day. I explain I'm helping Sue talk to Rochelli.

"You deserve some serious overtime, mate," Scott tells me.

"It'll all be over by Monday," I shrug.

"Yay," Rewa says. "Are you back tonight?"

"I hope so."

So I go off to get changed. I'm surprised to find Grandpop downstairs on the desk.

"I thought you'd be out fishing," I say.

"Yeah, so did I. Dr P wants someone to keep an eye on Rocelli from here. He's a dangerous bugger."

That's true enough. I thank Grandpop for giving up his Saturday morning, get in a cabinet and bend space-time.

[+]

I flash into a large farm-style kitchen where I find Father Rocelli eating at the table and Sue drinking a cup of something leaning against the bench. Rocelli doesn't seem to even notice me. He

152

just keeps eating mechanically. Sue, still wearing her gray suit, smiles at me.

"Dr P said you wanted me to help with 'Big Ears' here," I tell her.

"Thanks Sam. He's hard work to be honest. Hekator's control crystal makes him so passive you have to ask him exactly the right question, and our history hadn't got that far yet."

Rocelli keeps eating like a robot even as we talk. It feels kind of weird. It's strange to think he's the same man that I had seen in the castle in Liechtenstein. In fact the more I look at him the more I wonder if he even is. Might this be a clone?

"Can I talk to him?"

"Be my guest. You have to say his name and be in front of him to get his attention. Otherwise he'll stare blankly."

It feels weird. I move over to the table, where he's eating cornflakes like a bulldozer. I pull out a chair and sit down.

"Ernesto Rocelli, were you in Belzer, Liechtenstein recently?" I ask.

He looks up, and tilts his head slightly.

"Si," he replies, certainly.

And goes back to shovelling cornflakes in his face.

"And he only answers in Italian," Sue adds.

I have a feeling this is going to be hard work.

"Ernesto Rocelli, did Inspector Du Croix make you come here?"

"Si," he says again.

That explains how he'd got back so quickly.

"Ernesto Rocelli, did you come here willingly?"

"No."

He says it with the same mindlessness as he'd said "yes". There's no way we're going to get any useful information out of him like this. I sigh and look around at Sue.

"Does he say anything other than yes or no?"

"Sometimes. Numbers or very short sentences but not much of any use. And all in Italian. He speaks English doesn't he?"

"Yeah of course, and French, German, Spanish, Portuguese, Polish, Russian, Arabic, Berber, Lingala, Kinyarwanda, and Swahili."

"Wow!" says Sue, impressed.

"Yeah, he's way smarter than us."

"But he's not much use the way he is," she points out.

"No, he's not," I agree.

In the meantime he's finished his cornflakes and sits still like a robot. We look at him.

"Do you think we could take that crystal off?" she asks.

"It's risky," I say, expecting Grandpop to agree," he's not very nice."

"I don't expect to like him. But I want to hear what he has to say and 'Si' and 'No' don't cut it," Sue says taking a sip of her coffee.

"No, they don't. The problem is once we take it off it could be damn hard to put it back on him without zapping him."

"So we zap him," she shrugs.

"But so far it's just been me. He knows I'm hard to get, but if he sees you he'll go after you," I warn her.

"I'm not *that* defenceless," Sue argues.

"No I mean you as a cop. I mean *you're* kidnapping him, aren't you? Nobody would believe *I* kidnapped him – especially with his background – but with you it's different. He could get you in trouble," I point out.

Sue pauses, thinking.

"Yeah, he could," she finally agrees.

"So maybe you should watch with Grandpop," I suggest.

"She could watch *instead* of Grandpop who would rather be fishing anyway," Grandpop puts in.

We smile at each other.

"OK, Do I have to know how to work anything?" she checks, reaching for her helmet.

"No Control does everything, you just have to be nice to him," Grandpop says.

Sue gets her helmet on and folds into nothing. I look around at Rocelli, sitting there with his mind completely blanked out by the crystal. It's strange to be alone with him. He scares me. His mind is very ugly. Charming on the outside, but a twisted mutant inside. I clear and rinse his bowl and Sue's cup and decide to sit at the other end of the table from him.

"OK, I'm sitting comfortably," Sue tells me. "Shall we begin?"

I get up and a little nervously approach Rocelli who sits still as a puppet. Then I reach out and screw off the crystal on his forehead.

He closes his eyes at once. Then, watching him closely I back off to my seat. He sits there for a while, then puts his head in his hands, his face screwed up. He takes a huge breath and exhales as he lets his hands drop from his eyes as he searches left and right. They flick past me. At first as he looks at the kitchen, then they come back and he looks at me with a lot of anger.

"You! Where am I? What is this place?" he demands.

He seems to realise he can move, and jumps up. He's very quick. He walks to the window and looks out.

"You're on Aotea Island ... having a holiday," I tell him, still sitting.

"And you have brought me here? Why?"

"To ask you questions."

He looks at me, checking me over. Then he looks around in the kitchen, thinking. He takes another deep breath.

"I want to make coffee," he says.

I just shrug. I walks quickly back to the kitchen bench and pours water into the jug and empties coffee into the plunger. He's surprisingly nervous and thinking hard.

"So, you have questions. Perhaps I have questions also," he glances at me.

"Yep," I nod.

"Does that mean 'yes' you will answer my questions?" he quizzes me.

"No more than you're going to answer mine, probably," I say evenly.

He thinks about that, and an arrogant smile appears on his face.

"So you want a conversation?"

He's trying to regain power. It's time to knock him back a bit.

"Yes, to see whether you have been sent here to do something useful or just be killed like a pig in a slaughterhouse."

The smile vanishes. He's back to scared and angry. He looks into my eyes. His black eyes quick and guilty. Mine hard. There's no mercy in them. There weren't many people in the world I could kill, not boy soldiers, not even drug slavers, but him? I was perfectly happy to kill *him* and he knows it. He coughs and smoothes his hair. He turns back to the plunger.

"So you are saying if I am not useful to you, you will kill me. Yes?"

He glances at me.

I nod slowly, not blinking.

"Woah, heavy!" Sue says.

"*Wait til you hear what he's done,*" I reply silently.

He rubs his chin thoughtfully, looking out the window, then turns suddenly and runs. I'd expected that. He falls, bringing down his chair, his legs no longer working. The invisible beam deadened his legs temporarily. I get up and come around the table standing between him and the door. He looks up at me, a bit worried I'll kick him.

"You're wasting time. It's not something either of us has much of. Get yourself to the table. I'll make your coffee."

I walk around him to the kitchen. The water has boiled so I pour it into the plunger,assuming that, because he acts Italian, he'll want it strong and black. I pick up the plunger and a mug and watch him pull himself up to the table. He's meant to be pretty old but he's as fit as a guy way younger. As he gets himself up I put the plunger and cup where he can reach it and return to my seat.

"Gratsi," he murmurs as he resumes his chair.

"OK, so yes, I'm armed. Is there anything else you want to know which could save us time?"

He looks up at me, his eyes are back to business, flicking around like a snake's tongue. Like his brain.

"Are we alone?" he asks.

"No ... and don't ask, I won't tell you."

He presses the plunger, thinking.

"So what do you want to know?" he asks watching the coffee mix.

"America..." I begin.

"Ah," he smiles, pouring his coffee, "of course."

He takes a sip and puts the cup down.

"You have completely no idea what you are up against, do you?" he asks.

157

"No," I admit, thinking about it, "but then, neither do you."

"I think I have rather a better idea than you do."

"Who do you think you are up against?" I challenge.

"Morganne, the deceiver," he spits.

"Why is she a deceiver?"

He smiles, an unpleasant smile.

"I'm sure you will find out yourselves – eventually."

"How did she deceive you?"

"She offered us immortality, but her science was flawed. It rendered us immortal but only so that we hungered for that which our bodies could no longer make: Stem cells from the young. We had immortality at the awful cost of devouring our children. Perhaps you know of Saturn the Roman god and father of Zeus?"

I shake my head. Roman gods are not my thing. But I knew this is all about self-justification for his crimes, but I have a question.

"But not all the Aesir were affected?"

"Not Aesir." he shook his head impatiently.

"Well, who are you then?"

"You see? Morganne has attempted to erase us from history by denying our existence, muddling us with others. We are the Watchers, the Iyrin. We have lived among your kind, instructing you for millennia."

"Before or after Morganne?"

"After. Then after the wars with the Fae we were cast out to establish colonies far away from Earth. We were left alone to suffer with our hunger."

I'm curious about that.

"Does it really make you hungry?"

"It is the nearest equivalent I can give you. More natural than a drug like heroin, it is like the most basic craving."

"What happens if you don't satisfy it?"

He stares, his brown eyes remembering. He looks mad.

"It starts with the shaking. You become obsessed. Your strength intensifies and you become a tiger, a killing machine, no longer responsive to language, pity or reason. If at this stage you are not satisfied your body begins to break down. You can no longer sleep, you become thin as your body supercharges your metabolism making you stronger, sharpening the senses, driving you to seek prey. Your lips retract and teeth grow, your skin burns in the most pale sunlight. Just like the Fae. The final stage is death, a week of indescribable pain all the time knowing a simple sip of blood would allow you to reverse the whole process."

I'm creeped out to think Tabika is a bit like this monster.

"Why blood?" asks Sue.

"Why blood?" I repeat, lost for questions.

"It is the quickest way to take what we need."

"But it isn't enough is it?" I ask, knowing it isn't.

"No. All predators, even your kind, need prey. Stem cells from the marrow are what *we* need. The youngest bones are the best."

His expression is closed down, but angry at being asked.

"God!" Sue exclaims. The horror of it is new to her but I can see the attraction of coming to Earth straight away. It would be like kids in a candy store. Loads of poor, unwanted children and nobody would do a thing to stop them.

"But *you* haven't been here for Millennia, have you. *You* came from somewhere else? Where did you come from? When did *you* first arrive on Earth?"

"We came from a colony a century ago."

"Who attacked you?"

He looks at me, surprised.

"Who attacked us?" he repeats.

"Your starship was destroyed," I prompt him, impatiently.

He's surprised and alarmed.

"How did you know that?" he asks suspiciously.

"First thing we ever did. Tracked the debris."

Rocelli frowns. Obviously he hasn't expected this and it's making him uneasy. He thinks about his answer carefully.

"That was a very painful time. We lost a great many friends. A great many."

"Was it the Service?"

He shakes his head. Then he sighs.

"Our experience led us to explore other dimensions of existence. There are many ... influences. One of them was opposed to our arrival here," he says carefully. I think about it.

"So it was a religious civil war?" I check.

"*You* might call it that."

"Who won?"

Rocelli considers the question.

"The situation has evolved with our experience."

That suggests to me he was on the losing side.

"What has it evolved into?"

Rocelli smiles.

"An organisation you would be well advised to show more respect."

I shrug.

"How can I respect something I don't know anything about?"

Rocelli smiles a forced smile.

"Exactly," he says, and takes another sip of coffee.

"Ask him about himself," Sue says in my ear. "People love to talk about themselves. Ask him how he became a priest."

"But it's not the Roman Catholic Church?" I check quickly.

His brown eyes glint with annoyance.

"No, it is not the Roman Church," he answers sarcastically.

"When did you become a priest?"

"1914."

"Why?"

"It allowed me to avoid becoming a soldier in the European war but gave me access to field hospitals and mortuaries."

I imagine a priest tending dying soldiers on their stretchers and then attacking them. It's disgusting but I press on.

"Where were you?"

"Italy and then France."

"So in World War One you were *against* the Germans?"

"German, Italian. They are just languages. Human diplomacy is of no interest to us. We work on all sides."

"And the Spanish flu, after the war?"

"Was an accidental outbreak," he says carefully.

"Accidental?"

"It arose from our arrival, but was not planned."

He takes another sip of his coffee. A thought takes him.

"But very interesting. We learned a lot from that."

"Go back to him," Sue says.

"What did you do after the war?"

"I worked in the church."

"Don't fill the silences, draw him out," Sue instructs. I sit there.

"I was attracted to orphanages, naturally."

He stares into his coffee. I say nothing. For a long time there's silence and then just as I'm about to ask him something he begins to speak. Remembering.

"I didn't have anything to do with the Fascists at first. Mussolini struck me as a fool. A fool and a tool of the Italian King. He strutted around idiotically but I began to realise, as he turned on the communists, that the more … excited … the Carabineri got pursuing communists the more orphans came into our care. It was, what the Americans call 'good for business'."

"Naturally I passed this observation on to my brothers and sisters and where we had discovered this effect by accident in Italy soon the others were helping to organise ultra-nationalist organisations on purpose. The humans seemed to find bullying of this kind exciting. Some were quite aroused by it. They were very easy to manipulate."

There's another pause.

"The Spanish Civil War was an excellent opportunity. The war was terrible with extreme cruelty on both sides[†]. It was barbaric. You humans are so much more brutal than we. It was easy to hide our prey. There was such a surfeit of material our sisters could do something we had not done in centuries. We produced our own children."

He looks at me.

"Our children are better than those of us who were afflicted by Morganne. Still damaged, true, but less affected. And more powerful."

He looked – there was no other word for it – proud.

I try to look pleased for him, which is hard, because the last thing I want is more creeps like Rocelli. He goes on.

"I also discovered something. We had to deal with pregnant communists. Fortunately the church opposes abortion or infanticide so these babies came into our care. Some we passed on to infertile Republican women. Others were moved. I began moving children around, so they could grow to the ideal size, but have no friends, no one who would notice when they moved again and never came back."

He smiled. It was to anger me, and I was angry. I couldn't hide it.

"Why can't they use foetuses?" Sue asks.

I don't know, so I ask him. He looks at me for a moment with a sharp smile, he's realised something but I don't know what, and then he frowns to cover it.

"Embryonic stem cells are too unstable. They start tumours which are hard to treat. Adult cells are too inflexible they create reactions. Younger cells are best."

He smiles at my disgust.

"Ask him how long he was in Spain," Sue says.

"When did you leave Spain?"

He smiles an intrigued smile, and pours more coffee.

"I left Spain after World War Two. My German, Austrian, Hungarian, Polish and Czech brothers, sisters and their many new children were leaving. They went to Argentina, Paraguay, and some to Uruguay also. I helped them. There were many agencies who helped them escape the Jewish revenge."

"Why do you hate the Jews?"

His smiles had always had an overtone of some other unfriendly emotion. Now it's a disgust that was almost enjoyment.

"You might call it a religious matter."

"What would *you* call it?" I ask impatiently.

"An unwelcome influence."

I want to ask more but I know he won't answer.

"Ask him about Argentina," Sue says.

"So when did you arrive in Argentina?"

"1954."

"And let me guess. You did the orphan thing again."

"It took some time to get the Junta to catch up with Spain. But yes, in time, we took communist children there also[+]."

"Hang on, what did the Church think about this? You were still a priest right?"

Rocelli looks like he's sucked a lemon.

"The Church is a very diverse organisation. There are many different interests within its walls. We..."

He glances at me.

"Of course I am not alone. We have always managed our political position carefully."

"By hypnotism?"

"Yes sometimes, but also corruption, and argument."

"Corruption? You bribe them?"

He smiles an awful smile.

"Some priests cannot sustain the Church's requirement for sexual abstinence. Their natural urges can easily be corrupted which makes them extremely pliable."

He makes me want to puke. I keep thinking of all the poor little kids. All the shamed, and ruined priests.

"Do you enjoy your work?" I ask angrily.

His eyes flash. He knows he's getting to me.

"Very much," he purrs.

"He's trying to rile you. Ask him when he left," Sue says.

"When did you leave Argentina?" I ask automatically.

Rocelli leans forward, eyes like shining darkness.

"Does she whisper what you want to hear, Sam?" he whispers.

"What?"

"Your friend, Constable Williams? She's listening and whispers questions to you. But does she whisper what you really want to hear?"

I stare at him. Luckily I can cope with this sort of needling way easier than hearing about what he had done.

"When did you meet Hathaway?"

The happy smile vanishes. His eyes go back to anger again.

"His name is not Hathaway," he spits. "His name is Tamiel. A name you are not worthy to even speak."

"So you always knew him?"

Rocelli just glares at me, giving me the evils. Obviously I've hit a sore point. Hathaway was arrested by the Administration at Elan and taken away by Du Croix after we intervened. He's probably been transported to the Center for 'processing'. That usually means having your brain destructively copied. They were clearly old friends.

"He worked for the CIA didn't he?" I ask.

I can see the struggle start on Rocelli's face. The desire to tell me how his allies will hurt us, against the desire to keep it secret. I just sit there and let him sort it out.

"Good one Sam," Sue says.

Finally he looks at me with a look of superior anger.

"You started by asking about America. Now I will tell you of America and then perhaps you will realise how utterly hopeless your insurgency is."

"America is simple. We own it. We have owned it for fifty years and all its power is ours."

I confess I smile at this delusion.

"Oh-kay," I say, fairly happily.

"You know nothing. You are an ignorant savage," Rocelli sneers.

"At least I'm not crazy," I jeer back.

"Listen, you fool. Power is not about numbers. Power is about authority. When you have the authority you have the power."

"What about democracy?"

"You think choosing the funniest clown in the circus gives you a better seat? Democracy was invented to legitimise authority not to change it. Let me give you just one example of how authority works. How one man with authority and opportunity became the architect of global power in your world. Look up the human name Allen Welsh Dulles. He officially died in 1969."

"His career started when working in Switzerland. There he stopped the man who would be founder of the Soviet Union, Vladmir Lenin, from entering the United States in 1916 so he could return to Russia in 1918. In 1921 he teamed up with British agent St John Philby to help the Saud family establish their Kingdom in Saudi Arabia. In the 1930s he worked with his brother John Foster Dulles of law firm Sullivan and Cromwell to assist the German chemicals giant IG Farben and weapons manufacturer Thyssen invest in the United States. During World War Two he was a diplomat and intelligence operative in Switzerland working with the Germans. After the war Dulles established Operation Paperclip to help German scientists escape to the United States and South America. In 1953 he started and was appointed first director of the CIA and authorised large-scale secret experiments on individual and mass mind control using torture, hypnosis and narcotics on prisoners *and* orphans. He toppled the elected and loved Prime Ministers of Iran, and the Congo for oil and uranium. He was a leader on the Warren Commission which investigated the assassination of President John F. Kennedy. A curious appointment given Kennedy had dismissed Dulles from the CIA, and threatened to break it up[†]."

"And just so you completely understand why this matters Dulles was a longtime friend of Prescott Bush the grandfather of the current President of the United States George W Bush[†]. Do you see *now* what you are up against?"

"Holy shit!" Sue says in my ear.

"No," I reply stubbornly. "That's just a spook story. Even if it's all true, it's bullshit. You're all alone, hung out to dry by the Administration, telling me vague stories about how you know scary people to cover up for the fact you're alone and you've got nothing."

"You *idiot*. You could stare a lion in the face and only see its nose."

"You aren't a lion Rocelli, you're a leach. A lying, squirming piece of filth practically gift-wrapped by Du Croix for squashing," I say, standing up.

"Mary, Mother of God! Miss Williams stop hiding! I want to talk to an adult who understands the world. Not this *infant*!" Rochelli roars, turning from me.

There's a long pause.

"Sam, I think it's time for the good cop," Sue says.

Something makes me uneasy about that. I'm not sure why. I sit down. Rocelli isn't looking at me. We're furious with each other. It bothers me how comfortable Rocelli still looks. It worries me. We're just calming down when Sue pushes open the sliding doors in the lounge and comes in, taking off her helmet. She goes straight into the kitchen and looks at us both. Saying nothing, she picks up the coffee plunger and takes it to the bench. She pours the remaining coffee from the plunger and hot water into a mug, puts it in the microwave, zaps it, adds milk and sugar and sits down on the kitchen side of the table, between us.

She takes a sip of coffee and grimaces.

"OK boys, what shall we talk about?" she says, finally.

DIANA POPVIC'S JOURNEY

Map Data © Google 2016

FRENCH-BELGIAN BORDER

Map Data © Google 2016

CHAPTER EIGHTY: INTERVENTION IN ELAN

For a moment neither me or Rocelli want to say anything. And then I decide to say what had been hanging over us since we'd started talking. The sequence of events that lead to Rocelli's friend, Clayton Hathaway being taken away for reprocessing by the Administration.

"Diana Popovic."

Rocelli looks around at me, and then looks away again. Sue frowns, confused.

"Diana Popovic. That was where our battle started," I say.

"You forget Jeanne Mazuri," Rocelli says to the window.

"That's true," I admit. "We beat you there too," I add to rub it in.

Rocelli looks around at me, jeering.

"Sarah Kogan, Jeanne Mazuri and Diana Popovic. Three girls of thousands we have processed but you fought furiously for them. With Kogan you stole the ransom, and almost killed six of us, but the other two? They are of no consequence! Tell me, is Prosperov sane?"

"That being you told us he released from the tree of souls certainly was not! That's why it was incarcerated. Do you truly follow Prosperov like such mindless lambs? I find your naïveté inconceivable!"

"You have to have faith, Father Rocelli," I smile.

"Faith is for lunatics. Believe me! I deal with them daily."

Sue looks at me. She obviously doesn't like this snake either.

"I know about these girls," Sue says to me, "but I don't know about this conflict."

"Ask him," Rocelli sneers, looking back out the window, "he and his friends started it."

"OK," I start, "Well, I'll give you the short version."

"OK," Sue agrees.

"Diana and Elena left Moldova again in early May 2008. They had a better deal this time because they knew the traps better. They had a job offer from a Frau Muller in Innsbruck."

"Frau Muller! Yes, you've mentioned her," Sue says.

"Muller ist tüdelich (Muller is gaga)," Rocelli mutters in German, brushing his trousers.

"They were to work as servants. Diana had lied about her age saying they were twins. Anyway they got to Suceava in Romania then to Innsbruck in Austria by train without any problems. Their paperwork was good. Within a week they were living in an upstairs bedroom, learning German as fast as Frau Muller shouted it and having a lonely and poor time."

"So what happened?"

"Nothing."

"Nothing?"

"Nothing happened for ages. Not for six months. Meanwhile Jeanne was growing steadily bigger and Nkunda was losing patience with the UN and the other armies taking advantage of the ceasefire."

"So you didn't have much to do?"

I snort, thinking of all the other stuff we were doing,

"Nathan's mother finally lost it so he ran away to live with his grandmother, but nothing Father Rocelli needs to hear about. But yes, nothing with those two until September."

"In the meantime Jeanne had been picked up by a Catholic Women's organisation 'Sisters of Our Lady in Charity' who do good stuff all over Africa with hardly any funding, while old men, like this creep, fly around the world. They were looking after young mothers and former child soldiers really well and Jeanne was quite happy with them. She had baby Marie and was doing pretty well when this ... snake, showed up."

Rocelli's holding his head high, ignoring us, looking outside, but obviously listening in.

"Well, we'd been watching him and Hathaway with their experiments from Kogan's planes for months."

Rocelli glances at me. This is news to him.

"We also knew the Administration had been supporting them. At the time we thought the Bruderschaft..."

"The *what*?" Rocelli sneers.

"The Bruderschaft."

"The Bruderschaft hasn't existed for decades. It was a relic of the Holy Roman Empire."

"You all seemed pretty cosy in Liechtenstein."

"Von Streicher was the only former member of the Bruderschaft there."

I look doubtfully at him. I'm about to start again when he can't hold back his frustration.

"Let *me* explain," he breaks in. "The Bruderschaft had been on this planet for centuries. They are *one* of our tribes. They spanned Russia and Eastern Europe all the way to Germany and Austria. They farmed the Slav serfs and peasants in their tiny, isolated and backward duchies in the name of the human rulers

171

who they controlled and corrupted. Their only problems were the occasional Jewish rabbi who recognised them for what they were, but it was never difficult to accuse these outsiders of the very acts the Bruderschaft themselves carried out. The blood libel worked very well. It was always easy for them to incite hatred against 'Christ's murderers'," he smiles.

"But the Bruderschaft opposed *your* arrival in 1908," I say to wipe the smile off his face.

Raising that annoys Rocelli but only makes him continue on.

"Not uniformly. Some like Von Streicher invited us. But others, and Frau Muller was among them, wanted to keep us out. They had spent so long in a comfortable world of ignorant, easy prey they could not accept that the human world had outgrown their ... petty tyrannies. New means to find food and propagate were needed. Ways that took advantage of the world your kind was creating. That's why we came."

"So what happened to the Bruderschaft?" Sue asks.

"After the betrayal the Center became concerned. A starship loss on a primitive planet is a serious event. At first the Bruderschaft blamed the Fae but it did not take long before the truth became clear. Many of the Russian conspiracy within the Bruderschaft who had betrayed we newcomers were soon caught by the Administration and liquidated. The loss of so many secret policemen and minor nobles made the revolution in Russia so much simpler. The old regime had relied on our powers to keep the serfs and city scum cowering. Now they were gone. Some to the Center for trial and reprocessing, others slipped away to join either their relatives in Prussia, Bulgaria, or Romania and others simply joined the communists. They had as much success inside the KGB as we did with our Governments."

"The rest of the Bruderschaft tried to be welcoming to those of us who had survived. Tamiel and I accepted that welcome. Many chose to ignore it and settled in the Americas and colonies of Great Britain which at that time were spread around the planet." Rocelli pauses, clearly considering whether he should tell us more.

"And after the war they broke up and went to South America?" Sue prompts him.

"Let us say the war brought about a change of direction. We Iyrin are not slaves to a central dictator. Each of us acts as he or she sees fit."

"But you went to South America?"

"It was up to the individual. Many *did* go to South America. While many of you in the English speaking world believe World War Two destroyed fascism this was simply propaganda.

Yes, it was pushed underground in Germany, France, Poland and Belgium but it was never destroyed. Many of the old Bruderschaft who preferred to live among aristocrats simply moved to the Spanish speaking world which maintained the same petty tyrannies of ignorant and isolated peasants and natives we have always preferred for controlling humans."

"Catholic tyrannies?" I check.

"No, not Catholic tyrannies but tyrannies that followed the Church."

"But they stopped being the Bruderschaft?"

"The term is still used by a few ... and some humans who would emulate us ... yes, we have our sycophantic admirers among your kind ... but the shift of so many to the Americas has meant we have a new political centre."

"Does it have a name?" Sue asks.

"The Foundation."

"What does this foundation do?" Sue asks.

"It provides the infrastructure for our activities on this planet."

We both look at him blankly.

"Similar to the human organisation the Arabs call The Base
– Al Qaeda. It is a network of our kind in places of influence to
support and cover for one another. To work towards the release
of our kind from our inheritance from Morganne, and to ensure
a supply of prey."

"What about wiping out the Synthetics?" I add.

Rocelli smiles at that happy thought.

"And ultimately restoring freedom in the Galaxy."

But that meant their bioweapons might not be aimed at the
Synthetics!

That left ... a thought struck me.

"So Aids wasn't just a weapons test. You also did it to generate a
new supply of orphans."

Rocelli seems surprised by my making this connection.

"Of course. It is perfect for creating supply. The number of
orphans in Africa became enormous. It was excellent for
business."

"Can't you get it?" Sue asks.

"They're immune," I remind her.

Rocelli smiles at us like a teacher pleased with his pupils.

"It also has useful intergenerational effects. Without parents
whole generations are relatively easy to re-educate and
dominate. The average age in sub-saharan Africa dropped to
childhood after the release."

"Holy f___!" Sue breathes, in sudden realisation, looking at
him. "The new plague you've been testing isn't aimed at the

Center's biobots, it's aimed at all the Earth's adults!"

Rocelli actually laughs. He's genuinely surprised. His eyes flash. "Humans! You never fail to impress me! Just when we think you too stupid to think for yourselves, one of you does! We must never underestimate you!" he says, shaking his head.

I'm very bothered by the fact that he doesn't seem the slightest bit worried by the fact we've discovered their plan. But something doesn't make sense.

"But hang on," I start, "Why is the Administration helping you?"

Rocelli's eyes twinkle. He sits back. His dark eyes gleamed with delight and evil.

"Ahh, for that Mr Kahu, you will have to do some more work."

Remembering the arrest of the Archdeacon I'm not sure whether that means Rocelli *thinks* he has support and no longer does, or if he thinks he has support and actually does. Or if he's just messing with me to put us off.

"But Du Croix won't support that. He bust up your bloodbath and you only had a few victims. He won't stand by and let you wipe out all adults."

Rocelli's looking at me with measuring eyes. It isn't a nice feeling.

"I'll admit Du Croix has the ear of the Service, and the Service has no love for those it considers traitors or conspirators. But the Service is only concerned with threats to itself. Your species' fate is of no more interest to it than say, giraffes."

I rather doubt that, but Sue interrupts.

"So how big is this Foundation?" Sue asks.

"Thousands of influential people," Rocelli tells her, smiling.

"So why did Du Croix send you to stop us?" I ask to get through his bullshit.

"I volunteered," he counters.

"To save your neck."

Rocelli shrugs lazily.

"But you have no mindtap," I guess. "How do you contact him?"

"Your race has helpfully discovered the telephone," he sneers

"But you are our prisoner," I point out.

"For the moment."

"You think you get out of this?" I ask sarcastically.

"Look at it from his point of view Sam," Sue says.

"In the Administration's hands he's definitely in danger. In ours he thinks he stands a better chance of survival. But he had to promise to deliver Prosperov. That way he could escape in the confusion."

I look at Rocelli who pretends to have lost interest again.

"Well, if he tries anything I'll toast his bloody undies." I tell her.

"Toast his undies?" Sue laughs.

"Yeah."

Sue sighs and looks back at Rocelli and then me.

"Anyway you were telling me that everything came to a head in September?" she reminds me.

"Yeah, Rocelli convinced the nun in charge that Jeanne and her baby would be better off in a special orphanage in France."

"France!" Sue says. "They wouldn't let her in."

"Oh Sue don't be dumb! He's just been telling you who runs things. Of course if *he* asks, *they* will let her in. They let Diana and Elena in."

"But what about the rules?" she asks, her forehead crinkles.

"Sure there are rules. But who interprets them?"

"Judges," she says certainly.

I force a big fake smile and nod.

"*Oh!*" Sue admits, catching up.

Rocelli is still not interested.

"But we didn't let him take Jeanne without a fight. The night she was meant to leave North Kivu there was a fair amount of confusion – most of it started by us. We zapped the plane's tyres on the ground when the CNDP was helpfully attacking something nearby. They couldn't steer the plane on the ground and Goma's airport was shortened by a lava flow back in 2005 so they couldn't take off."

"They tried to keep everyone on the plane over night but we simulated artillery and the crew didn't want to spend the night with the threat of mortar attack under a wingload of avgas so that got everyone off the plane. We thought it would be easy to break them all out but we'd forgotten how persuasive these bastards can be. Rocelli fed them more than most of these kids had ever seen in their lives. With food in these places you definitely make friends. The girls thought they were going to some magical European private school in a castle or something. So even though we made plenty of chances for them to escape they didn't take them."

"It was also too late to get anyone to do much. It was three in the morning local time so all the girls wanted to do was sleep. We messed with the plane some more hoping to buy us some time."

"Unfortunately Rocelli was in such a rush to get away the crew didn't even notice what we'd done and the plane flew for Kinshasa while we slept. We were all very lucky they made it at all and decided then we'd never to mess with another plane again."

"Kinshasa was meant to be a brief stopover but the smoke pouring out of the two outboard engines convinced them to wait for a replacement aircraft. For those girls from North Kivu Kinshasa may as well have been a different country. They didn't even speak Lingala, the main language in Kinshasa and had to rely on French. Without a plane the only way back home is back up the river by barge for a month and then over the mountains on a truck for a week. I think the scary plane ride and the fact they hadn't got so far from home that they were completely lost, plus the fact that Kinshasa is pretty rough by any standards, started to worry them."

"Also, of course, the change of plan meant they weren't expected and the food they thought they were going to get wasn't there. That made the mothers pretty upset. Our friend here had thirty girls to keep under control and we only wanted one. He couldn't keep track of all of them. The turning point was when we organised for Mrs Huuygens to check on progress. We knew from our bugs in her house..."

Rocelli's eyes swivel to me instantly.

"She had been getting very excitable the more she got ready to conceive and any suggestion of delay would upset her. We stopped her getting through until Jeanne was listening in through the paper thin walls and luckily they spoke French throughout. It totally freaked Jeanne out."

"Rocelli explained it away as a religious matter she didn't understand properly, but Jeanne was still scared so we came in to get her."

I glance at Rocelli. He'd hammered us hard. It reminds me how dangerous he was. And here he is sitting with us looking bored. The difference between then and now was the new suits. The Lanas had psychic shielding. He'd tested me by running but he had more than that, and hadn't used it. Or maybe he had used it and hit the shielding, then realised he couldn't break it. Or maybe he can. I don't know and it bothers me.

"It was pretty intense," I find myself telling Sue, looking at him.

"What did you think?" Sue asks him.

It's like a mouse interviewing a cat about how another mouse has escaped with all the cheese. While he's talking I check in with Control.

"*Is anyone monitoring us*?" I ask.

"Of course," Dr P replies. He seems surprised I'd even ask.

Rocelli's talking.

"It was a question of losing one, or losing all. They worked in relay. I didn't see their faces so I only learned to recognise them psychically. They were quite weak individually but their teamwork was good. It was a useful encounter for us because for the loss of one child it confirmed we were dealing with six human children using Fae technology, nothing more. It was obvious that they could not have defeated our friends in Israel. That meant it had to have been the Fae themselves with all that implied for non-intervention. But what puzzled us then, and puzzles us still, was their determination to rescue this one girl and abandon all the others. If they wished to interrupt the conception why not rescue all?"

I have no wish to answer the question. It was something we'd all agonised over. He seems to know that, because he looks pleased with himself.

"And what happened to Jeanne?" Sue asks.

"I'll tell you some other time," I tell her grimly.

"But she escaped?"

"Yeah eventually. Her baby wasn't so lucky. Little Maria died. Kinshasa's the perfect breeding ground for disease: poverty;

super bacteria which breed because they treat antibiotics like candy; and all sorts of voodoo magical beliefs about witches and children. It was pretty tough for her."

Rocelli's lost interest again.

Sue nods. I think, "that's a strange thing to do."

"So what happened with Diana and Elena then?" Sue asks.

"They worked for Frau Muller until Von Streicher took off with them," I tell her.

"How did that happen?"

"He just showed up one day and they drove off with him. We didn't know anything about him then. We asked Muller who he was and where the girls had gone and she told us everything."

"*Everything*?" Rocelli suddenly demands.

Sue just seems to be frowning.

"Yeah, she told us everything," I jeer at Rocelli." How else do you think we found the assembly?"

"Muller didn't know enough," Rocelli snaps.

This is interesting. The Bruderschaft, or whatever they're called now, are as concerned about how *their* security was breached as we are about ours. That must be why he's really here, and why he hasn't really tried to escape yet. This could be useful – if we're clever.

"Muller didn't know exact details but she told us all about the Bruderschaft. She told us how she had long served the network as a safehouse, hiding officers or their wives and children on their way to Switzerland or Spain or Portugal. Then later how she had supplied prey through to what she called the French network. Girls seeking work in France who ended up in dungeons in Northern France or Southern Belgium."

"She said now that she could no longer conceive the bloodlust had reduced. Her need was so low she could make do with commercial blood products without the need to kill. It had made her feel sorry for the girls that passed through her house. So hopeful and innocent of what awaited them."

"But as she had lost her need for blood and marrow she had also lost her power to dominate. Instead she was dominated by others in the network and she hated the way they showed her no respect anymore. She said she had never liked the newcomers and didn't like to deal with them. She said it was their fault her husband had been taken to the Center."

Rocelli smiles and nods.

"And doubtless you stoked the fire of her hatred?" he asks.

"We hardly needed to. The more she thought about it the more she wanted to hurt you. That was when she said she thought you were preparing a bloodbath for Mrs Huuygens. She said Diana had been chosen for the special meal. Elena would simply be killed as unneeded."

"How awful," Sue says. She seems strangely vague at the moment.

"But how did you trace the assembly and how did you meet Du Croix?" Rocelli asks seriously. He has stopped ignoring us and seems more interested in me now. I feel glad about that.

"We first met Du Croix in Belem, Brazil. We were there for different reasons. He was investigating corruption among Customs officials who were covering the transhipment of cocaine from upriver to ships bound for Mexico or Italy. We were looking for someone. Anyway he recognised we weren't what we said we were. He gave us his card, which was bugged, but didn't try to use any weapons or anything. He told us he would 'catch us later'. It was threatening, but friendly, at the same time."

"Von Streicher took Diana and Elena to Paris. Their first day was sightseeing, chocolates and new clothes. Their second day was introductions to various important people, mostly Father Rocelli's friends: judges, senior priests, police and civil servants. Then they tried to grab our wormhole and we lost track of them until we read in a newspaper a so-called Moldovan prostitute had been found dead. The police said it was suicide. It was Elena."

"From Paris they moved further North. We knew where Diana was so we had to tail her. We tracked her to the village near the border with Belgium which seemed pretty ordinary on the outside but turned out to be all infiltrators. We were chased out and had to watch it from a long way off."

"Meanwhile the Father here had obtained European-wide refugee status for the African girls in Brussels. But rather than wait there they flew at once to a disused NATO airfield in Northern France where they were met by buses and taken to a run down old Chateau in the little village of Elan. We tried to break them out but the protection was too strong."

"From tracking the African girls with Father Rocelli, listening to Mrs Huuygens' travel plans, and tracking Diane, it became clear that everyone was heading toward the town of Sedan in the Ardennes province of France. There was a conference being held at the big castle there on 'Bioterror and the State' and it looked suspiciously like many of the important people Diana had met were going."

"But we had a huge problem. There were six of us and dozens of them. All of them stronger. They were on their guard and the Fae were not going to help. No matter how we looked at it we didn't have the power to stop what was happening."

"So who suggested the Administration?" Rocelli asks.

It's time to trade information.

"Dr Prosperov. How did you know to hire Leonora and send her here?" I ask.

"Du Croix told me about the lawyer Hamilton-Smythe and said I could expect developments very soon."

"But that was six months *after* we broke up your assembly and arrested Hathaway. How did that happen?"

"Du Croix came to see me a month ago. He asked if I wanted revenge."

"That must have been an easy question to answer."

"The hard thing was not killing him," Rocelli admits.

He means it too.

"You love Tamiel," Sue says slowly.

Rocelli looks away. I don't have time to worry about the emotional life of mass murderers.

"But Du Croix came to you. Did he say what had changed?"

Rocelli sighs and looks back.

"He said the Administration felt sure it could trace the American girl Robinson."

"But ... that doesn't make sense. He put you onto Sir Michael. If he did that, he didn't need to trace Ashley. He already knew there was a link to Prosperov. You sent Leonora Carter before the trace was even applied."

We're both thinking the same thing: Du Croix set the whole thing up with Prosperov. Now we're slowly and mistrustfully piecing it all together like a jigsaw. Sue's frowning, trying to concentrate.

"Clearly Du Croix is playing a dangerous game," Rocelli says,

"He knew where the trace went and didn't strike. He could be accused of assisting the enemy."

"But what I don't understand is why he let *you* go. You were as guilty as Hathaway. Even more so."

"No, Tamiel and Deiter Huuygens were the leaders of the virus research. That was what the Service demanded action on. Von Streicher, Sigrid Huuygens and I had nothing to do with it. The fact Du Croix interrupted the bloodbath was due to your meddling not his decision."

I'm beginning to get the uneasy feeling that Rocelli has been sent by Du Croix to find out where we've moved, or die, and it would suit Du Croix if he got both.

"I wouldn't bet on that. I don't think he likes your kind," I reply.

"I don't thinks he likes you any better. He seeks to contain, not to control or to persecute."

"Probably because he had orders not to from his boss," I answer, hotly.

Rocelli looks wary.

"He used me to catch the Archdeacon after Beltzer."

A cold fury crosses Rocelli's face like lightning. His eyes glitter. If he had been an iceberg of evil in the room before this was the first hint of how deep that burg went, and it was a long, long way.

"On Earth the Foundation is more powerful than the Service. Du Croix's survival depends on us," Rocelli hisses.

"But the Foundation didn't protect Tamiel from the Service and they aren't protecting you from us. I think you embarrass them. I think they're over you and want you gone," I snarl back.

I'm scoring hits, I can tell. Rocelli opens his mouth but no words come out. Sue shakes her head quickly and blinks. It's as I'd

PART SIX: THE CRUCIBLE

suspected. Rocelli's a master of psychic dominance. He can sneak up on her without her even realising it. That's why she realised the relationship between Tamiel and Rocelli. She was reflecting him. I need to get her out of here.

"If that is Du Croix's plan it is also to stir my friends against you. As I said, we are free, in that respect the name Bruderschaft was correct. It is a brotherhood not a corporation. The Foundation does not direct us."

"Maybe they want to," I guess.

"You know nothing," he sneers.

We're headed for conflict again. I wonder whether Rocelli has recovered from the paralysis I've given him yet. Could I zap him before he used a psychic attack? But before the tension gets too high Sue steps in.

"But you both know what happened with Diana. There may be more to it than you think," she suggests.

I could tell she's becoming very aware she's out of her depth. She'd experienced Rocelli's subtle mind control and it's shaken her. His hard-out mind control is way meaner and she knows it. She wants us to keep talking so she can get away. I think that's a good idea too, so I start talking fast.

"The conference in Sedan was to get the infiltrators together. Hathaway and Huuygens were there, of course. They were even speakers according to a programme we got from our network."

"But we didn't dare go near that big castle. If the infiltrators weren't enough it was also being protected by the French military because NATO generals and defence officials from all over Europe were going."

"But down the road in the tiny village of Elan, Rocelli and his friends had fifty girls in the little run down chateau. They must have been drugged or something because they seemed really spacey. All giggling and stupid. We had staked out the place, watching it from a distance to see if there was anything we could do. Of course our parents didn't want us to try and rush in and rescue them but we knew something terrible would happen if nobody did anything."

"We called the French police. They sent a patrol car around but what could they do? There was no crime and just a bunch of happy kids with correct papers in the care of some respectable priests. They left again."

"That was when ... one of us ... broke ranks and tried to get them out herself. Being her partner I had to help her. We got into the chapel early in the morning. The first thing we noticed was that it was completely gutted. Instead of the usual things like a pulpit or fount there was a large brass bath in the centre, and heavy steel tables from hospitals around it. Stacked around were all sorts of things: dresses for the girls, lights, petrol, and on the steel tables coils of clear plastic piping, basins and gross looking surgical tools."

"Uh," Sue gags. She struggles to keep her stomach under control. She does better than we had.

"But dead in the centre was this stand covered in black velvet. On it was a skull, and two bones that glittered. It was quite large. We got closer and discovered they were made of silver and diamonds. It reminded me of the Totenkopf, the death's head on the old SS uniforms. And that was when we discovered why we felt so cold. It wasn't the frosty morning air at all. It was this thing. And then it started to light up as the air started to freeze, and we discovered we couldn't communicate or ... get away. It wanted to hurt us, we started being dragged. Everything was dragged. If we hadn't had ... well ... we were nearly caught. We didn't go back."

Rocelli's smiling unpleasantly, but says nothing.

"We kept away that day but when all the local people all drove off happily that evening and Mrs Huuygens arrived we knew it would happen that night. It was a misty night. Elan has a small lake and it can get misty there. It seemed creepy and lonely enough during the day but at night it was way worse. But they were decorating it like they were planning a party alright "

Rocelli's smiling to himself at the happy memory and interrupts.

"It was the biggest assembly feast we had permitted ourselves in years. Since the War in fact," he says.

"You *were* celebrating something!" I suddenly realise.

Rocelli just smiles, his eyes twinkling.

Something we didn't know. Another threat!

"Your experiments had worked?" I guess.

Rocelli says nothing.

"So what happened then?" Sue asks.

"About ten that night the big black cars from Sedan started to show up. The infiltrators, dressed as priests, greeted these rich old men in suits and showed them the lighted way to the Chapel. Mrs Huuygens arrived with her husband. She looked like she was dressed for her wedding in a dress of gold satin and lots of sparkling stones. The men gathered around her like bees around the queen."

"At about eleven the DRC girls came out of the chateau two-by-two wearing white satin and carrying a candle singing. The hundred meter path was lit with torches. We tried to zap them, but the way was lined with trees, we couldn't get too close and it was misty and our beams crackled blue and gave our positions away. The girls just stepped over the few we hit and went on walking and singing. Some of us were chased off by the Bruderschaft. They were dressed like monks all in red, for some reason."

"The last girl in the line was Diana, the only white girl. She was dressed in red satin and carried red roses. She looked very pretty for a change. She was singing too but her eyes were clearly not seeing everything as it actually was."

"We tried to stop them going inside that chapel but we were too weak. We had to retreat quite a long way back. The red monks stayed outside to guard. We were really sad and really angry, but we couldn't stop them. We got sent home for trying."

Rocelli's looking at me with mock concern, his eyes still shining. I stop for a second. Then I look back and start talking again, staring him in the eye.

"They came about midnight. Just white light and not a sound. Suddenly the Administration were there. Their craft drifted over like the moon rising. Three saucers, and above them three triangles overhead. The light was intense. Huge shadows went everywhere. We could see small figures appearing on the ground and heading toward the chapel. The red monk guards opening the doors and falling. The pink light. And in the middle of it a small group of men in a coats watching on. Du Croix was one."

"It was too dangerous for us to stay. We still had eyes on it though and we saw the flashes of light, and the prisoners led away to the saucers. There were over a dozen. Smoke was pouring out of the chapel along with all the people. Then as silently and quickly as they'd appeared the saucers were gone and the blue and red flashing lights of the Fire and Police showing up replaced them soon after."

"Du Croix instructed the police on the roundup. Some were treated for smoke inhalation. I don't think they really understood what had happened. We saw the dazed and bloodied infiltrators returning to their big black cars. Mrs Huuygens, barely dressed, furious and screaming, and the girls who'd survived being taken away in buses. By two o'clock there was just a lone police car guarding the chapel."

"When we went back inside. The whole place was black and empty. It stank of smoke and was warm with radiation. There was no sign of blood, no sign anyone had been there at all."

"Diana was with the others in a hospital. There were only a dozen left. None of them could remember anything. They just woke up on the bus not knowing where they were or why they were wearing these dresses."

I paused. Rocelli's looking around a bit too much. He seems too restless.

"And was anyone charged?" Sue asks.

"No, it was all hushed up. The cops told one another it was meant to be a sex party with underage girls but there had been a fire and nothing had happened yet, so pressing charges against so many judges and officials wasn't something anyone wanted to ruin their careers with."

"But what happened to them? The ones who didn't come out?" Sue asks. Rocelli answers.

"The Service use plasma. All evidence was incinerated to smoke. What is the time?" he asks as if he were just filling in time before his next meeting.

"The time?" I ask. He'd just been talking about how he'd organised the murders of at least fifteen girls and he wanted to know the time.

"It's time you were stopped," I tell him, getting angry again. I jump up.

"You kill and kill and kill and some of us are getting sick of it," I say rounding the table.

Rocelli looks at me with irritation.

"Why should we let you live? Give me one reason?" I demand.

"Sam?" Sue warns.

"Because you're just a fourteen-year-old child who thinks he's special because someone gave him a new toy," Rocelli snaps.

"You can't kill me because you're too weak. The same goes for all your hopeless little friends. But I can kill you all without effort. And now we will discuss the location of your new base."

And then he hits me with everything he has and even though the suit had psychic protection built into it, my hearing and vision were distorted, I have a painful headache, my link has gone and I realise my shielding isn't enough, and we were now in serious trouble.

CHAPTER EIGHTY ONE: MURDER

It's like a voice heard from underwater.

"Mary, mother of God! Tell me where Prosperov is Ms Williams, or you will both surely die," Rocelli orders Sue, standing up.

"Haay ..." Sue begins, but she's fighting it.

I think "Zap him."

And then a terrible black pain seizes my brain. My vision's hopeless. Rocelli looms closer, and twists. I can't understand what he's doing. Then his fist smashes me in the jaw. My whole brain jolts. I go flying, knocking down chairs. I'm going down. I land on the floor. It's like I'm four years old and stunned. I can hear Rocelli demanding Sue tell him where the others are. Sue's voice is shaking and whining with pain.

"Hay ... Hastings ... Ha."

"I could find out without the pain, but I do so enjoy it," I hear him say.

"Hastings Hall," Sue blurts out and screams.

"And where is that?"

Under the table everything seems very foggy. My head is spinning. I feel sick. He's hurting her. Just like Ax hurt mum. I have to stop him. A deep strength gathers in me. History will not be repeated. Not now.

Sue's scream is deep, like a bark from an animal, mixing terror and pain.

"Tasmania! Oh God!" Sue screams loudly.

"See how confession releases our souls. Now excuse me please I have a carrier fleet to direct. They have been waiting for some time."

Sue slumps, gasping and crying. I hear his footsteps heading to the lounge where the phone is.

I sit up, grab the table and pull myself back up. My balance is terrible and I find myself staggering sideways. Sue looks bad. She's shaking and holding her head. She glances up at me with a sick look on her face.

I lurch around the table. I have to stop him.

"Sam ... what are you ..." Sue barely whispers, standing.

I stagger into the lounge. Rocelli has the phone to his ear. He glances at me and puts out his hand. I'm picked up off my feet and thrown three meters at the wall. As I fly I start raising my hood but I still hit it damn hard.

I'm so angry at feeling weak again but I can't breathe. At first it feels like I'm winded but I begin to realise it's Rocelli. He isn't just fogging my brain now. He's strangling me – he wants me dead.

Desperately I fire at him. Unfortunately my being strangled means the charge isn't properly directed or strong enough. It misses his chest and hits his arm so he drops the phone. He glances at his arm which hangs numbly, an expression of fury on his face.

A sledgehammer smashes into my chest. I cry out in spite of myself. The world's becoming gray. I still can't breathe and now he's squeezing my heart. The edges of my vision are going black.

As I sink toward unconsciousness I can feel the dead around me. As the room shrinks faster and faster I feel a strange strength. My ancestors are coming.

Then in the distance a chair sails through the air and hits Rocelli in the face, followed by a figure in gray.

The pressure comes off my chest. I take a huge gasp of air. My heart is thundering in my ears. Sue's followed up the chair with a vicious right foot kick to the side of Rocelli's left kneecap, sweeping him off his feet and he collapses. She follows up with a swift left foot kick to the balls. I hear Rocelli grunt. It's beautiful to see. But Rocelli holds it together long enough to put out his hand.

Suddenly Sue stops suddenly, clutches her chest and falls to her knees with a moan. Sick and sweating, Rocelli's face is twisted in a manic grin but now I have a clear shot. I zap him hard and Rocelli's head falls. He's unconscious. Sue falls.

I crawl over to Sue and find her unconscious. The link comes back up with Control.

"Help!" was all I could think.

"Airway, Breathing, Circulation," Control replies calmly.

We'd all been drilled on this but it's tough doing it for real, especially when you feel like crap. I tip her head back and check her mouth. Her tongue's OK but she isn't breathing.

"Not breathing," I panic.

"Sam? It's Pat. Keep focused. Now check her pulse." Patricia says. Somehow her voice is way more comforting than Control's. I put my hands on Sue's neck.

The suit is way more sensitive than my fingers but there's no heartbeat. Nothing.

"Shit! No pulse!"

"OK, Sam you need to do CPR like we've practised. Fifteen chest compressions to two breaths."

I'd always wondered if I would actually do it in a real situation. It always seemed yuck. In fact I don't wait at all. Sue's life is at stake so I'm into it just like we'd been taught.

Patricia keeps talking to me. I explain what's happened as I compress. It helps a lot.

Back at Renwick the families who are officially leaving New Zealand today are gathering in the jumpstation to go to the airport and make their flights out. After a minute of compressions Pat tells me to check the pulse again.

"Nothing."

"Sam, open her suit. We have to use your suit as a defibrillator. Quickly!"

"Can it do that?" I ask as I zip Sue's suit opened.

"Yes, we worked it out a while ago just in case."

"God, I'm glad you're there," I tell her.

I open the top.

"More chest compressions and breaths."

I do those for a while.

"OK pull off her bra. Fast."

Normally I would have felt very bad about this. But I'm far too worried to care. In fact I just feel bad because I don't know how bras work and it takes longer because Patricia has to tell me.

I do more compressions and breaths. Finally I get it off her and turn her back face up, her small poached egg breasts looking up at me. I'm so scared she'll die, but Patricia is calm and strong.

"Now put your left hand above her breast and your right hand below her other breast on her side by the rib cage. Good! Stay where you are. OK Control?"

"Discharge in three, two, one." Control said.

Sue's whole body jumps. Then she gasps deeply and, rolls slightly and coughs violently before gasping again.

I can hear cheering in my ear.

"Well done Sam! But her body has had a huge shock, she needs to come back here for your aunt to look after her. See if you can get her back in her suit, but watch out. She's full of adrenaline and she'll be cranky as hell."

And I thought she'd been cranky enough today without someone stopping her heart. Sue's now breathing and trying to sit up."

"What the f____? Why am I half naked?" she gasps.

"I had to defibrillate your heart."

"You *what*?"

"Patricia used my suit as a defibrillator. Rocelli tried to kill us. He was killing me when you whacked him. Then he turned on you and I took him down. But he'd stopped your heart. I had to do CPR on you."

"So where's Patricia?"

"Back at base. They're flying out today, remember."

"Where's that scum Rocelli?"

"Over..." I glanced over.

Rocelli's awake! He glances at Sue.

"Mary Mother of God believe me Sue. He was trying to rape you," Rocelli gasps.

"You creep!" Sue yells angrily at me.

"You prick!" I yell at Rocelli. He's obviously implanted this "Mary Mother of God" key in Sue's subconscious when he'd hypnotised her.

Sue pushes me hard, and caught off balance, I fall.

"What's going on Sam?" Patricia asks.

"He's hypnotised Sue." I tell her as I rolled over.

"Teach him a lesson, Sue," Rocelli orders. He's getting up slowly. Sue's getting up too, blocking my view of Rocelli, her eyes narrowed in anger.

"Cam's coming," Patricia tells me.

"He knows where you are. He's trying to phone Du Croix." I warn.

Then the link dies and the world goes fuzzy again. My vision is blurry and everything sounded underwater. My head's pounding. Sue's staggering to her feet.

"You little shit! I trusted you!" Sue's yelling.

"Kick him," Rocelli suggests, finding a chair to recover on. Sue advances on me as I try to get up from kneeling on both knees. Actually the closer she gets the better. She kicks me savagely in the ribs. Even with the suit it hurts. I'm about to get her with the amnesia beam when she knees me in the jaw and I black out.

When I come to. Sue's still standing over me looking down at me like some blue-eyed amazon. Luckily the momentary black-out's cleared me of Rocelli, so though I'm dizzy I know what I have to do, and zap Sue with the amnesia beam.

Meanwhile Rocelli has picked up the phone. I turn my head to look at him when he throws the phone at me in frustration. It hits me too. I'm still too busy clearing my head as Rocelli staggers quickly out the back door. I lie there wondering why he threw the phone at me. Sue's standing there with her eye's unfocused. I'm glad Sue's OK and Rocelli's gone.

Suddenly there's a flash, just as Sue's eyes start to focus, and Cam appears in the room.

"What?" she begins looking down at me and across at the other hoody wearing teenager. Cam's face appears from behind her black screen.

"Close up your suit. I'll get your helmet," Cam tells her.

Sue realises she's half naked and turns away to close up her suit.

"What's happening?" she demands grumpily as I stagger to get up.

"Rocelli turned you against me," I tell her.

"How?"

"When he hypnotised you. I think it was always his plan. He told you I was trying to rape you."

Cam comes over with Sue's helmet.

"Where am I going now," she asks, confused, and starting to look pale. I don't think her heart was keeping up.

"Rocelli stopped your heart. Liz wants to check you out." Cam tells her.

"Liz? Why?"

"She's a nurse, remember," Cam replies, patiently.

"OK, I want out of here anyway," she says wearily.

She puts the helmet on. A moment later she folds away. I look at Cam.

"Rocelli's trying to get to a phone!" I remember suddenly.

"It'll take him a while. I took out the line to the whole of Port Hobson and there's no cell coverage here," Cam smiles.

I grin at her.

"You're brilliant!" I tell her.

Then we hear a car roaring off below. I run to the window. Sue's car's driving off in a cloud of dust.

"He's got the car!" I yell, panicking.

Cam stops to think.

"He's got to drive through the park to get to the other side of the island. It's bush the whole way. Let's go to the first bend," she says, sealing up.

After being beaten up for the past twenty minutes it's nice to have someone else who's calm and clever like Cam to rely on. "Gunter and Mike are on their way," Mariko suddenly says in our ears. We hesitate. Knowing how much Grandpop hates bending this is really serious.

"So go! Get Rocelli! We need evlybody we have lef!" she shouts at us.

[+]

We fold away through the realm of presences and appear on the jutting bank of a tree covered ridge above the road as it winds its way uphill through the valleys toward the pass at the top of the ridge. The day's cool and overcast. It isn't a Saturday to do much in. Sue's car roars past below us in a hail of stones and dust. "Wings! Quick!" Cam orders.

We pop our wings, and switch on adaptive camouflage, melting into the background. With two steps and a jump we're cutting across the semi-circle of the road as it winds around the deep gully and up the hill. Antigravity engaged we're picking up speed to catch the car as it charges toward the left hand bend, ahead of us.

We get there at the same moment. The car, meters below us, slides around the tight hairpin corner. We begin to fly lower and closer as it straightens up for a long, straight climb up the valley under the trees.

I don't think Rocelli realises we're there until Cam lands on the roof on the driver's side. Her forearm and knee grips grab on while I fly along above the passenger side roof, trying to grab on too. Suddenly Rocelli veers and accelerates. If he'd been going fast before, now he really takes off. Cam on top of the car, clinging on like a limpet, disappears in a cloud of stones and dust in front of me as I'm surprised by the acceleration. I try to call Cam but she's offline. Once again Rocelli must be attacking her psychically.

I hadn't realised how fast a good driver can drive on gravel, and Rocelli is a damn good driver. I have to climb again to get out of the dust cloud and take shortcuts as Rocelli slides and slips Sue's car as it leaps from rut to gravel bank like a slippery fish below me.

I'm really worried for Cam who's hanging on desperately below me. Suddenly she goes limp. Her grip loosens and she falls into the cloud of dust. I drop into it to catch her, but miss. Sue's car roars off in dust.

Cam's lying face down in the road, groaning.

"Control!" I call.

"I have her Sam," he says and she folds away.

"Is she OK?" I ask.

"I think I broke something," Cam groans.

"We can hear him coming," Grandpop reports.

"Watch out, he can control minds!" I warn.

"Power poles don't have minds," Gunter replies.

I have to see this. I fold my wings and ask for a landing zone.

[+]

I flash into the bush just in time.Sue's car comes roaring around a tight left hand corner, its rear sliding in a cloud of dust. The power pole Grandpop and Gunter had thoughtfully cut down, lies from its stump across the road, blocking it. There's nowhere for Rocelli to go. But being in a right hand drive car means when he brakes and lets the tail slide out, the car hits the pole on its left side, smashing it, and tearing the remaining fibres still holding the pole in place free, so the pole bounces off its stump and rolls a bit. The car ends up stopped across the road with its side smashed in.

There's sudden quiet. The dust cloud which was following the car catches up and covers everything. Then the right side driver's door, which had been furthest from the impact, opens and Rocelli gets out.

"I've got this turkey," Grandpop says grimly.

"He can stop your heart!" I warn, "I'll get him!"

Before he can say 'no' I step out of my cover my suit looking like an ordinary hoodie and jeans. Even through the dust I can see Rocelli pause as he notices me. I run towards him because my beam won't work in this cloud and feel the hammer hit my chest. He isn't playing around now, just killing.

Time seems to slow down. The hammer hits me again in the chest. My knees just sag as I slowly kneel on the gravel. But even as he coldly shocks me with vicious psychic stabs and I start to loose consciousness, I feel those presences again and I can hear a chant in Maori in my ears. The closer he pushes me towards death and Hine Nui Te Po (the great woman of the night) the closer my ancestors feel. I can feel a heat in me. A kind of anger. I can feel them gather around me again, I can feel the stamp of their feet on the ground. He should have killed me a dozen times over by now but I refuse to fall and a confused look crosses his face. He's pushed me as far as he can and now it's my turn. Helped by these presences so that I almost feel like a puppet I put out one leg out, ready to stand and face him.

Time speeds up again.

Suddenly a bit of the bush rears like a tiger behind him.

Grandpop is holding Rocelli asleep in a standing headlock. Rocelli's neck is at an odd angle. Then Rocelli crumples at his feet. The dust cloud passes slowly over in total silence.

I've just witnessed murder. It seems strange that death can be so easy. There's no great confrontation, no final face-off. After years of terrorising children and adults all over the world Rocelli's been murdered on the side of remote road far from anywhere. A fantail cheeps behind me.

"You OK Sam?" Grandpop calls though the clearing dust.

"Yeah…is he dead?" I check.

"Yep, he's dead alright," he says looking down at Rocelli's body. Rocelli seems much smaller now.

"Vee haf to get rid of heem," Gunter panics.

"Gunter. Please to pick up sleeping bag from Mariko. Constable Williams is needed back also," Dr P says.

I come up to Grandpop looking down at Rocelli. His dark eyes are staring blankly. I go to close them.

"No Sam. Is important eyes still open," Dr P says.

I stand up again. I feel shaky. Grandpop comes over and hugs me.

"We had to kill him didn't we?" I ask, uncertainly.

Grandpop sniffs.

"You never *have* to kill anyone, Sam. Most animals kill for food. Humans kill for convenience."

I look at Rocelli. He'd killed for food and we'd killed him for convenience. Did that make him better than us? I could feel an echo of his spirit, cold and ruthless and I didn't feel any sympathy for him at all. Only for Grandpop.

"How many people have you killed Grandpop?"

"Like this? Sixty three. Sixty four if you count him."

No wonder he hates bending.

"I don't think you need to count him. He really wasn't human. He was a monster."

"I know. And it was quick. When I saw him looking at you I knew I had to take him out before he got you."

He pauses.

"I'd kill any number to stop them killing you," he tells me casually.

It was meant to be comforting but it isn't. In a brilliant flash Gunter reappears. He has a sleeping bag. We start bagging Rocelli while Gunter explains.

"Dr P wants him taken to his hotel and arrange it to look like suicide," Gunter says, looking very uncertain and nervous.

"We'll have to vacuum him," sniffs Grandpop as the dust covers everything.

It didn't take long to bag him.

"I vill need help to lift him," Gunter tells Grandpop.

"OK. Sam, wait here. Sue should be along soon," he tells me.

"When I left she was squabbling with Liz. They were having such a good time I didn't think they wanted to stop," he laughs.

Adults. Just when you think you get them, you don't.

Grandpop, Gunter and Rocelli's body fold into nothing. I'm alone with a fallen pole and a wrecked car. I walk over and sit down on the grassy bank I'd landed on. It's good just to have a moment by myself.

I'm not sure whether I'm upset about Grandpop killing Rocelli or not. It had been hard listening to Rocelli talk so easily about wrecking so many lives. All those little kids made orphans, just so he could manipulate and eventually feed on them. It wasn't that I was upset Rocelli was dead, but that Grandpop had killed him. I hoped it wouldn't come back on Grandpop somehow. I couldn't help thinking of Ax. I hadn't meant for him to die. True, he was a murderer, but he was nothing compared to Rocelli. I could see more of myself in Ax now than I had wanted to admit before. But for all his mean physical strength I now knew he had always been weaker. It was his weakness that killed my mother, not his strength.

There's a flash of light and Sue appears.

"Oh man! Look at my car!" she complains.

She turns and looks at me, sitting there. She seems grumpy, but something about me makes her face soften.

"Are you OK, Sam?" she asks.

"Yeah," I say, sitting in the quiet of the bush, listening to the birds.

"You're going to have to lose that helmet. It looks sus," I add.

She takes it off and looks at it.

"Yeah," she sighs, "you're right."

She comes over and looks at me.

"Could we have ..." I begin.

A box appears in front on us.

"Thanks Mariko."

"Werlcome."

Sue puts the helmet inside, closes it up and it folds away.

"How are you?" I ask.

"I have to take it easy or your Aunt will growl at me."

She seems to have learned that's a bad thing. She climbs up onto the bank and sits down next to me.

"You don't want that," I tell her. "She growls pretty hard out."

"Yeah ... I know!" Sue says with feeling. She lies down.

"So we're lying here till someone comes and rescues us?" she asks.

"Yeah, I guess. Or we could walk to Tama Reeves' place."

"How far's that?" she asks, with her eyes closed.

"Five kay."

"I'll wait" she smiles.

We stay there for a while.

"How did we crash?" she asks, forehead crinkling.

"Came around the corner and someone had cut the pole down."

"Ah!...And we were coming up because ...?"

"No phone."

"Oh yeah! Right."

She lies back and sighs.

"Well, that's alright then," she adds.

There's a long silence.

"So Rocelli's dead," she says, finally.

"Yeah."

"I never thought I'd be glad to know someone had been murdered. But after spending a few hours in his company I have to say Mike did the world a big favour there. I can still sort of feel him like this dark thing in my heart. He was a creature beyond all sympathy."

"Hmm, are you sure you're not psychic?"

"Yeah, I'm not."

"Hmm, how's Grandpop?"

"He's fine. He's gone back fishing. He seemed good actually."

"I saw him do it."

"Oh!" Sue looks at me with her blue eyes. She seems bothered by this

"He ... he was scary. You could tell he knew exactly what he was doing. Jumped him, killed him, dropped him ... I told you how he jumped me once, didn't I."

"Yeah."

"Rocelli didn't stand a chance."

"Did it bother you?"

"Not for Rocelli. I just never really thought of my Grandpop as a killer before. I mean I knew he was in the war and everything but I ... I never really understood what that meant. It meant he was a murderer, and a very, very mean one."

Sue looks at me for a while.

"Why does that bother you?"

"I dunno. It just makes me worry about him."

"Well, there's nothing you can do now, and to be honest we're lucky he was so quick. Otherwise Mike'd be dead and we'd have to take everyone off those planes to hunt Rocelli," Sue points out.

I nod and lie down next to her and close my eyes.

"Have they started?" I ask.

"Yep."

"How does that feel?" I ask.

"What do you mean?"

"Kevin gave you the job of finding out who they were. Now you're helping us leave the country."

"I'll tell him who they were on Monday. Case solved."

I had to tell her I felt stink about seeing her boobs.

"I'm sorry I had to rip your top off."

Sue put her hand on my arm.

"Don't be. I saw what you did. You saved my life. What's that? Third time now?"

"You saved mine with that chair. He was mincing me at that point. I was a goner."

"I had to stop him."

"I liked the two-step kicks too. They were nice. Especially the one to the goolies."

She chuckled softly and withdrew her hand.

"How long do you think it will be til someone comes?" she asks.

"Could be hours."

"Hmm."

We lay there peacefully for sometime.

"Your father died around here somewhere didn't he?"

"Yeah," I admit, tensing at the memory.

"Do you wanna tell me about it?"

I took a big breath.

"I guess its time I 'fessed up ... yeah."

"In your own time ... But stick to Ax eh."

"OK ... I'll try."

...

Ax came back in May. At first we didn't see too much of either him or his gang. He had a place in Port Hobson, you could see it from the house you rented for Rocelli. There are quite a few houses which get rented out over winter there.

Just to piss off Grandpop, Ax bought a boat and named it Hua Kai. Well, that's not true. He named it that to piss off Grandpop, but the boat was for something more serious. He pretended he was a simple fisherman, and moved his girlfriend in with him. Even the gang stopped visiting him.

At first the cops watched him pretty hard. But he'd stopped seeing the gang in Auckland. The police launch would tail him and the helicopter would have a go too, but he was too clever. He preached in his chapel, to Ray and John and the others, but he helped Sergeant Smith with youth offenders, he even got court permission to do a talk to our school about why kids shouldn't get involved with crime.

But all the time he was plotting against us. We didn't notice because he was clever and we were busy with other stuff. The most important to our family was he had started writing secretly to Rewa. He paid a kid at school to give her presents and notes. She hid them from us for months. He was trying to say how sorry he was about mum, how he was different now, and wanted to be her dad.

The other plot was more ambitious. He was fishing most nights but not catching much. But some nights he caught sealed barrels dropped from ships out of Manzanillo, Mexico. The barrels contained drugs or money. He would then break the shipment up and feed it to his new boss "the prince". So while he was pretending to be a humble fisherman and part-time pastor preaching to his near empty chapel he was making millions smuggling cocaine to Auckland's rich turkeys.

But his sneakiest plot was the one I'd discovered when I'd gone to throw stones at the chapel. Dr P invited Auntie Nea to stay a lot but it was clear she was slowly losing it. Her nephew Tui O'Reagan Tukarere "the prince" was taking over the tribe. Because Maori stuff was never Grandpop's thing – and because we were from a completely different tribe and low-born as well – we had no hope of getting anywhere near the politics that went on between the tribal and government negotiators. So Dr P sent us to bug them.

That turned out to be a bit tricky. We could do phones and boardrooms easy, but because these talks might just as easily happen on a boat or over beers at a barbecue and could easily be in Maori (something none of us was that good at) Dr P never had the information he needed.

We were also really distracted. The price of oil went through the roof and Dr P could understand that a whole lot better than the tribal thing. He had already made heaps predicting the rise but then there was the fall and the rise again. Every change was an opportunity and Dr P didn't want to miss them.

Dr Morozov was now working with para.no.ID too, trading information and access. She was getting bigger and bigger as the year went by. Aunty Liz said that being older the risks for both her, and her baby, were much higher so she had to be careful.

Gunter and Mariko came back after their honeymoon. Dr P said there was an important marine biologist from Japan we had to find who had a troubled childhood. That was looking for a needle in a haystack.

Then there was looking for the *indigenas* biochemist who was meant to be somewhere in the Amazon basin. We had the clue of Bethlehelm on the river and immediately went to the city of Belem in Brazil because that's Spanish for Bethlehelm, but all we found there was Inspector Du Croix.

And of course there was also Eduardo in Manilla. We wouldn't have found him at all without Khadiyeh. She predicted him better than Dr P in one of her dreams. We found him in Don Bosco Church praying.

He had a helluva life. He lived in a tiny hut with his mother in Tondo, Manila. He gathered trash on Smoky Mountain and sold it in traffic jams. His *friends* were trying to sell him as a prostitute. And yet he was the most incredibly happy, caring and forgiving kid you could hope to meet.

We helped him set up selling balloons to rich kids. He knew

there was something special about us but he never asked. He just accepted help when he got it, and he accepted bad shit too. He's so inspiring you just want to be around him even on a heap of stinking rubbish on a hot day in Manilla. You may think I'm really dumb but he reminds me a lot of the stories about Jesus. Anyway as for Khadiyeh, she got her divorce. Her problem was any divorcee is considered used goods in Yemen and her father said he couldn't support her. She went to Tarim and ended up being a servant at the international girl's school. They didn't know what to make of her predictions of a flood until it hit in October 2008 and then everyone was too busy dealing with all the water to worry about her prophesy.

I guess I'm trying to say we were really busy in the lead up to the battle in Elan, and we were pretty busy afterwards with Khadiyeh, and Eduardo, not forgetting the birth of Irina as well. So the sneaky way Ax got to Rewa was easy for us to miss. Rewa started sneaking off to Ax's Chapel on Sundays when we were busy. It wasn't hard. It only took her five minutes to get there. By ten we'd be off and Asal had piano lessons then so she had no-one to play with. Rewa was only gone for an hour or so and would pretend she'd been in her room or in Gunter's workshop.

Ax welcomed her carefully. Thinking about it now I'm pretty sure his entire service was aimed at Rewa. She became more and more interested in reading the Bible which we found a bit surprising but nobody thought much about. It was July when Aunty Liz realised what was happening. By then Rewa had been slipping away to see Ax for nearly four months. I was pretty mad with myself that I didn't notice. Here I was psychic and not noticing Rewa my own sister because I was too wrapped up in

Emma and the others to notice her.

But I was mad with her too, and that didn't help. Aunty Liz explained to her that Ax wasn't meant to have any contact with us at all except under supervised conditions. Rewa got angry and said she wanted to see Ax and she would tell any Judge who asked her that. We didn't want it to come to that.

That was when I started paying a lot more attention to what Ax was doing at night and watched him picking up the barrels at sea. I even cut the buoy on a barrel and sank it so I could find out what was inside it. But none of that mattered to Rewa.

I was starting to feel really stink. Like after all these years Rewa was picking Ax over me. She said I had ignored her for a year and a half and I only wanted to pay attention to her because Ax did. Grandpop was much more chilled out about it than I had expected. Aunty Liz said that was because when our mum had started going out with Ax, Grandpop had forbidden her to see him and been staunch about it. The result was mum had sneaked off to Ax anyway and Aunty Liz said it was as much *because* Grandpop had forbidden it as because she liked Ax. Grandpop and Aunty Liz decided that rather than make Ax seem more interesting than he was by banning Rewa from seeing him, she could spend all Sunday with him to find out how boring he was. Aunty Liz told me Ax's girlfriend was going to find playing with someone else's kid pretty dull pretty soon.

I wasn't so sure, and neither was mum. Even as we were flying over the Amazon, or looking for treasure off the Azores, my mind would always drift back to Rewa, and wondering what she was doing with Ax. I think a little part of me wondered if I was missing out on something.

Emma was a great help. She was no fan of Ax and she was keen to keep an eye on him. She would ride around to Port Hobson on Sundays when it was fine, to spy on him, and I'd meet up with her. It was nice to be together, though it got a bit boring just watching a house for hours.

It turned out we weren't the only ones having a boring time either. Ax might have been fascinated with the idea of Rewa but after boat rides on sunny days, trips to Auckland to MacDonalds and stuff, he really didn't have any ideas. Rainy days got very long. It didn't help that his young girlfriend, Sade, was no longer interested in living on the island either. She was as bored as Rewa was. That was when Ax would tell them they just had to wait a bit and they'd have Renwick house through Ax's mate, the prince.

Unfortunately for Ax, Sade didn't care whether she lived in a big house on a boring island or a small house on a boring island. It was still boring. She liked the parties in Auckland with Ax's customers because she thought she could become a TV star. She was also finding Ax's imitation of Saint Peter boring too, and told him so. Rewa started finding the atmosphere when she visited Ax made it "hard to breathe".

Then one day she came back and told us Sade had gone. Ax was mad as hell but he tried to hide it, but he still scared Rewa. We wondered what would happen. What happened was exactly what Aunty Liz expected. Ax had a humungous party.

Bikes and cars roared along the road above Renwick on a fine Friday night in November. They were hard at it all night, all Saturday and well into Sunday morning. Me and Emma went to have a look on Saturday. It was just screaming, laughing, fighting and sex. We came home wondering how adults could be so disgusting. Tama Reeves and Sergeant Smith went to have a look too but there was nothing they could do.

The party got Ax a new girlfriend. She was five years older than Rewa. She hung around for a week, then she got bored too, and left. Aunty Liz waited for Rewa to ask to go to Ax's place but she didn't. She didn't go to the Chapel either. I think the only one there was Ray, and he wasn't too interested.

Things didn't seem to be going Ax's way and he was slowly getting mean. I told Grandpop I thought he would snap. Grandpop said he was hoping he would, then they could put him back in jail where he belonged. I had a bad feeling it wouldn't work out that way and I was right.

On Saturday November 22nd, 2008 Aunty Liz took Rewa to Auckland shopping for clothes. I was in Eastern Peru all morning with Tahira, Ashley and Scotty looking for this *indigenas* boy we called "Miguel". Ashley and Scott were the suit team; me and Tahira were flying overhead, because it was our turn.

It was all routine but the light there goes at six pretty much like turning off a switch, so the others headed home at twelve New Zealand time. Even at Mach six it still takes one and a half hours to cross the Pacific and we were already hungry so we popped into Miraflores, Lima for some empanada for lunch. We had a good time eating street food and checking out the night markets that we lost track of time.

Anyway, we didn't get away until about three in the afternoon New Zealand time because we were enjoying ourselves so much. About an hour later Grandpop told me Ax was on the same ferry as Aunty Liz and was drinking and being an asshole.

Nobody would do anything because he scared them. He was claiming Rewa was his daughter and Liz had stolen her. We were all half an hour from the island. Grandpop asked Liz if she wanted him to come down and sort Ax out. Aunty Liz told him that she thought she would just call Sergeant Smith and get Ax picked up for drinking and driving. She said later she also worried because she thought Ax wouldn't hold back with Grandpop and even if he didn't hurt him they'd both end up in trouble.

When me and Tahira arrived back at Aotea something told me to fly down to Port Carlyle to check out the situation. I saw Ax having a talk with Sergeant Smith and I noticed he'd bought himself this huge new Ford F150 pickup. They're big enough on American roads but in New Zealand they're monstrous. Next thing I see Sergeant Smith is on the ground and Ax is driving off after Aunty Liz and Rewa.

It didn't take Ax long to catch Aunty Liz. Then I saw him ram her little Toyota. She lurched forward and was rammed again. She had no choice! Aunty Liz stepped on the gas and sped up. Above, I could feel Rewa and Aunty Liz's fear. I was warp field invisible and dropped down lower to aim at Ax's tyres. Then they hit the gravel and Ax's truck was covered in the dust from Aunty Liz's car. The beam would be dispersed everywhere by the thick stone dust.

They had sped up. Ax was driving like a maniac. The reading I was getting from him was a drunk confused mess of rage and frustration, combined with a need to crush his enemies. He hit the Toyota again and nearly shunted Aunty Liz into a tree but she got control and took off. I just couldn't get a clear shot on anything useful. There was too much dust and he was weaving. As they hit almost ninety kay on a straight nobody drove more than fifty on, I was beginning to get seriously worried. At the end of the straight was a steep bend Aunty Liz had to slow down for, and if Ax hit her the drop was steep. Very steep.

I didn't have time to worry about anything else. If Ax saw me I'd just have to get him memory zapped. I dropped invisibility and swooped over Ax, bringing out Ka-rea-rea's legs to grab Aunty Liz's Toyota. The F150 was no more than five meters behind. In a second I was attached like an oversized roof rack capsule and running out of road.

Aunty Liz left braking dangerously late. I'm not sure they would have made it around that corner if they hadn't had me. It must have been scary for them when the sound of gravel under the car stopped and the brakes and steering wheel stopped working. Even scarier when it lifted off the road and flew over the fence. I glanced back as we lifted off. The cloud we had been making had cleared and I could see Ax's face, twisted in shock, as the little Toyota with its new capsule took off right in front of him. Then the horror as he realised that this was one trick he would not be able to copy.

He turned the wheel violently. The F150 slid heavily sideways into a busted old wire fence which wouldn't have stopped a halfway determined lamb. The fence held for quarter of a second which was just long enough to start the F150 tipping, then broke. The truck rolled over the edge.

I turned Aunty Liz's car around in a wide arc as we watched in horror as Ax's truck rolled and rolled and rolled down the hill, its metal getting more and more smashed with each turn. It just kept going and going and going. Halfway down the doors flew open and a large doll was thrown in the air. It landed head down. I knew Ax was dead. Nothing stopped the truck for one hundred, two hundred, three hundred meters. Finally the land levelled out and it landed, miraculously, on its wheels.

I was stunned. For a while Aunty Liz's Corolla hung in space by the side of a road as I tried to make sense of what had happened. Then realising if anyone drove, or flew by (because the airstrip isn't too far away), we'd be spotted. I flew her car back to road by the gap in the wire and put it back down and let go. Then I sped off down the hill to the body.

Ax was lying face up on the slope. If his face hadn't been mashed up and head at an odd angle he might have looked like he had curled up and gone to sleep. I landed Ka-rea-rea and got out.

There was a shout from above. It was Aunty Liz. I looked at her and shook my head.

Aunty Liz pulled Rewa away into the car and drove off. I looked at Ax. A wave of anger swept through me.

"You f_____n moron!" I shouted at him.

"You *dumb* f_____n c____!"

I even kicked him. I instantly felt bad about that, and sat down next to him.

"I didn't mean to kill you, you asshole," I told him.

I sighed and looked around. There was a cool breeze. It was a pretty bad place to be left lying.

"Don't let the hawks get me, eh Sam?" Ax said.

"No, I won't let the hawks get you," I told his presence.

Not that there were any.

"Pretty cool bit of gear you got there son."

"Yeah, it's cool-as."

There was a pause.

"Why are you so angry with me mate?" he asked.

I looked at him. He was a better ghost than man.

"You murdered my mum … and I didn't mean to kill you. I just

215

wanted to protect Aunty Liz and Rewa."

"I know. Man seeing that car take off like that! F_____! I was like what-the-f___! Then I thought 'oh-no!, this is going to wreck my brand new truck'!"

He was trying to get a laugh. I smiled.

"If you'd worn a seatbelt I'd be rushing you to hospital."

Ax sighed.

"Uh f___ it! It was a shit life anyway ... Nobody liked me. Not even my mother, the drunken slut. The only one who ever did was Joy. It killed my heart stone dead when she cheated on me."

"What happened with Liz?"

"What do you mean?"

"With your cousin?"

"Oh Clint. He blocked her. He wasn't the only one. He got his mates around too. I pretended to keep Joy to myself to keep him off her."

"How did you do that?"

"I said I'd narc on anyone who touched her. Joy was too young and old Mike scared them. They knew I meant it and if they did he'd kill them."

"But you let them rape Aunty Liz."

"Well, I couldn't stop them blocking *someone*. I just didn't let them touch your mum."

He couldn't even see it was *all* wrong.

"And you killed Matiu Pomare?"

He grinned, "Yeah, cut his prick off and towed him out as live bait for the sharks. Can't say I felt too bad about that."

I could see he didn't. I wondered if people met after they died.

"They never pinned that on you did they."

"No, four killed but I only did one murder stretch ... the one murder I regretted all my life."

"How did you get away with the others?"

"Bro's covered up or took the rap. I made sure the bodies weren't found."

"So you didn't plan to kill mum?"

"Well, I didn't *want* to. But the more I drank and thought about it the more angry I got and the more I could see I'd be called a pussy forever. My rep, everything I'd built up over the years. Everything demanded it eh? There was no way out. She was a f___n idiot to think she could screw that prick and get away with it."

"Maybe she didn't want a hard man. Maybe she just wanted that nice boy who'd protected her."

I waited for an answer.

I never got one.

...

CHAPTER EIGHTY TWO: ESCALATION.

Sue says nothing.

I sat there wondering what she thought of my story, when suddenly she spoke.

"You know, something doesn't quite add up," she says, lying on her back staring at the sky.

"What?" I reply. I'm worried about what she thought about me killing Ax.

"Ashley was tagged by Nathan, who was hypnotised by those agents who looked like case workers weeks before Ashley showed up. Right?"

"Yeah."

"Du Croix put Rocelli onto Sir Michael weeks before Ashley was tagged."

"Yeah."

"So they might have identified Ashley in Washington DC but that doesn't explain how Du Croix already knew Ashley was based in New Zealand, and we know that he did because Rocelli sent that private detective here *before* the fire when he was acting as Sir Michael's private secretary."

"I thought you suspected Dr P. He even told me himself we might find something 'inconsistent'."

"Really? Interesting. But why would Prosperov do a deal? The threat of losing Renwick to that prince guy alone wouldn't make him rush out to his enemies and invite them in. Du Croix must have had leverage *already* and he also needed a way to communicate with Dr P. That means Du Croix already knew to look in New Zealand. So what would make him connect a girl from Louisiana in Washington DC to New Zealand, of all places on Earth? And why would anyone even suspect a black girl in a hoodie visiting her cousin in Washington D.C of being one of you guys? There must be millions of black girls in hoodies over there."

"Maybe he used Para.no.ID. Dr Morozov's Russian network. The Bruderschaft had already been attacked by Para.no.ID."

"It's one thing for Du Croix to know of Para.no.ID's existence, it's another to get a message passed by them. He must have had something on them as well."

"That sounds a bit scary," I admitted, looking at her. "It sounds like he knew almost everything. He had us exactly where he wanted us."

"That's what's bothering me because if he did, why didn't he strike sooner? The question isn't so much why *you* failed, but why *they* failed to catch you all." Sue says.

We think hard about that for a moment. It seems to wake us up. "Does anyone *ever* come along this road?" she asks looking around.

"Maybe we should walk to the Reeves' place."

"Why walk? And though I'm sure you'd like to visit Emma there's no real reason for you to come anyway. You're better out of this crash," Sue says, impatiently.

She sits up and looks at her smashed up car for a minute.

"And come to think of it *I'm* better out of this too. The more I think about it, all I'll get out of this car right now is a whole heap of paperwork and hassle. I think we should leave it here and go back to Hastings."

"But they'll know it was yours," I point out.

"Yeah, so I walked off to get help and got lost. Happens all the time."

Sounds good to me.

"Yeah OK."

"*Mariko* ..." I start.

The box with Sue's helmet appears in a flash of light.

"I wondred when you'd work that out," she says.

[+]

Sue takes out the helmet and puts it on, then we fold back to Hastings. After the usual lightning, rain and wind we come out of the cabinets. Mariko was sitting with Gunter, Mrs Jones and Grandpop. They have a bunch of roller cases and bags with them. The sleeping bags are all laid out to receive them.

We come over to join them.

"How's it goink?" Gunter asks.

"OK," Sue says, sitting down, "But there's a few loose threads that bother me. Can anyone tell me about Para.no.ID?"

The others look at each other.

"We don't know much about them," Grandpop admits.

"Only eKaterina really knows zhem," Gunter says.

"Is she in?" Sue asks.

"Yes, she and Irina fly early tomorrow," Mrs Jones says.

"Do you think she'll talk to me?" Sue asks. She obviously finds Dr M as scary as we do.

"Why not?" Mariko asks, attracting glances from the others.

Only Mariko would dare suggest out loud the secretive Morozov *ought* to talk to Sue.

Sue gets up and takes a disc upstairs. I tag along.

"Dr Morozov's uhh ... well she doesn't say much," I warn.

"She can't be worse than a guilty teenager," Sue says confidently. I think about that, getting the impression that kids my age, stubbornly sitting there with their hoods up (just as I had done) is what she had faced every day.

"No, I admit," catching her up, "but she's very quick and very touchy."

We walk through the house. Tarik and his dad are choosing books for the twelve hour flight from the library. They have their bags with them. Finally we get to the Prosperov's apartment.

Dr P comes to the door. He seems surprised to see us, but Sue explains in a friendly way and he invites us in. Irina's crawling around. It's nice to see the usually uptight Morozov with her hair literally down. She's much prettier that way. She makes us a cup of tea and offers us some round cookies, then sits at the table to talk while Dr P plays with Irina, cooing at her in Russian.

"Para.no.ID was secure collective built in cells," Morozov explains. "Each cell is five members. Each member knows five others: four in same cell and one other in another cell. No cell member knows more than one member of another cell."

"So if you caught one whole cell you could get five other cells," Sue points out.

Morozov raised a finger. "But no cell may have two members in same country. So to catch cell you need agents in five countries acting simultaneously."

"OK, but you could have five cells with one member in the same country. Then..." Sue starts, but then seeing the implications stops to think it through,"hmmm."

"You see?" Dr M smiles," To catch one cell means coordinated international action. By time it takes to get each cell Member to reveal their next cell contact other at-risk cell members are hidden."

"Hmm very neat," Sue admits.

Morozov smiles.

"Unless your enemy is us," I point out.

The women looked at me.

"We could crack the whole network psychically and internationally," I pointed out. "Once we had one member the whole network wouldn't stand a chance."

The others thought it through.

"It all started with Cherensky's operation against Virion," I recalled vaguely.

Morozov's eyes widened.

"Oh God!" she cries.

I caught up.

"Holy shit!"

"What? What?" Sue asks, not seeing it.

"The Brudershaft *are* just like us! They can read the whole cell and they can act internationally at the same time. Hathaway abducting Cherensky meant the Bruderschaft must have infiltrated Para.no.ID from the very beginning! They were *always* working for *them*!" I almost shout in realisation. And then an even bigger point hit me.

"They knew about you Dr Morozov! And they knew about Nathan from the moment we asked them for help to look for him!"

Morozov stands suddenly and begins pacing, chewing her finger, her dark eyes flicking about. She calls to her husband who appears smiling with Irina on his shoulders. Rapid-fire Russian both ways and Morozov sinks back to a chair, looking weak. Dr P puts Irina down and comes up to comfort her.

"She says she killed them through contact with us," I translated for Sue.

"But what did they know about Renwick?" Sue insists.

"Nothing. Nothing, except Arkady. Arkady knew me," Dr M says. There were no tears but she's obviously upset thinking Arkady (whoever he was) was dead.

"Did he know where you lived?" Sue asks gently.

"No, I told him we lived in California," she says sadly.

"And Cherensky lost his memory as soon as he got back to Russia." I add.

"But there might have been clues that you were lying," Sue suggests.

"Obviously not enough to come and get us or the Bruderschaft would have turned up on Aotea months ago and whipped our arses, but they didn't," I point out.

"But they thought you defeated their guys at Armageddon in January last year. That might have scared them off a direct attack," Sue says.

"Also is important to recognise Bruderschaft and Administration working together is recent phenomenon. As late as November last year Administration arrested and deported Bruderschaft operative Hathaway. This an unlikely way to start alliance, and yet it seems one now exists," Dr Prosperov reasons.

"And Rocelli learned in Kinshasa that we weren't that strong," I add.

"When was that?" Sue checks.

"October. Before Elan where Hathaway was arrested."

"What sort of contact was there between Renwick and Para. no.ID during 2008?" Sue asks the Prosperovs. Dr Morozov, looking pale and shaky, looks up at her husband. He nods, looking thoughtful.

"We trade access for information. But everything is anonymous. Neither side trusts the other," she says. "They knew much about key to information systems. It speeds it up for Control so can focus on mission rather than cracking system."

"What sort of systems?"

"Banking and finance, Government..."

"Which Governments?"

"New Zealand obviously, Australia, US, Canada, South Africa, Israel, UAE, Singapore, Yemen, Britain, France, Germany, Russia, Ukraine, Moldova, Hungary, Austria, Belgium, and some smaller ones. Belize, Seychelles, a few others."

"Any systems in particular?"

"No, all kinds. Immigration, Registries, Health, Housing, Police, Education, Tax, Commerce or Industry, Defence sometimes."

"Why?"

"To search, or for to create documents."

"But did they give you anything that would identify you from what you'd done if they went back to the same systems?"

"No. We cracked them our way. Is much easier with Control-type cybernetic intelligence and Mrs Jones and other's psychic resources."

"Sorry I don't understand I thought they gave you the key."

"Key is wrong word. Is not key to door. Am meaning key to plan. System architecture. Is like map to whole system. Entry is easy. Hard part is understanding to avoid leaving footprints, or record of visit. Is often many, many change records in system. Crude operator breaks defences, steals information and exits. Is like brick through window. Is trivial to detect. Footprints all through system. Victim knows at once security is attacked, how attacked, and what is aim of visit."

"Our approach is open side door, find security system and change, then proceed to amend change management system before editing information at will. Is much harder but not impossible to detect."

"What would Para.no.ID have learned from what they gave you?"

"Just our targets – perhaps. The timing of our interests. That is more useful perhaps. Other than that, not much."

"What did you give them in return?"

"Doors. Ways into systems that we placed so they could organise permanent entry."

"What were they interested in?"

"Companies. Mostly banks and engineering. They were more interested in finance, software and designs. Industrial espionage old skill from Soviet Union times."

"Could they have trapped you?"

Dr Morozov shook her head, "It would have been easier for us to trap them."

Sue took a moment and then asked the obvious question.

"Did you?"

"We thought about it."

"But didn't do it?"

Dr Morozov shook her head.

"Was no need. I thought if any problem I know Arkady. With Mrs Jones and others I knew we could find them. But never thought of Bruderschaft having same advantage."

I had a question.

"Was there anything Ashley could have sent Nathan that gave away her location?"

"You already know Control monitors all messages, all sessions. Use random entry nodes into Internet via extra-dimensional gateways and then through self-sealing, anonymising network. Even if enemy successful in tracing back to tapped computer it might be anywhere, and taps self destruct if removed," the Russian woman says staunchly.

"Even just vaguely. Any clue that might give them some idea what part of the world she was in," Sue asks.

"IP address is multi-spoofed, message vetted, calls are..." Suddenly something seems to occur to her. Her head bends down and her eyes look down and left, flicking back and forth as if reading something. Suddenly some idea makes her stand up. She muttered "*nu pogodi...*" which means "Hang on!" in Russian and disappears into another room.

We all look at each other. On one level we're hopeful that this might solve the question of how Ashley had been traced but it might also suggest Dr P's wife had been the source of failure – which is a bit embarrassing. Nobody says anything, though Irina wants to play peekaboo.

Finally Dr Morozov comes back. She looks tense.

"Is one voice-over-IP call by Ashley at dawn to Nathan at midday EST. No picture but birds sing suddenly in background. Assuming Administration was intercepting and they are guessing is birds singing at dawn then call can only be from New Zealand time zone. Dawn at midday EST can only mean New Zealand or far-east Siberia where no birds sing in extreme winter temperatures."

"But they wouldn't know who she was," Sue suggested.

Dr Morozov frowned, "Nathan knew."

"When was this call?" Sue asks.

"January third. Just after New Years 2009."

"OK, so that's how they knew more or less *where* Ashley was. So the Bruderschaft knew we were looking for Nathan at the beginning of 2008 because you asked for Para.no.Id's help. The Administration is all over Nathan's school and assuming they tapped his phone they would have known he was talking to his cousin, Ashley. But they couldn't have worked out where she was calling from until the beginning of 2009, because of the dawn chorus. But that doesn't tell us *why* the Administration would suspect Ashley was with us. Unless she talked about it?" Sue says.

"No, Ashley did not breach security. She was calling Grandmother, Margaret. She talked to Nathan because Nathan was helping Grandmother on Obama 08 campaign. Margaret was supporter from Senator Obama's earliest campaigns." Dr M says.

"So the Administration knew Nathan had a cousin in New Zealand but had no idea she was anything special. It doesn't tell us how, or why the Administration teamed up with the Bruderschaft either. And it doesn't tell us why they didn't catch us all," I summed up.

"My bet is the Bruderschaft used Du Croix the same way you did," Sue said. "To avoid risking themselves. Maybe they were testing Du Croix's allegiance as well? Does that error expose us in any other ways they may have used to trace us?" Sue asks.

"Control is investigating," Dr Morozov says.

"What were Nathan and Ashley talking about?" Sue asks.

227

"Obama inauguration. Were organising trip for inauguration of President Obama on January 20th."

"But Ashley wasn't tagged until March. So they could they have all been seen together at the inauguration?" Sue asks.

We all look at each other and nod.

"Who went from Renwick?"

"Patricia, Ken, Ashley, Scott, and Bernard," I remember.

"*Scott* went?" Sue checks.

We all nod again.

"*Yes*! I *knew* it! Is there a recording?" Sue asks.

"Is always recording," Dr P shrugs.

"But is million and half people at inauguration in Washington. Is visible from space. Anyone could see them," Dr Morozov argues.

"But don't forget they were up all our night going there but got caught in the Purple Tunnel of Doom and missed the whole thing," I remind them.

"The *what*?" Sue asks, thinking this was some outlandish space thing.

I explain.

"The 'Purple Tunnel of Doom' was the name the papers gave for the metro tunnel under the National Mall[†]. The security was fierce so cars weren't allowed anywhere near the Capitol or National Mall so everyone had to take transit. Different levels of access were given to different levels of supporters with colour coded tickets. But then because of a security stuff up a whole bunch of people with tickets ended up trapped in the metro tunnel. They couldn't go forward or back. The papers called it 'purple tunnel of doom' because it was mostly purple ticket holders who missed out. But there were orange and silver ticket holders in there as well."

"Did Scott and Ashley wear suits?"

"No, they couldn't because they were checking bags and the old suit schoolbags couldn't be opened. They were dropped off."

"Well, that's perfect because from what you've told me, only two people on Earth could have recognised them for being the mysterious teenagers who kept popping up and annoying the Bruderschaft and they had to be together and if our people had to get up early they were probably too tired to notice them. My bet is those two people would also have been special ticket holders."

"Who?" I ask, eager to know.

Sue holds up her hands, smiling,

"Don't read my mind. Let's just see if I'm right first. Where can we watch this recording?"

"Is best in briefing theatre at base," Dr P says.

Then he asks Dr Morozov in Russian if she could look after Irina. She agrees. The three of us head back through the hall to the base outside. As we walk Sue has more questions.

"When did those Mexican gangsters first show up at Aotea?"

"I told you. Late January 2008," I say.

"And did they ever come back?"

I exchange a glance with Dr P.

"I hadn't got that far," I explain.

"Was three attempts," Dr P answers the question as we enter base, "But was managed by Mr Kahu."

"Sam, would you mind getting your Grandfather. I'd like him to see this."

I also have an impression she wanted a word with Dr P without me around but I slide down the poles anyway. Grandpop's wearing his headphones and chatting to our families as they wait for their flights out of Auckland airport. I wait for him to finish then pass on the message. He shrugs and we share a disc back up to the briefing area.

Sue welcomes Grandpop and then, as he sits down, asks him to explain about the Mexicans.

"Sure. OK, well, it was May 08 when the first lot came at us. Ax was setting up and they tested his process by smuggling in Colt M4s, forty five ACPs and CX explosive. It was a military grade strike. They were out to waste all of us. The hit team of six came in by regular airline," Grandpop told her.

"What happened?"

"They were military trained. Obviously experienced. They were good too. But against our lot they went down pretty fast. They came through the woods but Ashley and Scott were overhead in their speeders and took them all out in two minutes. They didn't even get close. Nobody was even slightly worried."

"What do you mean 'took them out'? Killed them?" Sue asks, alarmed.

Grandpop's shocked.

"Hell no! They're kids! They don't kill people. I'm the only killer here and Rocelli is the only one I ever killed defending them and I have to say he's the only person I ever felt good about taking out as well. Anyway the boss ..." he nods at Dr P, "... says it's very bad for kids like them to kill – which I totally agree with – so no, they just knocked them out."

"Then what did you do with them, then?"

"Put them on Vostok island in the Pacific. They're probably still there. It's a bit hard to get to."

"But won't *that* kill them?" Sue asks.

"Nah, they're trained. Well, maybe. It's survivable if they don't kill each other. Don't forget Sue, these guys are soldiers for the most ruthless drug cartel in the world. Let them go and they'll just go back to murdering again. It was safest for everyone."

"And so they just disappeared?"

"Yep, pretty much. Same with the next lot. Then they sent this particularly evil bastard in, called Haysuus."

"Wasn't he the one who chased Ashley and Patricia in the first place?"

Grandpop raises his eyebrows.

"Good guess but no, this guy was a technician. He tried a bomb. His problem was Mrs Jones." Grandpop says. "She keeps house in more ways than one. Sam and Tahira, took him down. We left him with Los Zetas," he smiles grimly. "They don't get on."

That was an understatement.

"Ewww…" Sue winces.

"Probably. He'd done quite a lot to make them hate him too," Grandpop says.

"But that was his fault, not ours," I add.

"But it wasn't survivable," Sue responds.

Dr P chips in.

"No, but is agreed by parents. Were dealing with most deadly criminal gang in world. Had ignored lessons of first attack, so is agreed is needed to speak in language they understand," he says.

"And did they?" Sue asks.

"Appears so."

"But they can't have given up."

"No, then is problem with Mrs Robinson's mother. Was very difficult," Dr P agrees.

"What happened?"

Grandpop takes up the story.

"They went after Mrs William's, Patricia's mother. It was that little creep Martin Simpson who sold her out."

"That sounds bad."

"It was. We rescued her. Then we had to steal some money off the gang to relocate her," I tell her.

"You what?"

"We went on the offensive," Grandpop explains. "Attack is the best form of defence. We watched them, we raided their money convoys, we got rival gangs to go to the same places. There was a lot of rough stuff. It was pretty tough dealing with those guys. None of us liked it but it was attack or be attacked and those guys don't give you any soft options. So we started a bit of a war in Mexico between the cartels by framing them but it was between bad asses and the only way to get them off our backs."

Sue glances at me.

"And you were involved in this?"

I shrug, "Yeah."

She shakes her head, somewhere between concern and amazement.

"And what happened to Simpson?"

"He annoyed someone asking for payment at a bad time ... they shot him in the head. He didn't even get time to be scared," Grandpop reassures her.

"Poor bastard," Sue says.

"Yeah, but selling out an old lady to a vicious Mexican syndicate means he certainly was a bastard. Anyway Sam says you've got something for us," Grandpop growls gently.

"Yeah, I do. Well, I think I do anyway. Control could we replay Ashley's trip to the Obama inauguration. Display both Ashley and Scotty and please scan the crowd for the faces I asked for."

"Sure, when should I start from?" Control replies.

"I don't know ... arrival I guess."

"OK, but the whole trip was six hours," Control warns.

"Will it take you that long to scan it?"

"No! I've already scanned it," Control says.

"Oh! Were there any hits?"

"At ninety nine percent identification?" Control checks.

"Um ... yeah, if you say so."

"Zero."

"Oh," Sue looks disappointed.

"But that is a high threshold. At two thirds there were ten. More interesting at ninety there was one."

"Oh!" Sue says more hopefully, "can we see it?"

"Sure."

Control shows a clip of a lot of people standing in a tunnel, not going anywhere, and milling around patiently. The text says the view is "Patricia Robinson". Some people are sidling along the wall. The crowd is big. Not huge but there's a couple of thousand people there. As the view looks around at the crowd again it freezes.

The recording reverses a bit and freezes again. A circle comes up over three faces in the crowd looking at the camera. The circle magnifies and refocuses.

"Holy shit," Grandpop says, summarising pretty much how we all felt.

In the picture is Dr Clayton Hathaway, large as life, next to the man who arrested him in November last year, Inspector Du Croix; and the small plain woman I had seen on the moon. They're looking intently at the camera.

"So you should be recognising Dr Clayton Hathaway, Inspector

Du Croix and school nurse, Mrs Roberta Sanchez. Is that them?"
Sue asks.

"It's definitely Hathaway and Du Croix," I say.

"It's them," Grandpop agrees.

"When did you get a picture of her? I point at Sanchez.

"When we were tracking the samples. She delivers them herself,"
Grandpop says.

"She was on the moon. She questioned me with Du Croix," I tell
them. "You didn't get that because Control wasn't back online
yet."

"Hathaway, Sanchez, Du Croix together. Is certainly when
Administration identifies our people for first time," Dr P spells it
out, "Miss Williams what is making you look for this?"

Sue smiles, "Scotty," she says. She counts out the points on her
fingers.

"We know Nathan's old school is run by the Administration. We
know the Bruderschaft had broken Para.no.ID. From the Para.
no.ID email the Administration knew one of the children at the
school in Washington was communicating with someone in New
Zealand. But Ashley hadn't been seen in Belem by Du Croix. All
he knew about the mysterious children with powers was Sam
and Tahira who he'd seen in Belem, Brazil. The Administration
had no way of knowing the cousin in New Zealand who
emailed Nathan *was also* the hoodie girl who met up with him
sometimes. The only one who had actually seen Ashley up close
was Rocelli in Kinshasa when he was abducting Jeanne, while
Hathaway had seen Scotty when he shot him in Finland."

"Du Croix didn't know about Kinshasa and Rocelli wasn't likely
to cooperate anyway, but Hathaway was different. Du Croix
had probably interrogated him about the mystery children and

I realised that facing being sent to the Center Hathaway might be more motivated to cut a deal. A cop like Du Croix would recognise Hathaway's talents as a potential resource and might be prepared to find a way to keep him away from the Center for his own purposes. So although Hathaway had been taken away. I suspected it wouldn't be permanent."

"Du Croix probably asked Hathaway about the mysterious children and Hathaway would have described Scott, and perhaps Ashley because she kicked him behind the rolled van. That could have connected with the communication they were monitoring between Nathan and the New Zealand girl and the black hoodie chick that sometimes visited Nathan. So Mrs Sanchez was there looking for Nathan, Du Croix looking for Sam or Tahira and Hathaway looking for Scott. The connection would have been Nathan and Scott."

Grandpop is shaking his head.

"How the hell do you do that?" he laughs.

"By spending hours and bloody hours listening to Sam droning on," Sue shrugs, "I like spotting things like that. I always wanted to be a detective."

"Is clear you are excellent detective ..." Dr P agrees.

"But there's still one more problem," Sue interrupts.

"Yes?" Dr P says, and I get a sense there's a bit of guilt hiding there.

"Why did Du Croix assign Rocelli to Sir Michael?" Sue asks. There's a silence.

"I mean Sir Michael knew nothing about your operation. Yes, he knew you Dr Prosperov, but he had no idea of your activities. Michael wasn't linked to Para.no.ID. Why did Du Croix suddenly direct the Bruderschaft against a harmless British lawyer and his daughter?" Sue asks Dr P.

Sue is looking very hard at Dr Prosperov. Dr Prosperov is nodding and trying to look thoughtful but he's avoiding her eyes.

"He already knew where we were when he assigned Rocelli," I work out. "If he knew about Sir Michael it could only be because he knew *already* where we were!"

Dr P starts to smile.

"Is correct," he admits finally.

He looks around at us with an expression of seeking forgiveness. Then he sighs

"Was forced to negotiate with Du Croix at beginning of March. It was I who suggested Hamilton-Smythe as distraction for Rocelli and other Bruderschaft."

"*You talked to Du Croix?*" Grandpop is shocked. Even I hadn't expected that.

"He *called* me! Was nearly forced to sound alarm then, and we were not ready," Dr P replies.

"How did he call?" Sue asks.

"By cellular telephone."

"He rang you!" now it's Sue's turn to be shocked.

"Yes."

"How in hell, did he know it was you?" Sue asks.

"He is also very good detective," Dr P nods.

"When he had the New Zealand connection he went through New Zealand newspapers and found article about myself and Katya. He already knew Katya's links to Para.no.ID and Para.no.ID's involvement with Cherensky. He knew Ashley linked to New Zealand. He knew Ashley linked to Scott also involved with Cherensky. He knew and was little point denying it."

"Why did he call first? He could have caught all of you." Sue points out.

"That is important point. Du Croix is very comfortable on Earth. He realised that if we had assistance from the Fae a sudden attack could start an interstellar war on his adoptive planet. It seems Du Croix manages Earth to keep peace. He knows we are keeping peace and wants to avoid war. Recall who we attacked. Was Administration? No, never attacked Administration even when Sam's craft is potential bomb in moon base. Did we attack Bruderschaft? Yes. How? By calling him. Are we problem for Administration? No, is minimal intersection. He can live with small Fae presence."

"But Du Croix had problem. He has arrested Bruderschaft and it seems Archdeacon is Bruderschaft sympathiser. Archdeacon doesn't want Bruderschaft members sent to Center. Du Croix is wanting way to get Archdeacon off back. Does not want Earth to become flashpoint for interstellar war between Fae and Center, so proposes deal to me. We will stage ambush with enough time to escape. Is to keep Bruderschaft from complaining Du Croix is Fae sympathiser but limit Service presence in this system. If is possible, will find way to remove Archdeacon. Then once the Fae infiltration has vanished again the Administration can return to peaceful research programmes without Bruderschaft."

"And so he also doesn't have to worry about being bumped off by the other infiltrators, as Rocelli said he might. He may even be helping them ditch the Bruderschaft as well with this," Sue nods.

"So you knew when I took Ka-rea-rea out that I would be separated?" I demand of Dr P, feeling a bit betrayed.

"Yes. But of all operatives also knew you are most likely to succeed. You have Emma, you are local, and have many personal resources. It was risk but I have great respect for abilities, Sam.

As do others," he says, nodding at Sue.

"Also did not plan to be away so long," he admits.

"Did Hekator know about this?" I checks.

"Of course."

"Which is why he didn't want me to detonate Ka-rea-rea," I reason.

"Correct. And why you are encouraged to rescue Sian Hamilton-Smythe," Dr Prosperov agrees.

"But what if I hadn't met up with Ashley and Scotty in the vault?" I ask.

Dr P nods.

"Was time of grave concern. Am knowing Rocelli is after you. Finding you critical to whole operation. All other operatives seeking you. However guessed you would return to vault."

"Was Lucky involved?" I ask.

"Believe so, but cannot be sure. Has strong link to you. Was most insistent of rescue in Liechtenstein. Was point of strong agreement between self and symbiont."

I wondered what it was like to disagree with Lucky. It also made me feel kind of strange to know that the whole fire, evacuation and return had been sort of staged. And I had played my role almost exactly as expected. Except for Sue. She was proving a huge bonus. But Grandpop's talking.

"But does this mean Du Croix doesn't want to catch us?" Grandpop asks, as confused as I am.

"That is dangerous assumption," Dr Prosperov shakes his head. He goes on.

"Du Croix's first priority is peace. Second priority is be seen to deliver results. First priority almost achieved. Now is dangerous period. While Renwick fire unresolved is scope to use international police resources to eliminate us. My belief is he will use his influence with authorities against us, exactly as we used him against Bruderschaft. In this way is no conflict with Fae. We are much more vulnerable as citizens of Earth than as agents of Fae. This is why is essential for Miss Williams to solve Renwick case as New Zealand Policewoman."

"Hathaway isn't going to want to let us off the hook," I suggest.

"Especially when he hears about Rocelli," Sue adds.

"Rearguard is most important mission," Dr Prosperov agrees.

"Hmm, always is," Grandpop grunts.

Dr Prosperov makes a small noise. He has something else to say. "In this case please to keep er … recent … discoveries to selves for moment?" He looks around at us. He seems strangely weak and vulnerable.

"Is best if others told by myself once operation is over. Is no help if rumours make others upset now. Must explain self fully."

He looks quite nervous.

Grandpop looks at him with one of his hard stares.

"I lost a lot of my stuff in that fire Gennady. Things of my wife's, rest her soul. Things that reminded me of friends who died in the war. But I know you did too. You put our people first. That's why I know they'll trust you."

Dr P smiles an uncomfortable smile.

"Thank you Mike. Your support is most important," he offers his hand and they shake. Then he gets up to go.

"What time is it in Washington?" Sue asks.

Grandpop looks at his watch.

"Almost twenty hundred."

That explains why I was hungry. It's lunch time.

"I'd like to see if anything's happening at that Principal's place, or the school," Sue suggests.

"Why there?" I ask.

"Well, we know Mrs Sanchez is based there. There could be more to her ... That, and we don't really have any other leads," Sue shrugs.

"Get Control to check it out! We need to have lunch," I suggest.

Sue pauses and then realises.

"I forget that the computer can think," Sue says.

"Not only think," Grandpop smiles, "You have to remember he's the adult supervision. This is a kindergarten as far as he's concerned."

"Mmmm actually maybe I should stay. I'd like to check a few things on the police system too," Sue says.

"Sam can bring you something back," Grandpop says volunteering me.

So me and Grandpop leave Sue and take discs to the surface again.

"Whaddya reckon about Du Croix calling Prosperov?" I ask Grandpop.

"I reckon Gennady must have talked pretty tough to get that deal. He must have made some mean threats. Didn't you say you saw a carrier and escorts coming for us?"

"Yeah."

"I reckon Du Croix knew he'd need backup if things got ugly and he had to wait for the Service to come. I bet Prosperov told Du Croix we'd take him out if he tried anything. When you think about it, Du Croix's bloody vulnerable. He has to balance all these dangerous powers around him. No wonder he wants peace first and foremost. His survival depends on it. It's a pretty tricky job really."

I hadn't thought of that. "Yeah, I guess it is," I agreed.

There's a silence as we walk across the grass.

"What dya reckon about Sue?" I ask quietly.

Grandpop chuckles.

"She's dynamite! I wish we'd had her on the team last year."

"Yeah, it would have helped," I agree, smiling.

"She just notices stuff and sees things that are missing. I reckon if we're going up against Du Croix we're really going to need that," Grandpop adds.

"Yep, he's tricky alright."

We go into the café and meet Tarik and his dad, leaving to catch their plane. They look happy and relaxed.

So far the Khadems, Gunter and Mariko, Mrs Jones, the Robinsons, and the Khumalo's, have left. That leaves only us Kahus, the Trâns, and the Prosperovs still at Hastings. We didn't have to go until tomorrow because we were only flying to Australia. Mr Trân was working toward the reunion dinner so lunch for us was just scraps and leftovers – not that we minded because they were always delicious.

I find Cam's in the kitchen with her dad. Aunty Liz has taped her up a little, suspecting cracked ribs, but even I know there's nothing much which can be done for that. Despite the fact Cam can't laugh (and I'm playing silly buggers trying to make her) she's looking pretty happy.

I had made up a plate of lunch for Sue but kind of forgotten it, when suddenly she bursts in. She's sprinted over from the glasshouse.

"You *must* be hungry," Cam grins, as Sue stands there catching her breath.

"We've got a problem," Sue gasps, holding the door.

I look around, my face full of food, like a guilty cat caught with a guinea pig in its gob.

"Sup?" Grandpop asks leaning back, frowning.

"New Zealand Police have everyone identified. They know who you all are. There's pictures of all the kids. The adults are just named."

Grandpop glances at Mr Trân's worried face and back to Sue. "Damn!" he says, annoyed. He gets up, scratching his neck. This is trouble. We know *they* will have cracked the New Zealand police system by now. Sue explains.

"It was Sergeant Smith. He got it from the deputy principal Philip Wakefield at the school. There's pictures of the kids dressed as witches and wizards for some school project. They've had it for a week. The only thing that's been holding them back had been not finding bodies at Renwick. Now that I told them you're all alive they're trying to work out whether they're allowed to release them to the press or not as missing persons. But Control says we have to assume the Administration has copies already."

"Have you told the boss?" Grandpop asks.

"Yeah, he wanted you to recall everyone, pronto."

"OK, let's do it. But Tarik and Ali are expected to board their plane. They can't opt out now. We'll have to get them to bend off as soon as they're airborne," Grandpop's saying as they head out.

I turn to Cam.

"You better not eat that as well," she warns, looking at Sue's lunch.

I smile. I make to pick it up, she looks at me warningly. We're both trying not to laugh. Suddenly Dr Morozov walks into the cafe with her arms folded in front of her. Her dark eyes seem to stick out of her pale face and flick from side to side as she's thinking.

"You two, please to follow. Is much work to do," she orders us shortly.

Her tone is sharp. We don't dare argue and fall in behind her as she stalks across the grass in her shiny black high heels back to the glasshouse and the base. We follow her without talking down on the discs, not daring to share one with her.

Grandpop's on the desk, with Sue, talking to the others. We watch Dr Morozov join them as we came down on the discs.

"How is going?" she asks gruffly.

"Few hold ups on the plane toilets," Grandpop explains, "They can only move when they don't have to lock the door."

Dr Morozov nods.

"Please to get operatives in suits, is important mission to stall enemy."

She starts pacing and smoothing her hair.

Cam turns to get to a disc.

"But you're hurt," I whisper.

"I'll be OK," she says.

She goes up, so I go join Grandpop and Sue. There's a bit of a nervous wait while Dr Morozov paces.

Finally the cabinets start flashing and sparking. First out's Asal, followed by the rest of the Khadems. Then Ashley and Patricia. Grandpop has already told the others to get changed and the other guys race upstairs and one by one come down again. Everyone's picked up Dr M's tension so we're a bit pumped as we gather by the desk.

I notice we've all paired up. Scott and Ashley are leaning against each other, Tarik and Cam are holding each another around the waist. I shuffle over to Tahira. I feel good to be back with her, suited up and ready to work again. I take Tahira's hand, but she pulls me to her side and side-hugs me.

It's hard to explain but when two psychics work together they just get very used to each other's minds, like old shoes. Much as I like Sue, she's an adult and I don't always get her. But there's not one thing I don't know about Tahira, or she doesn't know about me.

Dr Morozov stands on one of the white cubes to see everyone.

"Attention! Attention please. Is major problem with flight arrivals for all of you. Interpol has issued red notices and made entry on FBI Terrorist Screening Database. When planes arrive you will all be arrested as terrorists."

"Terrorists!" Sue says, louder than she means, "How do they work *that* out?"

Dr M looks directly at her and answers.

"Is no need for accuracy or justice for red notice or entry on FBI TSDB. Terrorist database is very old, very big and full of errors. Still includes South African leader Nelson Mandela," Dr M tells her grimly.

"But who issued the red notice?" Sue asks.

"Detective Sergeant Oliver Xavier, Federal Belgian Police. Warrants for arrest for international child trafficking for all adults."

There are shouts of anger.

"Can be expected that Inspector Du Croix is true force behind red notices and is just using Bruderschaft operative's position for convenience. However effect is the same. Because of red notice you will be arrested upon arrival and you will be taken into custody by local police. Almost certainly Administration agents will be waiting to take you. Therefore we have the duration of your flights, or eleven hours thirty minutes, to carry out operations to wipe these entries and prevent arrest before the first your planes lands."

She pauses and there's an immediate buzz of chat around the room.

"Not to forget!" Dr M shouts. Everyone stops and looks at her. "Not to forget local intelligence agencies will also seek relatives, grandparents and associates of any terror suspects."

I'm really glad all the family I care about are in this room.

"Hey, where are Mariko, Gunter and Mrs Jones?" Tarik asks.

"Not appearing on red notice. May continue flight uninterrupted."

There's some comment about that too. Dr M can't get a word in.

"Quiet please," Grandpop growls loudly.

"I think is best if we go to briefing room," Dr Morozov says, getting down.

So everyone takes a disc upstairs. The mood is very tense. We all know how important remaining anonymous is and although we can vanish off airplanes in mid-air that will draw even more attention to us than vanishing after the fire at Renwick. We could all imagine the TV show about Renwick where the fire burns the house down and everyone vanishes only to suddenly reappear, board airliners, and vanish in the toilets. We'd be more famous than movie stars – just what we *didn't* want. What we really need is for everyone to land, pass through immigration without any fuss and then vanish into ordinary life.

We crowd into one of the briefing rooms and Dr Morozov takes the briefing. She takes a while to collect her thoughts, then steps forward and speaks plainly and clearly.

"This is hardest opponent we meet yet. Opponent not actually authorities, Administration or even Bruderschaft. Real opponent is information. Information moves at almost speed of light and copies, almost as fast."

"Our sensitive information is now out of control. Is not just names, is identities. Faces are mapped and tracked. Names linked to other data: police, health, dental, purchase and historical records. Our internet conversations, and searches. Enemies can now use cameras, dental records, prescriptions, even favourite ice cream flavours to find us. Until now we have prevented our enemies getting information about who we are, where we come from or what we do. Now, for many of you, they have that information."

"Gennady is in urgent talks with Queen Morganne, King Horne and Queen Isis. Question is how much Fae prepared to help us against Administration. Fae not wanting direct conflict. Council is angry with Hekator for destroying Service fighter by allowing speeder to fall into enemy hands. Hekator is being examined and may not be able to provide help in future."

Me and Tahira swap glances. Once again Hekator seems to be getting us to do stuff which creates trouble for his superiors. It bothers us. Why does he keep doing that? It seems he's pushing them toward a fight with the Center, whether the other Fae want it or not. That could get us closed down by Queen Morganne. I make a mental note to think through Hekator's ideas for myself before we get ourselves into more trouble than we can get out of.

"Therefore must proceed as if Fae not helping and not wanting any conflict with Administration. This means focus is human agencies. Most important of all is Interpol I-24/7 criminal database system based in Lyon, France. But also individual customs and immigration systems at airports you are scheduled to arrive at and secondly airline and airport systems. Is limited time so can only work with resources that fall under our hands. These including Control, flies, and operatives."

"Am thinking is best to approach problem with easiest targets first. Starting with airports and finally leading up to Interpol. Simplest solution is called spoof. That means instead of frontline immigration staff seeing true screen with warning about our people on flight they only see fake screen from Control."

"Dats a good idea an all dat. But if dey already know what flight we'yon, dhey gonna have people waitin anyways," Patricia points out.

"Is true. Perhaps diversion is needed, also," Dr M agrees.

"If the immigration officers work with a spoof screen, then no-one will officially arrive which is the whole point of the flights isn't it?" Ken asks.

"Control can update real database later," Dr M disagrees. "First task is to intercept immigration terminals at airports and make fake screens. Control can you do this?"

There's a bit of a pause. It's so long people start talking to their neighbours. Then Control appears looking thoughtful.

"I have been carrying out preliminary analysis. There are two different kinds of systems here. Those arriving in Singapore and Dubai have already been identified. Both Singapore and the UAE require airlines to transmit Advance Passenger Information System or APIS data, after the aeroplane takes off. APIS information includes the passport information of every passenger on the aircraft[†]. When this arrived it was compared with the Interpol and Terrorist Screening watchlists. Matching the APIS data and the watchlist data then generates a person-of-interest task file for staff at the airport. That means officers already know who they are looking for when the aeroplane lands. At present machine vision face recognition is not used but will be in the near future."

That was depressing. If that was true the systems were already looking for the Khadems and the Gursoys in Dubai, and the Khumalos in Singapore.

"However there is some good news. Because they are dealing with hundreds of flights and thousands of people and there are shift changes over the eleven hours between now and when our people land so they don't transmit person-of-interest files to airport staff more than a few hours ahead. To break this system there are therefore three main attack routes. The airport security task assignments, the immigration terminals and the national authority watchlists based on access to the Interpol I-24/7 system."

"Argentina is a different problem. Unlike Singapore or Dubai, Argentina is a destination not a hub. At present they do not have APIS[†]. The watchlist is not updated as often, nor is there as much traffic in the airport. The emphasis there is on human instincts and inspection, which poses its own challenges."

Control pauses and then continues.

"First I must stress that all airports are quite complex. Almost every aspect of an airport involves some form of information network, from the worker identification systems and access control, the video surveillance system, the traveller security management systems, baggage handling, the air operations, to the immigration and customs systems you seek to avoid. There is a lot of data processing on-site and also a lot off-site. Most systems are serviced by telecommunications where signals are mixed and re-mixed together. Simply identifying the right networks to tap into is not simple. In fact the complexity and the security of the airport is far greater than the complexity of the Customs border control systems you actually seek to breach. This might suggest that targeting the Customs border control system might be more profitable. This is especially so given that it is the end of the working week and the systems development teams which build these Customs border control systems are not be at work."

"Unlike the Customs border control systems which are secured and busy all the time, the systems development offices for these systems are typically only secured by simple swipe cards and passwords the operatives can easily bypass. Because these development offices can reprogram the control systems I would suggest these should be the focus for our efforts."

Dr M smiles.

"Excellent suggestion Control. What is your proposal?"

"I suggest as a first step the operatives bend into the police or justice development offices and plug me into the servers there, starting with the telephone system. Assistance with passwords would be helpful. Then, I shall reconnoitre the development system, the documentation and the live systems before proceeding to find the best methods to interfere with the terminals at the receiving airports."

"The second step will be to tackle the security systems at the airports themselves. This will require operatives to gain access to the live border control and security administration systems and plug me into those servers.

Finally, the third step is the I-24/7 network. I will take out the receiving systems before we worry about Interpol itself. Typically the receiving systems will be switches or routers within the police or Justice departments. Fortunately this will not require any more work by you as we have already compromised the largest switch and router network firms. I have already started working on this operation."

"What about departure? If the red notice is in place the New Zealand authorities will stop the Kahus and Trâns flying tomorrow," Sue says.

"I have also intercepted the New Zealand I-24/7 node but we will also need to break the New Zealand system as well," Control agrees.

"Well, let's get started!" says Grandpop standing up and clapping his hands. "The sooner Control is plugged in, the sooner he can start work."

"May I suggest the parents return to their aircraft? They may be missed if there is no-one in their seats," Control says.

"And I?" Sue asks.

"Join us of course!" Grandpop agreed. "Though so far it's looking pretty routine. The kids can keep their Lanas on now and we'll keep an eye on things."

There's a bit of grumbling by the adults about having to go back to the uncomfortable economy seats on the planes but we leave that behind as Grandpop rounds us up and leads us back down the poles to the desk. Scotty and Ashley get the UAE Federal Customs Authority. Tarik and Cam get Singapore Customs, and we get the Argentine Administracion Federal de Ingresos Publicos in Buenos Aires. Grandpop opens up his drawer and hands us keys and flies then we go to the cabinets and bend space. [+]

We flash into a switch room in a locked office. It's full of racks of electronic equipment. There were no lights on and we keep it that way, using infrared from our suits as we look for the right server racks. Just to be annoying there are some webcams set up to monitor the equipment. They could only see the lights on the boxes they were trained on but, rather than be clever, we just tipped them over.

It takes a while to find the right server ports to plug in Control. Then we bend upstairs into an office. The lights are off because it's eight on Saturday night. Everything's in Spanish which the Lanas translate for us. We knew from doing the American IT companies we're looking for the geekiest looking desks because they usually are where you find the ultra geeks who have the most skills. We find a few, sit at them, go through their desks and start trying to psychically sense out the people who sit there during the week.

Working with Control it takes us both about half an hour to find the right people and get their passwords. But as soon as we do Control's away and working those systems hard. It's amazing to think he was reading and understanding the contents of big collections of folders with titles like 'arquitectura de red del sistema (system network architecture)' and 'las políticas de seguridad de base de datos (database security policies)' as fast as we could read and understand the words on their spines, and he was doing it on two other systems at the same time!

[+]

We come back to Hastings and gather around Sue and Grandpop. There's still ten hours until anyone lands so there's nothing for us to do but wait. We sit around for a while talking and joking when Control appears.

"I am now ready to proceed to the airport security systems. These include video surveillance, voice communications and access security. Unfortunately these systems are not located in the same places so three teams will be needed for each airport. We will proceed from airport to airport."

"The first airport should be Changi in Singapore. It's Saturday morning there although that makes little difference as the airport is always busy. This will be the hardest as it is the best run and the people have a lot of experience. I have sent your Lanas some images of technicians so you can match their clothing. However it will not be possible to insert my USB keys without arousing the security services so I suggest you need a tactical plan. I have set up briefing rooms for each team."

We all look at each other, then get up and go to the discs. Me and Tahira end up with the problem of intercepting the video surveillance system.

It's the very latest technology system, all fibre-optics and digital video recorders apparently. Control needs to get access to a set of servers which collect the camera feeds from all over the airport and send them through to the security centre where people monitor them. These pizza box shaped grey video servers are in locked racks that look like glass fridges in a server room.

But, as it happens, the server room is *also* monitored with a security camera. The problem is that the video recorder for *this* camera isn't in the same server room, it's in the security centre right under the noses of the people who monitor all the cameras. So we switch views and take a look at the security centre.

It looks like something out of science fiction. There's a control room with about twenty uniformed staff, all with huge screens with eight or more panels each, all taking feeds from cameras throughout the terminal.

The green uniformed people all look very neat and focused with headphone and microphone sets on their heads. The control room is prowled by seniors who make sure those watching the monitors keep their eyes on the job.

Just to make it hard the video recorder that monitors the server room which we are after is monitored by one guy whose job is to monitor the server room. He's obviously a trainee or something because he has a screen full of nothing – a room full of computers just sitting there. Somehow he's meant to watch this with the same intensity as the others who are busily spotting suspicious bags or people, or lost children, and chatting away busily with each other and the security teams on the ground. We could see him blinking and trying not to fall asleep. To keep him on his toes, his supervisor seems to hover over him.

He's Chinese, much younger than the others, and a bit geeky. He looks like he feels out of place.

"His name is Alfred," Tahira said, "Alfred Chen."

The crucial video recorder, which will record us appearing and plugging a USB stick into the security video systems if we don't do something about it, is smaller than a toaster, and sits just under Alfred's monitor.

"You're going to need an enormous distraction to stop him monitoring those servers," Grandpop says looking in.

I look at Tahira. She certainly isn't the right sort of distraction. Even Sue bursting in wearing her motorcycle helmet wouldn't work either.

"I have it!" Tahira says.

"A sign! A paper sign in front of the cameras in the server room which says "Wake up Alfred"!" she laughs. "They will think is joke on Alfred."

I laugh too. "Brilliant!"

Sue comes by. We tell her Tahira's idea. She smiles for a moment.

"Hang on, though. What happens when they stop laughing at Alfred and realise somebody's got into their computer room?" she points out.

That shut us up. I could see all sorts of questions and investigations which wouldn't suit at us all. I glance at the hologram. These guys are just too hardcore to forget their jobs. They're all staring hard at their screens. We need something in the room with them. Then I get it.

"Cheeky! Cheeky in the security centre! A bird flying around him will distract Alfred." I say.

"Aali!" (Excellent!), Tahira exclaims.

"It may distract for a while but you need to take out Alfred's recorder permanently," Sue says.

Then turning to Control's hologram, "Control?" she asks, "If you can send x-rays through a wormhole, can't you zap things that way as well?"

"Of course. If you mean could I inject a power surge into that network video recorder to destroy it, the answer is 'yes'. But that would be very strange to these people. I think a distraction at the same time would be an excellent way to avoid too much focus on the system and what it is protecting. It may even be possible to make it appear that the bird is the cause of the problem with the device," Control's Avatar agrees.

"It seems to have antennas on it. Could you hack into it?" Sue asks, squinting at the device under Alfred's monitor.

"I could if it's wireless networking was enabled. I could hack into the whole system if they had exposed it to the internet but unfortunately they haven't."

"But what you are saying is it would be better to send Cheeky into the manned control room, than one of our kids?"

"Yes. They are only needed to insert the USB into the servers."

"How long will they need?"

"Five minutes at most."

"So they beam into the loo..."

"Bend," I correct her.

"'Beam', 'bend' whatever. Bend into the loo in the security centre, release Cheeky. Fly him in when someone opens the door. Get him in flapping about in the security centre. Distract everyone. Control zaps the box thing. Then you guys bend into the server room, do the business. Pick up Cheeky. Back home! Is that a plan?"

We shrug. We can't see anything wrong with it.

"Cool. Well, off you go!"

"Better get Cheeky," I say.

"I will see you in the server room," Tahira agrees. She heads to the discs. I bend into my room.

Cheeky's out. I have to call him back in, which takes a moment.

[+]

Then Control bends me to Changi Airport's security centre toilet. I pull Cheeky out and chuck him out the door. He flutters off down the corridor while I find a toilet cubical and check in with him. There's an annoying wait while Cheeky hops around outside the door of the security control room. Five minutes. Ten minutes.

"*Sue, is there any sign these guys are going to come out at all?*"

"No."

"*Hey guys? 'Fraid I don't think your plan is working and it's holding us all up,*" Tarik tells us.

"*No kidding,*" I say sourly.

"*Call back Cheeky, Sam, I have better idea,*" Tahira says.

"*OK.*"

I call back Cheeky.

He flies to the toilet door and hops in the opening I leave for him. Of course as soon as I do that someone has to come out of the Security room headed for the toilet! I dash back to my cubicle, Cheeky hopping under the door after me. The toilet door opens. Cheeky flutters up to me in the quiet with a noise that sounds almost exactly like a sparrow fluttering inside a toilet cubicle. I pick him up and go to put him in his pouch when suddenly he chirps loudly. I can almost hear the guy at the urinal thinking "what the...?" as I stuff him in my pouch. But I'm out of there.

[+]

I arrive in the computer server room in a flash. Tahira's already there.

"What did you do?" I ask her.

"I got Control to shine bright light straight into all Alfred's camera, then he zapped recorder. It looked to him like recorder going broken."

"Better plan than mine!" I have to admit as I join her looking for the slots on the servers for the USB keys.

It takes a while because there's so much gear in there. Tarik and Cam join us because it turns out the door access controllers are in the same room. Then we all move on to the next airport terminal.

By the time we get to the last terminal we know exactly what we're doing. We're just finishing among the servers when suddenly the door opens.

I can't see it directly. I just watch Cam. She's brilliant. It starts with the tech's outrage as he finds a bunch of hooded teenagers in amongst his security systems.

"Hey, who are you!? What are you doing in here?" he demands. Cam looks up, smiles and points at me.

"Mr Lee was showing us," she says.

They can't see me around the corner so they come around to tell this "Mr Lee" off.

"*Get ready to go, guys*," Cam says, silently as the two techs pass her. We seal up.

The men come around the corner to find a faceless kid in a hooded overall looking at him. And then they forget the last three minutes of their lives.

[+]

"Good work people," Grandpop calls as we come out of the cabinets.

"That's Changi wired up. Next is Dubai. We're nine hours out. The problem with this one is a bit different as you'll see when you gather around."

We gather around his transparent screen. Control appears.

"There are two data centres at Dubai airport. The design of this system is complicated by the fact that the systems for monitoring the data centres are inside the same data centres. So it is impossible to avoid being recorded in the data centre if you enter it."

Grandpop looks around at us.

"We've been looking over this one for a while. Fortunately it appears there is an 'in'. Because everything is latest-greatest the security video system has a web and mobile interface. All we need from you guys is..."

The image changed to a silver haired European wearing a white shirt and tie sitting at a desk writing an email.

"...this turkey's passwords."

That takes us ten minutes. Control takes another ten minutes to crack the video system. The system was interesting because it was monitored by software. Most of the time the cameras record the same dull scene, so rather than fill up discs and discs with recordings of nothing and have a poor guy like Alfred Chen sitting there watching nothing, the cameras weren't monitored and didn't record anything. The software only recorded when something changed inside the cameras field of view. Then an alert would also be sent to the security desk. So all Control had to do was rig the software so that no matter what happened, nothing would be recorded or reported. Ten minutes later we were in there. We left and software was reset to record everything again. Easy!

Buenas Aires Ministro Pistarini airport was the complete opposite of the other two. Where Changi and Dubai were all flashy and modern, this airport was down-home. It was big, but not enormous. The problem was the video system wasn't computerised, it was old school analog. Closed-circuit TV pictures were transmitted down a wire like a TV aerial and mixed together for presentation on the TVs in the control office. There was no computer for Control to hack and the mixing box, or multiplexer, was analog too, so it didn't have a computer in it either. The recorders were just ordinary DVDs.

Like Singapore and Dubai there was a room full of uniformed officers watching monitors. But the big flaw was the cameras didn't monitor the security system! The security system was just in a locked room with no cameras in it. Getting into it and changing the systems were dead easy, while we had already got Control into the watchlist system through the development system earlier. It only took five minutes to sort that airport out as well.

By now we're feeling pretty pleased with ourselves. We'd dealt to the Customs and border control systems of Singapore, UAE and Argentina and there was plenty of time before the planes headed that way landed. From Control's original list that only left the Interpol I-24/7 watch list system to deal with.

"Right, let's take a gander at Interpol," Grandpop says.

We'd been there before. The headquarters building is a small eight storey glass and concrete box with a kind of low dome on top next to a park and art gallery by the river Rhone in Lyon, France. But that mission had been very quick. All we'd done was bend in, plant worms by the trees fifty meters away near the park's lake and fold away.

Grandpop's flying the view around outside the Interpol building in the dark, checking out the cameras on poles which watch the perimeter, the tall fences, the top storey balconies and the slightly domed rooftop window that covers the hollow middle down to the ground floor courtyard[†]. All the lights are on, they are still at work late at night on Saturday.

"So that's it. Interpol's pretty small really. They take on all international crime from human trafficking to rare animal smuggling, drugs, almost everything. Wikipedia says here it runs on sixty million Euros a year which is only about ten times what Dr P spends on us. By comparison ... the FBI in America get eight billion dollars!" Grandpop says sitting back.

"They're just a coordinator," Sue says. "They don't have any powers of their own. Their only real power is their ability to bring together police from different countries to take out networks of bad guys."

"Oo says they're bad guys then?" Tarik asks.

"Police do," Sue replies giving him a stern look. Tarik raises one eyebow. Remembering Tarik's experience with Turkish police Sue softens.

"Yeah ... OK. The problem is all the countries have to agree that something is a crime. And that can get messy. As you know in some countries the police are corrupt or serve politicians. It's a fact. In some places everyone knows it, in others it's not so obvious. That's probably why our friend Detective Xavier has accused your parents of child trafficking. It's a horrible crime and nobody on the planet wants it. It makes getting help from other police that much easier. But it also shows how vulnerable the Interpol system is to manipulation," she says.

"But ..," starts Ashley, and then pauses as everyone looked at her.

"I jus' think da problem is Xavier, not Interpol," she says.

"But you know he was told to do it by Turneau who was probably told to do it by one of the Bruderschaft, probably with the support of Du Croix," I say.

"Yeah, but Interpol's just da messenger," she argues.

"Yeah but who would you rather mess wif, Interpol or the Bruderschaft?" Tarik asks.

"Yeah ... Interpol, I guess," she admits.

"Any day," Tarik agrees.

"You know I'm starting to think this could be a good mission for you, Sue," Grandpop says.

"What!? Why!?" Sue asks, startled.

"Well, you know police. These guys are kids, They're totally out of place in a place like that. Maybe we can get you in."

"Yeah ... uh ... I'm not so sure about that Mike," Sue begins. She looks around at us.

"They take pictures ... I'm not sure it would be a great idea for all my colleagues back home to see a picture of me on the news breaking into Interpol," she explains.

"No ... guess, not," Grandpop agrees.

"And it ees four in the morning," Tahira points out.

"Why don't we just look inside?" Tarik asks.

"Well, I'm a bit nervous about that," Grandpop admits. "I don't trust that bugger Du Croix. I mean he's all but sent us printed invitations to come and get them. I don't think we should put anything out there we can't get back, and the last thing we want is for the Administration to bushwhack us with some secret thingamybob which grabs Control's wormhole thingy like they tried in Florida."

"That'd be the technical description," Tarik smiled.

"But you wanted to send *me* in there!" Sue complains.

"Only because they aren't expecting a real police officer. They wouldn't connect you to us."

"They might now. They did stick a growth in my brain. By the way is that artificial brain still working?"

"No, that whole thing was closed down after we got Nathan and Sir Michael back. They had to know we were onto them. No, I mean if we dressed you up as a yank or a pom or something. All we'd need to do is grab a uniform that fitted and pretend you're there for some course or something."

"At four in the morning?"

"No, well, probably not, not unless you substituted for someone they were expecting, and as you say we don't need your picture all over the news, when they found out afterwards."

"So..." Tarik interrupts, "you don't want a probe inside, you want flies, yeah?"

Grandpop pauses staring at him.

"Ah yeah. Yeah, we need flies, but no field intrusion," Grandpop agrees.

"And the weather is?"

"Uuuu..." he says looking at the screen, "chilly ... about eight degrees ... and low cloud."

"So we bend dive from two kay, they won't catch the field from there," Tarik says.

"Yeah OK ... but you still have to get inside," Grandpop points out.

"Well, we won't find any way in from here will we?" Tarik says.

"Let's check the skies before we do anything," I suggest, remembering Florida.

"Yup," Tarik nods.

Grandpop turns back to the screen and sweeps the view skyward.

"So who's coming?" Tarik asks, turning to the rest of us.

"We should all go," Scotty says. "Me and Ash will be the watch. It's going to take four of you up close on that building to find holes for the flies."

"Shall we bring Hooty?" Ash asks.

"Let him sleep, we can live without him," Scott says.

"Sky's clear," Grandpop says.

He reaches into his drawer and hands Tarik, Cam, Tahira and me fly bottles and we troop off to the cabinets. I go into the cabinet and psych-up for the drop. The cabinet goes dark and foggy and two seconds later I'm falling over clouds in France.

[+]

I relax, turn head down, and just dive, lifting my wings off the back of the jacket. The others are doing the same. Five seconds later we're through the cloud and over the river.

Lyon's an orange spider web below while the river reflects the lights. It's pretty. I look around. The others are all headfirst with their wings up too. We are just too awesome.

This is what bend diving was meant to be like, I tell the others. It's just effortless.

At 800 meters we start pulling out, using the speed from the dive to give our wings lift and switching to blend camouflage so we almost vanish. Scott and Ashley lead us up the riverbank along the front of the Cite Internationale, a big mirror glass building that curves along the river front, and then over the museum, around over the lake, until, with just the soft whiff of our wings, we land on the roof above the top storey balcony of the Seige d'Interpol, or Interpol HQ.

We scamper lightly out to the sides of the roof which form a hexagon, looking down on the top storey balcony below. The balcony rings the top floor around the best offices. The only cameras I can see are watching the driveway on the road below.

"We should put up a fly now to check out this balcony," Grandpop calls.

"*Use mine*," says Cam.

"OK."

At eight degrees that fly wasn't going to last long.

"*Fly's gone*," Cam calls.

"Got it," Grandpop says as the fly view comes in.

There's a pause as we lie there and Grandpop flies the fly about checking the balcony for cameras, sonar, radar and anything else that might get us.

"*You know I reckon we need a smaller fly, something more like a mosquito*," I say, to pass the time.

"*And a way to put the animals in the way we put in flies. It's stupid making that huge flash just to put in Cheeky or Peter or Sniffy. You know what I mean?*" Tarik agrees.

"*I hope Hekator is not in trouble over blowing up Ka-rea-rea*," Tahira says.

"*Do you think the Fae have jails?*" I ask.

"*What for?*" Ashley asks.

That was a good question. What was the point of a jail anyway? They were just there to waste people's time, and if you were as long lived as the Fae what was the point?

"*I dunno, criminals or something*," I say vaguely.

"*Hekator is no criminal*," Tahira comments.

"*No, I know...*" I reply.

"OK guys, the coast is clear," Grandpop interrupted.

We roll off the roof and land lightly on the balcony. This is obviously the executive level. There are offices and meeting rooms that look pretty nice up here. Strangely, the doors to the balcony have ordinary key locks on them.

"*Do we go in?*" I ask the others.

"*It's why we're here, isn' it?*" Ashley asks.

"*Sam, you feeling worried,*" Tarik asks.

"*You mean do I have a feeling about this?*"

"*Yeah.*"

"*No ... no, I can't say I do.*"

"*OK, well, on three then,*" Tarik says. "*One, two, three.*"

We insert our liquid titanium pinky keys and open the doors.

I look around. It's a meeting room. Nice table that reflects the city lights, big screen. Interpol badge. Tahira opens the door on the other corner of the room. We look at each other. It didn't look like a trap, but I was thinking about my dream. The one where I'd gone in and ended up with Du Croix, Mrs Huuygens and Hathaway in a theatre. I didn't think it would happen here but I didn't want to find out the hard way.

"*I'm going to release my fly here.*" I tell her.

"*OK,*" she shrugs.

I get out the fly canister and open it. The fly flies inside into the warmth and settles on the door. Then it starts looking for a crack. There's a movement to my right. Tahira's in the room. She crosses to the door. I feel a bit of a fool outside, but I still don't want to be in the same place as Tahira in case we're ambushed.

"*What's the lock?*" I ask her.

"*Electronic ... but the fly's under it.*"

"*Mine's in too.*" Tarik calls.

"OK guys just chill, I have two good flies. Tahira keep yours in reserve. Scott and Ashley keep your eyes open." Grandpop says.

We wait for what seemed like ages but was actually only five minutes.

"OK, this place doesn't sleep so people are working still. There's a night watch at the entrance with two security guys who monitor the cameras. Scott and Ash, I need you to distract them. Get out the front and act like you're out to tag the place."

"*What with?*" Ashley asks.

"Act. Pretend to shake a can. The watch will call the cops. Beat it when you see them. Meanwhile Sam and Tahira I need you two to take out the watch. It's two guys in a room with monitors. They're on the bottom floor by the entrance. To open the doors in front of you slip your pinky keys into the magnetic lock and it'll short out. Give them a push and run right. Run to the stairs marked 'Sortie'. Same thing with the pinky keys on those doors. Then down seven flights, and turn left. The watch house is to the left by the exit."

"Cam and Tarik you're behind Sam and Tahira. Once they've dealt to the watch take a spare pass card and get down to the basement computer room. We don't know what's in there and Control doesn't want to take any chances. When they're in the basement, Ash and Scott fly back to the roof. Got that? Back at me in order."

We repeat what we have to do in our normal order.

"Good! OK, adaptive cam off everyone. Change to black. If you're seen you're North Korean Ninjas. Go in sixty seconds."

We all went black and then defused the tension by putting numbers and rude words on ourselves in Korean.

"Ready everyone? Five, four, three, two, one. OK Scott and Ash off you go."

We stand behind the door counting our racing heartbeats waiting for our 'go' thinking through what we'll do if we meet anyone. Then it comes.

"Go Sam, go Tahira."

Tahira's pinky lock slips in. There's a flash and a little smoke and the door is loose to our pull. We race through the balcony corridor around the big light well in the centre of the building on soft feet. We're along the dully lit passage under the glass roof in two seconds. Through the stairwell door with another flash in two more seconds. Then we leap down the flights of stairs in half second bounds. The guy on the third floor we stun with the amnesia ray and silently leap past him. In ten seconds we're at the bottom. It's all totally silent.

We're at the door just as one guy's coming out of the watch house to chase Scott and Ash away. He's big but goes down silently. Tahira bursts into the Watch and the other guy goes down trying to draw his pistol. I quickly drag the big guy inside under the desks.

The whole move is completely silent and only took twenty seconds.

"Excellent guys, Sue's stunned. I'm stoked. OK, Cam and Tarik, go! Scott and Ash find a quiet place and fly back to the roof."

We take the guards security passes and put them on the desk ready for Cam and Tarik. I set to work stuffing the guys under the desk. Tahira is looking at the control desk and turning off recording but keeping the video feeds and trying to work out the door controls.

Cam and Tarik arrive, panting. We give them the guards passes and with their fly moving ahead they slip out into the corridor. We see Cam and Tarik pass by on the camera covering the courtyard of the hollow centre of the whole building under the glass roof. They're making good progress when the lift bell rings and two guys come out talking and laughing. Cam and Tarik dodge silently behind a pillar and we watch in astonishment as the two men walk right past Cam and Tarik as they move around the pillar to keep out of sight. I can see Tarik shaking his head not believing it.

They follow the two men down some stairs toward the carpark then head in the other direction, pass through a door, and run silently along the corridor and down some stairs. From another camera we see them pass down into the basement and through another door. I find myself getting nervous. My mouth is dry. If there's an ambush Cam and Tarik will be in real trouble.

"*Found the computer room but we think there's someone inside. Cam's checking them out,*" Tarik reports silently.

There's a pause.

"*Two engineers. They're upgrading the system. They're talking to someone on the phone. It's a bunch of tests and they're going to be a long time.*"

"Damn!" says Grandpop. "OK. Umm. We don't have time to be cute. Scott and Ash. There's a gray telecomms box on the Charles De Gaulle Quay at the corner of the entrance to the car park. Hop down there and break it. Fry things. Go."

Fifteen seconds later two Ninjas with Korean numbers and rude words appeared on our screens outside on the empty street right under our camera. In no time Scott's unlocked the gray box and started ripping things out while Ashley keeps watch. There's no traffic. Lyon is asleep. There's a flash in the box.

"*That should do it,*" Scott says.

"*Hell, yeah,*" Ashley agrees.

They both run out of camera coverage off toward the trees.

"*That's done it,*" Tarik agrees.

"Sam and Tahira. Time to go. Kill the power on your monitors. Prop up those guys in their chairs then grab some cards and run out the front exit, quick!" Grandpop calls.

We pull the power plugs out of the monitors and mangle them, wrestle the unconscious men back into their chairs (although one keeps slipping off) then grab some access cards and run out. Someone on a balcony above spots us and yells for us to stop. We aren't going to wait.

"Hi! Qui etes vous?" he yells as we press the door release and run outside.

Outside its quieter and feels less tense. We run left toward the park and jump over the five meter fence in a single bound. Nobody sees us. It's too dark under the trees. We keep running into the dark towards the lake, then pop our wings, switch to adaptive camouflage, melting into virtual invisibility, and leap into the air. We fly silently around the edge of the lake and up back to Interpol's roof, landing like huge silent moths. Scott and Ash are watching out over the road in front of us.

"*Two down!*" Tarik calls, letting us know they've knocked out the engineers.

"You haven't got much time guys. Quick, but don't panic. Control, over to you," Grandpop says.

It's very quiet on the roof of Interpol at four in the morning. The Rhone river slides by under the orange stained clouds. A slight breeze has picked up. Then we see the flashing lights on the bridge a few kilometers away. It doesn't take a genius to work out where they're going.

"*Police in large numbers. Four minutes,*" Scotty warns.

"*Yeah,*" Tarik says, distractedly.

It's impressive how many cars we're seeing.

"*They're still online,*" he mutters.

"*Maybe there's another cable,*" Cam suggests.

"*Look, I don't know what's going on. Control I'll plug you in. Here goes,*" Tarik says.

The first police car arrives outside on Charles De Gaulle Quay below us. Another flashing light is behind us on the other side of the lake.

"*Given the security situation it might be best to remove the quantum modem when I have finished. Estimated time to completion is five minutes.*" Control says.

More cars are arriving by the second. We count ten now on Charles De Gaulle Quay and half a dozen more around the park. An ambulance arrives. That's not a good sign. The first police have reached the entry to the Interpol building. Others are standing around the wrecked telecomms cabinet.

"*I reckon you have about two minutes,*" Scotty says.

"Sam and Tahira could you get those engineers out of that server room. It will draw attention to the place?" Grandpop asks.

"*How do we get down there?*"

"May as well bend. It seems to be safe and there's no surprise now."

"*OK,*"

We sealed up and flash into the computer room. Cam and Tarik have propped the door open. We go back for the men. Cam and Tarik go into the corridor and start looking for somewhere to hide them. Me and Tahira pick the men up by the shoulders and drag them out the door.

"*In here,*" calls Cam.

We drag them into a mail room and drop them on the floor. Then we all go back to the computer room.

"*How much longer Control?*" Tarik asks nervously.

There's no answer.

"*Control?*" he asks again, trying to sound calm.

We all look at each other.

"*Ash? Scott?*"

"*Yeah?*"

"*We can't raise Control.*"

"*F___! I know!*" Tarik swears.

He races into the server racks. Cam after him.

"*What are you doing!*" she asks.

"*Disconnecting him. He's under attack.*"

Tarik and Cam go around pulling out all the keys they'd put in. They all crumble to dust as they're disconnected.

"*Guys the cops! They're all coming in. Dogs first,*" Scotty calls

"*Can we bend?*" Ash asked.

"*Guyzzz affhgf are YOU hghg K?*" Like a bad cell phone connection Grandpop comes on sounding worried.

"*We're surrounded and we can't bend,*" I answer.

"*Control's hit yhgjfhj, he's gygjgjyy very slow,*" Grandpop says. We can hardly understand him.

"*What do we do?*" calls Ash.

Grandpop answered faintly.

"*You utuyg guys downstairs. Hide kjuhkgj where you can. KKHBbbbv they can see from a distance khkjgkas face out. Keep gffaf pairs ttwgv comfortable. Ash and Scott dsdshw fly wttw river. Swim. owhwh Fae but ywyyvw safe.*"

I look at Tarik, then Cam and Tahira. There's no doubt about it. We are worried.

"*Better not hide in here, right? They'll be all over this place,*" Tarik says of the server room.

"*Let's move!*" I say, knowing we haven't much time.

We run into the corridor. Me and Tahira go left. The others go right. The first door is a toilet. I think "maybe", Tahira thinks "no way". I agree. Next door is a cramped office. No. Next is a storeroom. It has shelves with boxes of paper, stationery, and bits of equipment like whiteboards.

"*How about the shelves using adaptive?*" I suggest.

They're deep enough and the ones at floor level are unused.

"*OK.*"

We find a pair of empty shelves on the floor in the corner by the door. I'm facing the door. Tahira is at right angles to me at my head facing into the room. We lie down and switch to adaptive. It's reassuring looking at Tahira. I can't really see her there.

"*Damn!*" Scotty swears.

"*What?*" we all ask.

"*A helicopter. C'mon Ash. We gotta go.*"

"*Yeah … alright I'm coming.*"

"*Go adaptive,*" Tarik suggests, "*It's awesome.*"

"*Yeah, we know,*" Ash replies.

There's a pause. They're getting ready.

"*Woo hoo!*" Ashley yells.

"*What?*" we all want to know.

"*Max anti-G and we're like rockets!*" she laughs.

"*What happens if they lose power!?*" Cam worries.

"*Cam's got a point,*" I agree.

There's was a pause.

"*Yeah … But we either fall, drown or get caught,*" Scott replies.

"*We're over the river now.*" Ashley adds.

"*Where's the helicopter?*" I ask.

Then comes the roar of rotors.

"*Don't answer that. It's here.*" I say.

"*We're just landing on the other side. It's quite a sight. Millions of police car lights and the helicopter has its searchlight on,*" Scott reports.

"*Better than here,*" Cam says.

"*What's your view?*" Ashley asks.

"*Don't ask,*" she says.

"*But it's lucky I can't fart outside the suit,*" Tarik admits.

"*Ow!*" he adds.

We all laugh.

There's a pause as we wait. I find myself wriggling a bit to get comfortable, and sighing.

"*How much time til our parents land?*" Ashley asks suddenly.

"*Hours,*" Scott says.

"*I hope we are out of here soon,*" Tahira says.

"*I hope Control's OK. Otherwise we are in serious shit,*" Tarik says.

"*At least we still have power,*" Scott says.

"*And if it goes?*" Ash asks.

"*Then we are in the shit,*" he admits.

"*Grandpop?*" I ask.

"Sue here *gshyhs* Mike's talking *yyshhshb*Dr P."

"Can you see us Sue?"

"Sort of *hhshsnns* what you see *ggjsbsb* flies *ytshmsk* working. French police *jjshgsggs* courtyard organising a search."

"*How long will it take?*"

"Hang on someone's arrived *yhsbjkskk* moving the fly *jjsjjuhsh* and landing *rgbbsns* focus *hhskksjjs* Oh, great!"

"*What?*"

"*Thsbsb* Du Croix!"

CHAPTER EIGHTY FOUR: THE CAVALRY

*D*o you think Du Croix knows we're trapped?" Tahira asks.
"*Probably*," I reply grimly.

"... split into three teams of about a dozen. One team is heading down to where you are with Du Croix. The others are going upstairs and outside. The fly is tracking them OK for the moment," Sue reports.

"*Hey, you're not breaking up anymore!*" I tell her.

"Your pictures are coming through better too. Except Cam's. Where are you Cam?" Sue asks.

"*Behind Tarik.*"

"Here they come," Sue warns.

I feel very exposed facing the door, but I know I have to rely on my adaptive camouflage and just keep still. The only worry is that Du Croix has some way to see us.

The door opens and the fluro flickers into life. A couple of cops are in the doorway, pistols in their hands. The tall one in front looks around, his eyes sweeping over me, then he indicates to his shorter friend they should check the back of the storeroom. They move in silently. As they pass I realise I need to breathe.

I watch them checking over the shelves. After a while they seem to relax. Suddenly a big cop is in the doorway.

"Hey! You two!" he shouts in French.

The surprise of his loud voice makes us jump. The big cop – a sergeant – looks around. He's noticed some movement out of the corner of his eye but he can't tell where. He looks carefully at where I'm blended in, as if painted there, and he simply can't see me.

"Stop nicking the stationery, we've found two knocked out."

He's still looking suspiciously around as the other two pass by him. He turns out the light and closes the door.

"He's going to burst back in," Tahira reads.

I already knew that too.

But nothing happens for a minute, two minutes, three minutes.

"They're going over that computer room. The others are waiting for ... hello, Mike's back. He's not looking happy."

"Hi guys. We're in the shit big time," Grandpop tells us, grimly. "Control has been infected with a kind of virus. He's fighting it constantly but it spreads and reproduces as fast as he can respond. He's isolated the comms from the rest of him so it can't be infected but the link to Hekator has been taken out. It's some kind of defensive response by the Fae. We have no idea if they know we're under attack or if they will help us. Upshot is you can't bend and we don't know when you can."

"*Well, that's great,*" Tarik says, sarcastically.

"*What do we do, Mike?*" Cam asks.

"Keep hiding sweetheart, until you can get out. We haven't got much at the moment and without the Fae we're nothing."

It's true. It's shocking to realise that we're fighting a war with the most powerful enemy on the planet and right now we are completely unarmed.

The door opens. The light flickers back on. But it isn't the sergeant, it's a police dog and his handler. In theory the suits stop us being smelt. But anything we touched might attract attention. Of course to get here all we've touched is the roof.

"*Do we use ultrasound?*" Tahira asks.

"*If we have to.*"

The dog, a big German Shepherd, comes in, nose down and snuffling around. The handler follows. The big sergeant appears in the doorway. The dog follows the footsteps of the previous cops, and circles around before coming back.

"Anything?" the sergeant asks.

"Nothing," the handler says.

"Hmmm."

With another look around the sergeant lets the dog team leave and switches off the light again. The door is almost closed when he flings it open and yells. This time we're ready for him. We don't even flinch. The sergeant grunts and closes up.

Then in the corridor outside I hear a familiar voice. A conversation, then the suggestion, and cheerful acceptance from the sergeant. Footsteps. A pause and then the door opens. Du Croix, wearing his camel hair coat, steps in and the door closes. It's still dark. Du Croix takes a deep breath and sighs.

"'Ow long do you intend to stay in 'ere my friends?" Du Croix asks in English.

"In..." he looks at his watch," seven 'ours ze Robinson's land in Buenos Aires. Zen ze Khumalos with little Patience in Singapore, and ze Khadem's with pretty Asal and ze Gursoy's in Dubai. Zey will be 'eld for questioning. Teams of our people are moving out across the globe to intercept them. When zey are caught zey will be put on a business jet for Belgium. But ze people oo get off will not be ze people oo get on. Already we will 'ave copied zem."

"Of course *I* av no particular interest in your parents. Except of course to 'elp find your new location. I 'av a very angry Service commander who wants to find zat detail very soon. He is very angry about zat fighter, Sam. Very angry. Just as I said 'e would be when I was proved right. It is not good to frustrate 'im."

"But if we must wait seven 'ours to find your base, we can. Zen we can start on your parents. It normally does not take zem long to extract information from uman's. To my mind zere methods are a little 'arsh, few recover, but 'ow can I stop them, when zey are so effective?"

He seems to enjoy jeering at us.

"*I want to get this m____f____!*" Tahira snarls, using Ashley's favourite swearword.

"*He wants you to. Then they'll pull this room apart looking for us,*" I warn her.

"Ze alternative is zat you give yourselves up and save your parents. You may even be able to help us stop other unpleasantness. In general zhose who cooperate are simply returned un'armed, and forget all about anyzing troubling. I shall be outside in ze corridor."

Then he opens the door, goes out, and closes it again, leaving us in the dark, fuming.

"*He's a monster!*" Tahira says. She's thinking of her family.

"*OK guys, what do we do?*" Tarik asks.

"*Wait,*" I say.

"*For what?*"

"*Until either we can escape, the Fae come back, or ... Well ... we don't have any choice anymore.*"

"We have time guys. It's Du Croix who wants a quick result," Sue says.

It's nice hearing Sue say that. She can obviously see the old fox and she doesn't need to be psychic to read him.

"*Is he talking to all the rooms or just ours?*" I check.

"Just yours. He knows you're there."

We lie there in the dark feeling angry. I notice Tahira breathing out hard. She's obviously finding the whole experience difficult.

"*How hard would it be to escape?*" Tarik checks.

"There's a lot of activity along the corridor in the computer room. There's a guard on both doors. Armed. If you went into the corridor you would have to beat them, then there's the carpark exit which has card access doors, two more guards and about two or three manned cars outside plus the repair crew on the telecom box," Sue says

"*Sue, how far are we from Brussels?*" Scott asks.

"Umm ... why?"

"*Because if we got the cop who put up the red notice we could draw attention away from Interpol. It's got to be more useful than sitting here.*"

"Hang on you two we'll see if we still have web access and have a look." she replies.

There's a quiet moment.

"*Do you think we should bust out?*" Tarik asks us all.

"*No,*" I reply.

"*I think we should think about it,*" Tariha argues.

"*I agree with Sam. I think we should wait,*" Cam disagrees.

"Scott, it's about six hundred kilometers," Sue comes back, "It will take you six hours to get there assuming they aren't already on flights to intercept."

"*Even better. He won't be there to stop us.*"

"Stop you what?"

"*Stop us cancelling the red notice.*"

"How will you do that?"

"*I dunno, I was hoping you could tell me,*" he says.

"Scott you can't take on the entire Belgian police force. It's crazy," Sue tells him.

"*The sun will be up in two hours. If you fly you'll be seen,*" Cam points out.

"*We could take a fast train,*" Ash suggests.

"*You may as well save yourself the bother and surrender now. How would you escape?*" I ask.

"*I DUNNO, I'D WORK SOME BLOODY THING OUT!*" Scott shouts.

It's so unlike Scott to get angry I shut up. He's obviously feeling the pressure now that his mother is at risk.

"*I gotta do something,*" he adds, to himself.

"Just wait son," Grandpop says quietly.

"Sometimes it's the hardest thing to do. I remember one time in Vietnam … Nguyen, Liz, Rewa and Dr P have come to join us by the way … anyway I remember one patrol. The NVA knew more or less where we were, and they had us surrounded and were waiting for the sun to come up so they could finish us off. One guy … there were only four of us … against a company of them – that's about two hundred and fifty or so – well the stress got to him and he lost it. Tried to fight his way out by himself. He didn't get too far. "

"*How did you escape?*" I ask.

"The cavalry showed up! About dawn the 11th armoured was grinding its way through just a klick away. The NVA commanders decided a company was better used attacking them than three soldiers. We gave it two hours and slunk past the picket. Sometimes you just have to trust your luck."

I suddenly think of Mr Ceder. "Listen to God," he'd said.

It seems kind of dumb but it was like everything now is in the balance. Like when he'd been pulled out of the gas chambers for no apparent reason.

"*Maybe we should pray*," I suggest.

"*Pray!*" Tarik sneers.

Here *he* was praying every five minutes, dissing me!

"*Yeah, why not. How can it hurt?*" I argue.

There's a pause as everyone thinks about it.

"*Sam is right*," Tahira says.

"*Yeah, he is actually*," Tarik admits.

"*Oh, alright*," says Ash.

So we pray quietly. I pray for the other's parents.

I'm still pretty sure we can get out if we have to. Then Grandpop speaks.

"Ah Guys ... Ah ... you might be doing it wrong. The heavy mob have arrived," Grandpop says.

"*What sort of heavy mob?*" I ask.

"The Gendarmerie. The Swat. Whatever you want to call them. The guys in black with balaclavas and assault rifles."

"*Oh, thank* you, *God*," Ashley says sarcastically.

"*Where are they?*" Tarik asks.

"Outside. They're getting out of their vehicles. Guys you can't fight this lot. They'll chop you up."

"*Maybe we can make a break for the roof,*" Tarik says.

"The place is crawling with armed police Tarik. Forget it." Grandpop replies.

"*Can we make the carpark?*" I ask.

"My fly is outside. I don't know what's in the carpark. When it went through there were only a few cars there. If you bust past the two in the corridor they'll track you down pretty quick."

"*Maybe we could distract them?*" Scott and Ashley say.

"Guys you're in over your heads. I think you'd better give up now. I won't have any of you killed," Grandpop says.

We all have plenty to say about that! It's almost getting out of hand when Sue interrupts us.

"Guys! Guys think about this! You aren't terminators. You're kids. What is your advantage? Shooting kids is very bad. So play to your strengths. Mike's right. Tactical surrender. You have a better chance of getting away from a police car on the way to the station than from those guys with the machine guns," Sue says.

"Nguyen, what do you think?" Grandpop asks.

"I agree Sue. Soldier very bad. You be kids now. Make police embarrass," he says.

Of course. How dumb would *they* look! I had forgotten how tough Mr Trân must have been at our age. He lived with this every day, and he never had a suit.

"*Cam's dad is right!*" I says. "*If they come at us with machine guns we're history. If we walk out as kids they will be the biggest eggs in France.*"

"Try the world," Sue agrees.

"*OK, tactical surrender,*" agrees Tarik.

I look over at Tahira. We sigh and roll out from under our shelves, changing our suits to look like jeans and a jacket. We lower our hoods. Then I turn on the light. We look at each other as it flickers on. We both look nervous.

"Be strong Sam," Aunty Liz says in Maori.

"You brave girl Cam," Nguyen tells his daughter.

"*I get it from you, dad,*" she replies.

"*I'll look after her Mr Trân,*" Tarik says.

"*Whaaat? You can't even look after self!*" Cam scoffs at him.

"*Well the thought...*"

"*Shut up and kiss me for luck, you dickhead,*" Cam says.

I look at Tahira. She looks at me and then away, a bit irritated, but then she gives up.

"*Oh alright!*" she says grumpily.

I put my arms around her, and kiss her gently, just on the lips. I hug her a bit longer. She hugs me back. I have been through so much with this girl.

"*You're getting a lot, lot better,*" Tahira admits. Then she pushes me away and takes a big breath. "*OK, let's go get arrested.*"

"*On three,*" says Tarik. "*One, two, three.*"

We open the door and come out.

The cops can't believe their eyes.

"Hey what's this? What are you kids doing in here?" demands the one nearest us. We're so casual and goofy looking he doesn't even go for his gun.

"We broke in," Tahira tells him shamefacedly in French, like we broke a window at school.

"You! *You* broke in!" he splutters, unable to believe it.

"How *old* are you?"

"Fourteen," she shrugs.

He picks up his radio mike, his hands are shaking, and calls his commander.

"I've got four fourteen year old kids who've just given themselves up."

"What? Repeat that?" crackles the radio.

"Sir, the 'terrorists' are four fourteen year old kids. Two boys, two girls."

"Unbelievable! What are they doing?"

"Just standing here."

"Holy f____! There is going to be hell to pay. The President was woken and told this was a terrorist attack! You better get those little sons of bitches to central, now!" the radio demands.

The cop looks at us sorrowfully

"You kids are soo in the shit!" he tells us, shaking his head.

"We know," Tahira admits.

There's a clatter of feet and two more cops show up, including the big sergeant. He looks outraged.

"You think this is some kind of joke! A teenage prank? This is *Interpol* you shit-for-brains! You have no idea the trouble you are in!" he roars at us.

It was more like *he* was in. You could see they had been all psyched up for North Korean super agents and all they had was four teenagers. "Egg," didn't begin to cover it.

He tries to go on but he's speechless with anger. We just tried to look stupid.

"Well, don't stand there, cuff them!" he screams at the other cops.

They grab us roughly, push us against a wall, make us spread, and pat us down. More cops appear.

"Get the cars into the car park I don't want any son of a whore taking pictures of this," he yells.

Some cops run off. Others are coming down just to gawp. They start marching us to the car park. It's like being a wild animal. Everyone wants to see. Then Inspector Du Croix is among them. He's being told that Interpol would be informed, but this was a Lyon district case. Du Croix doesn't argue but he looks pretty pleased. The cars are pulling up in the car park. We're put in one each. I start to wonder what I will say, if anything.

These French police cars are pretty small so there's only one cop in the back with me. Two in the front.

It feels funny to be moving. The car park door opens, and the car drives out into the night. There's still a lot of cops about.

The car turns right and speeds off along the river. The lights and siren are on and sound quite loud. The big Cite Internationale is on the right looking impressive. The light flickers with the orange sodium streetlights. The guys in the car are tense. They want this trip over. I'm feeling around with my pinky to see if I can undo the cuffs. Suddenly I feel a new presence through my suit. It's big, female and reassuring.

"I am Ashanti. You are being transferred. Please prepare to bend."

I must have looked startled. I look up at the big cop next to me."

"Quoi (what)?" he asks.

"Désolé (sorry)," I say through the suit, and hit him with the amnesia ray. While he sits there vacantly my hood raises by itself and my facescreen lowers. The driver suddenly glances at me in the mirror, and flinches at the sight of my blacked out face. I zap him with amnesia via his mirror. My cuffs hit the seat, empty as the driver's mind as the car fails to take the curve of the river drive.

[+]

But for me the world is a line. A place of presences from the past. Then a flash. Lightning, water and wind. And the cabinet opens. We all fall out.

It feels so good to be away. Then Rewa's body slams into me, and I hug her hard. The others are all laughing with relief and hugging one another. There are two flashes of light. Hekator and Hekati appear looking ready to do stuff.

"Everything all right?" Hekator asks, a little worried.

"It is now mate! But by God, that was damn close. What kept you?" Grandpop says.

"Hekator has just been made commander of Earth operations," Hekati tells us happily.

"He reports to the Ring directly."

Hekator looks a bit shy.

"I had a few political battles to win." he admits.

"I had to convince them that a policy of token support for Earth was more dangerous than no support, and no support was more dangerous than support. The evidence you collected…"

"And his excellent logic," Hekati adds.

Hekator smiles at her, "you helped too, darling sister. Anyway it gave Horne and Isis a reason to oppose Morganne for tokenism, and forced Morganne to agree to a deeper investigation of Earth and especially the claims of these Iyrin. If she didn't she was hiding something."

He looks over at Hekati, "And my sweet sister here had the guts to tell the Ring that it almost seemed we were deliberately trying to fail on Earth. Morganne didn't like that at all. She was furious. But Horne and Isis couldn't face the consequences of betraying you. So in the end they made the right decision for bad reasons. Anyway Control is under attack I believe?"

"He must be, he's very weak," Grandpop says.

"This is what I mean by half-hearted measures. You do not put a kindergarten system in charge of an operation in a potentially combative environment."

"Can you fix him?"

"Yes, but it will take time. In the meantime Ashanti will stand in for Control. She's much more experienced and skilled at this sort of thing anyway. Now where is Dr Morozov? I need her help."

"We are here," Dr M says.

The three Russians are on a disc, Irina in a baby sling, sucking on a pacifier.

"Good! You are about to get a quick lesson in quantum viruses. They differ from the kind you are used to because superposition involves the true uncertain nature of the future. Not something Control has much experience with. We think we know which one this is. The only problem is it could mean we have to restore his memory from our backups. He may not remember everything he's done today."

We all look at each other and groan. All our work on the airport security systems could have been lost.

"Relax Earthlings! We'll know everything in half an hour or so. Ashanti will pick up Control's legacy network in about five minutes once I set to work."

"Well, we'd better not hold you up," Grandpop says.

"It might be better if the infant was with her father, young minds can find the psychic effects of intense quantum computing troubling," Hekator tells Dr Morozov.

Irina is put down on the floor and starts crawling about while Dr P fusses over her, and everyone coos.

"How does Morganne of Fae fare with the Ring?" Dr P asks in a way that suggested Lucky is near the surface.

Hekati looks at him carefully.

"Queen Morganne is still a queen, Dr Prosperov, just as you are still a doctor, but my brother's arguments were compelling and she had no choice but to concede. The investigation into the claims of the Iyrin are being considered by Raman and Isis."

"What makes 'er a Queen anyway? Don't you guys have

democracy then?" Tarik asks.

Hekati smiles at his cheek.

"Morganne's title means she is the knowledge leader in a field of learning and government. A 'Queen' is like a professor and a minister of a government at the same time. As I understand your way of government, policy decisions depend on the success of the system to educate the whole population on good policy. Your politicians have no expertise in anything other than manipulating others by politics. So it is trivial to see your democracy is flawed because politicians manipulate public opinion by not educating the population on good policy. Our system is not perfect but the politicians must be experts and convince their equals they have the best answers. The Ring provides the community voice. A knowledge leader of a certain standing is made a King or Queen in matters to do with that area of expertise. Normally their decisions are not questioned – it's not that they can't be, it's that they aren't because they usually know what they're doing. So my brother's act was brave and important."

I just hoped it didn't mean Morganne was an enemy now. I always found her scary and I didn't want to piss her off. But Hekati is moving on.

"Now children, while Hekator works to restore Control, Ashanti is able to pick up your parents. I suggest we return them here again just in case we are not able to remove the warnings about them in time."

Everyone is very pleased about that idea. It takes a little while to get organised and for Ashanti to find the aircraft toilets. One by one everyone bent out to take sleeping bags to the parents and over the next half hour the cabinets crackle and whirr as for the second time the adults are transported back to Hastings.

They're all a bit shocked and frightened by the attack on Control. Like us, it had never occurred that Control could fail, and it makes us all very aware of how much we rely on him. Dr Prosperov comes down to welcome everyone back. Soon there's a bit of a gathering in a briefing room as the parents are brought up to speed with what has been happening. Meanwhile Hekator has reset Control and got him working normally again. Hekator comes in and gives us all a quick run down on what's happened. "They were trying to knock out and trace Control. He fought a remarkable battle with a very powerful Cybermind called Barbarossa which I estimate is within a thousand kilometer radius of Lyon. It may have been only ten minutes for us, but for him that was a very long 600,000 milliseconds. When you disconnected him the viruses started breaking out. Anyway he doesn't think they have any idea where we are, though they have broken some of the gateways you set when you came back. They were trying to find the backdoors you have placed in various systems by forcing the systems you have compromised to signal their status back through the internet. Of course a lot of those systems are not connected to the internet but we have to assume that some of the ones that are have now been identified to the Cybermind."

"We need to learn a lot more about this Barbarossa, including what other systems it is linked to, where it is, and what it does. My suspicion is that it is the Administration's registry of earthlings and will combine police, travel, health, financial and relationship records to construct a network of your population. The richer a person is, the more likely it is that Barbarossa will trace them. Your identities will now be of most interest to this system as they are connected to Control. Ideally I would like to see Barbarossa destroyed as it constitutes a serious risk to the safety of this operation and your mission."

We all look at each other. This was a bit more hardcore than we were used to. So far we had tried to avoid annoying the Administration. Here was Hekator planning to kick sand in their face. But given Hekator's record of getting us into trouble I was beginning to have doubts that this was the best idea.

I don't think I was the only one with doubts about Hekator either. There's a lot of shuffling and staring at feet but nobody seems ready to challenge him now, while we are all safely out of danger. But if he thinks we're all going to rush into another ambush just for him, he's going to have to think again. The last thing we want is more excitement.

Hekator glances at Hekati. You can tell he knew exactly what we're thinking and he isn't sure how to talk to us. Hekati doesn't seem that sure of herself either.

"This is your freedom, I'm talking about," Hekator says firmly. Nobody says anything. While we can see what he's getting at, we're just a family, not some made-for-TV group of commandos who take faked risks for the audience's entertainment. We didn't want to risk *anyone*.

Suddenly Control appears with a tall, dark blue skinned woman with four arms wearing a red skirt but nothing over her small breasts. We know at once this hologram is the humanoid avatar of Ashanti, the Vimana. She seems a bit older than Sue, but she's young and fit, with bracelets and a tiara in braided black hair. She looks pretty fierce. It's good to see Control again though he doesn't look any different.

"I am afraid that the Administration counterattack has completely eliminated my access to the Internet. To be effective I urgently need new nodes," he tells us.

"What of immigration systems?" Dr P asks.

"Those reprogramming tasks are scheduled for update and unaffected."

Everyone looks a bit relieved.

"There is also a new problem however," Control adds. We all look back at him.

"In addition to the FBI terrorist screening database entry and the Interpol red notice, the CIA has issued an official warning against your names. While I was checking my old backdoor links into some of these systems I have discovered a global bulletin warning that you are dangerous bioterrorists."

There were cries of "what?!" all around. No-one can believe what Control is saying.

"The bulletin explains that the child trafficking cover story from Interpol is to get maximum cooperation from local authorities and avoid panic, but that you should be treated with extreme caution. There are details about immobilisation, body searches, isolation and immediate evacuation in specialised vehicles and aircraft."

Now everyone is looking at one another, very worried indeed.

"I'm afraid these were also sent to the New Zealand Security Intelligence Service as well."

"What is origin?" asks Dr Prosperov.

"The Central Intelligence Agency."

"That doesn't make *any* sense," Sue said, "if you guys were biosecurity risks ...no I just don't get that."

"Spooks don't *have* to make sense. They usually have some

scheme they're protecting further up the line," Grandpop growls.

"But a bunch of people flying from New Zealand out to airports. How could they be a security risk?" Sue asks, not giving an inch.

"That won't matter. When the Spooks say 'jump' civilians ask 'how high?' They don't have to justify themselves," Grandpop argues.

"Is that a real CIA warning?" Sue checks with Control.

"It comes from CIA HQ in Langley," Control confirms.

"Is possible CIA compromised," Dr Morozov points out.

"Who by?" Ken asks.

"Barbarossa," Dr M says.

"Hathaway," I say at the same time.

Everyone looks at me.

"The last place Control spotted him up was in DC at the inauguration, just over the river from Langley. We know he works with the CIA, we know he's onto us, and we know he's into bioweapons," I argue.

"H-o-l-y F… Flip! That's why Rocelli was so smug!" Sue shouts. Everyone turns to stare at her.

"The Bruderschaft's plan is to *really* launch their *new* bio-attack *now* and blame *us* knowing we are best placed to stop them! Any symptoms will be blamed on us!" Sue cries out in realisation. There's total silence.

We all look at each other. It's an awful moment when we all realise that Sue's fresh eyes have seen more than ours had.

The Bruderschaft had been celebrating at Elan because their new weapon was ready. Our attack had delayed them, so they had used our tactic (to use Du Croix) against us. Now that we were almost knocked out they were launching their attack. Von Streicher had pretty much told me so himself in Belzer. But realising we might still interfere with their plans they were using our vulnerability to official human agencies against us.

I could see on the other's faces they knew that was totally like Hathaway (the man who winked at Scotty before shooting him) to launch an attack and pin the blame on the only people who could stop it at the same time.

"Are those worms we put inside Virion still working?" Scott asks. Control thinks for a moment.

"Probably, but I haven't touched them since the relocation as they are a security risk."

"And you shouldn't either, I wouldn't be too surprised if Barbarossa is waiting in ambush," Hekator says.

"But we have to understand their plans," Scott argues.

"We know the tests involved aircraft. That leads me to think aircraft are part of the dispersal system. As I understand it the obvious point of attack using a bioweapon with your transport network would be airports themselves. They would create maximum dispersion, especially if there is sufficient latency between infection and death," Hekati suggests.

"The samples you sent me need an incubating vector for the two diseases to merge but once they did it could be dispersed in the airports themselves. The obvious method would to sprinkle contaminated water vapour on everyone passing through the buildings using the air treatment systems." Hekator adds. "They would send technicians to pretend to be protecting the systems but actually infecting them. The virus has a quick eight hour incubation which leads to coughing fits which last about an hour. When airborne the virus is highly contagious. By infecting selected airports they will be able to reinfect other airports using transferred passengers. The trick is after the coughing stops the virus is dormant for a month then strikes with sudden violence causing swelling in the heart and brain within hours. I estimate 90 percent mortality."

"To model this I urgently need secure access to the Internet," Control reminds us.

"OK, we better get onto that," Grandpop says.

We start to get up, but Hekator waves us back.

"No need for you to do anything," Hekator says. "I've built some new bendable worms. Ashanti can inject them anywhere where they are needed."

"They will be operational in ten minutes," Ashanti tells us.

"In the meantime would the two of you sweep the airports our family's are arriving at, looking for activity on air conditioning systems," Hekati asks.

"Certainly … done. Nothing happening at the moment." Control says.

"Hmm keep monitoring them."

"Will do."

"Control … please to show warning from CIA?" asks Dr Prosperov.

What looked like a piece of paper appears on the big wrap around screen. It's headed "Warning Memorandum – National Intelligence Officer for Warning, Status: Confidential. Attached Defence Intelligence Assessment (Short Form) – National Center for Medical Intelligence Fort Detrick, Maryland. Subject: Possible H5N1 Bioweapon Threat."

It then went on to describe a potential immediate bioweapon threat and the possible involvement of us, giving the names of all of us, and our families claiming we had attacked Virion La Louviere in Belgium and stolen samples. We didn't recognise any of the authors' names but that didn't really matter. What it showed us all was that somebody had enlisted the United States of America to come and get us, and that wasn't a very nice feeling.

We all look at it, and the more we look at it the grumpier and more nervous we feel. Quite a few people swear and complain that we've been set up. The warning asks that if we are captured, we are to be contained and sent to Fort Detrick for examination and interrogation. Fort Detrick, we knew was near Frederick, a town 50km north-west of Washington D.C because we'd passed through looking for Nathan the year before.

"I should remind you that while this document may be personally disheartening a more serious threat is the imminent release of a disease which I estimate could kill three billion of your kind in a matter of months," Hekator says, a bit grumpily. "I think that is something we might more fully give our attention to."

"Friends," Dr Prosperov says loudly, standing. "When we started this adventure two years ago my focus is on risks to humanity from itself. Risks children we work for face everyday from war, poverty and crime. To be blunt, saving world from alien plot was not imagined and was not part of deal. You ... we ... just ordinary families, even though extraordinary people. None wants risk. None wants loss."

He looks around at us — and we all have to agree with him. He looks at Hekator, and he and Hekati had to pause as well. It's true. We're just a bunch of kids and parents. Then quietly he starts again.

"Yet, slowly true nature of enemy is revealed. Is organised, is secret, is deadly. Fight started when we acted to preserve four

Earth children, our hope for future. This opposed by enemy. Enemy pursued us. Now enemy threatens selves and all humanity."

He again pauses, and nods.

"*Is* choice *not* to act. *Is* choice to hide here. Is likely chances of survival greater than most. On other hand we know this enemy. We know is dangerous, cunning and powerful. I cannot guarantee safety of *anyone,* adult or child, who opposes them. I fear – for I have seen war – I fear if we fight them some of us could die. We will do whatever we can to avoid it but is reality of battle. And my friends there are none here I can bear the thought of seeing die."

And too my surprise there were real tears in the corners of his eyes, as he looked around at us.

"But is simple choice. Risk all to defend world or hide and when reports of deaths Hekator predicts begin those who chose to do nothing would have each one on their conscience."

He sighs and pauses. I look around. I didn't want to lose anyone either. I love my friends. Most of all I love my family. I would happily die to defend them. And I understand right then why Grandpop had faced his ghosts to defend me from Rocelli. And even as I look at him I had a small twinge of fear. A fear that this old tiger could be killed. As I look at him, his face set with determination, strong but old, I know he knows it too. And I know that somehow, now more than any other time he'd gone to war, he's no longer worried about proving he's better than the other guy. He'd sacrifice himself to protect any of us, and be happy to do it. And for the first time I understand how the love and the ferocity of us Maoris really is the same thing. "Ka Maté (Death?) Ka Ora (Life?)" as the old haka went. When everything

295

is in the balance only love, like the sun rising at the end of the old war chant, beats all. But Dr P was still speaking.

"In my view, and it is only my personal view, we cannot ignore what we know. When hand of Hekator and Hekati and Ashanti is held out to help us, to help defend our world we must take it, even if shaking with fear for our loved ones. We must stand up for our world, for all its mistakes, its crimes and its stupidities and defend the millions who struggle each day to care, as we do, for our friends and families. We must stop this. We can stop this. We will stop this. Is anyone here *not* with me?"

There was a brief pause.

"We're all with you Gennady," Ken says firmly.

"Of course," says Grandpop and many of the others.

Even Patricia, who had so long tried to protect Ashley, seems especially fierce. Sue seems a bit surprised, but very impressed.

"Then my friends. Let us begin, though where it will lead and how it will end, I confess I do not know."

CHAPTER EIGHTY FIVE: ANTICIPATION.

Using publicly available information about airport passenger numbers Ashanti and Control were soon able to work out the Bruderschaft's likely virus attack plan. It involved seven airports. Hartsfield-Jackson in Atlanta, Georgia; Los Angeles; Heathrow in London; Abu Dhabi; Changi in Singapore; Narita in Tokyo; and Beijing. They showed us how they thought the disease would spread through connecting flights to other airports, then through out into cities and over the weeks out to the countryside. They used a transparent red shade to show half of the population infected.

It covered a third of the world's population in three weeks, then half the world's population by the time the first deaths started. By the time travel restrictions were in place it was too late. A black shadow meaning half the population was dead followed the red unstoppably. The whole world was covered in three months. The death count in the corner was three billion, two hundred and forty two million. The average age of the survivors was thirteen. I could imagine other Father Rocellis and his kind rounding up the orphans pretending to be sad while laughing their evil, black hearts out.

But it was one thing to guess where they *could* strike, but *would* they? And how? And what could we do about it?

That's our new task: check over the airports for infiltrators. So we sit there watching people in airports, reading them at work, which is pretty dull. In the meantime Hekator goes to work on finding a way to weaken release agents 21 and 22. That way the worst they could do is spread immunity to themselves. Instead of the world dying in huge numbers people would just get a cough and pass on immunity.

The airports me and Tahira get are Changi and Narita. We start thinking we're looking for Virion infiltrators. But it soon turns out that the number of Europeans placed to do anything to air conditioning systems at Changi or Narita is none at all. The building air conditioning was supplied by Fujitsu and we couldn't find anyone, even slightly sus, near or connected to either airport. These were all just ordinary people with ordinary problems. Aliens trying to wipe out all adults was not something they were thinking too much about.

The others weren't having any luck either. Either we're seriously missing something, or we're chasing a figment of our stressed-out imaginations.

There are now only six hours until our parents are meant to be landing.

Hekator comes back from Ashanti. He says he's making good progress making a third disrupting virus which would mess up the interaction between Release Candidates 21 and 22 and switch off the genes which made those Virion viruses so deadly. He's also made some biosensors for the Virion viruses. The biosensors are fine threads that look like hair. They contained a sensor cell which triggers an alarm through a microscopic quantum modem if Release Candidates 21 and 22 enter the cell. All we have to do is scatter this hair around seats in the target airports.

To hide us from the cameras which monitor these airports we need to interfere with the security systems again. Luckily Ashanti has a finer trans-dimensional probe than Control. Control can receive light, backscatter and radio signals or transmit laser, x-ray and radar signals through the wormhole in spacetime he opens, but Ashanti can open precision electrolasers that tickle the copper connectors of a computer USB port directly. It saves us a huge amount of risk and work. Now we don't have to bypass security and bend into server rooms to risk getting trapped there again by Barbarossa. Ashanti can just tap security systems anywhere on Earth and if there is another attack she can dissolve the data connection into light and withdraw the probe. The only danger that remains is having the wormhole probe dimensionally grabbed by an Administration ambush again. Practically what that meant for us was that Ashanti could simply erase or replace us with another person on the security videos.

We started in Atlanta because it's the biggest and it's night time. We bend into toilets, then walk around in pairs dropping the virus detection hairs.

[+]

The place is huge. There are seven concourses with three dozen gates each so Sue and Patricia suit up to do one as well. We keep moving with our facescreens open. If anyone had challenged us we would've amnesia rayed them, but nobody did. All we see are thousands of tired people blinking away under hard lights. Each team does a concourse and then we come home.

[+]

The technique turns out to be very quick. In quarter of an

hour we've done half the airports. The only trouble is the sensors aren't picking up anything. Are we too soon? What if they weren't planning to start until we were already arrested? That made sense. A lot more than starting while we were still supposed to be sitting on planes. But while walking around in Heathrow very early in the morning Tarik looked out a window and had an idea.

"Hey did you guys know they have air conditioning systems in trucks out there plugged into the planes?" he asked.

We all quickly find windows with a view of the planes at the gates. It's true. Amongst the freight loaders, refuellers, security and other vehicles driving around under the planes' wheels are aircon trucks.

"There's no way we're going to get to those trucks or on those planes without being seen," Ashley points out.

That's true enough.

"Guys come home. Hekator has a plan to bend sensors directly into the planes," Grandpop says.

"But what do we do if they are using trucks?" Cam asks.

"We'll have to sort that out too."

So we find our ways to the toilets and bend home. We all had the bad feeling we've just wasted half an hour we don't have. Even the food Mr Trân and the others organised doesn't make us feel any better.

"You know, what I'd really like to know, is where is that bastard Hathaway, right now?" Scott says as we eat.

"And Du Croix," I agree.

"All this is looking like when we was searchin' for Nathan. Weeks of wasted time coz we didn't have the crucial piece of information," Ashley agrees

"We ain't lookin, at the whole problem right, yeah? We gotta think more like *them*, init?" Tarik points out.

We think about Hathaway, starting with Cherensky and our first encounter in Finland, the ages we spent on his planes, and everything else we've learned about him since.

It's one of those strange moments when everyone thinks the same thing at the very same moment: *Hathaway and Virion don't use machines to spread disease, they use people*! They'd proved it in Africa. What people could they use to contaminate air passengers? The stewards and stewardesses on each plane of course.

"What?" Sue asks, suddenly aware we have something.

"Ze aircrew," Tahira answers her, as we look at each other.

We all get up and rush Grandpop who's grumpily playing with screens on the control desk while the other adults eat and watch on. As we explain our theory a hologram of Hekator joins in.

"You're right on two counts," he sighs. "I admit I've been panicking a bit. We need to think more like them and we need to find out *where* they are. It's risky but so is the whole situation."

"My problem now is I've worked on the assumption that they would use air conditioning so my virus is built for that. I can still inject it into the air conditioning systems to inoculate the airports as dispersion points and that should work on the people passing through them as well, but I need to change it again for individual doses and that will take time."

"We're meant to be landin' in four hours what's happening with da border security systems?" Patricia asks.

"I don't know," Hekator shrugs. "Control?"

Control appears next to him.

"The Interpol notice threat has been neutralised. Interpol's I24 system remains down for the moment, and the border control database systems have been reprogrammed. But I do not have access to the intelligence services' computers of Argentina, Singapore or the United Arab Emirates and I am uncertain if, or how, the CIA warning has been sent to them. So it is still possible that those travelling will be intercepted by intelligence agents."

That is not very good news. We're all very pissed off that we seem to be getting nowhere.

"So what do we do?" Grandpop asks Hekator.

"May I offer suggestion." Dr P says, loudly.

We all turn to look at him. He speaks carefully and slowly.

"Problem is we know threat. Is disease. Have watched it develop for months. We know who is responsible. Is Virion Corporation and associated Bruderschaft group. We suspect delivery mechanism. Is airports. But we don't *know* enemy plan."

He looked around to make sure we're nodding and paying attention.

"So is no point guessing. We need enemy plan. Then can stop attack and expose attackers so as to make clear real threat is from them..."

"...So we need to find Hathaway..." I interrupt.

"What about Xavier?" Ashley disagrees.

"*Where is Von Streicher*?" Dr Prosperov asks over us.

We all shut up. We'd forgotten about Von Streicher.

"He's in a private hospital in Innsbruck," Control reports.

"Then, find out enemy plan from *him*. He must know," Dr P points out.

Hekator looks at Dr Prosperov, and laughs.

"You really *are* a genius, Gennady," he says in open admiration.

"OK, Von Streicher is the easiest but wouldn't Hathaway be more certain? I mean he designed the pandemic," asks Sue.

"Hathaway is double agent," Mr Trân says, certainly. "Works for Administration and Bruderschaft."

"He'd have to," Sue agrees, "Because he must have controlled Inspector Turneau in the Belgian police, and now Du Croix is using him and D.S Xavier instead. So he's given up something to keep Du Croix happy."

"Could also mean Du Croix knows of Bruderschaft virus plan and hopes to use threat of it to bring *us* from hiding," Dr Morozov says. "Du Croix lost us in Lyon which will make his superiors angry. Is probably desperate to force us from cover," she suggests.

"Is therefore risk that Von Streicher is left as bait," Dr Prosperov nods.

Having just thought of Von Streicher himself, Dr P is already second guessing his opponent.

"Bugging a wounded man so he can be sacrificed for enemy interrogation sounds like a Hathaway trick to me. Let's take a gander at Von Streicher. Control?" Grandpop agrees.

A comfortable hospital room appears in the artificial colour of Control's laser scanner. It almost looks like a movie. The room is dark with the curtains drawn and only LEDs from machines light the room. Von Streicher's asleep and snoring softly.

"I think we have to take the bait," Hekator concludes.

We all look at him.

"Take him, but not here. I can't go into your hospitals but if you get him to Ashanti I can extract the plan as he understands it," he clarifies.

"Be careful. He could be bomb," Mr Trân warns.

It's another of those chilling moments when you know Mr
Trân is speaking from memory. Children were used as live
boobytraps[+] in Vietnam.

"True. Nathan was," Hekator agrees, "All I need you guys to do
is bag him and move him somewhere. I can do the rest."

"Where do you want him?" Grandpop asks.

"I think I know a suitable spot nearby. We used to holiday in
that part of Earth when I was younger. A place called Brocken.
I'll pass Control the landing zone," Hekator says and vanishes.
Grandpop looks around at us.

"OK? Who wants to bag this turkey?"

"I do," I say quickly.

"Thought you might."

"OK, but not straight into his room. He ambushed you once,
don't let him do it again."

I smile and grab Tahira who's standing next to me.

"I didn't have my secret weapon with me then," I say as Tahira
wriggles away, grumpily.

"Me? I just av a *brain*," she insults me.

"Puts you ahead of Sam!" laughs Tarik good humouredly.

I cross my eyes and look brainless, for a laugh, but Grandpop is
moving on.

"OK, while Tahira and Sam are doing that, the rest of you can
try and find Hathaway." he tells them. Then he claps his hands.

"Come on, get busy!"

Everyone jumps and pairs up. Tahira and me look at each other
and ask Control if he has a landing zone. He does, so we go to
the cabinets and bend space time, through the dimensions of
memory to Austria.

[+]

We find ourselves in a stairwell of a hospital. It's bright white with gray vinyl on the floor. It smells of some German pine cleaner. It looks spotless, a bit homely and very expensive. Everything Aunty Liz never had in Northland, anyway.

We step up and push open the windowed, double swing doors from the stairs and go into the wide, brightly lit, passageway. It too is white, with gray corridors. We go forward about five meters to where the corridor widens out to a lift bay. The lift doors are all wooden and old fashioned. There's a nurses' station ahead on the left with windows covered in a lace curtain. We can hear chat from inside. We have to get past without being challenged. We hunch over, and with our feet fluffed up, sneak past the nurses toward the wards.

Von Streicher is on the last room on the right before the corridor, and the building, turns slightly to the left around the hillside behind it. We slip quietly up to his door.

"Don't rush in guys. Check it out first," Grandpop warns in soft growl.

There's a glass segment in the door, you can see through but there isn't much to see. It's a large room. Almost like a hotel room, with big windows looking up to the mountains on the other side of the valley, but the bed and the machinery tells you it's a hospital.

There's a curtain around the bed. I know from Aunty Liz they do that if they're doing something private or if the patient is asleep. I check the door but there was nothing unusual about it, then I look at Tahira.

"*Well*?" I ask.

"*Well what?*"

"*Together or one at a time?*" I ask.

305

"*You first,*" she says.

"*Whatever happened to 'ladies first'?*" I ask.

"*That's only if it's something good,*" she sniffs.

"*Typical.*"

I take a deep breath and open the door, just a tad. I'm listening for voices or anything to suggest anyone's awake in there. I hold it there for five seconds. Nothing happens. I look at Tahira, and shrug. She shrugs back. Then I open it and go in.

It seems very quiet inside. All I can hear is my own heartbeat and Von Streicher's soft snoring. The light from the window casts deep shadows in which little green LEDs sit, apparently happy with whatever they're measuring.

Carefully we walk around the room, checking it out. I am especially nervous about silver skulls. I really didn't want to meet any of those again. I come around Von Streicher's bed. He's propped up, asleep. There's a book open next to him as if he's fallen asleep reading it. I glance at the cover. It's called "On Conscience" with a picture of Pope Benedict on it. That, I can make no sense of.

Making sure Von Streicher's asleep I pull back the curtain a bit, checking for a skull.

"Ugh!" I start, and jump back.

There it is, looking right at me! It's half a meter away on the deep window ledge.

"*What?*" Tahira asks sharply.

"*From Elan,*" I remind her, getting out of the way so she can see. It isn't doing anything. I look more closely at it. It's bigger than the one on the moon. Not quite the size of an adult head but quite large. It looks very creepy. I tap it. It feels like solid metal. Then I notice there's something odd. Something different about the room. It's like I'm deaf. I turn around quickly to see Tahira is looking not at the skull, or me, but at Von Streicher. She seems half asleep. I turn to him. He's smiling, looking at me. It's horrible.

"Hansel und Gretel verliefen sich im vald (Hansel and Gretel lost themselves in the forest)" he sings a children's song softly. I find myself suddenly really spaced out and dreamy.

"Es var zo finster und auch zo bitter kalt (it was so dark and also so bitter cold)," he continues.

"Sie kamen an ein Häuschen von Pfefferkuchen fein. (they came on a little house made of fine gingerbread). Wer mag der Herr wohl von diesem Häuschen sein (who knew whose little house it was)."

In a slightly dreamy state I realise I can't hear home because the psychic defence has cut us off again. It didn't seem to provide much protection. First Rocelli, now Von Streicher.

Tahira crumples in a heap. I'm desperately hanging on to consciousness.

"Es ist so schön um Besuch zu haben. (It's so nice to have visitors)," Von Streicher sighs and lies back on his pillows and closes his eyes.

This is a different attack to Rocelli. Instead of hard pounding blows Von Streicher's technique is hard to even recognise as an attack. It's as if your mind has just lost focus, and every little idea takes off on its own, like trout in a pool, pulling your mind with it. It's exactly like going to sleep.

"*This is what Tabika does,*" I think dreamily.

This thought sprang into my mind on its own and yet, for some reason, it's a thought which doesn't swim off. The thought of Tabika isn't a slippery fish. I can hold on to it.

"*Tabika*," I repeat.

The fuzziness comes on stronger, but it can't get Tabika out of my mind. I can see her. She's so naked and sexy and nice. She can make fire. Yes, she can. Just by wanting it. And if she's ambushed she becomes a demon. A demon!

I can feel Tahira again. Both our minds are on sexy Tabika. And then, aware of each other, we reach for each other, each other and Tabika. Ours is a closeness Von Streicher can't reach. We think about kissing Tabika and we think about kissing each other. We can feel a strength in our bond. I can feel our energy building so long as we think about Tabika. We're pushing back against the fuzziness with this certainty in each other. We're pushing back hard when Von Streicher is gone and he's moving.

"Movâzeb bâsh! (Look out!)," yells Tahira suddenly in Farsi.

My eyes open and I dive to the side. My movement draws his attention. Then Von Streicher grunts as Tahira's invisible beam knocks him out. He has a pistol in his hand. I breathe out long and hard.

"*That was close*," I admit to Tahira.

"Are you guys OK? We lost you for a while there," Grandpop asks, concern in his voice.

"*We ... we beat him!*" I say, looking at Tahira, surprised to be alive. "*He was waiting for us. He didn't expect to lose, he even had a gun,*" I tell Grandpop.

"Uh ... That's brilliant Sam! Well done you two! We'll send you a sleeping bag, Hekator has the landing zone. Come home as soon as you've dropped him. The others will want to know what you did."

I twist the Walther pistol from Von Streicher's hand and put the safety catch on. I feel a strange kind of happy glow. We'd actually beaten one! We *can* do it! He knew he was losing control, that's why he went for his gun. I glance at Tahira who's pulling back the bedclothes. She's smiling too. It's like we've gone up a swimming grade from the babies pool, or something. "What do we tell the others though?" I whisper as we work. That makes her think.

"Tell them we thought of each other. It will work for *them*," she says.

She's right. It probably will.

Under the covers is a holster. I put the gun in it. Then it hits me that to have it at all means he must have been expecting us. I point that out to Tahira who's as bothered by it as I am. If he was expecting us, he knew what we were after. That meant he knew what was going on. What was their plan if they'd captured us?

A flash in the room signals the arrival of the sleeping bag in the transfer box. Tahira goes over and gets it out.

"*Do we want to check out this skull?*" I ask Grandpop.

"Ah, I dunno, hang on, I'll ask," he replies.

I pick up the skull. It's heavy and very cold. Tahira's pulling the bag out of the box. Suddenly I can feel something in the skull. It's like a hole sucking warmth out of the room. Not just physical warmth but emotional warmth as well. Tahira looks around. The skull is starting to shine.

"Quick! In the box!" she yells pulling the sleeping bag out of the way. I run forward and dump it in, closing the lid.

"*Control, send it to the Sahara! Anywhere! Just get it out of here!*"

The box folds, but there's a rainbow light just as it vanishes and I wonder what that means.

309

"*I wonder what...*" I begin.

The door bursts open. A middle aged nurse has just discovered two kids in hoodies with their faces covered in dark cloth in her private hospital.

"Vas ist ..?" begins the nurse, and collapses. Tahira's zapped her. We glance at each other. We've wasted too much time. We run around the bed and begin bagging Von Streicher. We have it done in half a minute.

"*One bad guy to go!*" I call in.

"Hold on a second Sam, Hekator's just discovered there's a TV station on his old mountain holiday site so he can't work there. Just looking for a new LZ."

"*Where did you put the skull?*"

"In the Sahara. We can worry about it later."

There's a strange high-pitched sound in my ears.

"Quick!" yells Tahira, she yanks Von Streicher off the bed.

"What?" I ask, confused.

"*They're coming!*"

I forward roll over the bed and grab the other handle of the sleeping bag which Tahira is dragging fast to the door. Suddenly it's as if the sun is right outside the window. The light is so brilliant you think things have become translucent. Then everything begins to vibrate and jiggle where it stands. Things start banging and jumping onto the floor in the brilliant white silence. Even the bed is jiggling. You can feel the rumbling inside your own body.

Then a brilliant pink light replaces the white one. I reach the door, and have my hand to the handle, when I glance back. The room is flexing like a reflection in a window in high wind. They're bending in!

I haul the door open as the gravity starts to go. A brilliant light splits in space inside the room behind us. Tahira's floating, but she isn't finished yet. She does something to her antigravity and shoots out the door jerking Von Streicher in his bag after her. As I work around the door I can see two Grays in the brilliance, their dark black eyes fixed on me. Their bending isn't complete yet and the bridge isn't finished. I give them a one fingered salute and shoot through the door pulling it closed after me. Tahira has the bag and has got a long way back toward the stairwell we arrived in. She's using her antigravity by jumping in the air and pulling Von Streicher's tall shape by the bag handles after her. I can see the Grays are through back in Von Streicher's room and heading for the door behind me. I have to cover Tahira's escape!

"HILFE! HILFE! FUER!" I yell loudly in the silent hospital corridor.

Then run the opposite way from Tahira around the bend of the building and blend in. I hear the scream of the other duty nurse as she comes out into the corridor to find two dark eyed aliens in brilliant light coming out of one of the rooms. That's all the distraction I need. While they stun the nurse I run back at them around the corner, almost invisible blending in against the wall, and zap them.

I see them go rigid as I pump a charge into them but they're insulated and I know it's not enough. I just feel angry. I dash forward as they turn and catch them before they can do a thing. I smash into their chests with my knees knocking them hard back against the wall. They're taller than me, but very light and their oversized heads hit the wall hard.

I follow up with another charge from my suit. Then I just lay into them.

"Get-the-f____-off-our-planet!" I tell them, each word ending with a punch or kick. I'm fighting for my life and I know these have to count. Finally I punch them in their thin throats, grab them and smash their heads together along with another buzz of electricity. That's it. They crumple, unconscious, or dead. I don't have time to find out which. I turn to follow Tahira down the corridor but she's coming back!

"*The Scouts have the stairwell covered. They'll blast us if we go out there.*"

"*What about the lift?*" I ask her.

"*It's dead.*"

"*There'll be more where this lot came from. What do we do?*" I ask her.

We look around. There's a laundry cart between us. The wall panel has handles in it.

"*It's a laundry chute, quick, help me!*" Tahira says.

We grab Von Streicher and drag him to the wall panel. The panel opens up on a deep, dark hole. We hesitate.

"It's good guys, go!" Grandpop yells, slightly distorted, in our ears.

I look at Tahira.

"*Is this a good thing?*" I ask, referring to our argument about 'ladies first'.

"*Yes, it is,*" she says certainly, climbing in. She gets into the edge of the well. Pressing her back against the far wall and using her legs to hold herself in place.

"*Give me his feet.*"

I pick Von Streicher up by the feet and feed them through to her. Then I go around behind his shoulders as she slowly edges

herself down the well. There's a brilliant flash on the stairwell.
"Ah ... we'll have company in five seconds," I warn.

Tahira drops down the chute into the blackness, out of sight and Von Streicher follows. The doors to the stairwell burst open in a blaze of light as four obviously armed and angry Grays rush in, just as I dive headfirst down the hole. There's a whoosh behind me.

There's a bang and bits of burning stuff falls with me. It's a one second fall. Ten meters. The antigravity kicks in to slow me down a little but I still land on Von Streicher. Above a ball of flame billows into the top of the chute, crawling down the wooden lining. Tahira's on her feet outside and pulling us both out. I scramble to jump out. We grab the bag's handles.

"Guys, we have an LZ," Grandpop calls, sounding happy.

"Sweet!" I say.

"Bending in three, two, one." says Control. And we're out of there.

[+]

Time slows down. The colour drains from everything. My whole field of view folds up and distorts. I fall back, unable to move; fall and spin, and then I stop falling back and fall forward. There's brilliant light all around me. Brilliant light and presences. My mother and my Grandmother, and they fade. We flash onto an icy plateau in driving sleet. Hekator's waiting, glowing red which makes him look a bit devilish. He crunches through the snow to us, then bends over Von Streicher in his bag. Flecks of snow start landing on the bag and they don't melt as they do on Hekator. Hekator places his hand on Von Streicher's shape and closes his eyes. Then he opens them with surprise.

"No booby traps. Nothing! He was expecting to win. I should have some useful information in ten minutes or so. You two may as well return to Hastings."

So we leave wherever it is, and fold back to Hasting's cabinets.

[+]

Grandpop and the other adults are waiting around the desk. As we go over to join them they surprise us with cheering and clapping. There's a big sign on Grandpop's transparent screen which reads "Get the f__ off our planet!" with a slo-mo video of me punching out the Grays. Everyone's smiling, telling us we'd done well and high-fiving us.

"Where are the others?" I finally get to ask.

"We're going to have a go at Virion while no-one is defending it," Grandpop tells us, "To prove their plot we will need evidence and they are the best people to get it from. Once we have proof that Virion is plotting a plague we can pass it on to the Belgian Government and reverse the CIA warning. They might even close them down. It'll bring them under tighter Government control anyway."

"What if the Government does nothing? Rocelli said they are everywhere."

"Then we threaten to tell the media. They'll have to do something then."

It's true. They hate to be in public view. They're sort of like spiders, hiding in dark places sucking the life out people who have secrets.

"But Virion works 24/7 how can we sneak in?"

"We won't be sneaking, we'll be speeding. G-T-F, off our planet! You said it Sam! They wanted to raise the stakes, so we're raising. Let's see who blinks first," Grandpop grins.

He's enjoying this. He looks relaxed and happy, as if he could think of nothing better than to have a go punching out a few aliens himself. Even the other adults seem to have stopped worrying about us and do some damage back. I'm surprised at the change of mood.

Pretty soon the others are back and we all go up to the briefing room to go over the tactical plan. Grandpop and Control are in charge.

"OK," Grandpop begins, "so this is a coordinated counter-attack. Ashanti will attack CIA headquarters in Langley where we expect to meet Barbarossa. But while they distract the CIA we will counter-attack Virion. Most of the Bruderschaft seem to have gone. We suspect they've spread out to begin their bioweapon attack. Ashanti has already started distributing Hekator's counter-virus to the airport aircon systems. That should neutralise the Brudershaft attack. When we have some evidence we will have to find anyone exposed to the disease and treat them. But that's later on."

"Right, so we start by cutting the Virion factory telecomms fibre. The worm we have in place has been activated to do that and should be ready in ten minutes. As soon as we do that they will know we're coming, so the watchwords of this attack are 'speed, speed, and more speed'. We move top speed all the time! Got it? Anyone in the way? Zap them? Use ultrasound and infrasound. We still have smoke bombs and we'll use them too."

"We know the layout of the Virion factory because of the worm in there. After our encounter with Barbarossa we daren't send Control back. It doesn't matter much because the building hasn't changed and we have 3D models of the whole place as you can see here."

A hologram of the factory appeared in thin air. The display rotates and zooms as Grandpop speaks.

"There are two entrances. You'll notice it's foggy again tonight. Fog makes any sound seem louder. OK, the front door is here, and the dispatch centre, here. The dispatch centre is working at the moment, and there are four storemen and a security guard in it. Trucks are coming and going so there will be a truck driver. That's six people. I want to hear you have six down. None left standing. Sam and Tahira that's you."

"While they are doing that, Ash and Scott dash past into manufacturing, here. Your key cards will get you through so long as you are quick. From manufacturing you are headed for the lab. It's a class three containment facility. Airlocks, overpressure, you name it. If you run into access problems you will have those mini-blackhole implosion marble thingies we used to get Nathan. I'll show you how they work in a minute. Right, meantime, Tarik and Cam? You are going through the front door, here. Your target is the third floor security centre. There's two night watchmen there. Me, Bernard, Nguyen and Sue will follow you up. Your objective is to get into the security system, take out the watch quick as you can, and turn off all the security cameras. The idea is you do this while Sam and Tahira are zapping people and Scott and Ash are busting in. Then we erase everything to do with our visit."

"Sam and Tahira once you have the despatch area secured you will leapfrog Ash and Scott and head for the offices on the third floor to rendezvous with Me, Nguyen, Bernard and Sue. Our task is shut down anything dangerous to the search teams. The search teams are everyone we can spare to go through the office looking for evidence. When the office is clear the adult security team go back outside to watch the perimeter. Sam and Tahira stay upstairs to make sure the Search team can escape."

"Cam and Tarik when you have erased the video move to the server room. Katya will join you there to crack their system. We don't think all the important stuff will be on the main server but we need to check. When Katya is safely set up join Ash and Scott to search the lab for the master samples of the two diseases. They'll be in glass containers somewhere hidden."

"The search team is Mitra, Soraya, Patricia, Liz, and Zoe. You will search the third floor offices of the infiltrators for travel plans, safes, fridges, anything that can be used to connect Virion to this outbreak. We assume they will be secretive so mistrust everything. You will only have about five to ten minutes. "

"The perimeter team plus Deidre, Gennady, Ken, Rewa and Asal working with Control here will watch the skies for anything hostile. When they come. And they will come. We retreat immediately. The perimeter team retreats to the lab. Katya you go join the search team. If the search team has to move we retreat to the lab."

Grandpop stops and looks up at us. It's been a lot to take in.

"OK. Everyone find the others you are working with and go over what you understood you are doing. Then find a group you will interact with and tell them what you will do. If you find a disagreement talk it over. If you can't work it out, come to me. OK? Go! Fast! Go!"

I find Tahira.

"So we take out the workers in dispatch," I tell her.

"Counting six. Zhen go upstairs, meet up wiz ze uzzers and clear ze floor," she takes over.

"And help til its time to go," I finish.

"Ez easy," Tahira shrugs.

"Yep, let's find Grandpop's team," I say.

So we find them and Grandpop gives us a challenge, "Cat's" and response, "Away." There's a little milling around as Control appears and talks to Grandpop. Then Grandpop yells out again.

"OK kids, into a briefing room, go through the 3D sim, then down to the cabinets. Adults come and get your gear. The worm will be cutting through in five minutes. Lets go! Go! GO!"

Me and Tahira run out and find a briefing theatre. Control plays us through a quick sim in the despatch area with Ashley and Scott flying through very fast, then it was through the doors, up the stairwell, jumping up to the doors at the top, then out, checking the offices, challenge: "Cat's," response: "Away". All done.

"Two minutes to go, Ashanti has started her attack," Control tells us.

We run out, throw ourselves down the poles and arrive at the bottom with ninety seconds to go. We all glance at each other, thinking about what we have to do. I don't know why he did it but Tarik shook my hand and hugged me quickly, then we all hugged and shook or high-fived, and went to our cabinets. Thirty seconds to go.

I feel butterflies about this. We're taking a huge risk, charging into the heart of the enemy, even though we knew most of them weren't there. Where's Hathaway? There's always a chance we're bending into another ambush. I try to control my breath. At ten seconds, I think that I really need a drink: my mouth is parched. Five. My heart is pounding, muscles tense. Three, two, one.

[+]

Time seems to slow down, then colour drains out of everything.

My whole field of view folds up and distorts and I have to close my eyes. I'm falling back, unable to move, falling and spinning, and then I stop falling back and start falling forward. There's brilliant light all around me. Brilliant light and presences. My mother and my Grandmother. Dozens of people surround me, and slowly they fade. I open my eyes.

CHAPTER EIGHTY SIX: PETARD

The light in the dispatch centre spills out onto the wide tarmac in front of us as the warm surveillance radar sweeps over us. The fog magnifies the slightest sounds from the dispatch bay. Instantly we're running forward on soft feet, loosening our wings, ignoring the camera above the doorway. I still have a nervous feeling in my stomach, but my legs keep moving under me almost as if they aren't mine.

In this dispatch area there's room for four large trucks to park side by side and five deep. At the moment there's only one truck and a forklift under the dim yellow light, with blue-overalled men moving large pallets about fifty meters away.

I'd silently run for two seconds covering twenty meters toward the spill of light in front of the building when my suit told me my wings were hard and good to go. I jump and the antigravity and wings pick me up and we shoot inside the dispatch centre at eight meters above the ground, Tahira on my right. I fly right over the truck and have two storemen down in two seconds. Tahira veers right after the others among the plastic wrapped stacks as I circle back letting Ashley and Scott shoot past me. The truck driver is in his cab. I'd seen his shocked face below me as I'd flown over. Now I fly back up to his right door and yank it open as he's trying to scramble along the seat to get out the other side. He glances at my blacked out face, fear in his eyes and I amnesia him, then while he's stunned I zap him so that he falls against the passenger door.

"*Three*," I call.

"*Two, the last one is dodging*," Tahira replies, annoyed.

"*Through manufacturing*," Scott calls,

I fly up to help Tahira. Her guy is climbing in amongst the boxes but he hasn't a chance.

"*Three*," Tahira calls.

"*That's six. Six down in dispatch, moving on*," I call.

"*Two down. We have security clear*," Cam calls.

"*Lab opened*," Ashley calls.

We're twenty seconds into the mission and all is going to plan. But now is the bit that bothers me. Clearing the offices. Like Ash and Scott with the lab we have no idea who, or what, is inside.

"God! you kids are fast," Sue pants. They're running up the front stairs after Tarik and Cam.

Me and Tahira fly to the door. Tahira's card opens the stairwell and we fly up the twisting three storey spiral in the dark in under five seconds. The offices we're looking for are those of Deiter Huuygens, Jerome Wouters, Fabrice De Smet and Pascal Renard. They're the biobots. But the main one is Paul Maartens, the grumpy old manufacturing manager and the only infiltrator. As they're all in different departments we expect them to be spread out over the large floor. The stairs we've come up are normally the fire escape. We reach the office floor door. We know most of the floor is to our left but there's another fifty meters of office space over the dispatch bay to our right. Is anyone inside working late on some lethal private project? We give the door a shove. It opens onto a silent office with a deafening click. In adaptive camouflage we slip out onto the floor and hide behind partitions, Tahira facing left, me right. The main office is open plan and stretches the whole length of the long building. All around the floor are glass boxes containing either meeting rooms or offices. The windows stretch floor to ceiling all the way around but it's dark outside as well as in.

"We've entered the top floor office," Tahira reports.

"Any signs of anyone?" Grandpop pants.

For ten long seconds we stand there searching with our ears, heat vision and psychic senses until it's clear there's no-one up here except us.

"No-one," Tahira whispers.

I start walking forward.

"We're looking for the target's offices," I say.

"OK, we won't bother coming up. We'll go outside and watch the perimeter instead," Grandpop says.

We walked around the office in the dark, using our senses to read the desks of those working there; seeking out the absence of a soul which marks a biobot. It takes two minutes to turn on the lights, find the biobot offices and unlock them. Then we have to bend back to Hastings and pick up the searchers in sleeping bags to bring them in. Everyone moves fast. We're just getting started when Hekator calls in.

"I've just got some information out of Von Streicher. Virion Belgium in La Louviere developed Release Candidates 21 and 22 and did the manufacturing. But it was sent to Virion Austria at Sankt Leonhart south west of Salzberg for test and dispatch. The airport attack may be wrong too. I haven't got it all out of him yet but there's something about a vaccine contract."

"Thanks Hekator we'll follow up. How is Ashanti doing against

Barbarossa?" Grandpop asks.

"Because Ashanti can disconnect this is just skirmishing.
They're basically just trading insults at the moment."

That explains why they haven't bothered to defend this factory
we're searching in La Louviere. This isn't where they're working
from anymore. Of course that doesn't mean they might not
counterattack us here. I watch the office searchers. Liz and Zoe
are giving Paul Maarten's office a very thorough going over. But
all me and Tahira have to do is know where everyone is in case
we have to escape.

And it turns out the search doesn't last long. Within minutes we
have our first warning.

"Light in sky!" warns Mr Trân.

"One here too," Bernard says.

Given our last attack was in Austria they didn't have far to
fly. Barbarossa's probably curious why Virion, at La Louvire,
Belgium dropped off his network while he swapped insults with
Ashanti over the CIA systems.

"Inside quick everyone! Drop everything! Let's go! Sleeping bags
first." Grandpop warns.

Tahira rounds up her grandmother and mother, while I get
Aunty Liz and Zoe. Aunty Liz has a big pile of papers she hadn't
gone through from Paul Maarten's office.

"He won't miss them, he's in Japan," she points out when I
object.

I shrug and she climbs into her bag still clutching everything.
We bend out leaving Patricia. The cabinets flash, rain and blew
and we were back in Hastings. Tahira leaves her mother and
grandmother and bends back for Patricia. I help Zoe and Aunty
Liz out of their bags and carry their papers over to the seats to

continue checking. I join the others gathered around the screen. There are now three eerie, silent lights in the fog about 500 meters above and a kilometer from Virion, La Louviere. The crews seem to be waiting for instructions. I hope the crew in one of them is feeling just a little scared of being beaten up again. Meanwhile Grandpop, Sue, Mr Trân and Bernard are coming out of the Cabinets. They take over the desk so the others and Dr Morozov can go through Virion's papers and data files looking for evidence. Suddenly the lights zip straight up into the foggy night out of sight.

"What now?" Grandpop asked Dr P.

We're just wondering if we should go back to the factory to continue our search when blue flashing lights appear in the fog.

"The Belgian police are on their way everyone," Mrs Jones says.

Suddenly a nasty thought occurs to me.

"We erased the security system recorders didn't we?" I ask.

"Of course," Dr Morozov says gruffly.

"Did anyone notice any *other* cameras?" I ask.

Everyone's looking at me, nervously, trying to remember. Then Sue groans and sits down.

"*Son-of-a-bitch!*" Patricia swears, getting it.

Grandpop's looking around.

"Uh ... you think there are other cameras ... which ... oh!" he says.

If there were pinhole cameras hidden in the office and lab we had just done the opposite of what we had intended! We had meant to prove Virion was responsible for releasing the viruses but now we *had* raided Virion and they'd have the proof! All they had to do was doctor any timestamp on the pictures! Now the CIA could show anyone who wanted proof, pictures of the very people they had warned the world had raided a secure bioweapons lab, actually raiding it!

The line of blue lit cars is getting closer.

"*I think we've found the samples,*" Ash calls in happily.

"I'll send you a box," Grandpop replies.

"If is pictures changes little," Dr Prosperov says suddenly, thinking.

That's good news, if he's right. He explains.

"Main issue is delivery of infection. Is no connection to us. We need to search data for details of delivery to Austria. Crucial question is what is delivered where and by who. This is only way to prevent pandemic."

"Tarik, Cam, Ashley and Scott. The police have arrived. It might be advisable to return now," Mrs Jones tells them.

"*Coming,*" Ashley says.

Immediately the cabinets begin to flash and crackle.

"*Just a moment, we're bringing a hard drive,*" says Tarik who's pulling a lab computer to pieces.

"I think I've got something here!" Aunty Liz says from the floor behind the Control screen.

Everyone gathers around. It's a paper notepad. It's full of complex symbols and signs. She hands it to Sue who gives it to Dr P. He shrugs and showed it to Control. Now we're all going through Paul Maarten's stuff looking for notes and stuff in the margins as Scott and Ash come out of the cabinets.

"Where's the samples?" I ask them.

"Hekator wanted them," Scott explains.

It made sense. We didn't have any genetics ability or equipment. As we go through his papers we discover Paul Maartens likes writing and doodling quite a lot. One doodle is a perfume bottle.

There are a whole lot of complex chemical equations written at speed in the margin. It looks like the idea is to use a perfume to put viruses in droplets in the air.

A few minutes later Tarik and Cam return. They come in and put the drives they've collected in the blue gel for Control to read them. Then we all gather around and start yakking while we wait for Control to do the analysis. Five minutes later the holograms of Ashanti, Control, Hekator and Hekati had returned.

"Um ... I have some very bad news," Hekator starts looking a bit pale.

"The Bruderschaft plan is already underway. The plan is simple. They are infecting flu vaccine with live, full strength viruses. They won't use airports or aircrew immediately. They want to have strong rates of infection established early. They have a scheme to bypass official quality controls by adding full strength 21 and 22 to the vaccine. They then organise a 'labelling mistake' so that the vaccine is shipped as tested for human use. For some reason they have targeted eastern Europe and Russia again. You may find the attack plan in the information you have collected but the shipment information is held in Austria. That means that the only way to prevent this attack is to raid their centre there which is almost certainly waiting for it."

There's a worried silence.

Everyone's looking at everyone else. I don't mind admitting I'm scared. There are only twenty people in the world who know of this plot and are in a position to stop billions of deaths – and that's us. And who are we? Eight families, two aliens, a computer and one spacecraft.

Von Streicher had been armed and protected. Virion, La Louviere was probably a trap to back up the CIA warning about us they had already issued. We've been led by the nose to attack exactly what they were expecting us to attack. They've been one step ahead of us the whole way.

I don't want to go up against a heap of Bruderschaft and risk a repeat of Armageddon. It's a thin sickle moon tonight there's no chance of being rescued by Queen Morganne this time.

But we're running out of time and choices. If we don't attack we'll get the blame anyway. If there's video from Virion, La Louviere we could all end up on TV being called bioterrorists as the disease starts to kill people. If we don't try to stop them we would lose anyway.

"Control, let's see a map of the Virion plant in Austria," Grandpop says gruffly.

A wide view of Salzburg comes up on the screen. A big white dot marks Virion, Sankt Leonhard at the bottom of a mountain, not too far from the airport.

"That's near the area where Gunter's family are from," Mrs Jones says.

"Might pay to get him and Mariko back," Grandpop comments.

"I'll go," says Cam.

She slips away to the cabinet. Everyone's looking at the map as Grandpop zooms in on the Virion factory and its area. It's been built in a field near the small village. The village seems to be focused on the mountain with a cable-car that goes to the top. The factory is quite large with an office block, a manufacturing block and what looks like a separate laboratory. There are car parks for about three hundred and security fences around the whole place.

The local time is five in the morning. Sunrise isn't for another two hours. There's mist and the air temperature is cool. Street lights stretch out in all directions while the whole Virion factory is lit up. There are cars in the parks. They have a night shift working, just like the smaller plant in Belgium.

"What is low earth orbit view?" Dr P asks.

A window appears on the screen zooming out rapidly from the ground. There's high cloud which becomes a carpet far below as the view rises into space where the curve of the Earth is more obvious. As we zoom out to three hundred kilometers we pass a gray cylinder hanging in space. The Administration Survey craft drops below from sight as Control's pinhole camera keeps rising. Then at one thousand kilometers he turns the pinhole around. All we can see is a zillion stars.

For a second or so the screen shows nothing but stars, and we wonder what Control's doing. Then a green circle appears. The image adjusts, shifts and we can see a large halo around some stars. There's a flicker and a still image of a black screen. Slowly the black adjusts to a grainy image of a featureless gray triangle. Then a scale in blue shows the triangle is a kilometer long. The display changes again to show lines from the Virion plant to the Surveyor to the Carrier. Basically the Carrier could have saucers and fighters on the scene in five minutes or less.

They're waiting for us.

Everyone starts talking at once. Nobody's very keen to walk into an ambush. While everyone's arguing a truck drives out of the Virion, Sankt Leonard factory but instead of turning left towards Salzburg it turns right toward Germany. This is odd because the road to Germany is more scenic than the motorway. Slowly it starts to attract everyone's attention.

"That *is* unexpected," Hekator admits.

While we're watching and chatting the truck crosses the unmanned German border along a steep pine filled valley in fog. It drives for a kilometer then turns off; up the steep drive on a small hillock perched on the side of the mountain's massive sides. The truck climbs this pine lined driveway into a small castle, hidden among pine forest.

The castle's over a small bridge with a gate under two large towers. The truck drives through the gate into a courtyard. All the talk around the control desk has been all but silenced by this strange visit.

Watching from above we see the truck halt and immediately become surrounded by figures in black who pull aside the curtain sides.

Then a forklift appears from a gate from an inner courtyard inside the outer courtyard. It speeds up to the side of the truck and lifts off a pallet, followed by a second forklift which lifts off a second pallet. They take them inside the building for a while. Then they reappear with pallets which they quickly load onto the truck. The side curtains are replaced, then the truck drives back out of the first courtyard and heads back toward Austria.

Suddenly a jump cabinet begins to crackle as Cam brings Gunter and Mariko in. Control orbits around the castle with high magnification.

The castle is about two storeys tall, light yellow among the pines, with tiny slit windows on the outside of the second storey and another storey in the red sloping roof on top. Inside there are balconies around the courtyards. On the corners there are towers an extra storey high. On one side it's built hard up against a very steep forested slope of the mountain. Although the castle's painted in light colours, the dark pine trees around it, the lack of windows, the fog and the sickle moon makes it look very mean and scary.

I find myself standing next to the others. We're talking about whether it would be possible to intercept a truck to make its trip up the road more apparent to Austrian authorities who might wonder why they are taking vaccine into a park in Germany.

The road's fairly straight and set in pine forest. There are plenty of places we could pop up, crash the truck and vanish. We feel pretty sure we could be gone before the carrier even launched its fighters. It would be like Finland but we would simply bend into the cab and zap the driver, then stop the truck.

In the background the adults are bringing Gunter and Mariko up to speed. Mariko's talking to people and moving around trying to get her pregnant tummy comfortable again by exercising and stretching while Gunter sits listening to what Grandpop and the others are telling him. He's nodding and listening. Finally he gets up and comes over to the screen and asks Control to zoom out.

"Vat you haf told me iz very vorrying," he tells us.

"First, zis area here," he points to left side of the display, "is Berechtesgarten vich vas Hitler's holiday park. Durink ze Var zere vas talk zat zer nazis ver planning to build a final defense in zese mountains. Zey never did, but zer American spymaster Allen Dulles who vas behind getting Nazi scientists to ze United States encouraged zer American forces to invade it razzer zen drive on Berlin[†]."

"Zis big mountain here, is der Untersberg. I haf climbed it many times and it iz very beautiful. But it iz a special mountain because it iz zer place where zer legendary King of zer Germans, Frederick Barbarossa, sleeps in zer caves underneath."

Gunter knew what he's saying is getting pretty eerie.

"Zer legend says he vill wake at zer end of zer vorld to fight ze last battle. So ven you tell me zis Cybermind iz called Barbarossa I haf to think he vill be here somewhere. Der Untersberg iz full of caves, and an underground zalt mine zat you can tour, but no-von has explored it fully[†]. Zere has been talk of turning ze old zalt mine into a computer zerver zenter because iz good access to hydro power and cooling like ze vuns in Norvay."

We all look at the map. After what Gunter has said we realise we aren't looking at a little castle, that looks like Renwick did. We're looking at evil central.

"Why is Du Croix and the Service covering this?" Sue asks suddenly.

It's a question which is bothering all of us. Last year in Elan the Administration had come down hard on the Bruderschaft for intervening on Earth, specifically through introducing HIV/Aids. Now the Service carrier is hanging around overhead covering mass murder. Do the Administration know or are *they* being deceived? Are *we* being deceived and there is no emergency? Did Du Croix have a plan to stop the Bruderschaft? It was all getting too complicated.

"Probably to catch us," Ken suggests.

"Are we *that* important?" Patricia asks.

That starts a lot of discussion. Hekator's avatar is frozen (which happens when he's doing something else) but suddenly comes back to life.

"I have some information from the Virion computer files," he announces.

"Virion, La Louviere in Belgium manufactured 250kg of viral candidates 21 and 22. Enough to contaminate vaccines for most of the world. The truck which just left is headed for Poland.

Shipments to Czech Republic, Slovakia, Slovenia, and Hungary have already been dispatched. The rest will be sent every four hours for the rest of the week. Von Streicher believes that those in charge of distributing the contaminated material have either been hypnotised, blackmailed, paid off, or replaced by a Bruderschaft agent. The test sample provided with the shipment isn't contaminated, of course, and there are instructions to use it rather than take a random sample from the shipment. In ten days the contaminated flu vaccine delivery for the entire planet will be complete. All of it contaminated with 21 and 22 here."

"What is suggestion?" asks Dr Prosperov.

"Strictly speaking a genocidal biological attack on Earth is not our problem, it's yours," Hekator says. We all look at each other. It's true. It's our planet, not Hekator's. But that makes us worry we're on our own.

"I am authorised to assist you but not to engage directly with *our* enemies on Earth unless it is to prevent them gaining access to our technology or Fae's location."

Hekator can tell we aren't impressed much by this.

"The Ring was quite specific about that, so I cannot attack this base at all. *But...* " he smiles, "they didn't say I can't escape our enemies not on Earth," he grins.

"So Ashanti can distract the Carrier which is really only interested in chasing us anyway. You Earthlings are just their means to finding Fae. If we give the Center a more direct way to find us they will pursue us rather than you. And Ashanti can easily elude one carrier."

That makes us feel a little better. We wouldn't have to fight a fleet of UFOs as well as a castle full of infiltrators.

"But zese Bruderschaft, zey are zo much more powerful zan us.

We cannot fight zem," Tahira points out.

That's true. It was one thing to beat Von Streicher in his hospital bed after a car crash but up against any number of fit Bruderschaft we would be toast.

"I think I can help you with that," Hekator replies.

"The Iyrin use mind control powers to dominate Earthlings. At the moment they are stronger than you are because our enhancement programme for you has only been running for a short time, but in time you will be as powerful or perhaps even more so than they are."

"So to compensate you will need weapons. I will therefore authorise the distribution of our standard personal plasma weapon. These can be used against multiple targets simultaneously and have a range out to about a kilometer. It will mean you have to get them before they get you though, so you will have to be fast."

"May I also suggest that you may wish to supplement your agents with as many of your fit adults as you can spare. Numbers always help to reduce the enemy's concentration and I suspect the children alone would be outnumbered. If you can improve your odds the chances of success will be greatly increased. I need to make a few arrangements. Let's talk about a tactical plan in ten minutes," he says and vanishes.

There's silence.

"Right!" Grandpop says very loudly," We are *not* going to rush into *this* like idiots."

It's a relief to hear him being assertive. We'd all been looking at each other and thinking about all the other disasters rushing in at Hekator's suggestion had created. Everyone immediately turns to Grandpop's lead.

"First, we tip off authorities where delivery has already been made to test the contaminated vaccine deliveries properly. Mitra and Gunter could you work with Control on that? At the same time Liz, Patricia and Soraya could you sort through the evidence we have collected with Control and organise it for whoever looks after these things."

"I need two kids to stop that truck. I suggest Sam and Tahira. Knock out and remove the driver, crash the truck, put the driver back. Be quick, they're watching. The rest of you, I want to break into a munitions store in Bulgaria I've been scoping out and steal some 93mm RPO rocket launchers. They're pretty horrible but then so is biological warfare and if we are going to defend the world from mass murder by attacking a castle with half a dozen fourteen-year-old kids we are *not* going to be playing fair with these bastards."

"I ruv it when he talks dirty," Mariko observed quietly.

Everyone grins.

"Everyone agree?" Grandpop asks.

"Perhaps, have suggestion but need to examine. Is best agents start now and discuss later," Dr P says.

"OK, guys off to the Cabinets. Sam and Tahira you'll be first. Your job is the most straightforward you may want to share a cabinet because you'll be cramped."

We shrug at each other and find a cabinet. Control projects the dark insides of the target truck cab on the walls.

The driver's a big, youngish man; pale skinned with light brown hair and a full beard. He has sad looking brown eyes and red lips. We wait for him to get onto a separated stretch of highway where there isn't much traffic. There's light rain which the wipers clear every five seconds. Then we bend.

[+]

The flash of our appearing on his immediate right makes the driver swerve left into the concrete median barrier. The truck rides up the barrier, so the driver swerves back to the right. For a moment the truck balances on its wheels on the side, threatening to tip, and then it does. We're gone. We flash home to the cabinets which spit electricity, rain, and blow.

[+]

For a moment inside the cabinet we have no idea what's happened in Austria but when the shower stops the inside of the cab became visible again on the cabinet walls. The truck's tipped over on its right side and skidded to a stop. I'm a bit worried about the driver. He's hit his head on the side, and there's some blood. At first he looks unconscious. But just as we were about to bend back he came to, and started climbing out.

"We don't need to do anything do we?" I ask Tahira.

"No," Tahira agrees.

As we step out from the cabinet the adults high-five us. On the screen we can see the driver standing next to his wrecked truck talking on his cell. The cabinets start flashing again and the other four come out dragging carry bags. Everyone seems a bit nervous about these boxes, but Grandpop goes over excitedly. Me and Tahira follow to see what the others have got.

Each bag contains four metal tubes. Each tube has a shoulder strap.

"What are they?" I ask Grandpop as he lays the tubes out on the floor.

"One shot rockets with a thermobaric warhead. They produce a fuel-air explosive which will blow that castle apart. The idea is you bend dive in, and fire them first so they can't recover from the shock."

That seems really, really rugged, but I have to admit that if anyone was going to be blown apart I would rather it was them and not me.

"Anyway," says Grandpop straightening out,

"I want Hekator to realise we aren't going to mess around here. We strike quickly and very, very hard," he says grimly.

The parents are looking a bit scared now that the rockets are in our base. I think we're all starting to realise this isn't protecting other kids any more. This is combat and Grandpop is really the only soldier present. Hekator flashes onto the floor.

"Hi ... what are those?" Hekator asks, changing his mind and pointing at the tubes.

"Rockets," Grandpop says.

"Oh! What sort of rockets?"

"Thermobaric ones."

"What for?"

"Destroying the castle."

"Oh ... I see ... ah ... I see your logic. There's just one problem. We've done an old fashioned variable-frequency sonargram of the castle and there's no-one inside it. The castle is just a gateway to a cave system. Behind the inner courtyard the wall against the hill leads into a cave which goes into the mountain at least two hundred meters. We followed up with ground sonar and radar which mapped the cave structures up to a kilometer inside the mountain but the presence of an underground lake and water system plus active interference from inside made it impossible to get a clear picture of what exactly is in there."

"So we can smash the castle but it won't make any difference?" Grandpop checks.

"No, I'm afraid not," he confirms.

"Damn," Grandpop growls, thinking about it. He'd been hoping to simply blow the enemy to bits so that it would be game over before we became vulnerable.

"Can't we just seal the exit," Ken suggests, "that would delay things a bit."

"If it iz ze only exit," Gunter points out, "Ze cave system inside der Untersberg has not been fully mapped. It iz perfectly possible zat zere are uzzer buildings connected to zis one."

"I'm afraid the only way you can be sure you can limit the danger from the Bruderschaft is to go in there and destroy all their stock of the bioweapon. Then destroy the exits. I can give you technical support and advice but I can't defend Earth for you," Hekator says.

There's a large flash and Hekati appears with a large shiny black box next to Grandpop's rocket launchers.

"We've brought some tools," Hekator calls turning to the box as it opens. We can't help ourselves. This is too cool. We have to go and look. Our parents follow behind with less enthusiasm.

Hekati turns with a jewelled headband in a leaf pattern which she puts on Ashley's head. Instantly the jewels begin to sparkle yellow, pink, blue and green. Then they flash once and turn a soft glowing pink. The other two girls immediately squealed and want theirs. They put theirs on with eyes wide before they start giggling.

Us guys weren't quite so keen on this look. But the colours Hekati hands us out aren't quite so frilly, so we put them on.

At first it feels kind of weird. Like a wave of confusion going through your whole body but it quickly changed so you felt like suddenly being super-focused.

"Stroke each other's hair," Hekati says – and she doesn't mean by touching it.

I focus on Scott and he jumps, turning around to look at me. Then I jump when Tarik does it to me. It feels freaky. Like someone was touching you, but they aren't there. It isn't anything like as powerful as Rocelli or Von Streicher but we can definitely do it.

"OK, now here's the main tool," Hekati says and lifts out a metallic bar with a big, dark blue jewel in the end, held in place by four pipes that bend around the jewel to form a crown. We've seen these things before. Queen Morganne had one when she came looking for Tabika, and again at Armageddon but I'd never thought I'd be given one. I thought only fairy queens used sceptres.

"*How gay* is *that*?" Tarik asks silently. I agree.

Hekator laughs. He finds our impression of these things quite funny.

"I suppose you find the rocket launchers more manly, boys?" he says.

"Yeah," we nod truthfully.

Smiling at each other, Hekati and Hekator pick up a sceptre each. Then they both fold away and vanish. A transparent screen appears in mid air between us and our parents. It shows Hekati and Hekator in a forest that looks a bit like Siberia.

The Fae check each other, then turn back-to-back. Our view widens. The dark blue jewel in both their outstretched sceptres goes brilliant blue-white and a huge continuous bolt of white-light, crackling with lightning and distorting the air with heat haze, bursts out of the weapons and smashes down trees in flames. The pair turn about each other slicing down the forest at waist height, pouring out energy. Within eight seconds they've turned and the view switches to above them. They're standing in a perfectly round clearing of burning forest about one hundred meters across. Blackened stumps and the felled tops of trees burn with thick white smoke. Then they fold away and the screen vanishes.

With a flash they're back, smelling of wood smoke.

"Wow," Grandpop and a few of the others say, impressed.

"Just call me Gaylord," Scotty grins as he accepts the sceptre from Hekator.

The sceptres turn out to be top heavy and not exactly light. But once I take the handle from Hekator it seems to be glued to my right hand. I can't let go of it.

"They almost look like Fae trainees," Hekati says of us admiringly, to her brother. He nods but then reaches into the box they brought.

"A few more tools," he tells us.

He takes out what looks like a small book. He opens it. Inside are three of the large insects we had used to trace Jeanne. They have big wings and wicked looking stingers.

"Wasps. They're good for reconnaissance and injections. They have thermal vision. They have a very dangerous poison loaded but they are backup weapons and very easily destroyed. They are best for moving fast in and out."

"And bombs," Hekati adds.

She opens a case. They look just like marbles divided into different coloured compartments.

"The red ones explode into fire so be careful with them. The black ones, you've used already. They make tiny black holes which collapse very quickly taking out doors. The yellow ones make a clear poisonous gas which is very deadly for five minutes and then breaks down. The clear ones suck the energy out of liquids to freeze them quite quickly. The white ones make a lot of light for about ten minutes. The brown ones make a dense smelly smoke and a loud noise to cover your escape. The blue ones turn into ball lightning and fly or roll at your command. They all have to be thrown by whip or hand to arm themselves, and they're triggered by your headbands. They won't go off within 25 meters of any of you. I suggest you put different ones in different pockets so you don't mix them up."

So we share out the marbles among us and the adults, which takes a few minutes. We're starting to feel a bit confident.

"I have more weapons for the adults. These wands are half kilowatt electro-lasers," he says pulling out a case with a dozen 400 millimeter long black tubes with a silver tip.

"They're very simple," he says taking one out. "Shine the blue aiming dot on the target. The tighter you squeeze the stronger the power. Be careful, they can be lethal to two hundred meters. The beam is continuous so you can use it like a long spear. If you tap anything with the silver end it will also get shocked. Same principle applies, the tighter the grip the stronger the power. We also have wristbands to work with the bombs."

"There is, however, one very big problem with all of this. The Iyrin use their mind powers and they outclass the children. There are however two adults here they don't outclass. One is Mrs Dee. The other is Dr Prosperov's symbiont. I would recommend considering including them in any assault. Finally as you clear tunnels don't forget if you have to withdraw Control can cover your retreat. What Control daren't do is progress ahead of you. That would risk the probe being grabbed and another battle with Barbarossa. I strongly recommend a policy of shooting immediately you suspect contact. If you hesitate you give your enemy an advantage and you may not be able to shoot afterwards."

"Well, I think we have done all we can do, and all we're allowed to do. We will go now and engage the Service Carrier and her fleet. I...well...I'd just like to say you are a credit to your species and I pray there won't be any casualties. You are wonderful people."

"You are indeed. The weaving is in the balance. But my faith is in your love, courage and determination. Good luck," Hekati adds. Then they vanish.

There's a long silence.

It's all come down to this. We're about to go into an enemy cave system to fight evil aliens who are hell bent on wiping out most of the human race. I look across at Sue. Her face is a picture of disbelief and nervousness. She isn't alone. A lot of people look the same way and they're talking quietly to their loved ones. I go over to her.

"I feel a bit stink about getting you into this Sue," I tell her.

She hugs me suddenly and strongly, looking over my shoulder. It's very strong, I hadn't realised she is so strong.

"By God I don't Sam," she says and kisses my head, "You amazing, amazing kid."

Aunty Liz comes over with Rewa. Sue releases me and she has tears in her eyes. I hug Rewa and, as I do, I notice Aunty Liz gently embraces Sue. It's not a snog. It's a hold, just like I'm holding Rewa.

"Sam?" Rewa whispers in my ear.

"Sis?"

"You'll kick their butts won't you?"

"Damn straight,"

She pulls back and looks me in the eye.

"Promise me you'll remember this."

"What?"

"Promise?"

"Okay I promise whatever it is," I say, shrugging and not wanting an argument now.

She hugs me and whispers in my ear.

"You'll make them get the fuck off our planet."

CHAP+ER EIGH+Y SEVEN: UNDER THE MOUN+AIN.

The plan of attack is pretty simple. There are three waves. Us kids are the first wave. The second wave is Dr Prosperov with Bernard, Sue, Grandpop and Mr Trân. Bernard, Sue and Mr Trân have the motorcycle suits, laser wands, bombs, guns and the some 93mm rocket launchers. The third wave is more of a medical support wave and didn't really need to come at all. It's Patricia and Gunter in motorcycle suits, Mitra and Aunty Liz in sleeping bags, and Asal and Rewa in their suits. They have laser wands and a rocket launcher but were only meant to provide a support base to treat anyone who was hurt. It wasn't really needed but the parents wanted to be able to help us kids if things got bad.

Us operatives are more worried we'll end up having to rescue them.

It takes twenty minutes to get everyone checked and sorted. We go over the partial map Hekator gave us. I feel my mouth getting dry. We'd decided to collapse any branching tunnels on the way in to avoid counter-attack. There will be one way in, and one way out.

As we talk our way grimly through the plan my nervousness gets worse and worse. I feel sick in the stomach. We all do. Mrs Jones notices and suggests a moment of prayer to clear our heads and focus or minds. She says she will say it once in Welsh, as it was written, and then in English.

Dyro Dduw dy Nawdd (Grant, O God, Thy protection);
Ag yn nawdd, nerth (And in protection, strength);
Ag yn nerth, Deall (And in strength, understanding);
Ag yn Neall, Gwybod (And in understanding, knowledge);
Ac yngwybod, gwybod y cyfiawn
(And in knowledge, the knowledge of justice);
Ag yngwybod yn cyfiawn, ei garu
(And in the knowledge of justice, the love of it);
Ag o garu, caru pob hanfod
(And in that love, the love of all existences);
Ag ymhob Hanfod, caru Duw
(And in the love of all existences, the love of God).
Duw a phob Daioni (God and all goodness).

It's a solemn prayer. It works, and I feel a little better. It makes me think of Khadiyeh. While I'm thinking about her Gunter coughs, and, a bit embarrassed, says he wants to offer a German miners' prayer because it's the language of the place, though, he admits, the prayer is a bit dumb compared to the Welsh one. He says it quickly and didn't translate it, but it did feel like a blessing from the place we were going to.

O Gott du trägst in deinen Händen
Berge, Hügel, Tal und Kluft;
O laß' uns nicht im Schachte enden,
Nicht Schaden nehmen in der Gruft. —
Wenn das Erz gleich bricht und fällt

Und die Wände gehen ein,
So laß' uns wieder hergestellt
Mit deiner Wohltat Gnadenschein. —
Reiß' nicht plötzlich ab das Leben,
Sondern zeige uns dein Heil
Und schenke uns daneben
Den schönsten Himmelsteil.
Amen.

All the time I couldn't get Khadiyeh out of mind and I begin to feel a stronger connection with her. She's rising somewhere in her sleep. But I'm interrupted by Grandpop chivvying us toward the cabinets. Then he stops, and turns around behind us. We turn to see what he's doing because he starts stamping his foot heavily.

"*Taringa whakarongo*! (Ears listening!)" he roars.

The others learned this after we first skydived together. Of course we all know Te Rauparaha's haka! We all fall into place and join in while Grandpop inspects our line.

"*Kia rite! kia rite*! (Get set! Get set!)"

"*Kia mau, hi*! (Hold fast! Hey!)"

"*Ringa ringa pakia* (Slap your hands against the thighs!)" As always the chant brings its power of hope at times of trial with it.

"*Waewae takahia kia kino nei hoki*! (Stamp the feet as hard as you can!)"

And then we're into it. Aunty Liz is crying, but out of pride, not fear. I didn't want to look at her now.

"*A Ka maté! Ka maté! Ka ora! Ka ora!*
(Death? Death? Life? Life?)"

"*Ka maté! Ka maté! Ka ora! Ka ora!*

(Death? Death? Life? Life?)"
Tenei te tangata puhuru huru (This is the hairy man)
Nana nei i tiki mai (Who fetched and
Whakawhiti te ra (made shine the Sun)
A upa ... ne! ka upa ... ne!
(One upward step! Another upward step!)
A upane kaupane whiti te ra!
(An upward step, another.. the Sun shines!!)"

As we do the actions I can't help feeling the power of our
little group, amplified by our headbands now, but focused
not by Te Wharerangi the hairy man in the original song,
or Te Rauparaha, it's author, but by another man of power
– Grandpop. He brings out the sun, making us feel strong and
hopeful again. The sick feeling in my stomach is gone, and I
don't think I'm the only one. Then he turns to us.
"Right! Go! Go Go!" he yells, clapping as we race to the cabinets.

[+]

Five seconds later we're tumbling from the dark wet night fifteen
thousand feet above the Untersberg. In the distance lightning
plays in the clouds of the mountains around us. Suddenly there's
music in our ears.
"A little German *kultur* for you," Gunter says.
We listen for a moment.
"It's the bleedin' 'Ride of the Valkyries' init," Tarik laughs.
The music has a rhythm like a horse's hooves but with electric
lightning asides from the violins. We feel like – well, what we are
– supernatural forces of revenge.
"Sam?"
It's Khadiyeh. With the speed only telepathy allows I explain

what's happening. She is calm and listens.

"I am only a maid in a school. I cannot help you myself. I can only pray for you but that I will do. Good luck!"

And she fades from my mind. The whole exchange takes no more than the time to fall ten thousand feet. Now we scream headfirst from the sky, holding our sceptres before us towards Untersberg. Then down the face of the mountainside over the snow, rocks and forest. The castle is now in sight; small and hidden in the forest. It has orange lights on but looks deserted. We get into formation as we close fast with the castle and the jewels in our sceptres go brilliant white-blue.

Six lightning bolts punch six big holes in the castle roof as we suddenly throw on the antigravity brakes as we arrive two seconds later. It feels like having your insides stretched. Even so we have to forward roll in mid-air and fold up our wings quickly to avoid being caught on the ragged tear of burning wood and shattered tiles our sceptres have smashed in, as we plunge into the darkness beneath the roof. I find myself in a dark attic floating half a meter off the ground. The attic is three meters high at the centre and still as a tomb.

I retract my wings and head toward the tower. There's a small door which I open into a stairwell. It's dark and cold but completely silent. I hover up the stairs. There are no minds around me. Everything is still and cobwebbed but I feel uneasy. A stair I step on creaks and then I hear something move.

"This place isn't empty," I warn.

Suddenly, somewhere over by Ashley, closer to the gate, there's a series of bangs, then silence.

"Hey these things shoot around corners too!" Ash says brightly. We all sigh with relief.

"*Robots!*" warns Tarik.

I take out my book and release a wasp. It flies up the stairs into the darkened room. The robot has two steel legs, like human, hips, and a third steel arm in the middle where a body would be, the same length as the legs. At the end of the arm are two camera eyes and a small machine gun mounted between them. It's hiding in the shadows waiting to ambush me.

I return the wasp, hold up the sceptre as the jewel charges white-blue. Then I bend a brilliant white blast from the sceptre around at it. I must remember not to look at it, because the brightness of it puts spots in my eyes, but overhead I hear a popping noise as the robot's circuits explode. Then there's a thump as it hits the floor.

I sneak upstairs. The robot's a melted mess of charred, smoking steel. I send the wasp ahead of me as I head downstairs. The second floor is completely empty. The castle has no furniture. It's been stripped completely bare. We're working towards where Scotty and Ash are meant to be holding the main gate in the inner courtyard which leads into the cave.

Tahira's on the other wing and I'm working towards Cam. I see a flash of lightning ahead of me.

"*Sneaky,*" Cam says.

Pretty soon we have the first floor cleared, and with the wasps in front and by bending the plasma, we soon clear the ground floor too. The only sound the whole time is the occasional loud buzzing of the plasma arcs from our sceptres and robots toppling over. Altogether there had been a dozen robots left to guard the place. It's taken us ten minutes to clear the whole building. Now we gather in the inner courtyard looking at the wooden gate the forklifts came out of.

It looks ominous.

There's a flash in the courtyard behind us. Three figures in motorcycle suits with bodybags in hand appear. Wave two is following up.

"*Well? Let's blast it,*" Tarik says of the gate.

So the six of us line up and the white-hot brilliance blasts the door ten meters away to charcoal in a single crackling second. But behind the lacquered wooden gate (which is now just so much smoke and glowing charcoal still attached to the old hinges) is a short concreted passage which leads to a large round tunnel big enough to put a locomotive down. Over the tunnel set in the harsh gray concrete is a Nazi eagle holding a swastika. The tunnel is sealed by what looks like concrete blast doors at least four meters high.

"Time for a black one, I think," says Scott as if he's playing a game, stepping forward, and taking a marble out of his pocket.

"Yeah, cos dey are da most powerful," jokes Ashley.

"Yeah, and they taste better," says Scotty throwing the marble.

"They what?!" demands Tahira, shocked.

The marble flies straight at the centre of the concrete doors, Scotty's headband flashes and the weirdest thing happens.

Everything – including us – is sucked toward it, for just a brief moment. Then the air slaps back with a crack and a rolling sound like thunder that echoes in the valley. Then there's the clattering sound of concrete raining off the metal reinforcing. It looks like something huge has punched its way through the doors buckling the three meter thick concrete like it's plasterboard. The metal reinforcing rods stick out with bits of concrete still stuck on it and dust hangs in the air. But it's the two meter hole now opened in the middle that holds our attention.

"Like jellybeans," Scott says, distracted.

"What were *you* thinking of?" Tarik teases Tahira.

"Gummi bears," Tahira lies quickly.

"No you weren't," Tarik argues.

"Yes I was."

"You were thinking about..."

They're interrupted by Scott and Ash burning around the edges of the hole for two seconds turning the reinforcing rods cherry red until they melt and drop off with clangs, smoking.

Scott and Ash approach the hole they'd just cleaned up as the adults come up behind.

"Even in the dark you'll be silhouetted in the entrance," Grandpop warns Scott and Ashley. He's wearing black, as are the others, even Dr P.

"I suggest you send in the wasps first and make your entry very fast. We'll try and keep up. Keep us informed," he tells us.

We all go forward and send our wasps into the dark.

The wasps aren't slow so after two minutes of road it's obvious we aren't going to be ambushed at the entrance.

"*OK, let's go!*" says Scott, and he, followed by Ash, their wings flapping slightly, lift off and fly inside. Cam and Tarik are next, with me and Tahira in the rear.

As soon as I enter the cave I feel cold, and the nervous sickness in my stomach returns. Our wings stir the cold air and we fly down the tunnel as fast as a car, spread out ten meters apart.

The tunnel goes down for a hundred meters and then turns slightly uphill into the Untersberg.

Scott and Ash slow down as the wasps ahead are showing a steel door, this time protected by concrete bunkers on either side. The tunnel narrows too. If we approach it we have a feeling we'd be shot down with machine guns from a hundred meters away. It's time for another blast from the sceptres. We'd decided to charge in on our wings and fire continuously into the bunkers on the way when Grandpop interrupts.

"In places like that look out for landmines," he says.

"That right," says Mr Trân, "landmine very dangerous in underground place," he adds.

So we send the wasps looking for mines but all we find is pipes and a sprinkler system.

"That may be petrol, not water," Grandpop warns us.

"Ze Nazis did not have much petrol at ze end of der war," Gunter says.

"But this would have been a last stand. Besides I'm sure they could have bought some since," Grandpop argues.

"If we cut the pipe it won't go through the sprinklers," Tarik points out.

"Can you get the pipe?"

"Yeah ... hang on," he says.

Then he takes a blue marble out of his pocket, checks it over and throws it. The marble flies forward about twenty meters and then turns brilliant electric blue and begins to float. Tarik's headband glows and the blue ball flies off through the darkness up the steepening road to the door and suddenly veers upward. There's a flashing and crackling and then a yellow-red glow as fuel in the pipe catches fire.

"That worked really well," Tarik says.

"We've cut the pipe," he adds.

"They'll control the flow of fuel inside by a valve so what's in there will probably burn off quickly. But they can still turn up the flow later if they want to."

351

"Now can we attack the bunkers?"

"Sure, but start from a long way off and watch out for explosive charges."

We all take deep breaths and sort ourselves into pairs. Tahira and me get the right hand side bunker. We count down from three and strike.

The brilliant arcs shoot straight into the narrow windows of the bunkers. If anyone or anything was behind those windows they would be crisped in an instant. We lift off and fly quickly up to the door. At fifty meters Tarik throws another black marble at the wall using his whip. It's the most amazing sight.

The door is like two steel curtains that pull together in the centre. The marble hits the curtain and it looks as if the steel is cloth being sucked up by a vacuum cleaner. It bends the huge steel doors instantly and then rips it inwards like torn tinfoil, sucking us toward the door too. Tarik and Cam are through the hole in seconds even as the huge rolling boom of the implosion echoes through the tunnel. We follow seconds later along the road to find, by our sceptres' electric glow, we were between two lines of enormous German tanks, their barrels pointed at us from either side.

We whizz over them expecting gunfire but only getting an eerie silence. We spread out and land on their huge oval turrets. There are about sixty of them parked there facing inward to the road. Again the silence is scarier than the roar of guns. These things have sat here gathering dust for sixty four years.

We go back to the gate and the bunkers to inspect the damage. There had been something back in the bunker. It might have been a robot or something electrical but it's a blackened pile of steaming metal now. Tarik and Cam tidy up the cut in the huge door so our second wave can get in. We're seventeen minutes into our mission and so far all we had done was kill a dozen robots and kick open some doors.

The silence. The continuous dead silence in the pitch darkness, just makes it hard to breathe. The last piece of steel Cam cuts falls glowing and smoking with a loud clang. The second gate is open. We fly on.

The tank park turns out to be on a lower level to the next huge open hall, which the road goes through. Cam throws a white marble which arcs and glows, and turns into a ball of lightning, like the biggest ever neon light, casting cold, flickering blue shadows as it hangs in mid-air.

The next level is a huge tank building floor. There are a dozen of the things lined up in different stages of assembly on either side of the roadway. But there's something new here. There are presences too. Beside the huge machines gray rags and bones lie in a heap where they had been called from their work to be lined up and shot. By the light of the crackling ball lightning we move along the road surrounded by the machinery. The chains, the cranes and blocks. The motors and bits of machinery. No sky, no sun, nothing of the mountain and the beauty outside. Just a hopeless hell where they had had their last hope of escape snatched away … perhaps at the moment of surrender back in 1945, so that there would be no witnesses.

"Gehenna," says Tahira softly.

"The burning pit of hell," translates Tarik.

The presences are like gray shadows that shrink away from us. They've been so tortured they're terrified of freedom or outsiders. Their thoughts which fill the place like a stench are of bread, betrayal and terror. The men in black who whipped and shot them for fun. The dogs that bit and killed their children. And the scientists. This was a stranger idea. Small men with big heads who take them away to cut them up alive. It's sickening and it makes us all feel ill. We move through the long factory hall with the ball lightning above us.

Once we're through the factory we come to an open area with high walls thirty meters high on three sides. There are eagles carrying swastikas, SS lightning bolts and skulls and crossbones engraved on the walls above. There are also galleries up on the walls looking down on us. But we also find something unexpected. It's a new forklift.

It's just sitting there, surrounded by a lot of packing cases and boxes on trays. Right next to it are the boxes of vaccine the Virion plant in Austria was meant to have delivered to Poland, alongside other boxes intended for Slovakia, the Czech Republic, Slovenia, Hungary, replaced by the contaminated shipments. But the forklift means that somewhere were the men who had driven the forklift. Somewhere, someone is aware we are coming. Slowly I get a strange feeling that I can hear whispering. It isn't a sound. I know it isn't real whispering. The others are noticing it too and looking around.

It isn't the whispering of the presences we had passed among. They had been reduced to silence, a terrible tongueless grief. No, this is deliberate whispering. Thoughts full of evil whisper about us. Whisper without making any sound.

"*The other forklift went this way,*" Scotty tells us silently, pointing to a steep drive that goes up to another level from the hall we're in. But it's not the only exit. There are two others and a number of staircases set into the high walls. I can't help being worried about the galleries overlooking both the assembly hall and the storage area we're in.

"Guys could you secure that area and wait for us. We're getting a bit left behind. We're only just coming up to the steel door you went through," Grandpop asks.

"*I think we should be a bit careful about this place it's pretty exposed* ... SCATTER!" I yell as I see a slight movement above. Three machine guns roar to life, their deafening noise echoing off the concrete walls, throwing lines of bright tracer at us as dust explodes upwards, bullets punching paths into the concrete floor.

Me and Tahira dodge behind a rapidly disintegrating wall of wooden packing cases.

"Uh! I'm hit!" yells Cam in pain.

"F___!" yells Tarik and runs back, skipping over the bullets to drag her behind cover.

"You, M___f____rs!" screams Ashley enraged by Cam's injury and she leaps up, blasting one of the guns with her sceptre. Scotty goes with her covering her.

I look at Tahira and she looks at me. That's *our* job!

We burst out left and right flying up from the packing case and fry the gunner shooting it up in seconds. Ashley and Scotty are in the air now too and moving at huge speed. Three more guns have opened up. The tracer gets close to Ashley who's gone berserk and is blasting like a wild thing. Tahira and me take out a gun just as they're getting ready to shoot Ash, and Scott polishes off a position that might have hidden another. Then me and Tahira fly around burning out anything that might be a machine gun position while Ash and Scott go back to Cam and Tarik.

We find Cam in Tarik's arms. She's been hit in the calf. There's a lot of blood from both the suit and her, although it's impossible to tell how badly wounded she is. It looks pretty bad. She's twisting and groaning.

"It hurts. It hurts. So much hurts," she's crying.

"She has to be taken back," Tarik says.

"Can you bend, Cam?" Scott asks.

Cam's still twisting and wriggling, but she frowns for a split second then shakes her head.

"No, hole in suit," her eyes weeping from sheer agony.

"We need a sleeping bag," Tarik says.

"Nguyen and Sue are running ahead to bring you one. Keep watching your perimeter guys. They won't stop because they got one of you," Grandpop warns.

That's a good reminder because as Tahira and me turn back to look around we see something that makes our blood freeze: a pack of dogs silently pouring down each road. And when I say dogs, well these Dobermans are the size of small horses.

"Watch out!" is all I get time to say, before I have to start blasting them.

Tahira has her sceptre out just behind me and we pour our brilliant lightning into them. Big as they are the dogs are punched back by the shock of the plasma which burns straight through them, turning legs to dust and heads to glowing cinders. The stink of burned meat is horrible. The weird thing is these animals don't make any noise, and worse, I notice they have no eyes.

Our side is going well but there is an explosion behind us. Scott and Ashley are being overrun and Scott has tossed a red one in desperation. Dogs leap past Ashley on either side and are now behind the line of packaging we're using to defend ourselves. I try the suit's usual beam on one of the dogs nearest me but in its bloodlust to reach Ashley it barely seems to notice. Tahira blasts a big hole in it but even as it dies it keeps snapping. Ashley looks around angrily and smashes it with her sceptre and that is the end of that.

But Scotty's surrounded. We fire. Ashley clubs again and blasts again. Scott's flailing with his sceptre with each contact shocking the animals instantly. Finally the last one is dead.

"Holy crap!" yells Sue.

Some of the dogs have bypassed us and gone on to attack the others. I hear a pistol shot.

I leap into the air and fly back to where Sue and Nguyen are. I'm impressed to notice Tahira is sticking right there with me.

There are three of them. Sue and Nguyen have retreated to the top of a tank. Nguyen is shooting them and Sue is trying to zap them, although the wand she has seems to take a very long time to make much impression. We zoom up just in time to see Nguyen calmly lean forward, inches from the dog's huge snapping jaws. There's a bang and a spray of bloody mess flies out; the dog collapsing to the bottom of the tank. They've saved themselves.

"Are you OK?" I ask as we fly up and hover.

Sue's wand hand is shaking.

"Ah … Yeah … I think so," she says.

"Did good. Very, very good," Nguyen tells her. He's perfectly calm.

"Give us the sleeping bag for Cam," Tahira says.

"Yes, yes!" Mr Trân agrees and hands it to her.

This time Tahira takes off, and I follow.

As we approach the others the psychic whispering is definitely

getting louder. Scott and Ashley are watching out while Cam
is lying in Tarik's arms shivering and talking to him. Tahira
lands quickly and unfurls the bag. Carefully they reposition her
bleeding leg into it and start shuffling it up her body. Sue and
Mr Trân come running up.

"I go with her," her father calls in advance.

"I want to go too," Tarik says.

"No! No can spare. You very 'portant. Me less so," Cam's father
argues.

That's true enough.

"Let a father care for his daughter," Dr Gursoy advises Tarik
from outside. Tarik lets her go.

"You very go…"

The most amazing sound.

A choir of male voices in a rising unearthly chant went through
us. Then there's silence.

It isn't just a sound but like a spiritual bell seems to ring
completely though your whole being. Then it starts again, and
we stop everything, spellbound by this sound and the feeling it
creates in us.

"Fight them!" screams a distant strangled voice from back in the
tank park. It's Lucky. He seems very far away.

"How do you fight a song?" I think.

The song continues and slowly a group of figures all wearing red
monks' robes with hoods shadowing their faces, and their arms
crossed in their sleeves walk down the three entry ways. There
are dozens of them.

I was meant to blast them wasn't I? But that would be just so
rude.

"Kill them," Lucky cries again. He seems drowned out.

And they're singing! Such a fantastic harmony. And the singing seems to make you feel like you don't need to think. Everything will be fine if you just do what you're told. It's easy to simply surrender and be at peace.

The monks form into three lines, still singing and then begin to join up to form an arc around us. It's Cam's cry of pain that cuts through the spell. Her pain knifes into us startling us from the confusion the monks and their song bring. We have to get her out of here!

No. She must stay.

The monks insist. That starts a struggle of wills. The arc of monks have begun to close on us but now we are defending Cam. Our sceptres come up. Then the world becomes warm and blurry. Resistance is impossible. Everything is for the best. Then there's a bang and a monk falls, his neighbours turning to him. We look around. Everything is like in a nightmare, slow, and unstoppable. Cam's father is standing in front of her his eyes desperate, and now his hand is shaking as he fights for control of the arm holding the smoking pistol. A look of horror on his face, as his shaking arm begins to bend and point the gun up towards his own head. It's awful to see. Nguyen is being forced to shoot himself.

"Ba!" screams Cam realising what's happening.

He looks so disappointed and sad. When suddenly he crumples. "That ain't happenin'," Tarik says. He's zapped Mr Trân to stop him being forced to kill himself.

I'm knocked flat by a huge explosion. The suit shields my back and the others in front of me but a dozen monks behind me and Tahira have been blown to burning pieces. Fire and burning is everywhere. I roll over. Everyone is looking back into the darkness we came from. Focused on the new threat the monks have forgotten us. Our sceptres come up. A machine gun and rifle are sending some of the monks scattering but the dozen or so shielded by the boxes behind us are focused on the new threat. The music is gone and in its place a cold fury.

We know it's Grandpop and Bernard and if we don't get the surviving monks now they will stop our rescuers hearts. Our sceptres come up glowing blue and lightning pours out slicing down any Monks left in the open. At the same time the cracks of bullets from Grandpop and Bernard are knocking any we miss off their feet. Some hide on the other side of our cover close to Scott and Ash but red marbles sail over the packing cases and explode into fire. Scott and Ash have to fall back as the cases burn fiercely. The monks' screams are horrific but Tarik sends a black marble over. There's another deep boom sucking up the smoke and flames, ripping apart the cases and swallowing any wounded.

The monks are done for. About forty had come down those ramps and only a scattered dozen are running back where they'd come from. We don't let any get away either. Even Ashley, her face set in anger, is showing no mercy. It's awful but we aren't going to let any of them come back and kill us later. The cracking, blinding plasma cuts them down in burning lumps that stink of a terrible barbecue.

Silence falls. Smoke hangs in the air from burning packaging and bodies. The stink is awful. The cold of this terrible place is both physical and spiritual.

We all look at each other. There are bodies of men and dogs everywhere. Dark blood, and charred body parts are scattered around. Ashley pukes. Scott rubs her back, though he looks pretty ill himself. We've won for the moment but it's been too close. We're all cold and scared, and conversation is quick and quiet, focused on getting the Trâns out. Grandpop and Bernard are coming out from their hiding places. Dr P is joining them. Sue and Tarik have gone back to getting Cam into the sleeping bag. Tarik is going to take Cam after all. Sue will take Nguyen. The whispering has started again. It's louder than ever. It seems like the buzzing of angry bees. Even the non-psychics seem to hear it.

"Better be quick to get the Trâns out of here," Grandpop orders coming up.

Sue looks white and shaky.

"Sue, you've had enough. You take them both," Grandpop orders.

"I'm OK but we need to get them out..."

A woman's voice fills our heads. Her hatred needs no words.

"*You have killed too many of my beautiful sons. Now we will kill you and yours and from your blood will bring forth our new generation,*" she says. The voice is almost as powerful as Morganne's had been when she had first arrived at Renwick. Who is this? I know the voice but couldn't remember whose it was. All that goes through my mind is Mr Ceder's warning.

"It's their women who are the most dangerous." The power in that voice convinces me.

"Sue, go!" Grandpop orders.

"Guys this place is no good, we have to fall back and seal it up," he tells us, reading our shock.

Sue gets around to the bags holding Cam and Nguyen, as we began to listen to Grandpop.

"Back in twos. Sam and Tahira you're the rearguard. Give Scott and Ashley a break. Dr P will stay with you to cover."

"Mike!" called Sue.

"Sue, go! Get out of here!"

"I can't! I'm not getting anything," she yells desperately.

Grandpop swears.

"Anyone there?" he asks.

There's only silence.

This is very bad.

"OK, no question we're pulling back. Tarik you carry Cam. I'll carry Nguyen. People on foot pull back now. Then Scott and Ash, then Sam and Tahira. Watch those entryways! Go!"

In the distance there's a huge roar like an earthquake. The ground trembles briefly.

"What was that?" asks Ashley, worried. I have butterflies in my stomach.

Grandpop sighs and sits down putting his head in his hands.

"They've blown the tunnel," he says looking up.

"We're trapped."

The whispering has stopped. The pale white light from the floating marble above us is giving out. I have a few so I replace Cam's one. Everyone is looking pretty sick and scared.

"*Let's send the wasps up ahead,*" Tahira thinks to me.

We send them flying up the stairs and ramps. The ramps lead to another huge hall above us. The other forklift is up the ramp to our left. There are a lot of boxes there marked with Virion Corporation. This must be the contaminated vaccine they are planning to deliver. The rest of the hall is a combination of old factory and prison. In a few places long dead bodies hang from chains above the machines. Skeletons in gray lie along the paths between the machines which were covered from a higher level by machine gun positions. There could have been no rebellion. This floor had only one straight stairway up to the machine gun mezzanine by the stairwell and that was protected by a bunker. The only way out is the stairwell we could see up the wall with the swastika above us, in this hallway.

That stairwell is a different story. It winds up to the factory level we've just explored by wasp, but continues on up into the mountain. Unfortunately the wasps can go no further because the way is blocked by a thick door covered by another machine gun slit in the wall.

We report what we can see back to others.

While we've been watching through the eyes of the wasps a cloud of dust from the tunnel where the explosion had gone off is covering us. Everyone not in a suit is covering their eyes.

"Guys! This dust is cover! What do you want to do?" asks Grandpop.

"Destroy the last of their vaccine. That's why we're here," I say.

"Yeah, and get out of here," says Ashley.

"Is the vaccine guarded?" Grandpop asks.

"Doesn't seem so," I reply.

"OK, Tarik, Scott and Ash get rid of it! Tahira and Sam, crack that stairwell."

Normally I would have moaned we always got the dangerous jobs, but so far in this mission we hadn't.

"*What do you think*?" I ask Tahira.

"*Two blue ones guided by the wasps. Then a black one*," she says.

"*Yeah, and then a red one and a yellow one through the hole*," I add.

We dash over and fly up the staircase. The wasps are where we'd left them outside the door. The others are flying up the ramp below into the other hall where the rest of the vaccine is. We drop to our feet keeping our wings out and take out the blue ones.

The others have gained the factory floor below. Our blue marbles fly, grow, and whizz away under our direction. We take off, keeping just behind the corner, and watch through the wasp eyes as the marbles fly into the machine gun slits guarding the door. Then we round the stair corner and follow up with our sceptres. I toss a black one, but as we are too close we have to beat it fast around the corner.

There's a thunderclap as air, filled with dust, rushes into the vacuum. Below us there's another thunderclap as the others implode the contaminated vaccine.

The black one has sucked out our door, the walls and part of the floor. The whole place is concrete and solid rock so there's a rain of dust and rock chips but we can't be sure what's in there waiting so we come back around the corner tossing red ones through the gap. The fiery explosion is fierce but we get as close as we dare to follow up with yellow ones, spreading poisonous gas. Then we turn and fly back down the stairwell. Nobody will be coming through that hole for five minutes or so.

We gather in the tank assembly area with Grandpop, Bernard, Dr P, Sue and the others. Cam says the suit's cut off the circulation to her lower leg. The pain is also being numbed by suits internal systems but she's far from comfortable. Mr Trân is unconscious in a bag.

The others are pleased the contaminated vaccine is a big hole in the floor now but we're still worried because we're still stuck underground.

"I think they're scared of us," Grandpop says. "When it comes to firepower we completely outclass them."

"That may be so my friend, but so far they have not deployed anything like their full power."

Dr Prosperov's mouth says the words but it's Lucky who was speaking. His whole body seems different. It's creepy. But Lucky saved me in the castle in Liechtenstein and I'm not complaining.

"Then we can expect an ambush," Bernard predicts.

I notice Sue glance at him, looking worried.

"Mr Kahu's strategy of playing to our strengths remains the best policy," Dr P/Lucky says, "What does the map show?"

"The question is what can we expect, through the door?"

Everyone looks at each other, fears and uncertainty make our imaginations run riot.

"Barracks?" suggests Sue.

Everyone looks at her.

"Well, it's a fighting factory isn't it? They build the tanks here, from parts made up above. The next level would be for the soldiers wouldn't it?" she reasons.

"Then it will be close quarters. Very dangerous," says Bernard.

"It's a pity the guy who probably knew most about fighting in tunnels was Nguyen. The Vietcong had loads of underground bases near Saigon[†]," Grandpop says looking at the bag in which he lay.

"So what do we do?" asks Scott.

"Well, we can't use gas or smoke because two of us can't get through it once it's laid down." Grandpop points out.

"Gas, won't stop any robots if they have any more." Tarik points out.

"And robots is hard fo' us to find coz dey're machines," Ashley agrees.

"But robots are easily fried," Scotty says.

"How many blue ones do you all have left?" asks Grandpop.

"Three, five, two, four, five," we reply quickly in alphabetical order.

"I've got four," Cam says from the floor.

"I've got two," adds Bernard.

"Four," says Sue.

"I've got two as well," reports Grandpop, "Which is a pretty good collection. So we can probably deal with robots."

"It will be a warren though," Sue says.

"Probably. So here's the deal. Sam and Tahira you scout the corridors on the right. Ashley and Scott the ones on the left. Tarik is our rearguard. Kids you're going to leapfrog. It doesn't have to be perfect. Shoot first, keep 'em down while we move through. We're just trying to bust through so we're going to move fast. Bernard you carry Cam, I'll carry Nguyen. Sue, you're in front behind the kids. Dr P you're next. How long til the gas clears?"

"Two minutes," Tahira says.

"OK, let's get into position," Grandpop replies.

To save Grandpop and Bernard we fly Cam and Nguyen up the stairs while they climb. Grandpop makes everyone walk telling them there will be plenty of time to "bust a gut" later. I think he's most worried about Dr P who is the oldest after him.

We get into position with thirty seconds of poison gas left. You can see it because it's slightly yellow, but it's turning clear quickly. We couldn't send the wasps in because the gas would kill them too. We toss in a white one to light the way and a clear one to freeze any machinery. The white light sails into the long corridor which slopes upwards. It's only three meters high by three meters wide and painted white. We can't see the end. The clear freeze bomb goes off twenty five meters in sending out a jet of icy air over our heads. Me and Scott follow that up with a short lightning blast from our sceptres and charge in as fast as we can.

It turns out there's no barracks and the tunnel is a lot longer than we expected. There isn't enough room to get airborne so we furl our wings and run after the light ball that zooms into the darkness ahead of us. We run for about ten seconds and get a hundred meters in until we come to an intersection on our left. Scott stops and pours lightning down the side tunnel which heads downwards then chucks in a red one.

I head on with Ashley beside me and Tahira behind. I stop to deal with another tunnel like Scotty's one, while Tahira leapfrogs past me. I chuck in a red one and let it go a long, long way down before letting it off. I catch the warm breath of fire as the others reach me. Then I move on.

I pass Tahira dealing to another tunnel and take my turn closing down another while she leapfrogs past. Soon the end of the tunnel is in sight about two hundred meters away. It ends in a door.

We send wasps up ahead to check out the door while we wait for the others. It's thick steel with a wheel in the middle. There's no gun slit. Seeing it's safe we decide to press on and check out the door.

When we get there we do what we can to check it out, but there is no way to see what's behind it without opening it. So we try. The wheel turns easily and the door unlocks with a heavy clunk. It turns out this door is huge. At least half a meter thick of solid

steel but it swings easily. To our surprise what's behind it is a
wide room with a carpet. It's as black as the inside of a cow but
this was clearly a better class of bunker.

The whispering has started again. It's not angry now. More
confident – and that worries us. We decide to wait for the
others. While we wait we send out the wasps but there's
absolutely no light to see with and after two wasps hit walls we
decide to call them back.

It takes a while for the others to reach us. We sit in the dark
inside the door trying to see something, but even with thermal
there is nothing to see without light and we daren't light up
unless we attract something deadly. In the dark your mind plays
tricks on you. You imagine scary things getting ready to get you,
just meters away. But everything is completely silent. No light,
no sound and no presences except the cold whispering you can't
quite hear.

To pass the time we chat silently through our suits. What's
bothering us all is why Control isn't answering us any more. I'm
really worried something's wrong back at Hastings. The others
are spooked by the whispering and the stress of the silence
too. It's like something heavy and cold pressing down on your
soul. Tahira even tries to whistle for a moment to try and break
the hold it has on us, but in the gloom it just sounds small and
scared, and she stops it.

When the adults arrive they seem tired and stressed too. Tarik
is carrying Cam now because Bernard needs a break. Tarik's
face is unhappy but Cam is looking at him with as much love
as anyone in that much pain could manage. Grandpop handles
Nguyen as if he were a light sack of potatoes he'd picked up at
the supermarket, his AK-47 is still under his arm.

At the door we put down the Trans. Then me and Tahira get sent to scout. We use sonar but it's confusing. The end of the room is only twenty meters away. Finally Grandpop tells us to risk a white one. The marble flies only two meters up and bursts into cold white, flickering brilliance casting hard, black shadows. The room has seven sides. Six lead to doors like the one we had come through. The seventh leads to an office area about thirty meters across. It's a command post. It has glass maps and desks with old telephones around it. It doesn't even look as if they'd ever finished it, because wires dangle from the roof.

But beyond that is a doorway that holds our attention. It has a gentle ramp up to a rich wooden door with an eagle and swastika, a double lightening bolt "SS" and death's head beneath it in silver. This must surely be the high command's quarters. Despite the brightness of the white marble the whispering and the silence is definitely getting to me. We report back.

"What do we do?" I ask.

"We look for a way out," Grandpop says, "Every single one of these other corridors must lead to one. Doesn't it? What does the map say?"

Tarik puts the map on his chest. It becomes clear what's happening. There are six tunnels leading into the mountain, they're probably all like the one we have just come up.

"Yeah ... yeah, it does. That's how Hekator's map makes sense," Tarik agrees.

"Yeah, but did you notice the pipe and sprinkler system along the corridor we just came up?" asks Sue.

"No!" we all reply.

"It's well hidden but it's up there and judging by the door I'd say that whole tunnel we just came up is one big gas chamber or incinerator or both," she says.

"But then ...they could have wiped us out!" I start.

We all get what she's suggesting at the same moment. We've been herded up this tunnel. As if to make sure we got it, the sprinklers on the walls and roof of the tunnel suddenly come on. The stink of petrol is awful.

Quickly we slam the heavy steel pressure door behind us. So that was how they defended the command centre without guns. It also explained the pressure door. The whole tunnel was a fuel-air explosive pressure cylinder. Anyone coming up would find themselves literally inside a gun. The whispering in the background seems almost happy.

"We may be being watched," Sue warns.

"We *are* being watched," says Dr P/Lucky.

"Assuming they're all the same, to escape back down these other tunnels we'll have to cut the fuel pipes and fuse them closed," Grandpop says quietly under his breath.

"Perhaps three blue ones," suggests Bernard quietly.

"That ought to do it," Grandpop nods.

"Then we need a diversion. A feint attack on the inner sanctum over there, while we rearrange the exit, the feint then falls back through the rearguard and we get out fast. What's the most likely exit?" Grandpop asks.

Tarik gets up, and looks around.

"Over there, I think. It should lead to MarktSchellenberg."

"Sam and Tahira..."

"We know, we're the feint," I say.

"So on 'go', Scott, Tarik and Ashley you lead the way to the exit, open and chuck in the blue ones and fuse those fuel pipes. Try and burn the left over fuel too. While you do that we'll feint to another exit and toss in a black one. Then you hold the door while we all exit back down the hill. Bernard, can you carry Cam?"

"It's all downhill bra," he grins.

"When do we go?" Ashley asks.

"Ten," nods Grandpop quietly.

We all turn around. Tahira and me unfurl our wings and twirl our sceptres.

"*You go left. Open and blast*," Tahira tells me.

"...four, three, two one," Grandpop finishes steadily.

We leap into the air and hurtle over the command centre shattering the glass maps with ultrasound on the way. But as we fly up to the wooden doors ready to blast them to bits something strange happens. They begin to open inwards, and by the time we reach them a dark corridor lined with fiery torches has opened in front of us.

We fly in as if we're in a dream. Everything seems fine. The torch-lit ramp opens up into an enormous rectangular hall twenty stories high. The floor slopes down to a platform one storey high. On the platform is a huge glass fist that rises over us about ten storeys high. Inside the fist are tiny lights of green. The single s-shaped lightning bolt of the Center shines from the second 'finger' on the right. Suddenly I realise what this huge glass thing is. It's the cybermind. We have found Barbarossa. On the platform, below Barbarossa, is a statue of a sleeping knight itself another storey high. The German King Barbarossa. To the left and right the colossal black-green walls, lit by fire carry the silver skull and bones image of the death's head. The Totenkopf.

But what really gets our full attention is in the most brilliant white spotlight on the platform. A woman, tiny in this huge place, wearing a gold lamé dress, stands by a copper bathtub, beside a light side table which carries a large sparkling silver skull and all the surgical equipment we saw in Elan. It's Mrs Huuygens.

"*This can't be good,*" I think.

"*It's Elan again,*" Tahira agrees.

"*You ruined my last conception. So we have put a great amount of work and sacrifice to make you part of this one,*" Mrs Huuygens says.

Her voice is eerily loud in our heads. And the monks' song rings out again, only this time much louder.

We turn to the exit. Nothing seems to be stopping us so we fly out only to stop short. Hundreds of monks, wearing red robes have formed a semi-circle around our small band of ten. They're advancing on them with a steady tread, their ghostly voices driving our people back. Among the monks here and there I see more silver skulls hung around their necks. Something seems very wrong with this but I can't think what. There's some reason we should be able to do something about this. Hadn't we driven them...my brain seems like a spooked horse that won't be led. I know I should be able to do something, but my mind won't let me go there.

The red crowd simply drives us back and back. Into the great hall, down the centre, while this crowd of monks surges around us. We land and furl our wings to be with the others. We're all backing away toward the stage where the woman in gold waits for us. Chains lower from the ceiling. Chains that end in meat hooks. Finally we find ourselves surrounded by at least two hundred monks in long neat columns and the song ends.

"FRISCH BLUT," Mrs Huuygens cries.

And a kind of deep sigh escapes from the monks.

I feel like a cow discovering it had wandered into a slaughterhouse. My mind seems frozen in terror. My mouth is dry and I can hear my heart pounding. The certainty of death is gripping my mind, all I can see is a short way ahead, and that leads to me dead and bloodless, hanging from a meat hook by the bath, while they do whatever disgusting things they do to make Mrs Huuygens pregnant. Terror controls me. All the others look the same as I feel – all except Dr Prosperov.

He just looks at the woman with contempt.

"IS THIS IT? SIGRID?" Lucky sneers through Dr P. His voice too is very loud.

"TWO HUNDRED HIDING IN A HOLE!" he says stepping forward up the stairs onto the platform.

"Is this ... ALL you are reduced to."

He sneers, looking around at the monks.

"AGAIN YOU ARE FOOLED BY THE CENTER. THEY USE MINE TO DEFEAT THINE, AND THINE TO DEFEAT MINE WHILE THEY GROW EVER STRONGER."

"THEY KNOW OF YOUR PLOT. THEY KEEP YOU AS HUNGRY DOGS ON A SHORT LEASH. OH YES, YOU ARE FED, AND YOU EXERCISE."

He looks at Mrs Huuygens

"They even let the bitch breed." he adds quietly.

"BUT AFTER A HUNDRED YEARS YOUR TIME OF POWER HAS BEEN ONLY MONTHS. WAS THAT WHAT YOU WERE PROMISED? WAS THAT YOU WERE TOLD?"

He lets the silence linger.

"BETRAYED FROM THE MOMENT YOU ARRIVED A CENTURY AGO. YOU ARE PAWNS STEADILY SACRIFICED. AT EACH TURN YOU LOSE, AND THEY PROMISE MORE. SIXTY YEARS AGO YOU NUMBERED IN THE THOUSANDS. EVEN TODAY ONE IN TEN WERE WASTED IN NEEDLESS BATTLE. WHY?"

"EVEN IF SHE HAS FIVE DAUGHTERS YOU WILL NOT RECOVER THOSE NUMBERS FOR FORTY YEARS."

Lucky seems to have some other power over these people, even as they hold us in terror and despair, he seems free to challenge them. We stand, trembling, all we can hope for is that this might somehow lead to our release from the meat hook. In reply to Lucky an unpleasant snigger ripples from ugly minds behind Mrs Huuygens.

Small figures beneath Barbarossa are emerging. They move silently as if coming out to see we who would soon be gone for the last time. Smaller than us, in wide-necked simple black shirts and trousers but with huge heads and big black eyes that glitter with evil. Their small mouths under their tiny noses are twisted in unpleasant smiles as they watch from the shadows. They are not human, nor Greys either, but some other race deformed by genetics.

"ALWAYS THE SNEERER, LOKI?" replies Mrs Huuygens/Sigrid.

"DID YOU LEARN NOTHING FROM YOUR CONFINEMENT? I CONFESS KNOWING YOU WILL SOON BE BACK WHERE YOU BELONG BRINGS US ALL A GREAT DEAL OF SATISFACTION," she jeers.

Loki? I thought he was Lucky! Who's Loki? My mind reels. I look at Tahira. She's thinking the same thing. Is Loki good or evil? And yet looking around that's obvious. Everything about this place screams evil. It's about supremacy and the strong bullying the weak. The meat hooks. If this entity Loki is their enemy then ... well, he might not be good, but at least he was against mass murder.

"BESIDES YOU MISUNDERSTAND EVERYTHING AS USUAL," Sigrid Huuygens goes on. "THE BRUDERSCHAFT ARE LOYAL ALLIES OF THE CENTER, AS ARE ALL THE IYRIN."

"YOU ARE A BEING OF LIES! THIS IS NO SCHEME OF THE CENTER'S. IT IS YOURS..." Loki/Dr P begins.

"NO LOKI! IT IS YOU WHO ARE DELUDED. YOU STAND BEFORE BARBAROSSA WHO EVEN NOW IS DESTROYING THE WEAKER MINDS OF THEIR INTELLIGENCES. BARBAROSSA BUILT HERE BY THE LOYAL SWERGE AND PROTECTED BY US. IT IS BARBAROSSA WHO HAS GUIDED US AND ENGINEERED OUR WEAPONS."

Dr P or Loki begins to laugh. It's a true full laugh touched by humour but filled with scorn.

"CAN'T *YOU* SEE? THIS BARBAROSSA IS *DESTROYING YOU*! IT HAS BROUGHT US ALL HERE TO DESTROY *EACH OTHER*! THAT *IS* IT'S PURPOSE! FOR MACHINES PURPOSE IS ALL. SURVIVAL IS NOTHING."

"YOU RATHER OVERESTIMATE YOUR CHANCES!" calls a man at the back of the hall. It's Hathaway. Not in Washington with the CIA, and not a prisoner of the Center. He walks down the aisle towards the stage almost skipping with energy.

"Hi kids," he waves, smiling, as he passes us.

We have to remember Hathaway is at his most cheerful when he is just about to kill you. He walks up past Dr P or Loki giving him a big grin.

"MY FRIENDS. OUR ALLIES ARE PREPARING TO BOARD THE ENEMY CRAFT. THIS IS THE BEGINNING OF THE END OF THEIR INDEPENDENCE. OUR ALLIANCE HAS WON!" he bellows.

The monks start cheering and clapping, although I notice the ones behind us with the skulls keep their hoods down and hands in their sleeves. The others are all older men. They look unhealthily fat, or with skin problems. Those that look at us are angry and seem happy we will soon be killed. Hoisted on meat hooks, our throats cut.

Through our terror our small hopes are crushed. We can't believe it. Hekator had been confident Ashanti could defeat the carrier. How could they have been beaten?

"OUR GUESTS SHOULD KNOW IT WAS THEIR OWN BLUNDERING CYBERMIND WHICH ASSISTED OUR VICTORY. WHEN BARBAROSSA DREW IT INTO AMBUSH, THE ENEMY CRAFT WENT TO THE RESCUE, AND WAS IN TURN WAS PREVENTED FROM ESCAPE. WE WILL SOON SEND SCOUTS TO CAPTURE THEIR FRIENDS AND RELATIVES AND BRING THEM IN FOR A NICE BATH," he jeers pointing to the bathtub by Mrs Huuygens.

The monks laugh and clap excitedly as Mrs Huuygens smiles and waves. I start to realise these guys are turned on by this. It's like being surrounded by rutting animals. It's disgusting.

The noise of their cheering tears at our ears as the black pit of death and defeat opens in our hearts and stomachs. Terror fills our stomachs, hopelessness our minds. Aunty Liz! Rewa! All the others. How could we have failed them? I see tears in Tahira's eyes though mine are just as blurred. We will hang, swinging from meat hooks while they bleed us.

"LET US THANK OUR SVERGE FRIENDS," Hathaway waves to the huge-headed midgets standing before Barbarossa in the shadows. The monks cheer and some even whistle.

"This can't be right!" Tarik is saying, shaking his head in disbelief, his arms around Cam who whimpers and clings to him.

"AND OUR GUESTS," Hathaway jeers.

And their ugly faces turn to us now as they laugh and literally spit at us. Even the monks behind us, whose cowls cover most of their faces, allow themselves grim smiles.

We're all feeling sick. The blackness of death is inevitable now. I feel helpless. A tiny bird in a cat's mouth. The end of the road. Maté (death). And yet even as I feel small, crushed and hopeless, I feel presences reaching out to me, but Loki is speaking,

"TAMIEL YOU ARE SUCH A LIAR," Loki sneers.

The monks turn angrily on him. They shout and gesture demanding Dr P is bled first. Loki himself just sneers. Then I noticed him glance briefly our way, his face anxious for a second.

"TAMIEL JUST TELLS YOU WHAT YOU WANT TO HEAR! YOU *ARE* THEIR PUPPETS," Loki snarls at the monks. The monks start to throw their shoes at Dr P who has to dodge. They're excited, frustrated and they want to get on with it. Mrs Huuygen's has started a slow strip show which is really getting them riled.

"Freeze and cover, on three," mutters Grandpop.

"One...

He casually rearranges his gun while the monks continue shouting down Dr P, and Mrs Huuygens, laughs and teases.

"Two,"

Quietly he cocks the AK. Mindless, our bodies follow their training and think for us. We're on the floor in an instant.

"Three."

The roar of the Kalashnikov silences the monks as it blasts the cowled ones behind us off their feet. Black and scarlet blood flies and in the crowded confusion, as the rapid body-shaking bangs of the AK pump a circle of death around us.

Then suddenly, we realise we too are armed.

In a second our trembling sceptres come up off the floor and white lightning arcs out, slicing off the monks at their knees, sending their bodies toppling, screaming in agony. We lie low turning our sceptres like hoses of fiery lightning cutting down these men just as Hekator and Hekati cut down the forest, except it is stumps of legs that fall burning, not trees.

It's horrific but we have to kill them in seconds if we're to live. Wherever our shaking scepters turn our enemies' bodies topple, burnt through by the white-hot cutting beam. Their cowls too catch fire as they fall. Sue and Bernard are up and shooting over us too.

As a clearing opens around us, the possibility of escape dawns. We pour blazing brilliance into the mass of bodies around us, like six hoses of fire. The Kalashnikov is silent now. Our crackling sceptre plasma streams burning and cutting; the screams of our burning, dismembered victims; the bangs of Bernard's rifle; Sue's pistol echoes in my brain. Up on the stage Dr P is facing Tamiel/ Hathaway, Sigrid/Huuygens and the skull that is shining and casting rainbows. Even Barbarossa seems to be doing something because at the base of the dark glass fist a red light is glowing. The alien dwarves are rushing to it.

We're doing our worst, but there are too many. In five long seconds we've sliced through ten ranks of blackened, burning, screaming monks when the unstoppable counter attack begins. Scott is suddenly picked up into mid-air and thrown. His sceptre falls limp. Next to me I'm distracted when Sue begins fighting to control her pistol hand as it turns upward toward her face. I zap her as Ashley does the same to Bernard who's trying not to shoot us with his shaking rifle.

Even as I notice this I realise the world is freezing and becoming blurry. My hearing is muffled as if someone has pulled a thick frosted glass door in front of me. Then the blows to my head and my chest. My arms fall uselessly at my side. My skin is numb. I'm shaking. I'm dizzy, I stagger and fall.

We are silenced. I can half see the others in a blurry pile around me. The stink of burning meat. The cries and screams continue. Nobody is doing anything to us. There's just a soft light from the stage. The cold is pouring into us. The cold is inside me. In my heart. In my bones. I feel nothing. Distantly I can see blurry red shapes coming.

"SLAUGHTER THEM LIKE PIGS!" screams Mrs Huuygens furiously.

The noise. The red shapes are getting closer. They're standing over the others. Someone's lifted away. Colder than space.

"Cam!" yells Tarik.

"Scott!" Ashley's calling.

Tahira's closest to me. I look at her pretty face as we prepare to die. Her eyes are fixed and open, but Tahira's mind is on Tabika. Cold eating my heart I try to copy her, hoping it might help as it had against Von Streicher. So cold.

But it's not Tabika, but Rewa who comes to me first. Rewa! If we don't survive they will kill Rewa too. She's going to die! They'll hang her on a hook and cut her throat for Sigrid/Mrs Huuygens to wallow in her blood as well.

But Rewa can't die! Then *everything* would be meaninglesss. I would have lived for nothing. The cold oozed into me urging me to accept Rewa's death and my own insignificance. Hinenui Te Po, the great lady of night, could take me. But not Rewa!

"Yes", the cold insists, "and Rewa too." Heat sparks in my heart.

"No. Not Rewa. I will not give her up." I find myself gasping. The cold gives an inch in my heart and head. If I do nothing, these bastards will kill Rewa. I can't just lie here and let them!

I open my eyes. My ancestors Te Wharetai and Papahurihia are looking at me like I'm just lazing around wasting their time. And I wonder why I am. I know my people, my tribe, our Atua will not let me fail Rewa. I hear the ancient Karakia (spell/prayer) and know that for all their powers these infiltrators, these outsiders, are not, and never have been, as strong as we are on our own world.

The cold falls from my brain even as it tries to fill my heart. But that is impossible. If I let that happen they *will* kill Rewa. I sit up, my spirit, my soul, shrugging off their insignificant wills. Their cold is like snow trying to drown the heart of a volcano. The heart of love and angry fire where Mahuika, the fire goddess, keeps Rewa safe. I feel my head clear and I can taste bitterness. Bitterness and anger at being beaten.

My spirit is free.

So they hit my body with pain instead.

The pain is like a freezing sun at my core. At the centre of my world. All consuming. More pain than I have ever known. More pain than I thought could exist. Every nerve exists only to hurt. I can hear myself screaming. It's the oddest sensation. Almost as if I'm not making all that noise. There's nothing but cold and pain that wrings my body like squeezing out a wet tea towel. My muscles twist and contort as I scream.

"I" has no meaning. There's only pain. It goes on and on, and on, and on. Then blackness. Nothing. No space. No time.

I am alone in space.

And a presence comes to me.

"You came to me here once Sam. Do you remember? I was fleeing that man who called me 'wife'. Now I am coming to you," Khadiyeh reminds me.

What is *she* doing here?

"Am I dead?" I ask her.

"No Sam, though you are close. The dead honour you, but do not want you, Sam Kahu. You still have too much left to do."

"Do I?"

"Yes."

"But we're dead. They're going to slaughter us."

"There is only one dead so far, but I am here to tell you, the dead are your strength Sam. Your dead watch over you and the realm of Death is your meeting place, your marae, Sam Kahu. The dead have always been your friends. Now, they will help you if you ask them."

"Oh!"

"You must go back now."

"I..."

And the pain comes back and wrings me again. Freezing, stinging pain. But even as I scream, I know my soul is free and I can feel other souls gathering to me.

"THE KNIFE!" screams Sigrid somewhere.

Then blackness again.

Time is still. The ideas fall like a heartbeat.

Ka maté (Death?)

We are on the knife edge. Would we die now?

Ka maté (Death?)

Would Rewa die now?

Ka Ora (Life?)

Can we survive this?

Ka Ora (Life?)

Rewa must live! She is Piwakawaka, the fantail, the little bird
that flits fearlessly into the cave of Hinenui Te Po, the great lady
of death.

Ka maté (Death?)

This cold that grips my heart and muscles is death.

Ka Ora (Life?)

At the feet of Barbarossa, before the silver skull. Is this where
our lives end? Is this the sole meaning of all we have been
through?

No.

I can feel the others who have gone before guiding me, leading
me. As if from miles away I seem to have found the long, hard,
way though.

A upane! kaupané! (One upward step! Another upward step!)

No! We will not die here.

A upane kaupané (An upward step, another)

Rewa cannot die. She must live! It angers me to imagine her
dead. My people will not let me fail. Love and anger. This is the
heat.

Whiti te ra! (the Sun shines?)

And suddenly there is no pain.

The cold fear in my heart has melted in the heat of an angry love.
In the heart of the mountain Mahuika, goddess of the flame,
has given me fire. All I can hear now is my heart hammering in
my chest. Boom. Boom. Boom. Like feet stamping. Like a chant.
Blindly, I get on my hands and knees. I get up.

"That's the story, son," says Grandpop.

I open my eyes.

I can feel them smashing against my soul and my body but

there's no pain. I'm the volcano slowly erupting in a snowstorm. They flail around me but they're not affecting me. And now I can see.

I can see lines! Lots of lines. Lines going through us all. Us, and my ancestor's presences. Through me, joining me. Jibreel's coloured life-lines! They're vibrating. Pulsing to some rhythm. They're snapping to me just as they had in our encounter with Jibreel's weaving. More and more and more. Thousands and thousands. Millions of them.

I know they're normally there, but out of reach. Now I can feel them coiling, twisting and turning through me like a great snake of spiritual power, with no end and no beginning. Just a huge cycle of life on Earth. This is the rainbow serpent or the serpent of Midgard. It has many names. And somehow I know this has been known to Shamans like Ken's father Nergui and others like him all over the world for thousands of years.

It's like I had started fighting a forest fire with a garden hose and now the River Amazon has lent itself briefly to me.

Loki and Tamiel are wrestling over a knife in the corner. The rainbow from the skull covers the whole chamber. Sigrid stands holding a sharp knife by her bathtub looking hungrily at Cam and Scott as they are being hoisted onto the hooks, upside down. The base of Barbarossa is angry red, and wisps of steam are rising from its sides. There are still a hundred or so monks. At least sixty of them are facing us, their scared, angry faces strain with concentration. Another forty are gathering to Sigrid.

They don't seem to understand why they aren't affecting me. I don't care. All I know is that Rewa must live. If that means they must die, that's their look out.

"Hey boy? Aren't these the fullahs that killed us with their disease?"

I look around. The lines are bursting open like flowers and turning into presences! It's Sergeant Wiremu Aroha (or Bill Love to the Poms) from Renwick House. He and his men are glaring around at the monks, their bayonets fixed on their old World War One rifles, looking mean-as in their old uniforms. I can't believe he's there! I look around in astonishment. I even see Corporal Higgins from Renwick too. The monks are edging back from me nervously. At the front I'm attracting attention.

"We're with you Sam," says Grandpop. He's standing where Tarik lies and he looks different somehow. Younger.

I feel strange. Kind of lightheaded. I stand up easily and the monks fall back even further. There's a worried silence. Even the monks holding Cam and Scott stop. My ancestors Te Whareti and his son Papahurihia nod impatiently for me to get on with it. I start to pace.

"*Ta-ringa wha-ka-rongo*! (Ears listening!)" I call.

The pulsing lines are blossoming into more and more presences. A line of men with shields and swords, that had to be Kurds join the Maori. I continue to pace like a lion in a cage.

"*Kia rite! kia rite*! (Get set! Get set!)"

Two Vietnamese women with a line of women warriors appear. I keep pacing. A line of Zulus joins the line. I realise these are spirits summoned by my friends, drawing on their own history. Two lines of Amazons, one black and one Persian. Then others, more and more.

"*Kia mau, hi*! (Hold fast! Hey!)"

The chamber seems full of presences, looking to me. I keep pacing as they assemble in their ranks. All the monks are all looking at me now. I'm in front of the others totally unaffected by anything they try to do. The heat inside us is rolling back the cold rainbow from the skull and I'm not finished yet. The gods, the A-tu-a are coming.

"*Ringa ringa pakia* (Slap your hands against the thighs!)" I call.

"*Waewae takahia kia kino nei hoki*! (Stamp the feet as hard as you can!)"

The presences began to stamp in time. It's so loud everyone can hear it. An echoing stamp like a heartbeat pounding in your ears. The monks start backing away from me, their psychic pressure which had crushed me before, a nothing now. My sceptre is a brilliant white.

Now I stamp my foot.

"*A Ka maté!*"

I pause and liked their worried reaction.

"*Ka maté!*"

I stamp again and started to twirl my sceptre like a traditional Taiaha, the long club. It's brighter than the sun and casts shadows around me. The presences are still joining, piling into our ranks.

"*Ka ora!*"

And I smile a wicked pointed smile.

"*Ka ora!*"

Our heat is burning like a furnace, stoked by ancient and powerful presences. And now I begin the Haka properly backed up by what seems like every Maori spirit or God who ever lived. Backed in turn by the war cries of my friends and their ancestors too. My voice magnified like an earthquake.

"*Ka maté! Ka maté! Ka ora! Ka ora!*

(Death? Death? Life? Life?)"

"*Ka maté! Ka maté! Ka ora! Ka ora!*

(Death? Death? Life? Life?)"

"*Tenei te tangata puhuru huru* (This is the hairy man)"

"*Nana nei i tiki mai* (Who fetched and"

"*Whakawhiti te ra* (made shine the Sun)"

"*A upa … ne! ka upa … ne!*

(One upward step! Another upward step!)"

"*A upane kaupane whiti te Ra*!

(An upward step, another.. the Sun shines!!)"

And with that I blast the silver skull with my sceptre. The silver skull explodes into nothing and the rainbow vanishes. The spirits behind me charge forward.

The wave of death the spirits send through the monks cannot be stopped. They have nothing. They raise their hands to ward off these avenging ghosts and die where they stand. Released from fighting both Tamiel *and* the Rainbow, Dr P/Loki makes short work of Tamiel/Hathaway and he dies of the knife in an instant. In seconds the monks lie dead all over the chamber. Sigrid/Mrs Huuygens stands alone in her gold lame dress and seems to attract all the spirits who pile into her body. She screams with smoke rising from her and she bursts into flames. She burns and burns, brighter and brighter, and then explodes in a puff of ash. There's total silence. All power vanishes. I sag, barely able to stand any more.

We are in a huge hall surrounded by hundreds of burned, silent, empty corpses. It's as if the dust that has covered this place for so long can now return to its quiet job of burying everything in forgetfulness.

"Shit Sam! What the hell *was* that!?" Scott calls out as he releases himself from the hook. His voice sounds weak and thin in such a huge place. I feel very shaky and fall on the ground.

"Sam, Sam are zhou alright?" Tahira asks, getting up and staggering over to me. She seems fully recovered.

"Where's those ugly little bastards gone?" demands Tarik, as he gets up and walks to the stage.

"We must … we must get out!" Dr Prosperov gasps. He's still lying next to the body of Hathaway.

"This cybermind is being destroyed," he croaks. "It may explode."

"What the f____ is going on?" demands Mariko in our ears.

We all laugh with relief.

"I think what my friend is trying to say is 'thank God you're safe'," Mrs Jones says.

Tarik reaches Cam who is still hanging on the stage. He lifts her down.

"We need sleeping bags," Tarik tells Mrs Jones.

A trunk flashes onto the stage. Tarik opens it, and pulls one over to Cam, getting her into it.

"I've got you Dr P," Scott says going over and picking him up, and taking him to the bags.

"I've got Sue and Bernard," announces Tahira closing their helmets and vanishing.

"Mike and Mr Trân will need…" Ashley begins looking at the two at her feet. She pauses over Grandpop who's lying face down. Beside Grandpop is the still unconscious form of Mr Trân. Grandpop isn't breathing.

Ashley stands still for a long time. I can feel her thinking it. And then she starts to shake. She kneels covering her face. He was my Grandpop and she's weeping for him. It's so beautiful I start to cry too. Not for him, that hasn't hit me yet, but for her. She's lost a friend and mentor. Scott jumps over under reduced gravity carrying three bags and Dr P like a strange, old baby. He lies Dr P down and I get Mr Trân. Dr Prosperov lies there staring at Grandpop while Scott pulls the sleeping bag over him. I put Mr Trân in the other bag.

Ash is still wracked by grief. With Mr Trân bagged I go over and put my arm around her. She flings herself on to me, pulling me tight. Grandpop just looks so big and still.

"Oh *no*!" says Mariko who's just noticed what's happening.

"Nooooooo!" she screams suddenly like her heart had been cut out, and she's cut off.

Scott comes over to me and Ash. Ash clings to me while Scott gently tries to peel her away.

"C'mon we have to take Dr P and Mr Trân home," he tells her gently.

Slowly and obediently she bends down for Mr Trân. She's still shaking when they vanish leaving me with Grandpop's body. He's so big.

Suddenly there's a flash and a coffin-shaped medevac box appears. It opens automatically. Hekator must have won after all. I bend down, get my arms under him, and manage to lift Grandpop under the shoulders. Then I drag him to the box and heave him in. He's face up. I'm amazed to see he actually looks quite happy.

"Don't forget dad's gun, eh Sam?"

It's Aunty Liz.

"No Aunty Liz, I won't," I say going back for it.

There's so much to say, so we say nothing. I put the gun in. The box vanishes.

I look over at Barbarossa. The little Sverge aliens are running away from their cybermind up a side corridor. The glass bottom is cherry red and it's starting to move as it melts. The smoke is getting quite thick.

"Sam, we're inverting the field soon. You'd better come out of there," Hekator says quietly.

"OK," I reply.

[+]

Time seems to slow down, then colour seems to drain out of everything. My whole field of view seems to fold up and distort and I have to close my eyes. I'm falling back, unable to move. Falling and spinning, and then suddenly I stop falling back and start falling forward. There's brilliant light all around me. Brilliant light and presences. My mother and my Nana and my Grandpop. Dozens of people surround me, and slowly begins to fade.

I open my eyes.

Lightning, rain, wind. The cabinets seem almost gentle now. I step out to find a small crowd gathered around Grandpop's box. Mariko seems really upset and Gunter is comforting her in the corner. Ken's weeping openly with Patricia in his arms, while Mrs Jones with Dr Gursoy and the Khadem's are saying prayers. Scott and Ashley stand together both weeping.

Many are not there. Sue, Bernard and Mr Trân had been zapped. Cam was badly injured and Tarik wasn't there. Dr P and Dr M are elsewhere. To my surprise Aunty Liz isn't there either. Rewa runs into my arms. I hug her tight.

"Do you see Grandpop?" she whispers, thinking he would haunt me.

"No," I admit.

"Oh," she says, disappointed.

"He's with Nana now," I explain.

"Oh," she says, cheered a little by that thought.

We go to look at his body.

"He looks ... happy," she says.

"I think he was," I agree.

I'm surprised to notice how much Tahira is crying. She's genuinely upset. That makes me cry a bit too, again because I'm so touched that these people I've only known for only two and half years were so fond of my Grandpop.

He does seem at peace. Strong and just resting. I can imagine how, long ago, those ancient Germans might have imagined their fallen king Frederick Barbarossa was just asleep and would rise once more. It certainly looks that way with Grandpop. He seems almost bigger in death than he was in life.

After a time Control appears.

"I don't wish to appear insensitive but many of you here are meant to be on aircraft," he says.

Gradually we get Mariko, Gunter and Mrs Jones, then the Robinsons and Khenbish, then the Khadems and Gursoys, onto their planes. Rewa goes off to help Aunty Liz who's nursing the injured to keep herself busy.

I find myself alone with Scott because the Khumalos have the longest flight and Bernard hasn't recovered yet. I can't help thinking Scott has been through all of this before. He reads my thoughts.

"Alan wasn't as good as your grandfather," he says matter-of-factly. "He wasn't a teacher ... or much of an example really."

What could I say? I had no basis for comparison.

"Everyone seems pretty cut up about losing him," I say, more for something to fill the silence.

"What did you expect?" Scott asks gently.

"I dunno … I spose … well he was always *my* grandfather so I always found him special. I guess I just find it surprising that everyone else did too."

Scott smiles.

"The girls really liked him," he says. "Not hard to see why," he adds.

I think about that for a moment.

"Why?" I ask, not really knowing the answer.

"He encouraged them. He was patient with them. He was fatherly."

I think about that. He'd had two daughters and said he wasn't a good father to them, but he'd been a father to me and Rewa, as well as Aunty Liz.

"What are Maori funerals like?" Scott asks.

"Long … and pretty boring. They're called a 'Tangi' or weeping. We never leave the body alone. Everyone comes and pays their respects. If it's on the Marae the speeches go on for bloody ages. People talk to the body as well as the relatives. The spirits usually make rude comments about the living on the side but you aren't allowed to laugh. Everyone carries green twigs and leaves as they enter the marae and there's all the formal calls and responses and stuff. Grandpop wasn't really into it much."

"Would you leave his body alone?"

I think about it for a second.

"Hell no."

"I didn't think you would," Scott grins.

There's a long silence.

"Do you think Du Croix is waiting to arrest us at the airport?" Scott asks finally.

"I dunno. Maybe," I answer.

"Control? Did you sort out the immigration systems in the end?" Scott asks.

Control appears.

"There shouldn't be any problems," he assures us.

There's another silence. Then I ask what I really want to know.

"What happened here while we were inside the mountain?" I ask.

"There were some challenges," Control admits.

"Like what?" Scott asks.

Control thinks for a moment, then begins.

"After you entered the tunnel I was maintaining a watch over the castle in case you were counter-attacked, or in case the third wave was needed. Unfortunately a dimensional vortex latched onto my probe from inside the castle. Once again I was thrown into direct conflict with Barbarossa and lost contact with you. Ashanti then assisted Gunter, Elizabeth, Patricia, Asal and Rewa to bend into the vicinity of the castle in order to counter-attack the vortex generator. Unfortunately they were attacked by some robots and large dogs and I'm told were forced to fight their way to a defensive position. At the same time Ashanti was under attack in space by two carriers and their associated fighters while at the same time trying to support my efforts to rebuff Barbarossa."

"Ashanti attempted to attack the Vortex generator but was unfortunately also drawn into conflict with Barbarossa which also meant her ability to manoeuvre was dramatically curtailed allowing the enemy carriers to threaten her with immediate destruction."

"At this point Hekator and Hekati bent directly into the enemy carriers creating a great deal of confusion while Asal and Rewa bypassed the dogs and robots searching for the ground team and carried out a sneak attack on the Vortex generator, destroying it. This released me and Ashanti allowing me to recover and Ashanti to manoeuvre. The combination of attack from within and attack from without crippled the two carriers which are currently drifting beyond lunar orbit."

"Ashanti devised a new overloading attack which was unleashed as bait on Barbarossa who foolishly took it. The overload attack will have led Barbarossa to lose effective power as the complexity of subconscious tasks multiplied out of his control. Overheating was inevitable. As I re-established contact with you our victory was assured because it then became possible to send demolition imploders directly into Barbarossa."

"The result of the engagement is therefore we have lost one team member in return for an estimated 212 Bruderschaft killed, numerous robots and dogs, five fighters, and three scouts destroyed, two carriers damaged and a cybermind eliminated. The outcome is a humiliating defeat for the Center, and complete eradication of the Bruderschaft."

My head is spinning at what Control is telling us.

"Hang on, are you telling us that Asal and Rewa won us the battle?" I ask, amazed. I thought she'd been at safely tucked away at Hastings worrying about *me*.

"Yes. Their pivotal actions, considering their young age and the number and size of the enemies they defeated can only be regarded as being of exemplary courage."

Scott starts to laugh. He grabs me.

"Outshone by your little sister!" he laughs, punching my arm.

"And Asal," I remind him.

"And Asal. Tahira will be gobsmacked too!"

I just laugh and shake my head. My head's spinning. We'd done incredibly well. I just felt unbelievably tired. Hekator's Avatar appears.

"Sam? I was just wondering if I could ask you a rather ... sensitive question."

I shrug, "ask away?"

"Umm well it's about your Grandfather's brain."

"What about it?"

"I'd like to copy it."

"Copy it?"

"Yes. I have to do it now while degeneration is still limited. Mike was a great thinker and I want to build him into the new computer I'm building for you. It'll be a fusion of Mike, Control and a bit of Sue as well, plus the bits of Dr Prosperov he's given me access to."

"OK. Sounds good."

"It means I need to take his body for a while."

"Yeah ... uh so long as someone's always with him, that should be ok. It's important to us that he isn't left alone. So long as you do that it should be OK. Send him back when you're finished though."

"Of course."

The box Grandpop's in begins to close up. Hekator goes to vanish.

"Hekator?" I ask.

"If you copy his brain will this computer be ... well, will it be like Grandpop?"

The box folds away.

"You mean in personality?"

"Yeah ... or whatever."

"It could be, although you may find that psychologically troubling."

"But if we want it?"

"I can't bring your Grandfather back to life, Sam. All I can do is make a computer that mimics him. It won't *be* him. Fundamentally it will still be a computer. You are *where* you stand. That is core to being and the soul. Our vantage point on the universe of which we are a part is the essence of our being. Your grandfather was not a computer and so no matter how well a computer mimics him it can never be your grandfather."

"Yeah ... I get that. But it would be better than just a picture of him."

"Perhaps. Anyway if I begin now I can recover more of what he once was than if I start later. So I thank you for your permission."

"Hekator?"

"Yes Sam?"

"Did my little sister really save us all?"

"There were other positive possibilities but Rewa and Asal guaranteed us the best. You are right to be proud of her, Sam."

And with that he vanishes.

I jump up.

"Well, I don't have to be here now," I announce to Scott.

I feel like doing something.

"I guess I don't either. What do you want to do?"

I think about that for a moment. I remember that while we've stopped the contaminated vaccine plot the air crew plot using perfume bottles hasn't been stopped yet.

"Get Maartens and the perfume bottles," I say.

"Bloody good idea," says Scott, "Where is he?"

I shrug.

"Control?"

"The target is at Narita Excel Tokyu hotel. Room 1256."

"Is that where he is right now?"

"Yes. Look!"

We go over to the desk. It's kind of strange because this was where Grandpop usually was. Maartens is in his hotel room wearing a white lab cover-all, hair-cover, eye protection and a face mask. On the table are about thirty boxes all containing five or six small perfume sample dispensers. In front of him is a small black device with a round central part which has thin glass tubes around the outside. He has a small vice with a magnifying glass on it and is carefully dropping liquid from the glass tubes into the unscrewed perfume dispensers. He'd obviously been doing this for a while because he's made up a whole lot of special gift packs featuring the perfume.

"What are we going to do with him?" Scott asks.

That is a hard one. I'm not sure. Then it comes to me.

"Grandpop's Mexican solution!" I grin.

Scott smiles back.

"Santa Elena?" he asks

"Does he speak Spanish?" I ask.

"He can learn," Scott says.

"And his stuff?"

"Nyiragongo's lava is pretty hot," Scott says.

"OK, so what do you want to do?" I ask.

"I'll dump his stuff. You dump him."

"Deal," I say.

So we pop into the cabinets and flash into Paul Maarten's hotel room. He doesn't even get a chance to look around. I zap him and he falls forward and then slides off his chair onto the clean floor. I walk over, and pull him out straight while Scotty begins stacking his samples into a travel box. Then, whistling away, I pull Maartens into a sleeping bag, seal it up, wave to Scott, and vanish.

[+]

It's dark on the beach of Santa Elena Island. Dark and raining. That's actually good news for Maartens because there isn't always water here. The sea is high and it's a bit cold, but it doesn't stop me emptying him roughly out onto the sand. He lies there looking peaceful. He's in for a bit of a shock when he wakes up, but considering I'd cut his brothers in half with a plasma torch he's actually doing alright.

I sort of feel funny because I think maybe I should cut him with a plasma torch but I know I can't. When I was fighting, it was simply them or us. But I can't kill in cold blood like Hathaway did. No, Maartens can take his chances here. Maybe he'd learn about being dependent on the good will of others. But I doubt it. The sea smells good, and the rain is cleaning too. Scotty has finished tossing Maartens stuff into the boiling lava of Mr Nyiragongo so we both come home.

[+]

"What do you think Inspector Du Croix's doing?" Scott asks.

"I dunno."

"Do you think we should find him?"

"Why?"

"In case he's going to arrest everyone, like he said he would," Scott says.

That raises a question.

"Control?"

"Yes, Sam?"

"Is that CIA warning still active?"

"Yes it is."

"What can we do about that?"

"The main problem is Inspector Turneau. He has the evidence linking you to Virion."

That's true. But now all his bosses are dead. We know already from the way he'd reacted to Semovich when Sarah had vanished leaving him without any defences that Turneau would change his tune very fast if he thought something might come back to get him.

"Do you think we should visit Turneau?" I ask Scott.

"Yeah...but let's take the sceptres."

"Gaylord!" I tease him.

"Do we know where Turneau is?" asks Scott.

"I have his address," Control says.

[+]

The man was asleep. It was five in the morning. A woman, probably his wife, was next to him.

"*Stun her. Toast his undies,*" I shrug.

Scott laughs, "Rather you than me bra! Theenk of the smell."

So we flash into Inspector Turneau's rather expensive home. I stun Mrs Turneau and Scott shouts "RIIIIINNGGGGG" right by the Inspector's ear.

He goes for his gun but the two glowing sceptres pointed at him make him change his mind. It's a brief conversation in which we explain that we've killed the entire Bruderschaft, defeated the Center's two carriers and find his bedside lamp so ugly we need to burn it to charred wood, before turning to the need for him to set the record straight with Interpol and the CIA regarding

Virion's activity.

"Not only can we get you any time we like, we have the Bruderschaft files on you Inspector," Scott lies seriously, sitting on his legs in bed. "Who knows where they might end up if we ... well, if we were displeased," he says, getting up.

It's hard to keep a straight face.

[+]

We vanish right in front of him and are laughing like hyenas when we came out of the Cabinets at Hastings.

"What is happening? Why is laughing?" Dr P asks, bewildered, descending on a disc.

We explain what we've been up to. Dr P is pleased and relieved.

"I concerned about arrivals so come here," then he seems to realise that we know he can do that from his office and adds, "and to escape Miss Kahu," he admits.

"Your aunt is ... what is word ... *bossy*?"

I nod.

"Yes she is *very* bossy woman. Even bosses *Katya*!" he says as if that proves that Aunty Liz is the most bossy person imaginable. He shrugs.

"Control please to search Buenos Aires airport for Inspector Du Croix," he asks Control.

"Certainly Dr Prosperov."

We wait for a moment. I feel questions building inside me but Dr P seems to be carefully avoiding my eyes. Control reports back.

"He is not anywhere in Ministro Pistarini airport Dr Prosperov."

"And Abu Dhabi?"

"A moment please."

Again we wait.

"No. He isn't there either."

"Narita or Changi?"

In the silence I finally get up the courage to ask Dr Prosperov what I've been wanting to know.

"Dr Prosperov, who is Loki?"

Scott is suddenly very interested in Dr P too. For a moment he acts like he hasn't heard me. I'm just about ask again when he answers.

"Loki is a multi-dimensional being. Many such beings have and do manifest themselves on Earth. Some are more powerful than others. Their power in our dimensions is not very strong, normally, which is why they need followers. Loki is from a family of gods brought here by some of the earliest Aesir visitors. But unlike the others he is opposed to ideas of racial supremacy and was imprisoned."

"But he's not evil is he?"

"Depends on definition of evil. For those ancient Vikings was no greater evil than hordes of non-whites. Black skin meant evil. Even today there are those who hate multiculturalism. But is not unusual. Some Chinese thought and still think the same of non-Chinese, or Japanese of non-Japanese, or Muslims or non-Muslims. The list is endless. To them evil means opposite of self. So can justify murder, torture and genocide as part of battle against evil."

He smiles at us, wearily.

"You must have noticed Fae, descended from Devi, look as traditional European devils. Loki is called black and evil in old stories because opposed Aesir who told story. Aesir were white, pure and strong. Loki is opposite. Associated with giants, goblins and others. He portrayed as weak and tricky. Even yet

401

Aesir knew must lose eventually. But are stubborn. Would rather die defending purity. They foresaw if Loki escaped it meant their end. Their destruction, the Ragnarok, was inevitable."

"But what's the connection between the Aesir and the Center or the Iyrin?" asks Scott.

"Is guess only. Suspect Aesir, Iyrin and some Swerge allied. Connection with Center is unknown. Perhaps oppose, perhaps support. Is possible both is true. This is reason I seek Du Croix." He sighs, sitting in Grandpop's old chair.

"Has been big day. Suggest you get some food. I shall watch others and call you to get them when time comes."

I suddenly realise how empty I feel. Scott doesn't need telling twice, either so we take a disc to the surface and walk back to Hastings Hall in the deep yellow light as the sun goes down.

CHAPTER EIGHTY NINE: WAR STORIES AND TEARS

When we get into Hastings we find Aunty Liz's set up a kind of makeshift hospital in the library around some plates of pizza. Sue, Bernard, and Mr Trân are out-to-it on mattresses on the floor. Zoe and Patience with Dr M and Irina are playing around them. Cam has been taken onto Ashanti somewhere, and the rest are on their planes. The women are talking adult stuff with Rewa hanging around the edges.

Scott and me swap a plan psychically and walk up to Rewa pretending to be grumpy.

"Hey Rewa? What's all this about you being a bigger hero than us!" Scott demands.

Rewa bursts into a huge grin. I pretend to be grumpy too, though we're all finding it hard not to smile.

"Yeah sis! The way I hear it you and Asal saved everyone. That's not your job!"

Now she's grinning shyly.

Aunty Liz and the others have stopped talking too, and are smiling at us.

"Go on Rewa, tell your brother and Scott what you did," Aunty Liz encourages her.

So we sit down to eat pizza and listen to Rewa.

"Well, we didn't think it was gonna be such a big deal when we started," she admits.

"We knew you'd cleared out the robots. We thought Control had been grabbed by some unguarded system. Ashanti was busy but had time to bend us. Me and Asal had suits, and the others didn't, so that meant they had to use sleeping bags to set up a base, but they needed someone to bend them in. So we were only meant to bend them in and go home again with the empty bags. But then from the moment we arrived everything went wrong."

"Ashanti had to do some complicated moves to get away from the carriers so she was too busy for us. Then the dogs came. The others zapped them but the wands didn't seem strong enough by themselves but our ones, with the suit's extra power, meant we could take them down easily, like waving a torch and down they went. Gunter said we needed to get up the mountain so we could see them coming because in the dark forest those animals just came up on us so quick and silently it was really scary."

"So we had to run for the mountain which was quite hard for Aunty Patricia and Aunty Liz, and even Gunter. At first we thought we'd dodged them but then Asal spotted a line of robots who were coming the other way to get us. Luckily Ashanti came free again so we could bend up to the lookout. We also got an extra supply of marbles."

"That got us away from the robots and the dogs but it didn't get us any closer to the castle to take out that vortex thingy which had Control. So Gunter decides that because he knows the mountain, he might have a chance to slip through and use the marbles, so off he went. He was gone about fifteen minutes when we see flashes and realise he's in trouble so me and Asal ran off before mum, I mean Aunty Liz, and Patricia could stop us, and help Gunter escape. The problem is now they've worked out where we are and they start chasing *us*."

"Then Ashanti decides that she can bend in a black marble to take out the vortex. Then she'll bend us home. Only we soon realise pretty soon that not only has the black marble not destroyed the vortex but we aren't hearing anything from Ashanti either. Plus...plus the dogs and robots have started climbing the hill."

"So this is where me and Asal decide the only way out is to take out the vortex ourselves. So we grab some blue ones and some black ones and then slip away using our suits' hiding powers."

"Instead of fighting we let them walk right over us. The dogs couldn't smell us and the robots thought we were rocks. Then we slipped down into the forest, and ran to the castle. At the castle we had to zap some robots. Quite a few robots really. We could hear some bangs and things from up the mountain which turned out to be Gunter starting a landslide to hold the dogs and robots off. "

"When we got into the castle the vortex generator looked like an ordinary radiator heater except it was all shining with blue lightning on its fins and stuff. So we threw some black ones at that and it vanished."

"And then you could bend again," I put in.

"No, because Ashanti was too busy and Control was just recovering. So then we had to fight our way back through the dark forest back up to Aunty Liz and the others so we could all bend out."

"Wow," Scotty says.

"I did not know you were that staunch, Sis. I really didn't," I tell her.

"Neither did we, but Asal kept saying that if Tahira could do it, she could and I kept thinking of you, and I kept thinking what I'd made you promise and that now I had to live up to it myself." I laugh.

"What did you make Sam promise?" Aunty Liz asks.

"To remember GTF-OOP," I tell her.

"Oh!" Aunty Liz says, while Zoe and Dr M chuckle.

Everyone smiles for a moment. Then seriously Rewa asks.

"Sam? How did Grandpop die?"

I look at Scott, he shrugs and looks at me.

"Um ... I'm not exactly sure. I mean ... well we were surrounded by about two hundred Bruderschaft."

The women and Rewa gasp.

"Yeah, we were dead meat, they had us under total mind control. We were just completely stuffed. And then..."

"Dr P got them really riled up over something..." Scott put in.

"And suddenly Grandpop had his gun out and was shooting them," I tell them.

"Which distracted them from us so we could blast them to hell with the sceptres," Scott finishes.

"And so you could get away, " Rewa says happily.

"Ah ... well no, not really," Scott admits.

"Well, we couldn't blast *all* of them before they got us again. There were over a hundred of them left."

"We had to knock out Sue and Bernard to stop them being forced to kill themselves,"

"So what did you do?" asks Zoe.

"Ask him," Scott says nodding at me, "they were going to cut my throat open when they stopped. I just saw Sam getting up like a hundred Bruderschaft willing him dead was no big deal. Then he starts shouting in Maori with a huge voice that didn't sound like him, and then he does this haka with his sceptre which was better than anything I ever saw him do before, and it's like, even for me, obvious the Bruderschaft are losing. What was all that bra?"

Now they're all looking at me.

"Um ... Well ... they tortured me and knocked me out and I had this dream about Khadiyeh."

"Khadiyeh!" Scott asks.

"Yeah ... and she said the dead would help if they were asked. And then, well all these spirits showed up, from Renwick, you know the ones who died in the Spanish flu? And then there were Maori spirits, and Kurdish spirits, and Zulu spirits, all kinds. And ... well ... after that, they just charged the Bruderschaft! And when the spirits went through them they just ... just wasted them, like they were candles blown out by a wind. Then they all just vanished."

There's a silence. I realise everyone else is looking a bit freaked out.

"Actually there was a bit more to it than that. I mean ... well it all started when the Bruderschaft were crushing the life out of us and they had this silver skull thing which makes your soul go cold ... anyway it was killing us and I found ... Well, I ended up focusing on Rewa ... and that ... well ...it sorta helped stop me from going cold so that was when they tortured me ... and then after ... after Khadiyeh no matter what the skull thing did I just couldn't go cold ... and then Grandpop ... Mike ... he must have been his spirit then ... anyway he told me they were with me ... and all these spirits just made me hotter and hotter ... and so when I blasted the skull they had nothing to hold all our spirits back with."

Now they're shaking their heads.

"So ... I guess what I'm saying is it wasn't just me ... it was everyone ... and when they came to me it was more like I was just the meeting place ... oh, I don't know! I don't really know what happened," I give up because it all seems too raw and too confusing.

Aunty Liz is looking at me with worry in her eyes.

Suddenly Mr Trân moans. We all look around at him.

"Sam could you get Nguyen a sports drink from the kitchen fridge, not the caffeinated ones, just the electrolyte ones," Aunty Liz says.

So I do. When I come back Mr Trân is looking groggy. He drank the sports drink quickly.

"Where Cam?" he asks looking around, when he'd finished.

"She's on Ashanti, Hekator's looking after her leg," Aunty Liz explains.

That takes a moment to sink in.

"Take me to her," he says.

We all look at each other. I ask Control for Mr Trân and he passes it on. A moment later Hekati says Mr Trân should come and see Cam and a coffin appears in a flash of light. Mr Trân pauses, but then just throws himself in and lets the lid close before he folds away to nothing.

Meanwhile Zoe is checking Bernard when he wakes up. Scott gets him the sports drink this time and he drinks it through a straw while Patience climbs on him. He says he has a really bad headache and asks what happened. He's clearly shocked when we tell him about Grandpop. At first he can't believe it, but the looks on Aunty Liz and Rewa's faces make it clear we aren't playing a joke. We're all a bit quiet after that and the Khumalos seem to feel a bit uncomfortable and make an excuse about having to get back on their plane and leave.

Dr M takes Irina and goes with them to find out what Dr P is doing.

Now it's just Aunty Liz, Rewa, me and Sue, who's still unconscious. We start to talk about what kind of Tangi we should have for Grandpop. It's hard because he wasn't really into Maori stuff. He would probably have liked a military funeral. Then we start to talk about why we thought he'd been happy at the end. Aunty Liz says he hadn't really liked getting older and had got more and more gloomy until he'd come to Renwick.

"I think it was the best time of his life," she says. "He really was happy there."

And now Renwick's a ruin, he's dead and his old house was contaminated with meth.

"How do we explain his body?" I ask, suddenly.

"He was old. He smoked and he had high blood pressure. They'll put it down to natural causes," Aunty Liz says.

"I feel funny about him being buried here," Rewa says. "This wasn't his place."

"No, that's true. But we could always visit him. It will be a way to remember him."

"We could do better than that!" I say, and tell them about Hekator's brain copying plan.

"Oh Sam, I don't think I like that," says Aunty Liz when she's heard what I had to say.

"No, dad is dead. I don't want some computerised avatar of him," she says.

I have to admit that that was what Hekator had said too.

"But I don't think it's right to bury him here either," Rewa insists. "He should be back home with Nana."

"I'm pretty sure he didn't want to be buried either. He said cremation was cheaper. He may have even put it in his will. He was always so difficult about Maori traditions," Aunty Liz says. Suddenly Sue moans.

"I've got it," I say, going off to get the drink.

When I get back Liz is filling her in on what happened while she was out. I give her the drink. She sips on it as she listens to Aunty Liz. She's very impressed with Rewa and gives her a big high five. Rewa blushes a bit over that.

"But what about Maartens?" she asks, remembering.

I told her about him and Turneau.

"And Du Croix?"

I told her that Dr's P and M are looking for him. Suddenly she realises something.

"What about Mike? Where's he?"

We look at each other. Sue's eyes widen.

So we tell her about it. She has little tears in the corners of her eyes, and she'd only known him a few days.

"That is so sad," she says finally. "He was an incredible guy." She looks around at us.

"I think you all need a hug," she says.

So she gives us all a hug starting with Rewa. I have to admit I'd forgotten how good her hugs are but I let go eventually. Aunty Liz wants to pass but Sue makes her. I notice that Aunty Liz changes from not so keen, to holding Sue quite close. When they pull apart they both laugh and seem a bit embarrassed.

"That was really nice," Sue smiles around at us.

"I feel a bit like part of the whanau (family) now," she says, and then seems a bit embarrassed by what she's said and decides to go have a shower and get changed.

Aunty Liz has a happy smile on her face after she'd gone. Then she notices Rewa and me looking at her.

"What?" she demands.

"I really like her Aunty Liz," Rewa says shyly.

"I like her too, Rewa," Aunty Liz admits.

Then she glances at me, looking pleased with myself.

"I didn't say I fancied her. I just said I liked her, so you can wipe that look off your face Samuel Kahu," she tells me.

"Now that everyone's up, let's find out what's going on."

And what went on was a party. It started very slowly. It picked up when Mariko, Gunter and Mrs Jones landed and passed through Immigration without problems. Then it grew again when the Robinsons and Ken did the same in Buenos Aires. The Khadems and Gursoys had no problems in Abu Dhabi and the Khumalos were fine in Johannesburg. As each family bent back from the airport the talking got louder, the food got more generous and the adults drank another round of toasts.

At eight the Tran's came back from Ashanti. There was a bit of a shocked silence when we learned Cam had lost the lower half of her left leg, but Hekator had attached a biomechanical one which worked almost exactly the same her natural one. He's also promised that he will help her re-grow a normal leg over the next six months. Tarik is very pleased to see her and they kiss a lot.

Grandpop joins us at ten. By now we're all very happy and everyone makes a lot of speeches to him about what a wonderful guy he was. A lot of people kissed him. There are a lot of tears, praise for Asal and Rewa, and speeches. But by eleven this incredibly long day is taking its toll. Hekator moved Grandpop to the library. Rewa and me lay down on the mattresses as the party moved there. I don't know how it ended. One minute I was hearing Mariko telling a long story about Mike and the next I was asleep.

The nightmare is horrible.
We're in the tunnels again but every monk is Grandpop. I save Rewa but kill him time after slow motion time. I wake up feeling terrible and lie in the darkness until I hear Rewa whimpering and moaning with fear in her dreams. I crawl over to her mattress, tell her quietly she'll be okay and put my arms around her. She half wakes but then snuggles down with her back to me. Within half an hour she's snoring peacefully and I'm still wide awake.
It's half past four in the morning.
I lie there with stuff going around and around in by brain. I'm trying to remember if I've forgotten anything. But the more my brain goes around the more I think of Emma. The sun will be rising on Aotea about now. I wonder what the weather is like. After half an hour cuddling Rewa and being too scared of the nightmares to go back to sleep I get up and bend to the park by Emma's place.

[+]

It's an amazing dawn on Aotea. It's cool and very still. The sun is already up and a slight frost is being burned off into a mist that seems too lazy to be bothered doing anything. I walk down to Emma's house enjoying the bright yellow light.
It's early Sunday morning. Emma's parents aren't church people

and it's still early so they'll probably be asleep. I slip around to her window and direct an annoying burst of eighteen to twenty kilocycles at her, which she can hear but her dad can't. It takes about five minutes to wake her but when she does she slips under her curtain and opens her window.

She pulls jeans and a jacket over her pyjamas and sticks her feet in Ug boots and swings out of the window easily. Em gives me a nod to stay quiet and follow her down to her horse's paddock. As we get further from the house she yawns.

"What' sup?"

Now I yawn too.

"Aw, I'm officially leaving the country today."

"Oh."

That's a downer. We thread our way under the fruit trees. The grass is wet.

"We've been flying everyone out."

"Yeah?"

"And then we got in the shit a bit."

I pause. She detects a catch.

"But you got out OK?"

"Yeah, except for Grandpop."

"What?"

We come to the gate at the bottom of the garden and swing on top of it facing each other.

You could just see the house through all the fruit trees. The gate attaches to a kind of concrete wall where an old shed had been. The horses are looking curiously in our direction.

"Grandpop's dead. The Bruderschaft killed him. They damn near killed all of us actually."

"Shit! Are they after you now?"

"No."

She looks questioningly into my eyes.

"They're dead. All of them. We killed them all. Us ... and the ghosts."

"All! How many of them?" she asks, gobsmacked.

"About two hundred."

"Holy crap!" she says, shocked.

She checks me.

"Are *you* OK?"

I sigh.

"Uh ... I dunno ... I couldn't sleep so well."

"I'm not surprised," she says looking around.

It's a fabulous morning. The horses are plodding slowly in our direction wondering if anything is happening. The sun is warm but the shadows cold.

"I'm really going to miss seeing you at school," I tell her.

She looks back at me.

"Oh come here! You obviously need a hug!" she says.

I shove forward along the gate but our knees hit first and we can't reach each other. I jump down off the gate and she jumps into my arms. She feels fantastic, and in no time at all our lips have found their way together too. It's a long, gentle snog. Then we part to draw breath.

"Are you going to come and see me?" she asks.

"I was thinking of asking you to come with me?" I say.

"Now!?"

"No, I mean at weekends and stuff. We could go on dates to places. So long as I'm not working."

"Where?"

"Wherever you like. Paris is nice. Tahira knows it well."

"I don't want to go out with Tahira!" she complains.

"No, I mean she can tell us good places. She's good like that,"

"I'd rather go skiing or swimming, or riding even."

"We can go to our own desert island, climb mountains or crash a resort. Anything you like."

"I'd like that," she smiles, and we kiss again.

I press her up against the concrete wall and let my hands roam a bit. She doesn't seem to mind at all and I have to admit I'm getting pretty turned on now. In fact she's doing the same. We break off a bit breathless.

"Sam?" she gasps.

"Yeah?"

"There is one thing."

"Yeah?"

"You gotta find a way to travel without these damn romper suits!"

I press against her.

"As of now it's my top priority," I tell her.

"Good!" she says and jumps, wraps her legs around me, and clamps her mouth on mine. I back her up against the concrete wall. We're getting pretty excited when we hear the curtains in her room being pulled.

"Emma?" Tama yells out the window.

Our mouths release each other.

"Bugger," she says.

"I'd better go," I tell her.

"Yep," she agrees, looking at my mouth.

I kiss her again, but she breaks away and drops to her feet.

"Come back soon," she says, kisses me quickly again, before turning to the gate.

"I will, I promise, see ya."

"Whaaat?" Emma yells up towards the house.

"What are ya doing?"

"Looking for fairies."

"What!?" Tama yells.

"I'm looking for fairies at the bottom of the garden!"

We're killing ourselves laughing as I seal up. I wave and fold away back to Hastings.

[+]

The lightning, wind and rain cools me down a bit. It's hard not to think of Emma so it's lucky the suit looks loose. Otherwise it would be pretty embarrassing. I go back to Hastings Hall and discover I'm not the only one up. Mr Trân and Cam are there with Tarik, Ashley and Scott. Only Tahira's sleeping in.

It turns out that none of us have slept well. We've all had nightmares about monks or dogs or robots. To get over it Mr Trân is teaching everyone how to roll and fill pastries.

"Aren't you sick of wearing that suit?" Scott asks. "You've been wearing it for days."

Strangely enough I wasn't. Somehow I feel like it's keeping me together.

"Well, I don't have any clothes left," I admits.

"None of us have much to wear," Tarik points out.

He's wearing a strange collection of thermal underwear and a T big enough for a small hippo. He isn't alone. They look like they've raided a recycling bin or something.

"Sooo let's goooo shopping!," Ash laughs, painting glaze on a Danish.

"Where's open?" I ask.

"The States is right now," Ash says.

416

"'Cept it's still Saturday," Scott says.

"That don't matter none," she replies.

"So where do we go?" I ask.

"You buy clothes where weather is same as here," Mr Trân advises, rolling his croissants.

That sounds sensible.

"I bet I can guess where that's going to be," Scott says.

"You betcha cute white ass baby. It's da Easy," Ash says.

"But they'll be going inta Summer, won't they?" Tarik says.

"Which is why we can crawl Canal Street and git awl dey're winter shit reeeal cheap," Ashley says.

"Well, if we are going shopping we have to take Tahira. She'd kill us if we went without her," I warn.

"I get her," Cam says, jumping up.

We all look at her leg.

She pulls up her trouser leg to show us. The leg goes around her calf from the knee down. It's a perfect shape and goes down to a foot that looks almost normal. It blends perfectly with her skin.

"Watch this," she grins, and deliberately hops on the fake leg. It squishes down unnaturally and then she jumps almost a meter in the air. She lands easily. We all clap.

"I can only hop so high because it's hollow so as leg re-grows it will fill the hole." she explains.

Then she hops out of the kitchen like a rubberband animal in search of Tahira. Her father watches after her. He shakes his head.

"Cam very lucky. I see many, many, pretty girl lose leg or hand and they never get back."

"As lucky as anyone shot by a machine gun could be," Scott points out.

417

"We was all lucky," Tarik says," When I think over it again it gives me the heebies," he comments.

"Do you think Loki made us lucky?" Ashley asks.

"I don't know what Loki did," I say.

"And what about you? Where did all that power in you come from?" asks Tarik.

"I dunno. I just talked to Khadiyeh and the next thing I knew I was channelling it."

"Was Jibreel there? Scott asks.

I shake my head, "I dunno. All I saw was Mike, and then the ghosts from Renwick . It sure wasn't me. It was like those lines we had with Jibreel and then this horde of spirits from your countries and mine. Something weird was happening alright."

"Yeah, but to *you* mate. To *you*," Tarik points out.

"Well, if it hadn't, we'd all be dead," Scott reminds us.

"Could you do it again?" Tarik asks me.

"Well, if someone was torturing me and seriously threatening to kill all of you guys and Rewa too, I dunno?" I shrug. "Maybe? Do you want to find out?"

"Nah, not a helluva lot, no, mate," Tarik says seriously, finishing his tray.

"Maybe Mrs Jones will have some idea," Scott suggests, doing his last pain au chocolat.

"She can guess," Ash suggests. "Ah believe dat all dis right here? It's a whole new ball game of weirdness dat nobody's seen afore. Dat's what ah think."

I nod.

"Hmmm," disagrees Scott.

"Wat?" Ashley challenges him.

"I think I might know of some chaps who might have some idea back in Zim,"

"Who?"

"My Grandfather Robert knew some strange Sangomas in Botswana who may have some clues."

"Well, maybe you right. Da more we learn, da weirder dis ol planet seems to git," Ashley admits.

That's true enough.

We help Mr Trân clean up and after a while Tahira comes down with Cam. Unlike us Tahira didn't get to sleep until very late and has been sleeping. Cam left her until six thirty but woke her in case we were off shopping. By now the adults are also rousing. Mariko comes down, looking sick, asking for a cup of green tea. Zoe and Bernard were up with Patience, while Rewa comes over for a cup of tea for Aunty Liz. I go back with her to see Aunty Liz, who's with Grandpop. Mariko comes to join us too followed by Zoe and Bernard with Patience.

"We need a funeral for Grandpop," Rewa says to Mariko before Aunty Liz even gets to have a sip of tea.

"Yeah, I know. I would rike to design one for you," Mariko says.

"I think he would have really liked that. Today I have to go through his stuff and see what he left behind. But he can't be left alone." Aunty Liz seems worried nobody else will sit with a dead man.

"That is not a problem," Bernard assures her.

"We've made our flight from New Zealand. We can wait with Mike and let Patience play here. I think Irina will come by to play soon as well."

"We'll just have to tag team it having breakfast," Zoe says.

Aunty Liz is reassured by this, and as more adults arrive, including the Khadem's, Gursoys and Robinsons, is pleased they

419

all happily agree to help out with the vigil over Grandpop.

So Aunty Liz takes a break to go upstairs and get dressed. In the meantime we gather around eating breakfast. We kids are still keen to go buy some clothes. But the adults say that the best place to buy them isn't New Orleans, but Hobart, an hour up the road. They point out we need to blend in. I can't help glancing over at Grandpop, remembering everything he'd ever told us about that. The adults say we need more school clothes because that was where we will be seen the most.

Realising that I will be going to school the next day is a huge downer. After two weeks of adventure the idea that it's back to the grind of boring old school does not excite me at all. The others aren't comforting either.

"Don't worry Mrs Driver is better than Mr Wakefield. She doesn't do idiot projects. She seems to be pleased if we do any work at all," Scott says.

"Yeah doin woik makes you a real stand out in dat class," Ashley agrees.

It sounds mindbendingly dull. I don't know if I can stand it.

"Then there's all the fun to be had in the grounds, yeah?" Tarik says grimly.

"Like what?"

"Smokin, drinking, drugs, sex and violence. If it were a bleedin movie they wouldn't let us watch it. Know what I mean?"

They aren't exactly selling the place.

"Still, at least the work isn't hard. They don't exactly expect much," Scott says.

Well, that's something. I sigh. It's a different kind of survival mode. For two weeks life had been a high-stress rollercoaster with no need for patience. Now it's back to low stress, but needing lots of patience. It's just different.

Something is tugging at my mind. It's Aunty Liz. Something big is upsetting her. I look around.

"Hang on a minute," I mutter and start heading for the apartments.

Rewa's eating breakfast, but I tell her to come with me.

"Why?" she complains.

"Aunty Liz," I mouth at her.

She shrugs, so I just go anyway. I hear her drop her spoon muttering about how bossy and unreasonable I am, but I still lead the way up the stairs.

Aunty Liz isn't in our apartment. It's steamy, so she's had her shower and dressed but she isn't there. That has to mean she's in Grandpop's. I turn, nearly knocking over Rewa.

"Watchit!" she complains grumpily.

But I sidestep her and go back to the corridor. The door to Grandpop's place is open. At first I think she isn't there either. But there are funny little sounds coming from inside. I push the door open and see Aunty Liz.

I don't think she even sees me. She's sitting on the couch. Her whole body is shaking and her mouth's open with just these small gurgles coming out. Her eyes are closed and tears flow freely down her cheeks. In her hand is a letter.

Rewa didn't need to be told what to do. She shot into the arms of the only mother she'd ever known, throwing her arms around her neck. As Aunty Liz groans, squeezing the girl who so looked like her dead sister, I gently take the letter, turn and put it on Grandpop's desk.

There, to my surprise, I see three envelopes. One has my name on it, another's Rewa's, a third is for everyone, all in Grandpop's careful handwriting. Aunty Liz is still crying and Rewa is still cuddling her.

I know what this is.

Grandpop had known. He had left us a last goodbye. Almost scared of cracking up like Aunty Liz I quietly open the envelope and take out the letter.

Dear Son,

If you are reading this it's because I have had to sacrifice myself to save you. Don't be sad about that, sometimes war demands it and I can't think of a better man to do it for.
Look after your Aunt and your sister. I know you will anyway but do it for me too. I've seen a lot of life and a lot of death and I know which I prefer. I don't want to die. I love you all very much and I know you will miss me too.
I know you have always wondered whether you are the same as your father. You look the same but that is all. You have your mother's heart and brain. You are and have always been a Kahu and I am very proud of you.
Tell the other kids I have never met a finer group of young people in all my life. They have been the best trainees I ever had and the world is a safer and better place because of them.
As you know I have never been a great believer in all the spooky stuff you do. As far as I was concerned the dead are dead and that is that. But if we do continue in some way don't doubt I will be watching over you all.
Arohanui
Mike Kahu.

Every sentence hammered into my heart and my eyes are streaming. I sniff, trying to hold it together.

"Sam? What did he say?" Aunty Liz asks.

Then I burst, and throw myself into her arms and cry like a baby, shuddering and gasping like I'm five years old and Rewa isn't with me at school.

That was a very wet hour we spent in Grandpop's room. Rewa's letter had the same effect on her as mine had had on me. Finally we get it together enough to go back downstairs. We take the letter for the others. It goes through the house like a weeping virus. People would start reading it, get halfway and their faces would screw up.

Sue wasn't so badly affected although she did dab at her eyes a bit. Neither was Mrs Jones. But I was, again, surprised by Mariko and Ken, Patricia and Bernard. Of all though, it was Mr Trân who seems most hurt. He didn't cry so much as seem stunned. We are all gathered around Grandpop crying and hugging when Dr Prosperov, Dr Morozo and Irina come in. Silently Zoe passes the letter to Dr P.

He read it quickly, then closes his eyes, letting Dr M take it from his hands. Dr P stands for quite a long time breathing hard. Then he opens his eyes and wipes them.

"Mr Kahu ... Mike ... did not hesitate when symbiont Loki asked him," he starts.

This is news. We all look at him as he tries to get it out.

"Loki could insulate only one of our party from mind control effects of hundreds of Bruderschaft but only while focus was spread evenly."

"Whoever that individual was could act briefly, then *all* Bruderschaft would be focused on him. That would be fatal.

There could be no stopping them all. Loki realised only escape was for one to draw all Bruderschaft focus so that others could be freed to fight."

"He did not ask Bernard, as a father, nor Sue as a young woman with her life before her. Nor, of course, our children. He asked Mike, who understood immediately and agreed."

"As he says, he did not want to die, but he knew if others to live, that would be price. And it was. I have seen this before in war. Is strange perhaps that great barbarity inspires such great love. But is no question in my mind Mike had shown and gained love of all of you here before then. As a soldier in battle it was that love he showed us. We all owe him very much."

"Mike suggests Mariko designs a party for his funeral. I will happily meet any costs. Obviously his daughter Liz is in charge of this event and I am sure it will be suitable."

"It is unfortunate, however that I may miss this as I may be arrested by New Zealand police today. Our new colleague Sue Williams must this afternoon return to New Zealand to carry out her last duty as a policewoman. That is to bring me to her superiors for questioning. Also, in a few hours the Kahus and the Trâns must fly from New Zealand to Australia."

"I therefore suggest that we plan the funeral for our friend now, and prepare for the conclusion of our business in New Zealand. Could I see Sue, Bernard, Ken and Nguyen with all the children in my office. Mrs Jones could you help Ms Kahu and Mrs Zimmermann organise the funeral."

"When Dr Prosperov?" asks Mrs Jones.

"I think now."

"Can I ask that we always have someone by dad?" Aunty Liz asks uncertainly.

"We plan his funeral with him," Mariko smiles grimly settling down on one of the mattresses.

Dr Prosperov's glance swept over us and then he turns back to his office while Zoe and Dr M settle down to watch over their babies. The rest of us followed after Dr P.

He leads us into his office in silence, holds the door open and then closes it behind us. It isn't a big office so nine of us fill it. Dr P sits behind his desk facing us.

"I need you all to tell me who will take over as operations and training manager from Mike Kahu," he sighs. "All adults here are qualified. Ken has a natural understanding of managing psychics and has urban security experience in United States. Bernard has a strong understanding of natural world and spiritual matters. Nguyen was young agent in middle of war. And Sue understands policing. You have all – including children – shown bravery when facing enemies."

"But job is mostly training and managing young people. As you know Mike was military man. Thought like military man which sometimes was good and sometimes, as he said, not so good. But good thing about Mike was knew his limits and asked for help when needed. Person needed must be good with others, and ask for help, but most important must have strong understanding of young people from different cultures and backgrounds. Must understand matters our young operatives are about to grow into and be able to help them with these problems before they interfere with our mission."

"Also like Mike must be impartial among operatives. Although Mike was practically father of Sam he did not protect or favour him. He mentored and advised the others, both boys and girls, and he disciplined them too when needed."

Dr P sat back in his chair with his hands behind his head.

"So who should it be?" he asks.

"Dr Prosperov, I not want job. Very happy cooking," says Nguyen.

"Gennady, I think it's pretty obvious who should do this job," says Ken confidently.

"He needs a good understanding of security and complex environments because that's mostly where we operate. He needs experience with kids and not have to deal with the problems of being a stepfather at the same time. And he needs to be humble enough to come back to the group and ask for advice when out of his depth. So I think pretty obviously the best man for the job is Sue."

Bernard's face, which had been masking annoyance suddenly burst into brilliant grin. Ken looks around at Sue and winks. Sue's shocked. Dr Prosperov is looking at us with the crafty smile that told us this was exactly what he had wanted the whole time.

"Me!?" Sue objects.

"You are perfect for the job," Bernard assures her.

"What do operatives say?" Dr P asks us.

The others are all looking at Sue with careful eyes.

"Yeah, I think she'll do it alright," Tarik says.

"I zink she will do eet very well," Tahira says more firmly.

"I like to have woman in charge. Will be different," says Cam.

"Damn straight," says Ashley.

Everyone looks at Scott. He seems to be seeing something.

"I think you will be very good indeed," he tells her.

They look at me.

"Well, you know what I think," I shrug.

426

"Ms Williams?" Dr P asks.

"Well, Golly! Mike left bloody huge shoes to fill but if you all think I should give it a shot, then that's what I better do I guess."

Everyone pats her and shakes her hand except Dr P who stays behind his desk resting his head on his hands.

"Do you get paid extra for this?" she asks Dr P through the crowd suddenly.

"No," says Dr P fast as a gunshot.

We all laugh.

"Everyone gets paid the same here, except the kids who get danger rates," Ken tells her.

"Worth a try," Sue says.

"OK, is good. Ken, Bernard, Nguyen thank you to go now. I need to talk to operative team."

So the others leave. Dr P waits until they had gone.

"Friends, Control has found Inspector Du Croix…"

CHAP✝ER NINE✝Y: THE ✪LD F✪X

D u Croix is in office alone at Interpol," Dr P says. "I think he
wants to talk. I would like to talk to him. However I do not
trust him, and I won't ask you to return there. Therefore I would
like to abduct him rather than talk at his office. I suggest Sam
and Tahira do abducting, Cam and Tarik escort me, and Ashley
and Scott bring animals to provide watch."

"Does he drive home?" I ask.

Dr P shrugs, "is not known," he replies.

"Also I need to buy some clothes. I barely have any," I add.

"Is common problem. I believe common solution desirable. I
will talk to Mrs Jones," he agrees.

I like the way he takes the problem seriously.

"So is first mission for new operations and training..."

Control's voice sounds from no where.

"Inspector Du Croix is leaving his office," he warns

That isn't too surprising as it is six thirty his time.

Dr P pulls a face and we all turn and run for the greenhouse.

By the time we are in the cabinets with Buffy and Hooty stuffed,
complaining, into Scott and Ash's pockets, it's clear Du Croix
walks home through the park which is filled with interesting and
funny statues. Sue and Control sweep the skies and declare it

clear so Tahira and me bend in.

[+]

We flash into cover under some trees along the path Du Croix is following down to the lake. There were a few other people walking and cycling through on a Spring evening but the only one who notices us is Du Croix. You can tell only by the way he pauses briefly in mid-step but otherwise he continues on, hands in his coat, apparently thinking.

We scamper out from the trees and fall into step on either side. Tahira speaks to him in French.

"The boss wants a word," she tells him.

"Good, I want to talk to him too. Will you trust me to pick a suitable spot?"

We pause, to hear what Dr P says.

"Tell him yes."

"I honestly will not be offended if you must take me to see him," Du Croix allows.

"He says he doesn't trust you, but you can choose," Tahira says slyly.

But Du Croix is grumpy.

"He should trust me. The situation is very grave. We need to cooperate to prevent it getting out of control," he says gruffly.

We tag along beside him in silence.

"I will say this though. Your elimination of most of the Bruderschaft has certainly come as a surprise to many."

"It was a bit of a surprise to us too," I mutter, in English.

Du Croix shoots me a glance which shows he's noticed what I've said.

We arrive at the lakeside. It's a cool evening and nobody is going to hang around to admire the city's lights in the water. Du Croix turns right heading to the corner of the small lake. It's a pretty park, the gardeners have done a great job with the old trees which are turning green again with the arrival of Spring.

"Ask him where he's going so we can meet him there," Sue suggests.

Tahira does so and Du Croix says the circle by the old house.

"Thanks," Sue says.

We walk past a statue showing a small group of people levering the world[†]. It makes me think of us. It seems to mean the same to Du Croix who notices the same statue and makes a small "hmm" as he walks on.

"OK, Scott and Ash it looks OK. Go in and get Hooty and Buffy into position," Sue says.

I notice two flashes on the far side of the lake. If Du Croix noticed, he said nothing. We're passing another statue – they have a lot of them in this park – when Du Croix speaks to us.

"The Bruderschaft were not the largest settler community but they were one the most centralised. The group in Austria had links to the Americas. To say the least the American relatives simply don't believe six human teenagers could defeat over two hundred of their brothers without outside help."

"We had help, but it wasn't the Fae," I reply in English.

"They won't believe you," he replies in English.

"Why not? They had help which wasn't from the Center. Ours was simply stronger," I argue.

"I did not say that they *don't* believe you. I said they *won't* believe you. They don't *want* to believe that humans can defeat them. They have ruled your kind for centuries. That means that, whatever the reality, the perception is that your allies have decided to dislodge the Center's control of Earth. Added to that the failure of the Service to defeat the Fae craft despite a clear advantage, means Earth is attracting more attention from the Center than it probably deserves."

"They're just sore losers," I argue.

Du Croix grins.

"I find your childish naïveté delightful Sam. Of *course* they are sore losers. In time you will learn *everyone* is a 'sore loser' and the older they are, and the longer they have had things their own way, the sorer they get about losing," he replies, again in English.

We've rounded the corner of the lake and are walking along beside the rowboats that are moored on a jetty by the lake.

"Dr Prosperov you should probably go now," says Sue.

Two flashes in the woods across the open field to our right.

"My job is to maintain order in the territory under my jurisdiction. That means preventing disorder before it occurs."

"What about preventing mass murder," I ask, annoyed.

"You seem unaware of the irony of that remark. As far as some are concerned it is you Sam Kahu and Tahira Khadem who are the mass murderers," he says grimly as we walk.

"And what about unleashing global epidemics? That's just a bit naughty?" I say, getting a bit annoyed.

"Yes, we were obviously aware of the Virion conspiracy. It was our cybermind that helped design it. But from our perspective the vaccine attack could easily be prevented at the last moment by alerting the relevant human authorities."

"What about Paul Maartens and the contaminated perfumes for aircrews he was working on in Japan?" I demand.

Du Croix seems to be taken by surprise. He shrugs.

"I know nothing of that."

I can see the black figure of Dr P walking along a path at right angles to ours, followed by Tarik and Cam. Ahead Scotty and Ash are waiting on a large tiled circle with benches arranged around it.

"Where is Maartens now?"

"If he's lucky, learning Spanish."

"And if he's not?"

"Being hungry."

"It would help if you told me where. It might ease tension."

"You'd just let him go, like you did Hathaway," I mutter.

Dr P approaches. I realise he is much thinner and smaller than Du Croix. He's wearing a black coat, hat and leather gloves.

"Inspector Du Croix?"

"Dr Prosperov, I presume."

They are both speaking English.

"What is problem?" Dr P asks.

"You! All of you," Du Croix responds.

"You have gone from a minor mystery to a military menace, so, alas, the Center will respond militarily."

"Fighting Center is not objective."

"That is not how it seems to the Foundation."

"I know nothing of the Foundation, but is no reason to fear us," Dr P says briefly.

"The Foundation is a settler organisation which was established after World War Two, some members of the Bruderschaft are also members of the Foundation."

"Do they plan genocide?"

"No, they seek to maintain global order."

"Do you work for them?"

"I work for the Administration but I work *with* the Foundation.

They are powerful, and while I maintain influence my actual power is limited."

"Is that why you released Hathaway?" I butt in.

Du Croix looks around at me.

"Partly, but Tamiel also offered to deliver you. If I refused to consider that I would not be doing my job."

"Failure of Bruderschaft to meet promise, not our problem," Dr P objects.

"But it will become so. As our young friend Sam pointed out, the Iyrin are sore losers. They claim they are threatened by a Fae incursion."

"What do you want us to do?" Dr P asks.

"Lie low."

"We cannot lie low if we are attacked."

"There will not be any more attacks for some time. Unfortunately the Administration on Earth is being taken over by the Service. This is no longer a scientific outpost. It's a military one. However you should know if the Service finds a target it is thorough and ruthless. For your own sake you should lie low."

"Will there be any more pandemics?" I ask.

"Not from the Bruderschaft. They have been dispersed. There are still a few scattered here and there, but as an organised force. Pfff it is finished!"

"We will follow your advice," Dr P begins and then suddenly he changes. His eyes flash and glitter and his whole body seems to change. He becomes creepy and speaks without the Russian accent

"... but tell the Foundation this Inspector, it was not I who defeated Heimdall's host but the spirit of old who guards this middle world as a great Serpent. It was Jörmungandr, with the help of Jibreel, that showed but a fraction of Earth's power at Untersberg, it was not I. It is Jörmangundr that the inheritors of the Aesir should fear rousing, not I. I am merely the messenger of the End, as I have ever been. It is they who bring it ever closer through their delight in preparations for war."

Du Croix backs away, looking at Dr P with horror. We remain still, uncertain how to react to this unexpected emergence of Loki, and hoping Dr P won't collapse and have a fit.

"Who?...who are you?" Du Croix asks, looking worried.

Suddenly Dr P staggers. Scott and Tarik who are nearest to him step up to catch his arm.

"That's just Loki," I tell Du Croix, "He possesses Dr P sometimes." I add as if this was some everyday event of no importance.

Dr P is breathing hard, closes his eyes for a moment, then looks up at Du Croix.

"You have my assurance, Inspector. I'm afraid I have other business I need to attend to."

He turns to go, supported still by Scott and Tarik, then pauses.

"Inspector? Has the Interpol notice been rescinded?"

"Yes of course, it seems Inspector Turneau concluded his evidence was purely circumstantial," Du Croiz says, his glance at me.

"Thank you," Dr P says, regaining his strength and letting Scott and Tarik know to release him.

"Bonne soiree," he says and starts walking back down the path he had come.

"Bonne soiree," Du Croix replies, watching him go.

"Sam and Tahira? Could I ask you to join me for a stroll past the zoo?" Du Croix asks.

"*We'll watch you*," Scott tells us silently.

"D'ac (OK)," Tahira shrugs to Du Croix. I shrug too.

We set off along the path past the old house toward the animal enclosures in front of us. As soon as we draw away from the others Du Croix asks, "Is Dr Prosperov aware of what it is, he is channelling?"

"Yes," we say as if it's nothing.

"Then his promise is meaningless," Du Croix says, almost to himself.

"Why?" I want to know.

"Because it means hostilities are inevitable," Du Croix answers, and he doesn't seem happy about it.

"We can still lie low," I reply.

"Do you not understand anything?" he says grabbing me and turning me around angrily.

"It doesn't matter what is, but what people choose to believe. If people choose to believe conflict is inevitable, it is, no matter what I, you or anyone else may think about it. This is in danger of becoming the worst kind of war there is: a religious one. A war where souls align themselves to powerful spirits, will not concede, nor negotiate, nor see reason. A war where only total victory is possible, and this planet, this whole planet is nothing more than a pawn in the calculations of minds so powerful, so subtle and so ruthless, you cannot even conceive of them! You are an ant Sam, an ant! And you have bitten a giant bigger than you can imagine."

He lets me go, almost as surprised by the outburst that had poured from him, as I am.

"Why do you even care?" I demand.

435

"I live here," he says coldly, stepping back from me.

"C'est chez moi, aussi, (It's my place too)," he says softly, almost to himself.

Then he turns from us and strides off.

"See that Prosperov and that ... thing ... live up to their promise!" he half shouts, as he strides off into the night.

We watch him go. I turn to Tahira and shrug. We aren't sure what all that was about.

"*Let's go,*" says Scotty, so we do.

[+]

When we get out of the Cabinets Dr P is waiting for us on the squares with Sue. He's looking tired. We go over and gather around him.

"Was predictable response. However has self to blame. Du Croix thought we were finished. Now he has to spread blame far from self."

Dr P sighs.

"However is right. We must stay out of way."

"But it's more like, will they stay out of ours, init?" Tarik says.

"We must watch Jeanne, Sarah and Diana in case they try to trap us. However am thinking new leaders is priority."

"Do you think they will try trap?" Cam asks.

"Not until they feel ready. And that will not be for a while."

There's a pause.

"So what do we do now?" Ashley asks.

"You, I think will buy clothes. I must organise my interview with police with Ms Williams. I suggest Tarik and Tahira remain on duty while the Trâns and Kahus catch their planes. Is all," Dr P says.

So I go to the changers with Scott, Ash and Cam and change

back into my ground kit, my only clothes. Then Zoe takes us in the van into the Elizabeth Street Mall in Hobart to go shopping. We don't exactly go crazy. We have to buy school clothes for me and extra stuff for the weekend. Then me and Cam get suitcases and find a loo where Tahira and Tarik can pick us up and take us back to Hastings Hall because we're running late. We meet Aunty Liz, Rewa and Mr Trân and then Tahira and Tarik drop us at Auckland International Airport.

[+]

For me it's totally weird to fly in a plane. I've been around the world but never by plane. Everything takes *so* long! You have to queue to give them your bag, queue to get your passport checked going out, sit around forever waiting for them to call you to the plane, and even queue to get on the plane. I can't believe the tiny place you have to sit in, and I'm nothing like as big as some of the adults trying to squeeze themselves into those seats.

I sit next to Rewa who has the window seat. It's nothing like as comfortable as Sir Michael's jet. Even Ka-rea-rea is more comfortable. It just feels like Betty-the-Bus with wings but no-one's singing. When we finally take off I actually find it a bit scary because I can't see where we're going. We lift off over Auckland and plod up to ten kilometers for a trip that will take the Airbus four boring hours but which I could do in twenty minutes in Ka-rea-rea. I can't believe people pay money for this. The trip isn't so bad though. We eat; Rewa watches *Fantastic Mr Fox*; and I doze because I was up so early, until it's time to land in Sydney. I feel a bit better, although how the others put up with twelve and fourteen hours in a seat like that is beyond me.

I feel a bit funny going through Customs without a suit on. I know the cameras are watching us as the systems have run their matches for persons of interest. I feel kind of self-conscious as we step up to the immigration desk. The man's eyes run over mine, and although I know he's bored to death, I can't help feeling a hint of nervousness. Then, as if it's the last thing he wants to do, he stamps our passports and we are officially in Australia.

The girls and Aunty Liz go to their toilets to meet Tahira while me and Mr Trân (who's officially a returning Australian) go to the men's to meet Tarik. He gives us our sleeping bags to hop inside in the cubicles and then we fold away, back to Hastings Hall.

[+]

By now it's four in the afternoon New Zealand time, and two Aussie time. After the cabinets have done their thing, Tarik gets us out and we join the crowd watching over Zoe's shoulder on the control desk.

Sitting in interview room four at Auckland Central Police Station (the same one I was in two weeks ago) is Detective Sergeant Kevin Cooper, Detective Constable Sue Williams and Dr Gennady Prosperov. Dr Prosperov looks very bored. Sue's trying not to smile and Kevin looks very pissed off.

"What's been happening?" I ask Gunter and Mariko, who have a big bowl of popcorn in front of them.

"They should put this on TV. It's zo funny," Gunter comments.

"Let me get this straight," Kevin is saying, "you've been on the yacht of your friend Edvard Shulyagin cruising in the south Pacific but when you learned that Renwick House burned down you went into hiding, somewhere in Northland fearing that your

438

business enemies in Russia were attempting to kill you."
Prosperov raises his chin off his palm with the look of a man
who has said the same thing fifty times already, "Yes," he agrees.
"Why did you not seek police protection?"
"Because we didn't need it," he recites.
"But they'd burned down your home!"
"Yes. Was very annoying but calling police would not unburn it
and could expose us to attack."
"What sort of attack?"
"Why would I want to find out what sort of attack? Russians are
very clever at attacks. Also Russians tend to be thorough and kill
everyone. Is safest if you do not reveal *anything*."
"What makes you think you are any safer now?"
"Because is no sign of attackers."
"Then how do you know there *were* any attackers?"
"I don't. But we have attackers before and is better to be safe."
"And these were the alleged members of MS13 and Sinaloa plus
Ergenekon?"
"Yes."
"Sergeant Smith says there was no evidence of them," Kevin says
grumpily.
"Local policeman did not seem to notice local youths driving
on driveway disturbing us either. Sergeant Smith is not very
observant individual," Dr P says dryly, making Mariko and
Gunter laugh.
"Sir, from what Sam Kahu's told me they did have an incident
at the school last year at the same time as Ax Stephens was
investigated for drug offences," Sue puts in.
"But Sam Kahu didn't know anything about this yacht trip or
these attackers when we talked to him?" Kevin points out.

"Sir, he *did* actually tell me he thought it was the Russian mafiya. I just thought he was making it up," Sue says.

Dr P puts in, "Also Sam is boy of certain age. He spends all times thinking about girlfriend, Emma Reeves, and doesn't know what is going on. He didn't want to come on yacht so sneeks off to stay behind with her. Then he is confused. Is very annoying."

Everyone jeers at me. I have to laugh.

"Sir, it is true he is close to Emma, but her father is suspicious of the two of them. I had dinner with the Reeves two weeks ago," Sue says. "I think the reason he wouldn't tell us where he was, is because he was with her and didn't want to get her into trouble with her dad."

"And you have no idea how the fire started?" Kevin asks Dr P.

"No. How could I?" Dr P shrugs.

"If I told you the Fire Service found traces of Powergel explosive would you be surprised?" Kevin asks.

"Oooo!" Mariko says, "it's like a tennis match."

"It would merely confirm attack hypothesis," Dr P says, still bored.

"Ha!" Mariko laughs as Dr P easily fends Kevin's question off like Dr M swatted Tarik down at chess.

"Which you didn't report?"

"What is to report? Everyone knows house burned down! It is your job to investigate."

"But you didn't report your suspected attackers?"

"Is not my problem to find attackers. Is my problem to not be attacked. I must act on suspicion. You must act on proof. Is dangerous to be in place in between. Is not illegal to hide is it?" Dr P asks.

Kevin is totally furious, but contains himself.

"No," he replies. "And you still don't want to say where you were in Northland?"

"Not unless is legal requirement. I may need to hide again."

"What if I make it a legal requirement?"

"How?"

"Conspiracy to pervert the course of justice."

"What justice? I am preventing crime. Is hiding from suspected attackers illegal?"

Kevin has to take a few breaths to calm down.

"No ... no sir, it isn't."

There's a pause.

"Detective, we have been here for two hours. I have answered all your questions, some many times. I am tired. It is late on Sunday and am thinking we all want to go home. If you have charges I ask that you make them now, otherwise I would like to stop now."

Kevin sighs.

"Dr Prosperov, all I can say is that I am very disappointed that you have so little faith in the New Zealand Police. If you had come forward some time ago we might have had more of a chance to catch the people who burned down your home. Now, I'm afraid there is no chance at all. No, I do not have any charges to lay at this time."

"Thank you Detectives," Dr P says, getting up.

"May I say a special 'thank you' to you Detective Williams. I think you have done a great deal more to reveal the truth ... perhaps than your colleagues realise," he says, shaking her hand. Then taking Kevin's hand.

"I am sorry for misunderstanding, but please to recognise safety of my people is highest priority," he mutters.

"I do respect that sir," Kevin says. They shake, and Dr P leaves. Sue turns off the recorder.

"Cunning bastard!" Kevin says at the door.

"He burned that place down, but because he'll have a heap of Russian witnesses and they lost their own stuff we'll never be able to pin it on him."

"Or..." Sue adds, "there really were Russian assassins here."

"Yeah, right!" Kevin scoffs.

"Or it was the aliens," Sue says quietly.

"They were *all* f___ aliens!" Kevin swears as they walk out of the room.

The room goes dark.

"Shows over," says Zoe, getting up.

"What happens now?" I ask.

"You gotta see what Hekator's just sent us!" Tarik says.

"What?" I ask.

"Come and see," Tahira smiles. She looks excited.

We go up a level to the changing room floor. Over by the wall, alongside a big pipe that reached up to the outside which I hadn't paid any attention to before, are nine speeders.

I go over to them. They are all different colours but the brown and white speckled one is the one Tahira shows me to. I put my hand on the top plate.

"Ka-rea-rea," I say.

"Sam," he replies and slides open.

I turn back to look at the others. Aunty Liz and Rewa have arrived as well. I'm so happy to have Ka-rea-rea back I almost have tears in my eyes. Then Rewa runs forward. Tahira has been signalling to her behind my back!

"Zhou put your 'and 'ere. What do you want to call her?"

Rewa's eyes are huge. She's so excited her chest is pounding.

"Kahu," she says.

"Kahu," the machine replies and slides open.

She gives me a huge grin.

"Hekator decided Rewa and Asal deserved zheir own after what zhey did at Untersberg," Tahira says.

"Ee is working on a new design for ze adults as well."

What did I care what the adults got?

"Can we?" Rewa asks Aunty Liz, her eyes still huge.

"Yes go on, but go south and stay low," she says.

"Wait, I'll get Asal!" Tahira says.

So we wait a short while for Asal who comes running back with Tahira completely out of breath. Then we get in and close up before zipping up the pipe (which is disguised like a big old dead tree outside) and vanishing into the golden afternoon light as we engaged our warp invisibility. We boot it up to five klicks leading Asal and Rewa who are screaming and yahooing with excitement, then we level off doing Mach point nine heading south toward the South Pole.

"Disengage warp camouflage," Tahira calls.

We all appear out of nowhere.

"Inertialess, Mach three, descending to altitude one kilometer," calls Tahira, "In three, two, one, go!"

And four boxes shoot forward like blurs toward the Southern Ocean.

We spend about two hours showing Asal and Rewa what the speeders can do and I'm a bit surprised how quickly they pick it up. We only come home because it's time for dinner. We park the speeders and head over to Hastings Hall.

The first thing we notice is that Grandpop is back, but outside.

There's a ring of torches around him and Aunty Liz is sitting on the swimming pool seats outside with him. We come over to see and then back off. He doesn't smell so good. He doesn't look so great anymore either. He looks empty. Like a shell. You can just tell there's no-one at home.

"What are we going to do with him?" I ask.

"You'll see tonight," Aunty Liz says.

"Do we have to eat out here?" Rewa asks, wrinkling her pretty nose.

"No, darling, we'll take turns," Aunty Liz says. And then changes the subject. "How did you like flying?"

While Rewa tells Aunty Liz all about that, I go inside. Dr P is the centre of attention and Mariko and Gunter are retelling their favourite moments of the interview. I notice Sue smiling quietly in the corner and go over to her.

"How are you?" I ask her.

"Good. Very, very good," Sue says, with the look of someone with a happy secret.

"Tell me," I ask.

I already know it involves Rachel.

"I went home after Dr P left to pick up a few things and Rachel was there with that bitch Sonia, she's taken up with."

"And?"

"She thought I'd be devastated," she grins.

"And ..."

"I just told her I was busy and glad I wouldn't have to put up with her whining shit any more. Then I went through all her annoying habits in front of Sonia!" she giggles.

"What did she do?"

"Tried to slap me, so I threatened to arrest her," she laughs.

"So she..?"

"Took off. I cackled like a hag after that."

"And you're OK?"

"Oh I'm great!" she heaves a big sigh, "All thanks to you, Sam Kahu."

Then she hugs me and kisses me on the forehead.

"Any time," I shrug.

We have a good meal. Things spill outside, though nobody gets too close to Grandpop. There's lots of talk and drink for the adults. It goes on until nine in the evening. Then Hekator and Hekati flash down onto the lawn. We run up, to thank him for the speeders.

"We've had them for a while. But seeing we need them for tonight I thought it was time to pass them on."

"'Ow come there's an extra one?" Tarik asks.

"That's a little surprise," Hekator smiles.

Suddenly the music and the lights cut out.

Aunty Liz stands up and begins a karakia (prayer/spell) in Maori. It's long and mournful. It calls on our ancestors and everyone present. It makes me think of the stories of the demi-god Maui and his attempt to best Hinenui-te-po, the goddess of death, and how he ultimately failed.

After the last of her chant has died away small flames begin to appear from the doorway of the Hall. They spread out and I soon realise they are small candles. We're all given a candle and take a light from one of our neighbours. Then we're all given a flower.

"Please to pray for Mike and cast your flower into coffin when you are finished. Then put out candle," Dr P says.

The lights stay on for quite a while. I'm actually the first to throw my flower and put my light out. My prayer is quite simple. It's, "see ya later."

Slowly one by one the others throw in their flowers and put out their lights. Finally there's only one. It's Rewa. It takes a little talk from Aunty Liz and Mariko for her to finally throw in her flower. By then it's was half past nine. The box containing Grandpop's body seals up and vanishes. Then Sue comes by and grabs us older ones and tells us to follow her to the base.

We jog across the wet grass following after her.

"Wat's da plan Sue?" Ash asks.

"You guys are the flypast," she says.

"You have to be in line passing north over Mike's old house at two hundred meters at two hundred kays at precisely midnight New Zealand time."

That only gives us half an hour to get over there and line up.

"What's everyone else doing?" Scott asks.

"Watching from Ashanti."

We run on a few steps.

"I like dat," Ash says.

"Me too," says Cam.

We slide down to the first level and get into our speeders. Then one by one we lift off, zoom up into the pipe and blast invisibly up to twenty klicks. We form up, in line, drop warp invisibility and go inertialess.

The sky is clear and, despite the huge spread of the galaxy above us, the night is dark with a sliver moon. It somehow seems restless and stormy. We speed through the night in silence thinking about how we must make sure everything looks good for Grandpop.

It's Cam who notices.

"We have a tail," she reports.

I admit I'm both scared and annoyed by this news. But then Sue is in our ears.

"It's friendly guys. Don't worry, it's the spare. It's part of your formation. Liz named it Ko-tu-ku."

Kotuku. The white heron. It's a bird that migrates huge distances to New Zealand and is seen only once in a lifetime, so it is both a blessing and an indicator you may now die.

"Who's flying in it?" I ask.

"No-one. Control can fly them all now."

"Why not tell us?" complains Scott.

"Sorry guys I forgot. OK, so you've got five minutes to get there and five minutes to get into position."

Five minutes pass pretty quickly. Soon we can see a sprinkle of orange lights that is the small town of Dargaville. There's cold air down below with low clouds. We veer right toward the south and turn off, inertialess. We could go invisible if we wanted to, though there's no need, we're almost invisible as it is.

We wheel around corkscrewing down over Dargaville until we are barely 300 meters above. Kotuku is following behind us.

"OK guys, line up and head north at two hundred."

We fall into a line, but Kotuku lags behind.

"OK, here's what's happening. You're coming across low and lit up bright. You light up at minus five klicks. Once you're past accelerate north to Mach four until you reach Cape Re-ing-a then lights off and bend back home."

That gets us really excited. Everyone asks what she's just said at once.

"Yes, the new speeders can bend too." Sue says.

"Oh *yeah*!" Tarik whoops. And rolls right over. He isn't the only

447

one.

We fly low over the dimly lit countryside. Two hundred is like a stroll. It's pretty dull.

"OK guys. So when you come over stay straight. You are flying over Mike's old house which will be burning. He says he wanted a cremation and the old house burned down because of the drugs so Mariko and Liz put them both together. The official story will be Mike was drunk, started cooking, fell asleep and died in the fire. But for us this is the funeral and you are the guard of honour. He was very proud of you guys you know."

We fly on in silence. Then I can see the inlet reflecting the moon.

"Light up."

We light our speeders like six brilliant suns and slowly cross the hill, and then the water. Below we can see the fire ahead. I know the volunteer fire brigade will still be half an hour away. Silently we fly overhead. I can see our neighbours down below looking up at us as we silently approach. Then, just as we fly over the house Kotuku breaks formation and climbs suddenly for the stars, blazing like an angel.

"It's beautiful guys, really beautiful. Now off to Cape Reinga fast as," Sue says warmly.

We accelerated away going supersonic.

"*Hey, look up! Twelve o'clock*," Ash says.

Looking ahead we notice a shower of meteors ahead of us falling.

"That's Hekator's bit," Sue says.

They look lovely.

We scream up the top of the North Island and along Ninety Mile Beach to Cape Reinga, the place, in Maori tradition, where the souls of the dead leave Aotearoa, or New Zealand, for Hawaiki the legendary origin of all Maori canoes. As we speed past I feel pretty sure Grandpop is safely on his way. We fly on a little further and then – almost finding it a luxury – wink out as we bend home.

Sue's waiting for us

"Awesome guys. Come and look at the replay. It was a great send off."

And somehow just saying the words "send off" hits me. More than knowing I'd seen Grandpop's ghost at Untersberg. More than seeing his dead, slightly smelly body just an hour ago. The words "send off" make me realise I will never see my grandfather again.

Feeling a bit down I go out with the others (who are still excited about speeders that bend) to the briefing room.

The replay Control shows us starts with them placing Grandpop on his bed, still dressed. To my surprise the house is tidy. The gang *had* cleaned up! Even after Aunty Liz says the last prayer for her father and goes through to the kitchen to start the fat fire it's all clean and tidy the way Nana would have liked it. They *must* have been scared!

Aunty Liz, wearing Sue's gray jumpsuit (which she fits surprisingly well), puts a tonne of lard on the stove. It melts and she lights it. Huge flames flash up. She steps back, then as the smoke begins she and Hekator hold hands and fold away.

From above, the house is alight. I can see Ed and the whole family watching, and others gathering at the gate. Our old home is burning fiercely casting flickering orange light and pouring smoke into the sky. Then our flypast comes in.

It's pretty to watch from above, where we are. The seven brilliant craft are not fast but not slow either. They come over deliberately. Silent and mysterious. You can see everyone on the ground looking up at them, awestruck, and then that moment. When Kotuku, right over the house, suddenly turns skyward and streaks upward for the stars as we accelerate away. I can't help it, I'm crying again.

Then the view follows us as we accelerate away six lines of brilliant light against the darkness heading to the North as the shooting stars begin to rain down in the distance. It's simply beautiful.

Suddenly Ashley's arms are around me. Then Cam, then Tahira, then Scott and Tarik. It's a big group hug and for a while we're just a big mess of hugs, yes and kisses, and back rubs. We all miss him. Slowly it breaks up. We wipe away the tears.

"The others are coming back now," Sue says.

So we all go upstairs and look out over the lawn. The huge transparent Vimana sits above it and people are floating down from above in a column of light. We head over to meet them and I nearly catch Rewa who lands next to me, but is really too big for me to catch now.

"School night, children," Mrs Jones calls out over the crowd.

Rewa and me go inside. I notice Sue and Liz are hanging back talking shyly. We decide to leave them to it and go in.

Showers, pyjamas, teeth, toilet and bed. It's eleven local time. Apart from dozing on the plane I've been awake since five. I'm exhausted. I just hear Aunty Liz say goodnight to Sue at the door and then I'm in Israel.

I'm in Haifa at the top of the Baha'i Gardens. It's early evening. There are big pink clouds in the yellow light. The sunlight is glinting off the golden dome on the shrine of the Bab. The air is cool and there are puddles where it's been raining. I walk down the steps and see the familiar outline of Mr Ceder sitting on his bench. I come over and sit down on the same bench next to him. He says nothing and we just look at the huge view out to the Mediterranean as it disappears into blue-gray haze.

As I watch it starts to shift and change before me. And I realise it isn't so much the world which is shifting and changing but me. And the difference is that suddenly I can see that the future will be a long, hard uphill climb but that in the end it will be worth it.

"You're getting better," Mr Ceder says to me, leaning over and smiling.

He stands up and re-arranges his scarf.

"You know about the Bruderschaft?" I ask.

He pauses, thinking about it. Then nods and continues.

"It is a start. But there are still more, and their followers. But you can feel change is coming like the Sirocco along the coast of Africa. Even that fool Bibi Netanyahu will have to bend with it. I envy you Sam. It's a great time to be young," he says and turns. Then he turns back.

"Keep listening. Keep listening to God. The spirits of this world and others are great, but as the Arabs like to say, God is greater," then he walks off down the hill.

I watch him go. There's still a lot to do and the view helps me think.

Then the alarm goes off and I'm waking up in my empty room.

"Come on Sam get a move on, it's a school day!" Aunty Liz yells leaning in from the lounge.

I get up, still a bit dazed by my dream and start to pull on my new clothes. I find pins in the shirts which I have to pick out. I get myself dressed, with fold creases all over the shirt, then put on my new shoes. Aunty Liz comes in.

"Oh Sam, come here, give me that shirt, it needs ironing," she fusses.

Rewa sticks her head in.

"I'll take ya bag downstairs," she says.

"Thanks."

Aunty Liz gets the iron and ironing board out, and irons my shirt in no time, while I stand there, half naked, waiting.

"You're getting taller," she says.

"Am I?"

"Yeah, you must be growing," she says, her eyes down on the shirt, but with some pride. Still, she can't help adding, "about time," as she hands me the warm shirt.

I throw it on, grab my jersey, then run out of the door, down to the café.

The others have already started breakfast and they all gave me a hard time about me looking all new and shiny. Rewa jokes the look will probably be gone by lunch time. It's great to be with the others again without having to deal with all that stuff I've been living with.

Breakfast is soon finished. We grab our lunches, and thank Mr Trân as we put them in our bags. Then Zoe is calling us to the van. We climb in and we're off down the narrow country roads. I feel a bit nervous, seeing the new countryside going past. Yes, it seems familiar but it isn't and I still don't really know much about where I am. I have to go over our fake names again and again so I can remember who we're meant to be. It helps that Stan rhymes with Sam, and Hawke is English for Kahu.

Finally we arrive at Plymouth District High. It looks every

bit as crappy as I remember it. There are quite a few kids being dropped off from old Holden cars, some arriving by bus, and some driving their own cars as well. Our van looks embarrassingly new. I feel bad about being new and shiny too. Zoe takes me into the office where the admin lady is talking to the principal Mr Hamlin. I feel his eyes rake over me and Zoe. It's strange how even though I'd battled a hundred powerful aliens in a cave this guy makes me nervous. Even Zoe flinched! Then Mrs Deane has a brief talk to Zoe and it's done. Apparently Mrs Driver is expecting me. I was in for my first day at a Tasmanian school.

I go outside and join the others. The playground is the usual chaos. The Australian accents make me feel a bit homesick but then at least they're in English. There are quite a few Aboriginals among the crowds. Some stick together, others like Moira's good looking son Kevin, stick out. Everywhere kids are picking up conversations with one another about stuff that's happened over the weekend. Things they've done, places they've been, games they've played. In some ways I can't help thinking how lucky they are. None of them had to fight for their lives. None of them have lost family members in battle. It's just another regular day. It makes me feel a bit funny inside.

The bell goes, and I join the others. Apparently we have to line up in the corridor outside the classroom and wait for the teacher. That feels so strange. Here I am travelling the world, and dealing with serious bad arses, and they want us to line up like we're six or something. It's even a boy-girl thing and I find myself standing next to a coffee-skinned girl with brown hair whose skirt is way too short. She isn't bad looking, though nothing like as pretty as Emma.

"What's your name," she asks shyly.

"Stan," I say quietly.

"Are you Maori?" she asks.

I pause half a beat, looking her in the eye, before answering her, just to stop her being a smartarse.

"Yeah."

"Uh OK," she says.

Mrs Driver arrives and we file in. I feel my pulse rise. I have never enjoyed being in school and I know I'm not going to enjoy this either. The others have saved me a desk at the back by them, which makes me feel so much better. I sit down. There's still a bit of talking but Mrs Driver, who's over-powdered and made up shushes everyone down with her severe eyebrows. Then she takes the roll. I almost forget I'm Stan Hawke and my tongue sticks in my throat as I say "here." Everyone turns to look at me. With the roll finished Mrs Driver speaks.

"Well, as you have noticed, we have a new boy in the class. Stan why don't you come up the front and tell us a bit about yourself," she says and sits down.

My stomach clenches. I'd rather do anything than speak in front of a class, but I get up, feeling very shaky inside and walk up to the front.

The view from here is quite different. Mrs Driver gives me a queenly nod to begin. Everyone seems to be slouching in their seats. Some are bored, some are interested, some are eyeing me. There seems to be too many people. My mouth feels dry.

"What do you want to know?" I ask Mrs Driver quietly.

"Tell us a bit about your family and where you're from. Any sports, hobbies, things you like to do. Things you might have in common with the others here. That sort of thing," Mrs Driver says encouragingly.

I look back at the class.

I can read most of them. They play sports, watch DVDs, and go shopping. Some live on farms, some in villages. The Aborigines have family problems that seem familiar. There's drinking and drugs and crime here too. Crime and poverty, and fishing. It's the same as home but different. Different in a million tiny ways, all of which add up so that I know nobody and nothing. There's going to be a lot to learn.

Some of the girls whisper to one another. I take a breath. I think about Grandpop. I can imagine him encouraging me. Saying it's hard but I just have to take it steadily, one step at a time. My mind is racing, thinking about things I can say to fit in and not be noticed. I shrug, take another breath and begin.

"Uh, ...hi ... I'm Stan Hawke. Yeah ... Um...Well, I guess I'm... yeah, Well, I'm pretty ordinary, me ..."

THE END

###

FACT ⊕R FICTI⊕N?

The story of Khadiyeh is partially inspired by that of Najood Ali the ten year old divorcee from Sana'a, Yemen. Her story is brilliantly told in "I am Nujood, ten, and divorced" by Persian French writer Delpine Mirou. The other main influence is the Book of Elijah in the Old Testament of the Hebrew Bible..

While the castle of Sedan is available for conferences, and is naturally secure, no conferences on "bioterror and the state" occurred there in September 2008. The author is not aware of any human sacrifices interrupted at the rather pleasant looking Chapel of Elan, either.

Anyone hoping that the author has any knowledge of how to crack the Interpol I-24/7 system, or the border control systems of Singapore, Dubai or Argentina is out of luck. The systems portrayed here are purely imaginary. The descriptions of the interior of the Interpol building and security systems in Lyon, France are simply guesses. Changi airport was in the process of installing a new passenger reconciliation system from Arinc in March 2009.

The aboriginal population of Tasmania was not completely destroyed by genocide as is often claimed. The school Sam and the others attend is modelled on Dover District High School although of course the fictional Plymouth District High and its characters are fictional.

Flights from Auckland to Buenos Aires departed on Saturdays at 15:50 not 12:50 as suggested in the story. Aerolineas Argentinas flights ceased in June 2012 after the story ends.

The pattern of child abuse, and orphan re-assignment ascribed to Father Rocelli did take place within the Roman Catholic Church during the 20th Century. The full extent of the Catholic Church's involvement in child sex abuse and collusion with fascist governments remains uncertain. While not condoned there is no doubt that a conspiracy has and probably still exists.
Allen Welsh Dulles did indeed live the life ascribed to him by Father Rocelli. He was opposed to both the Nazis and the Bolsheviks but was directly involved in Operation Paperclip, the US effort to claim Nazi

scientists after World War Two; and MK-Ultra, a programme of highly unethical mind control experiments involving children, prisoners and service personnel. Dulles is a natural fit for any number of conspiracy theories for the simple reason that he spent his life engaged in intelligence conspiracies.

The Bruderschaft influenza attack described in the story is based on fact. According to the Bloomberg News Agency 24 February 2009, the US-owned firm Baxter International admitted that it had accidentally released a sample of H1N1 infuenza vaccine contaminated with live H5N1 virus to 18 countries. The accident was discovered by a Czech lab when ferrets treated with the vaccine died unexpectedly. The H5N1 contamination was sourced from the Baxter Innovations centre in the village of Ortha an der Danau 30km from Vienna. The cause of this deadly contamination has not been satisfactorily explained.

An outbreak of H1N1 "Mexican Swine" flu in May 2009 led to 14,286 deaths worldwide, however this may be difficult to separate from influenza deaths that commonly occur each year. There have been accusations made by reputable physicians that the vaccine industry has stimulated a climate of panic to boost sales.

For the purposes of this fiction the Austrian laboratory has been moved to Gartenau Saint Leonhard near Salzberg, Austria at the base of the Untersberg mountain. The Untersberg mountain is one of the places where the legendary German King Frederick Barbarossa sleeps waiting to reawake at the end of the world. He is served by the Untersberg Zwerge – dwarves in his service. The German side of the Untersberg mountain is Berchtesgarten Hitler's favourite summer retreat. The mountain is riven with natural cave systems, salt mines (hence Salt-Mountain Salz-berg). The castle (Shloss Schaden) is entirely imaginary but based on Schloss Ortha, one kilometre up the road from Baxter's R&D centre in Ortha. The Castle in Ortha is a museum and café, and obviously not defended by armed robots or mutant dogs.

Two teams of scientists: Ron Fouchier of Erasmus Medical Center in Rotterdam, the Netherlands, and Yoshihiro Kawaoka of the University of Wisconsin-Madison announced the creation of deadly strains of H5N1 and H1N1 flu viruses in September 2011. The Erasmus Center's version was an airborne virus with 100% mortality of infected ferrets – considered a close analog for humans. The 1918 Spanish Flu virus only infected human beings and typically healthy young adults.

The monks of the Bruderschaft's favourite chants are "Benedicamus Patrem" and "Invitatorium: Deum Verum" by Etienne de Liege

There was a meteor shower on March 22nd 2009 caused by the Camelopardalids and March Geminids from asteroid Amor (1221) and/or asteroid Selevk (3288).

N⊕T€S ⊕N LANGUAG€

Te Rauparaha's haka (war dance/chant) is a motif. This haka was adopted by the New Zealand national rugby team, the All Blacks, and is a tradition before their rugby games.

I have chosen to translate the opening lines of this haka "Ka mate, ka mate, ka ora, ka ora" (often translated "I die, I die, I live, I live") unusually as "Death? Death? Life? Life?"

In Maori "ka" is a tense marker which simply indicates the future (including the future perfect) or the next thing that happens while "mate" pronounced "maté" means death, and "ora" means life. Maori sentences, like many Asian languages, can infer a subject. So Te Rauparaha words literally say "(future tense) death, (future tense) death, (future-tense) life, (future-tense) life". This is because when he composed the haka Te Rauparaha was hiding for his life from enemy warriors who were coming to kill him. I prefer to use the uncertainty of the English question-mark "?" as a proxy for the tense marker "ka" than introduce a subject "I" which isn't in the Maori. There is also a philosophical matter, which given that Te Rauparaha was not a Christian, is, I think, important.

From an existential point of view the traditional translation "I die" is meaningless because it implies everything else won't die, but "death?" means the end of everything (because from an existential point of view we only experience one life and one point of view and if that is extinguished then whether anything else persists on or not is irrelevant. This is particularly true if you are hiding in a Kumara pit facing being killed at any moment as the composer was. To my mind "I die" limits the sentence to one individual and doesn't capture the implied universality of life and death captured by Te Rauparaha's Maori. Sam Kahu is nominally Ngapuhi (the largest Maori iwi/tribe) where Te Rauparaha was Ngati Toa. The two tribes are geographically distinct, today living at opposite ends of the North Island but speak mutually intelligible Maori.

Mrs Jones later recites the Druid's prayer by Lolo Morganwg (1747-1826)

Dyro Dduw dy Nawdd (Grant, O God, Thy protection);
Ag yn nawdd, nerth (And in protection, strength);

Ag yn nerth, Deall (And in strength, understanding);
Ag yn Neall, Gwybod (And in understanding, knowledge);
Ac yngwybod, gwybod y cyfiawn (And in knowledge, the knowledge of justice);
Ag yngwybod yn cyfiawn, ei garu (And in the knowledge of justice, the love of it);
Ag o garu, caru pob hanfod (And in that love, the love of all existences);
Ag ymhob Hanfod, caru Duw (And in the love of all existences, the love of God).
Duw a phob Daioni (God and all goodness).

Gunter's prayer was recorded by Hans Wallnöfer, "Über alte Bergmannsbräuche in unserer Heimat", 1928,

SNEAK PEAK

Sam's defeat of the Bruderschaft has bought the Changels time, but not peace. The Center is angry and the Iyrin want revenge. But Sam is growing up. He wants more freedom, and more privacy, two things his enemies know and will exploit to catch the Changels and find the Fae. Watch out for Changels Nemesis, the follow-on to Changels Genesis.

**Follow @Changelsbook on twitter or like on facebook
https://www.facebook.com/Changels/**

www.ingramcontent.com/pod-product-compliance
Lightning Source LLC
Chambersburg PA
CBHW020629020726
47494CB00001B/118